Nancy Drew

D I A R I E S ™

"Clearly, neither he nor the tiger has any interest in being caged."

—Nancy Drew

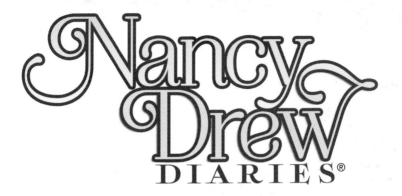

NANCY DREW DIARIES®

#8
"Tiger Counter"
and
"What Goes Up…"

Based on the series by
CAROLYN KEENE

STEFAN PETRUCHA & SARAH KINNEY • Writers
SHO MURASE • Artist
with 3D CG elements and color by CARLOS JOSE GUZMAN

New York

Nancy Drew Diaries
#8

"Tiger Counter" and "What Goes Up…"
STEFAN PETRUCHA & SARAH KINNEY – Writers
SHO MURASE – Artist
with 3D CG elements and color by CARLOS JOSE GUZMAN
BRYAN SENKA – Letterer
JEFF WHITMAN – Production Coordinator/Assistant Managing Editor
BETHANY BRYAN – Reprint Editor
JIM SALICRUP
Editor-in-Chief

ISBN: 978-1-62991-593-7

Published by arrangement with Aladdin Paperbacks,
an imprint of Simon & Schuster Children's Publishing Division.

Printed in China
May 2016 by Samfine Printing Co. Ltd.
Shenzen, China

Distributed by Macmillian
First Printing

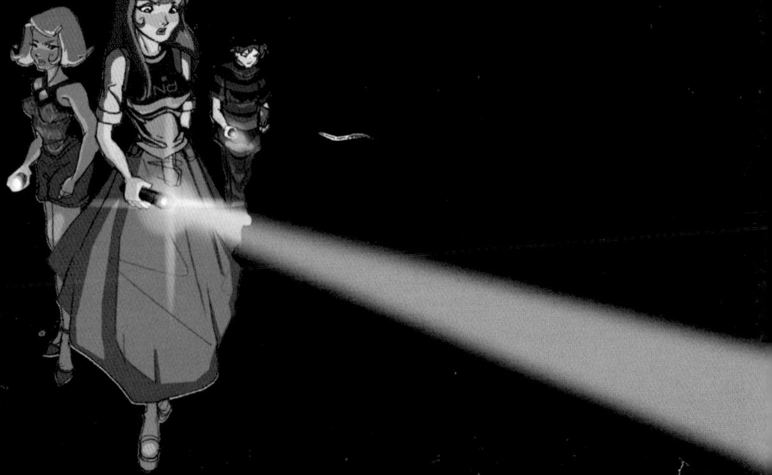

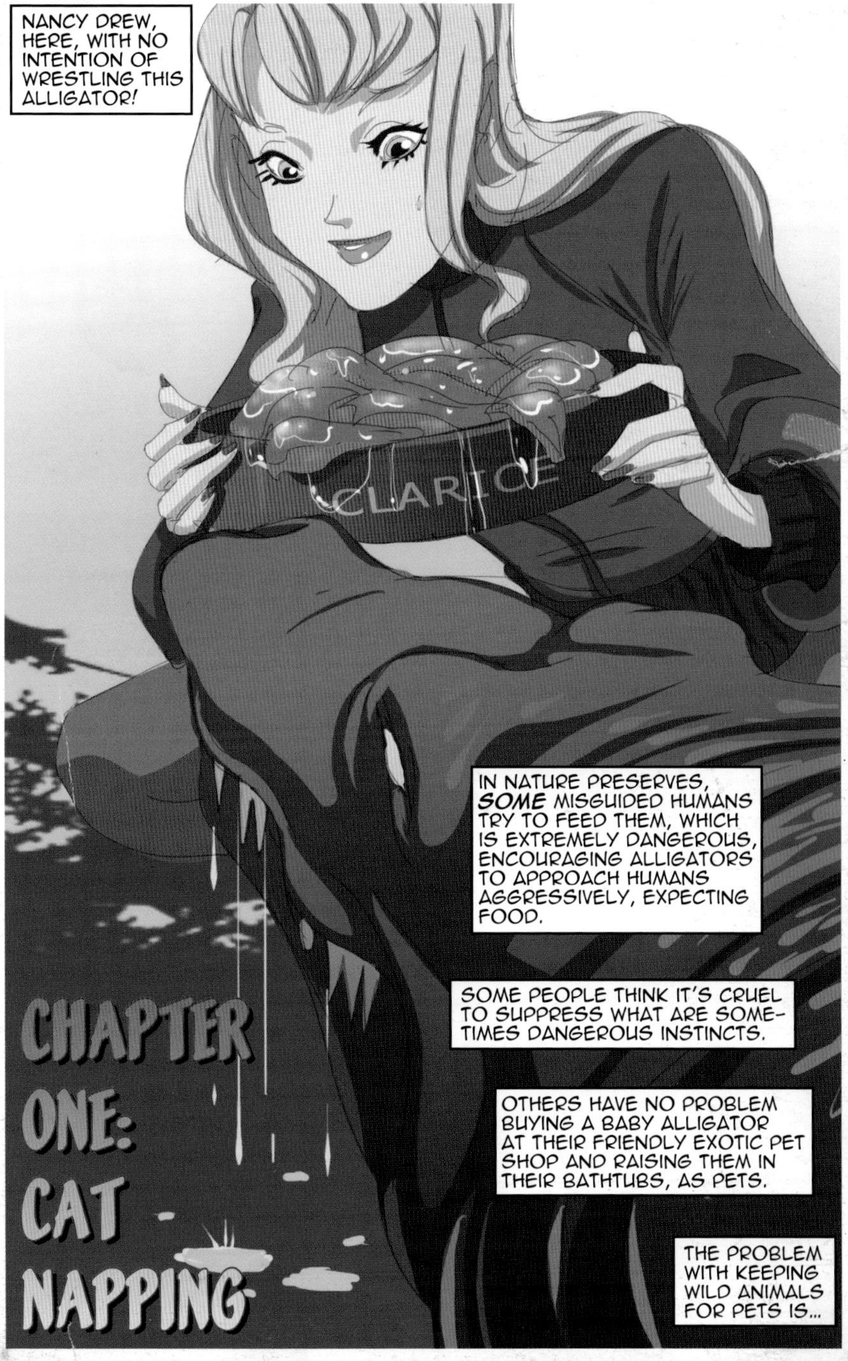
NANCY DREW, HERE, WITH NO INTENTION OF WRESTLING THIS ALLIGATOR!
CLARICE
IN NATURE PRESERVES, *SOME* MISGUIDED HUMANS TRY TO FEED THEM, WHICH IS EXTREMELY DANGEROUS, ENCOURAGING ALLIGATORS TO APPROACH HUMANS AGGRESSIVELY, EXPECTING FOOD.
SOME PEOPLE THINK IT'S CRUEL TO SUPPRESS WHAT ARE SOME-TIMES DANGEROUS INSTINCTS.
OTHERS HAVE NO PROBLEM BUYING A BABY ALLIGATOR AT THEIR FRIENDLY EXOTIC PET SHOP AND RAISING THEM IN THEIR BATHTUBS, AS PETS.
THE PROBLEM WITH KEEPING WILD ANIMALS FOR PETS IS...
CHAPTER ONE: CAT NAPPING

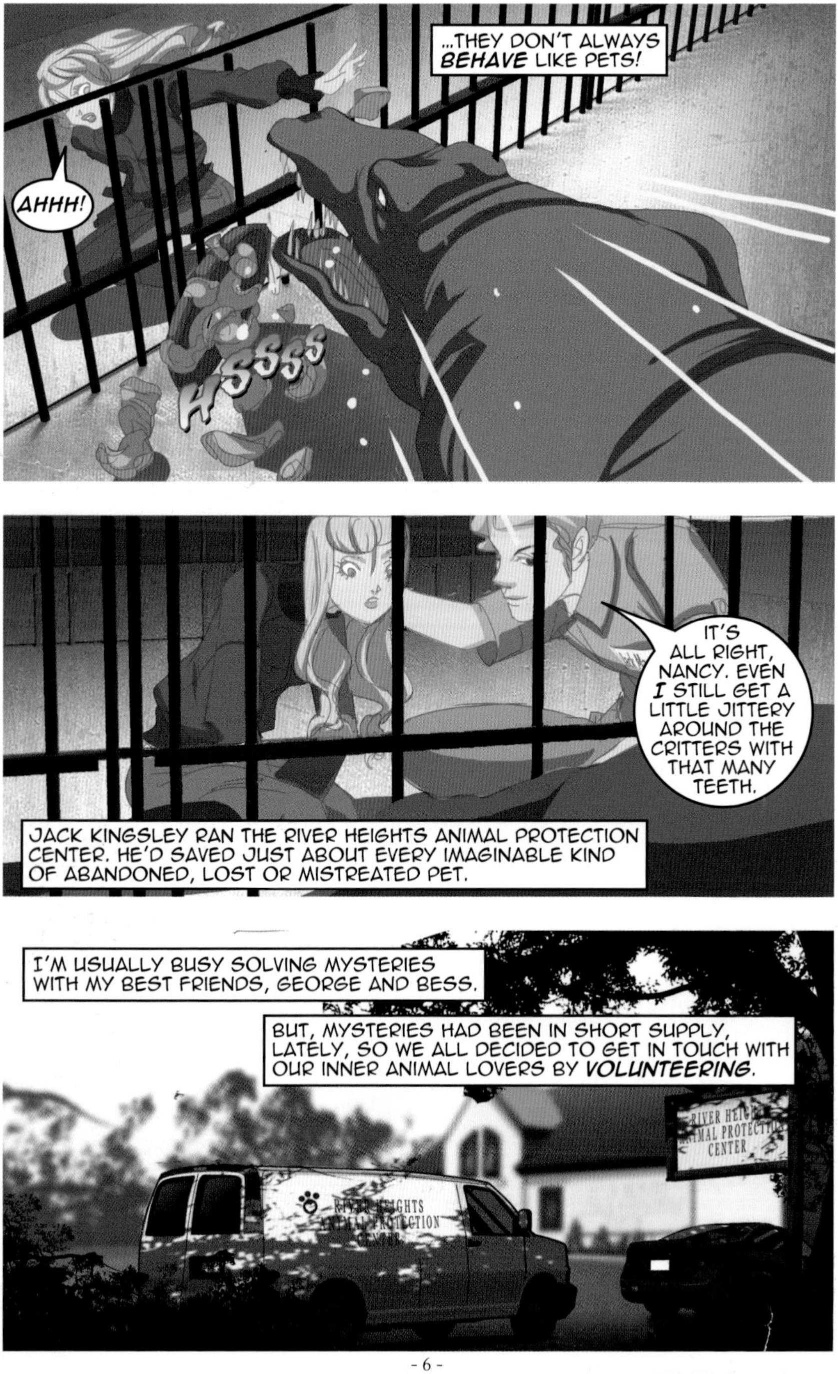
...THEY DON'T ALWAYS *BEHAVE* LIKE PETS!
AHHH!
HSSSS
IT'S ALL RIGHT, NANCY. EVEN *I* STILL GET A LITTLE JITTERY AROUND THE CRITTERS WITH THAT MANY TEETH.
JACK KINGSLEY RAN THE RIVER HEIGHTS ANIMAL PROTECTION CENTER. HE'D SAVED JUST ABOUT EVERY IMAGINABLE KIND OF ABANDONED, LOST OR MISTREATED PET.
I'M USUALLY BUSY SOLVING MYSTERIES WITH MY BEST FRIENDS, GEORGE AND BESS.
BUT, MYSTERIES HAD BEEN IN SHORT SUPPLY, LATELY, SO WE ALL DECIDED TO GET IN TOUCH WITH OUR INNER ANIMAL LOVERS BY *VOLUNTEERING*.
RIVER HEIGHTS ANIMAL PROTECTION CENTER

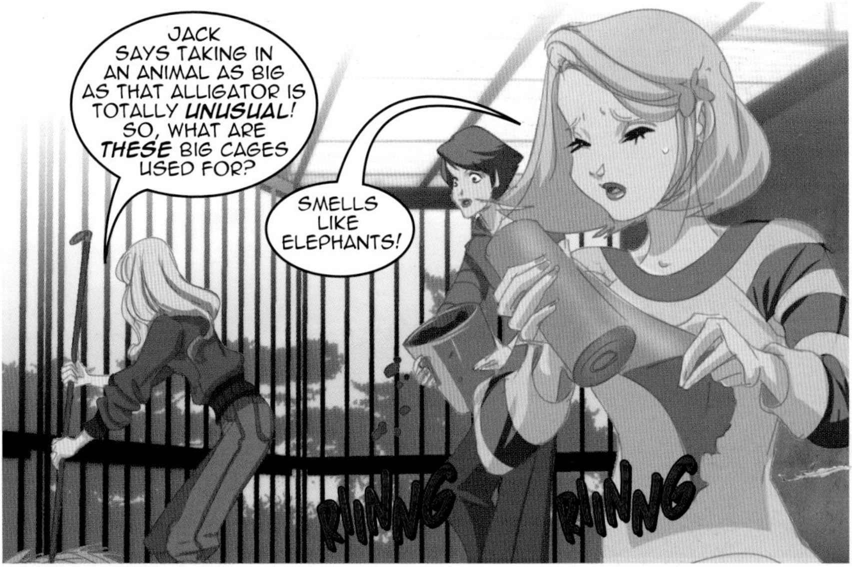
JACK SAYS TAKING IN AN ANIMAL AS BIG AS THAT ALLIGATOR IS TOTALLY UNUSUAL! SO, WHAT ARE THESE BIG CAGES USED FOR?
SMELLS LIKE ELEPHANTS!
RIINNG RIINNG

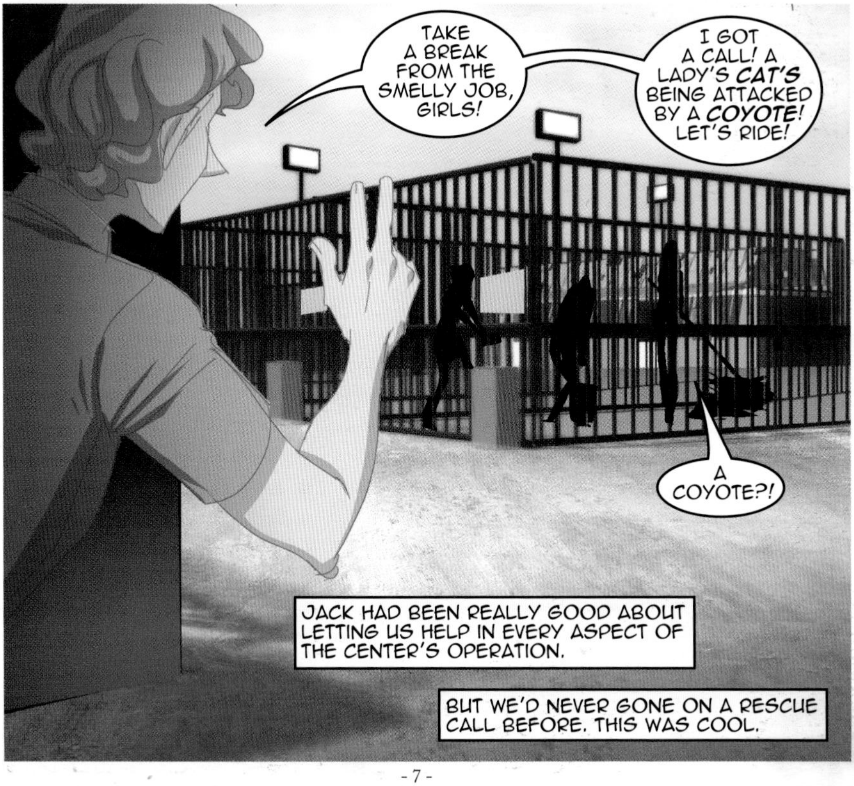
TAKE A BREAK FROM THE SMELLY JOB, GIRLS!
I GOT A CALL! A LADY'S CAT'S BEING ATTACKED BY A COYOTE! LET'S RIDE!
A COYOTE?!
JACK HAD BEEN REALLY GOOD ABOUT LETTING US HELP IN EVERY ASPECT OF THE CENTER'S OPERATION.
BUT WE'D NEVER GONE ON A RESCUE CALL BEFORE. THIS WAS COOL.

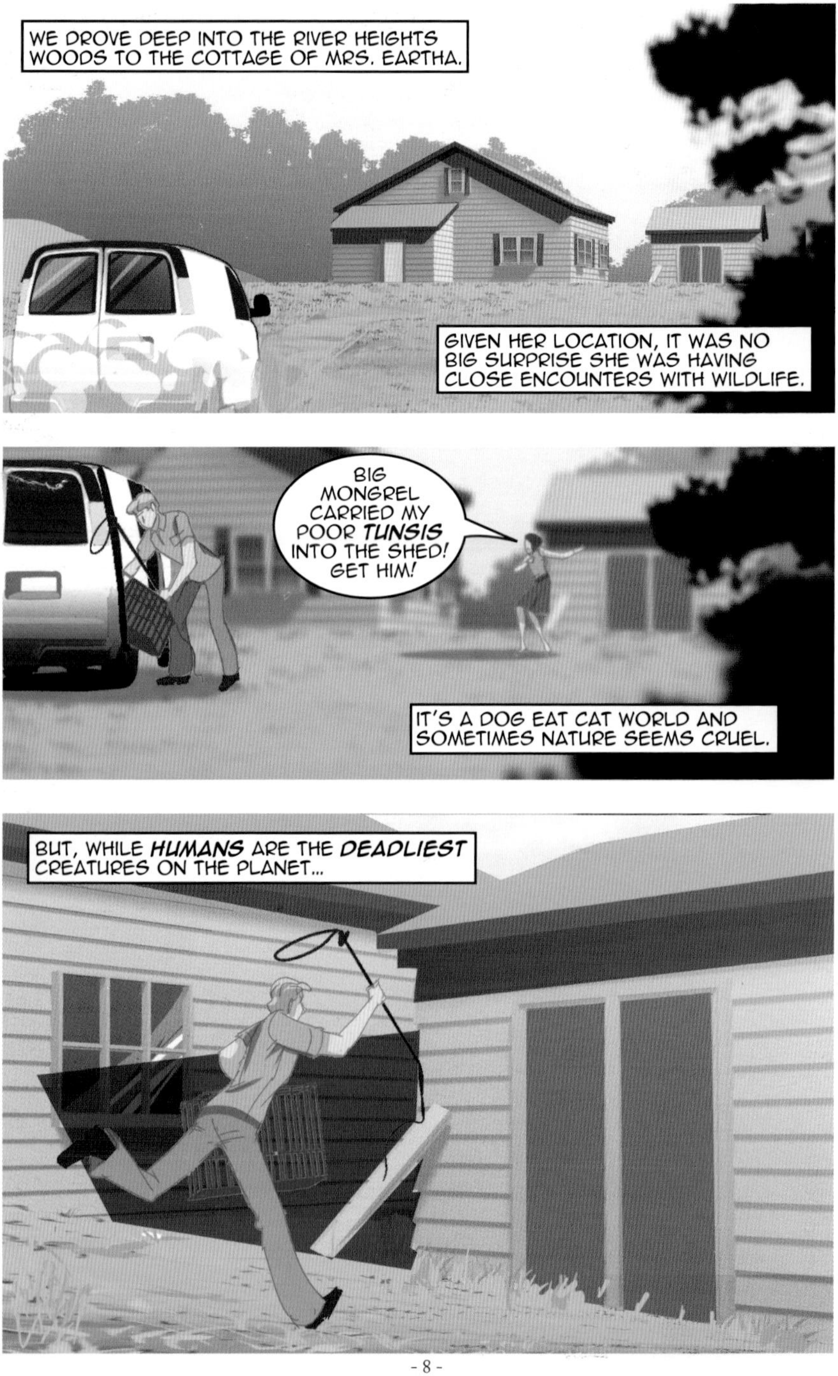
WE DROVE DEEP INTO THE RIVER HEIGHTS WOODS TO THE COTTAGE OF MRS. EARTHA.
GIVEN HER LOCATION, IT WAS NO BIG SURPRISE SHE WAS HAVING CLOSE ENCOUNTERS WITH WILDLIFE.
BIG MONGREL CARRIED MY POOR *TUNSIS* INTO THE SHED! GET HIM!
IT'S A DOG EAT CAT WORLD AND SOMETIMES NATURE SEEMS CRUEL.
BUT, WHILE *HUMANS* ARE THE *DEADLIEST* CREATURES ON THE PLANET...

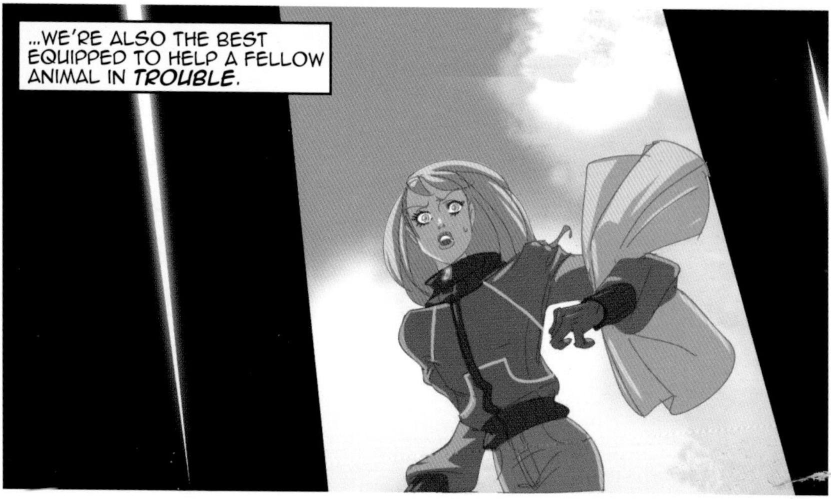
...WE'RE ALSO THE BEST EQUIPPED TO HELP A FELLOW ANIMAL IN *TROUBLE*.

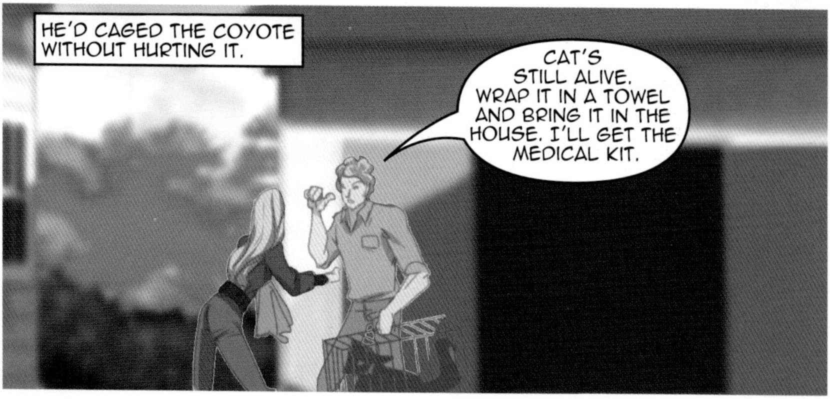
HE'D CAGED THE COYOTE WITHOUT HURTING IT.
CAT'S STILL ALIVE. WRAP IT IN A TOWEL AND BRING IT IN THE HOUSE. I'LL GET THE MEDICAL KIT.

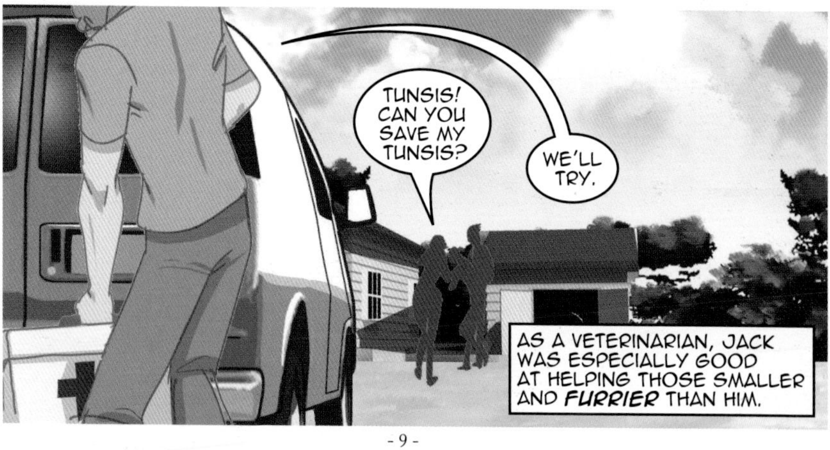
TUNSIS! CAN YOU SAVE MY TUNSIS?
WE'LL TRY.
AS A VETERINARIAN, JACK WAS ESPECIALLY GOOD AT HELPING THOSE SMALLER AND *FURRIER* THAN HIM.

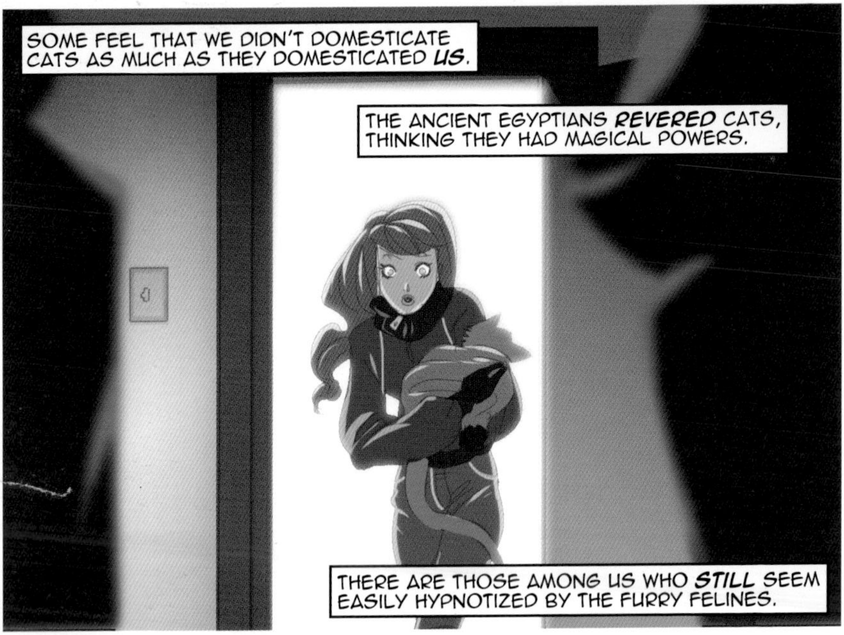
SOME FEEL THAT WE DIDN'T DOMESTICATE CATS AS MUCH AS THEY DOMESTICATED **US**.
THE ANCIENT EGYPTIANS **REVERED** CATS, THINKING THEY HAD MAGICAL POWERS.
THERE ARE THOSE AMONG US WHO **STILL** SEEM EASILY HYPNOTIZED BY THE FURRY FELINES.
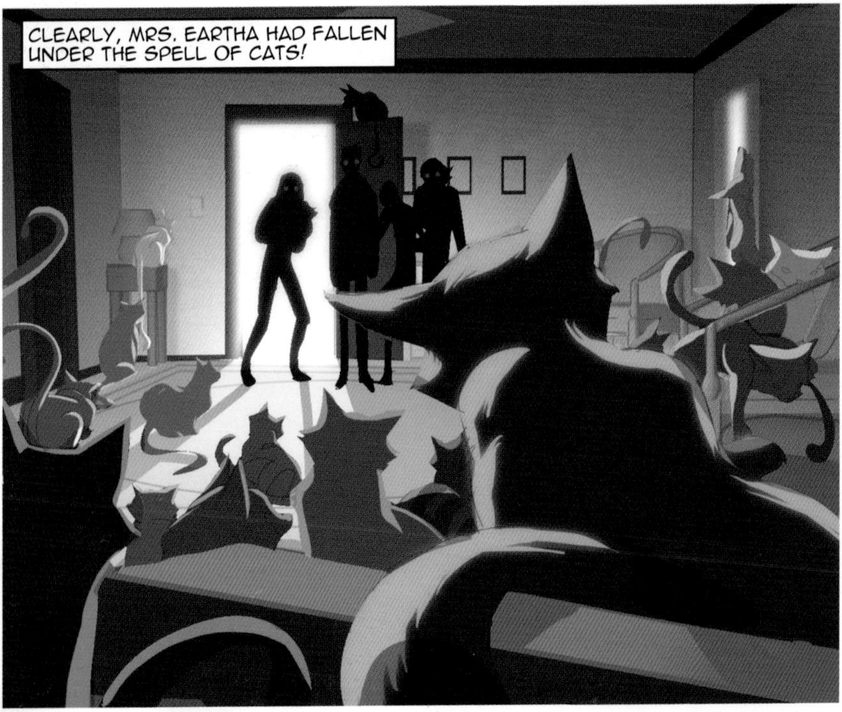
CLEARLY, MRS. EARTHA HAD FALLEN UNDER THE SPELL OF CATS!

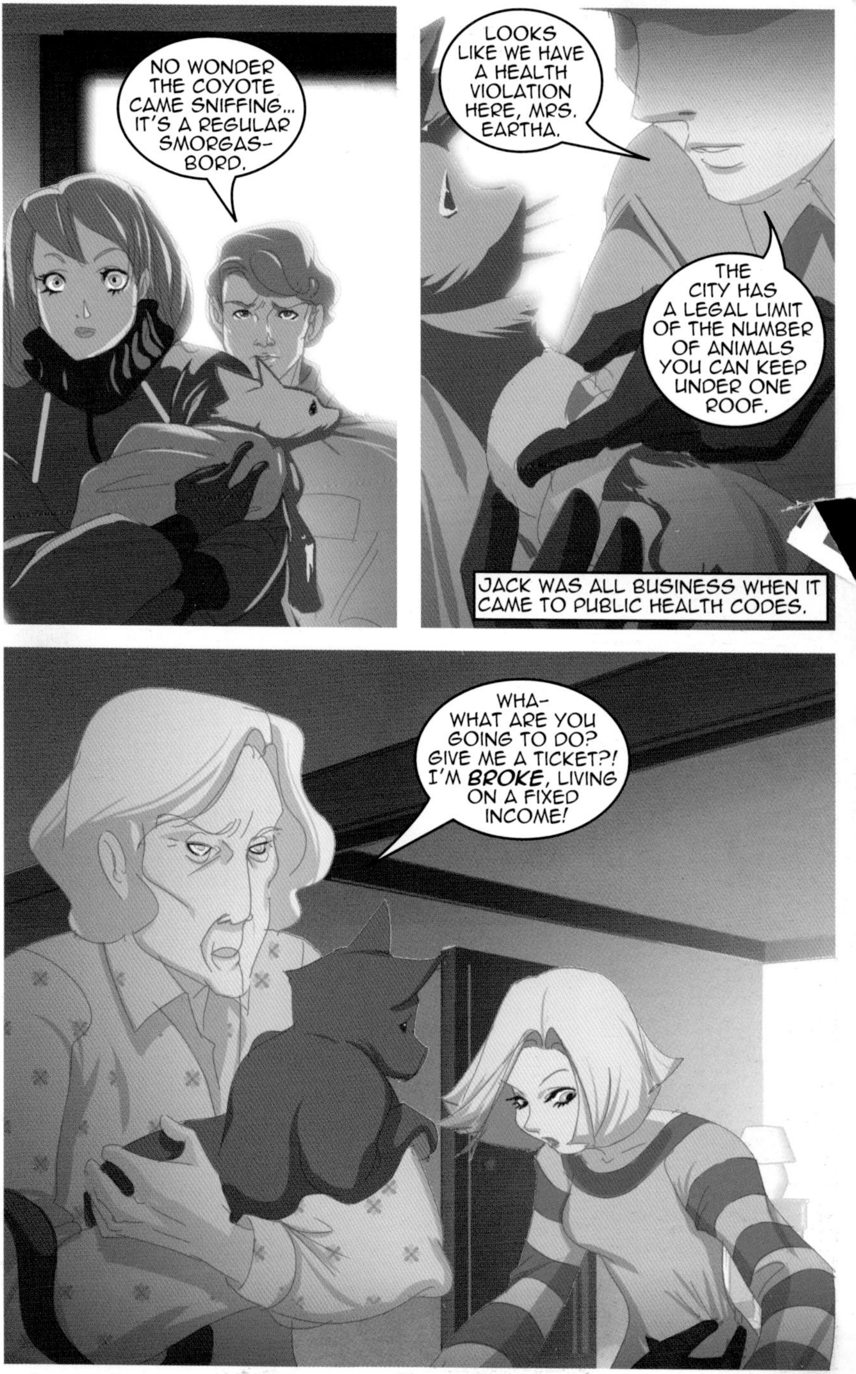
NO WONDER THE COYOTE CAME SNIFFING... IT'S A REGULAR SMORGAS-BORD.
LOOKS LIKE WE HAVE A HEALTH VIOLATION HERE, MRS. EARTHA.
THE CITY HAS A LEGAL LIMIT OF THE NUMBER OF ANIMALS YOU CAN KEEP UNDER ONE ROOF.
JACK WAS ALL BUSINESS WHEN IT CAME TO PUBLIC HEALTH CODES.
WHA- WHAT ARE YOU GOING TO DO? GIVE ME A TICKET?! I'M BROKE, LIVING ON A FIXED INCOME!

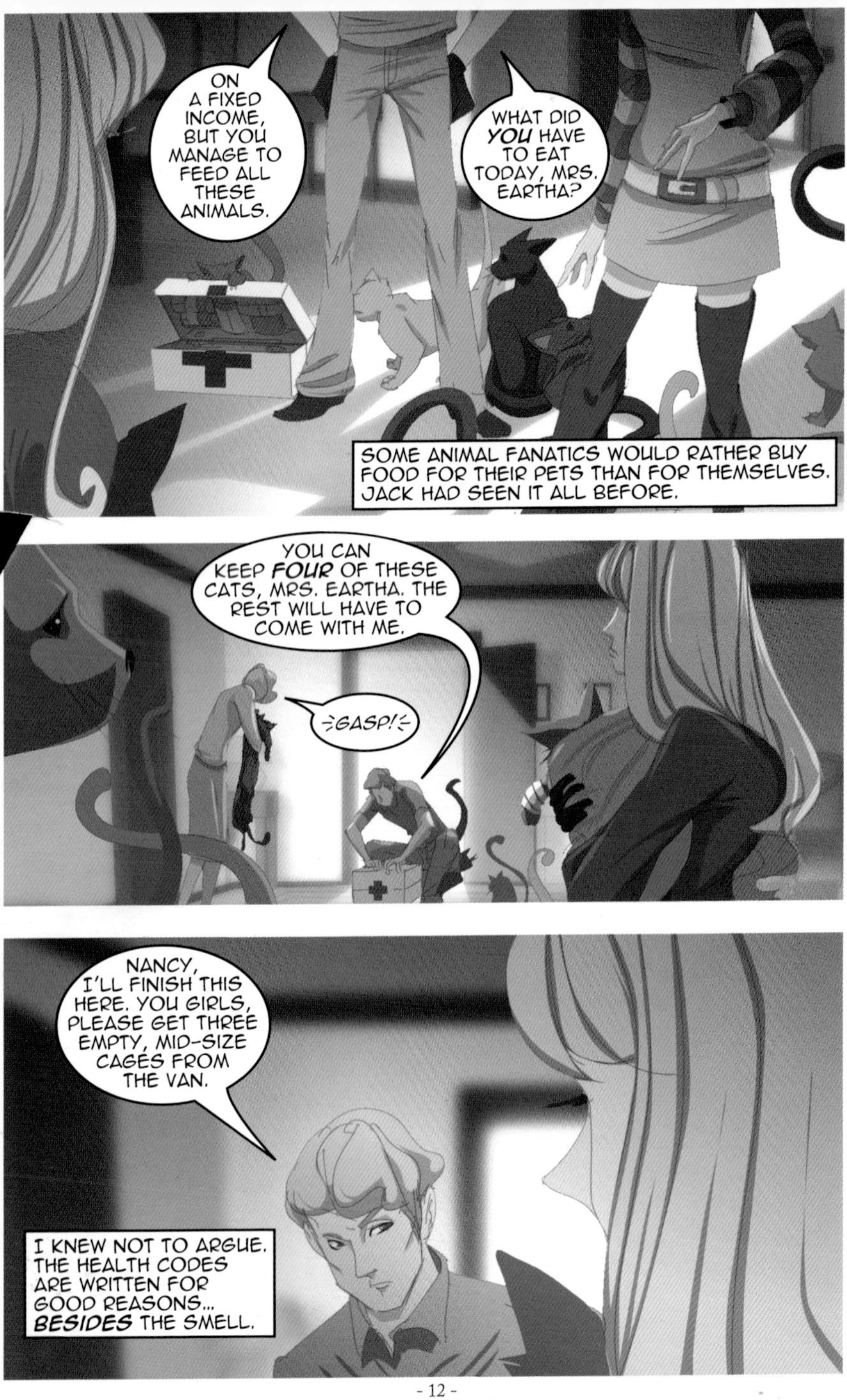
ON A FIXED INCOME, BUT YOU MANAGE TO FEED ALL THESE ANIMALS.
WHAT DID *YOU* HAVE TO EAT TODAY, MRS. EARTHA?
SOME ANIMAL FANATICS WOULD RATHER BUY FOOD FOR THEIR PETS THAN FOR THEMSELVES. JACK HAD SEEN IT ALL BEFORE.
YOU CAN KEEP *FOUR* OF THESE CATS, MRS. EARTHA. THE REST WILL HAVE TO COME WITH ME.
GASP!
NANCY, I'LL FINISH THIS HERE. YOU GIRLS, PLEASE GET THREE EMPTY, MID-SIZE CAGES FROM THE VAN.
I KNEW NOT TO ARGUE. THE HEALTH CODES ARE WRITTEN FOR GOOD REASONS... *BESIDES* THE SMELL.

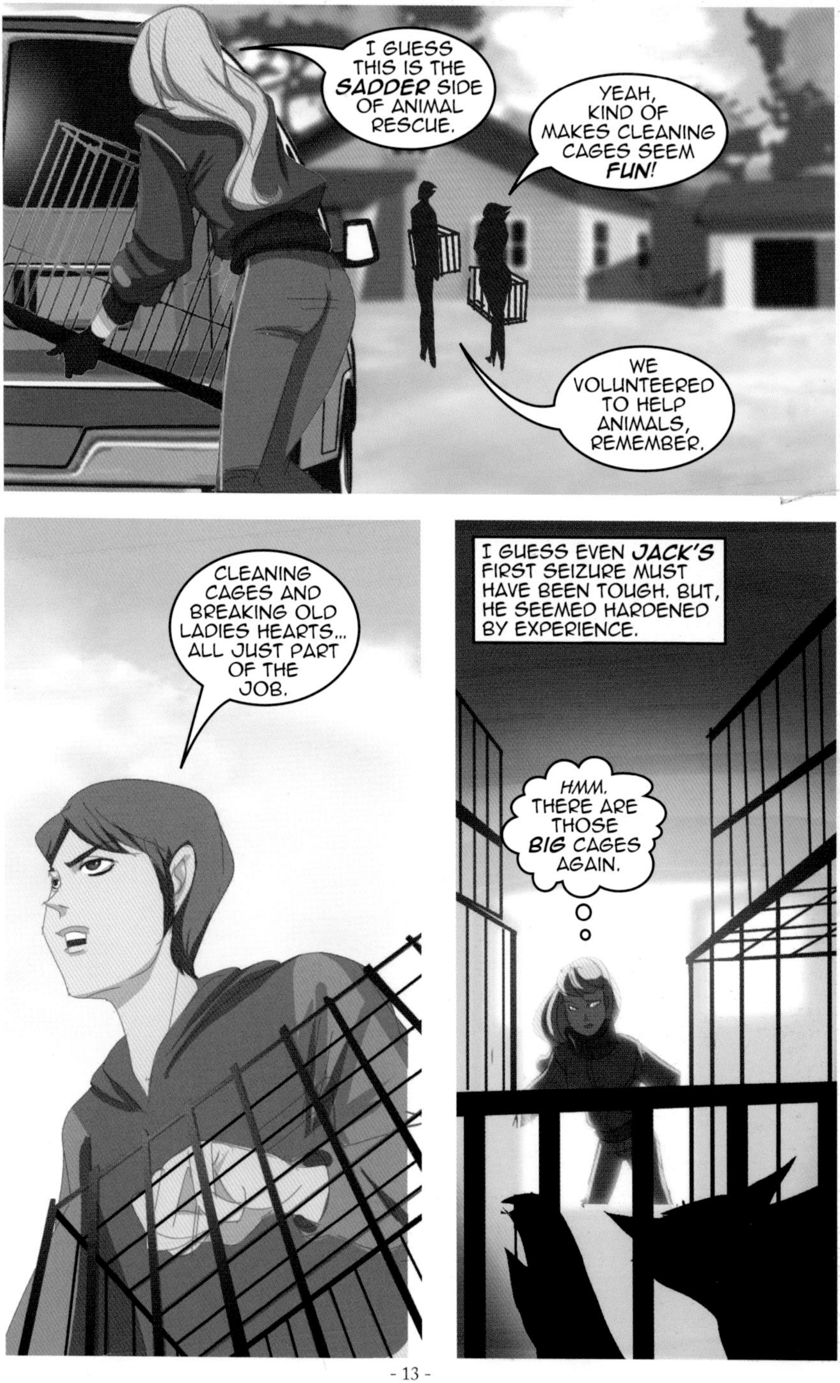
I GUESS THIS IS THE SADDER SIDE OF ANIMAL RESCUE.
YEAH, KIND OF MAKES CLEANING CAGES SEEM FUN!
WE VOLUNTEERED TO HELP ANIMALS, REMEMBER.
CLEANING CAGES AND BREAKING OLD LADIES HEARTS... ALL JUST PART OF THE JOB.
I GUESS EVEN JACK'S FIRST SEIZURE MUST HAVE BEEN TOUGH. BUT, HE SEEMED HARDENED BY EXPERIENCE.
HMM. THERE ARE THOSE BIG CAGES AGAIN.

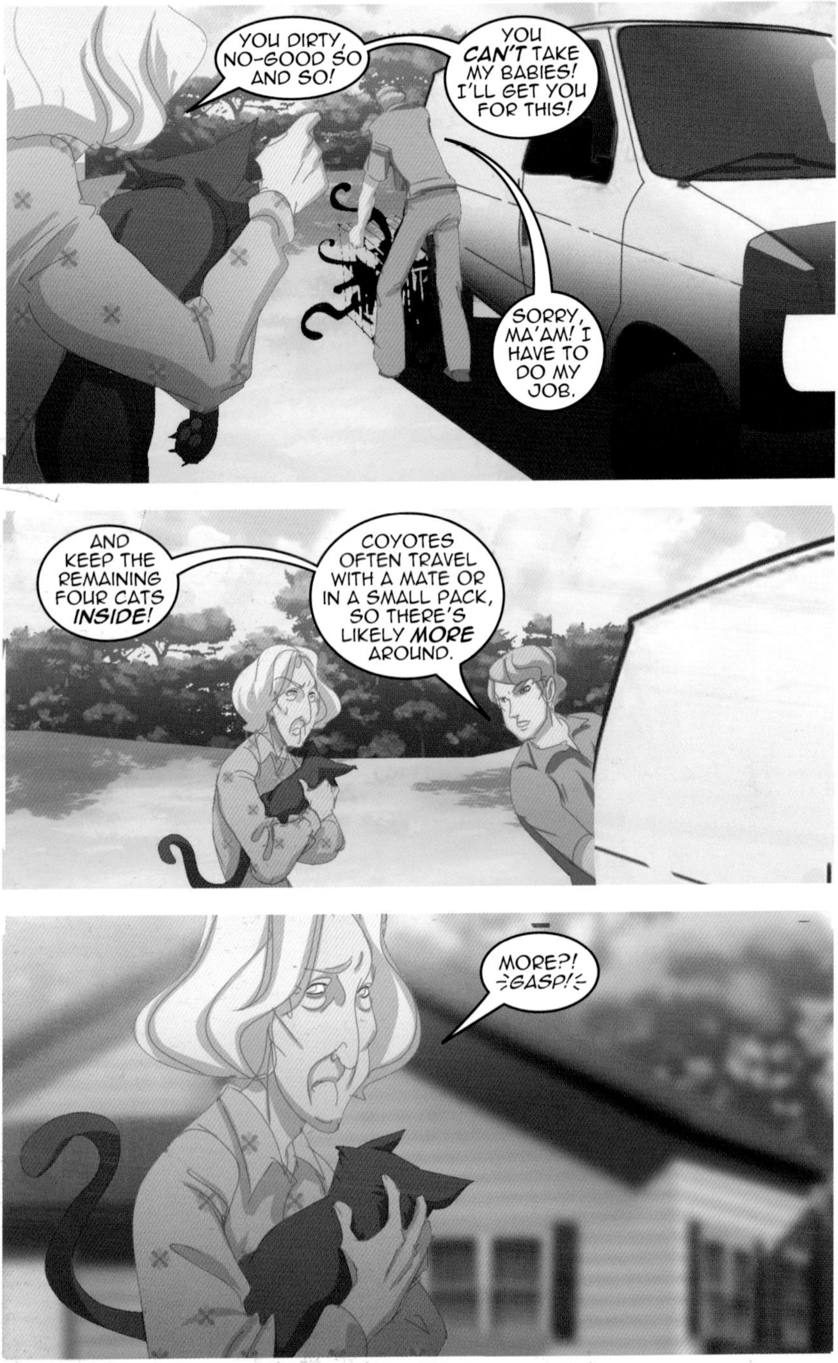
YOU DIRTY, NO-GOOD SO AND SO!
YOU *CAN'T* TAKE MY BABIES! I'LL GET YOU FOR THIS!
SORRY, MA'AM! I HAVE TO DO MY JOB.
COYOTES OFTEN TRAVEL WITH A MATE OR IN A SMALL PACK, SO THERE'S LIKELY *MORE* AROUND.
AND KEEP THE REMAINING FOUR CATS *INSIDE*!
MORE?! *GASP!*

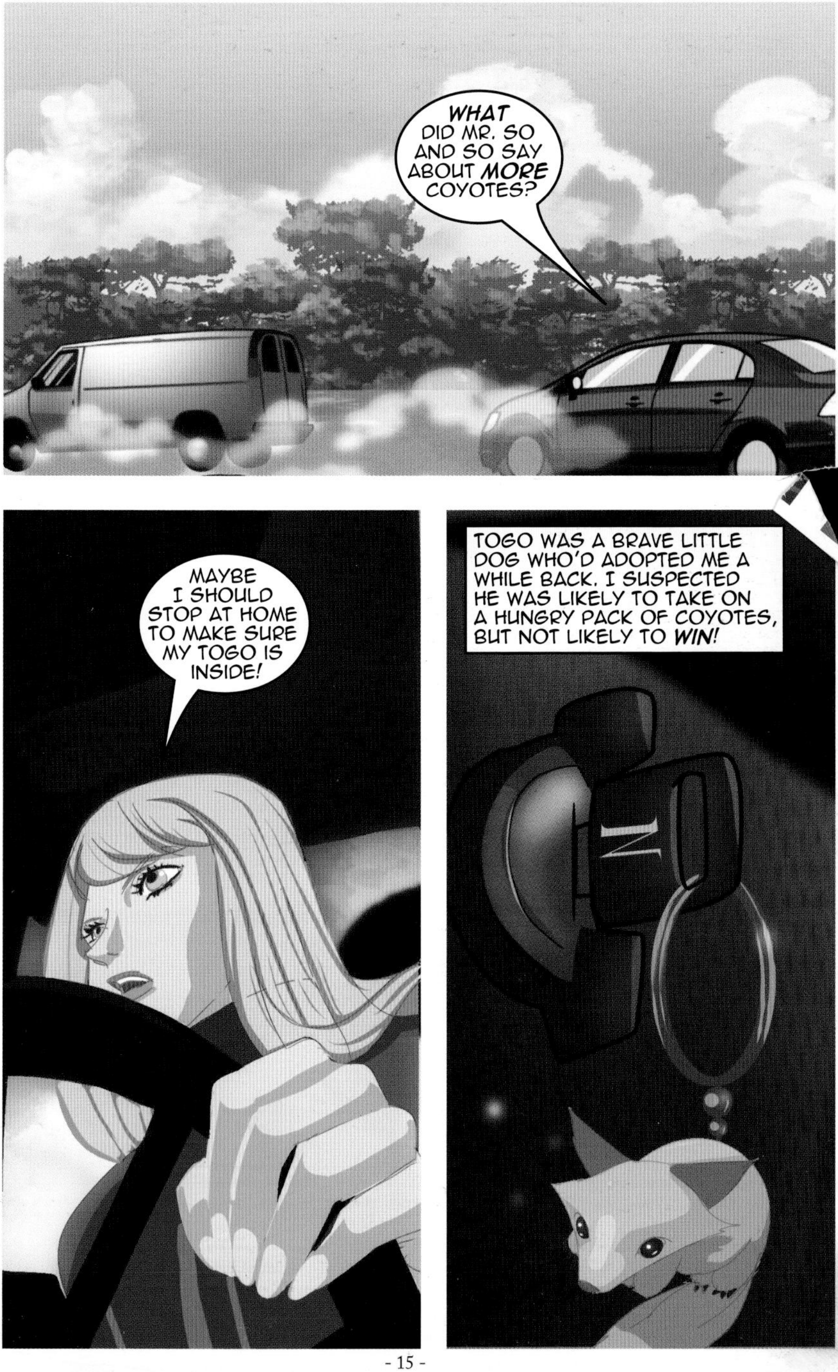
WHAT DID MR. SO AND SO SAY ABOUT MORE COYOTES?
MAYBE I SHOULD STOP AT HOME TO MAKE SURE MY TOGO IS INSIDE!
TOGO WAS A BRAVE LITTLE DOG WHO'D ADOPTED ME A WHILE BACK. I SUSPECTED HE WAS LIKELY TO TAKE ON A HUNGRY PACK OF COYOTES, BUT NOT LIKELY TO WIN!

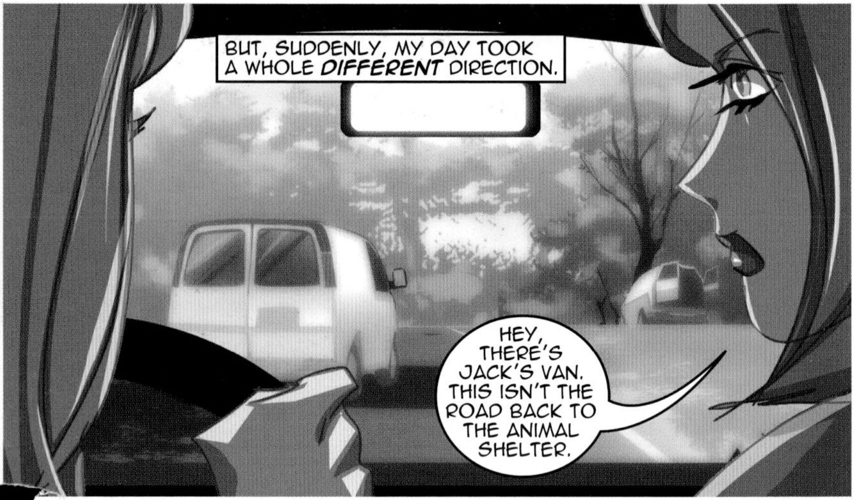
BUT, SUDDENLY, MY DAY TOOK A WHOLE *DIFFERENT* DIRECTION.
HEY, THERE'S JACK'S VAN. THIS ISN'T THE ROAD BACK TO THE ANIMAL SHELTER.

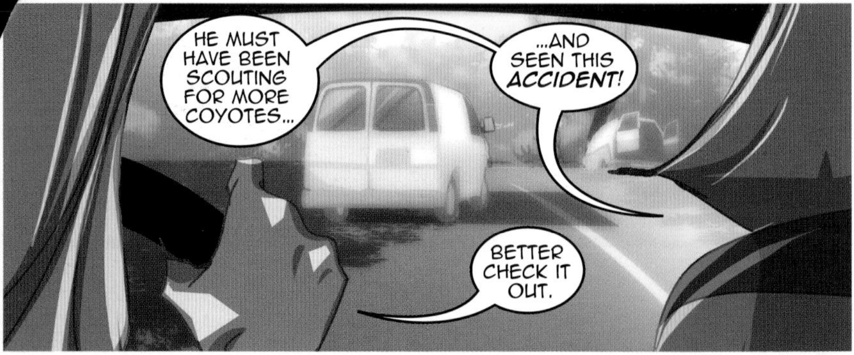
HE MUST HAVE BEEN SCOUTING FOR MORE COYOTES...
...AND SEEN THIS *ACCIDENT*!
BETTER CHECK IT OUT.

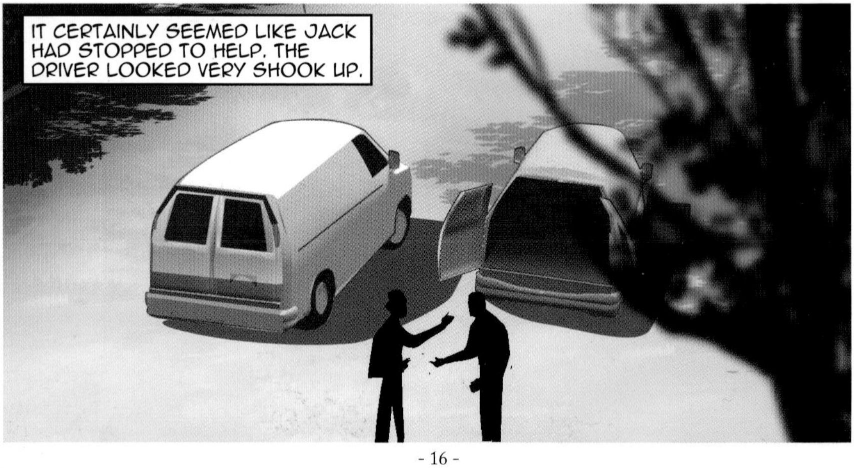
IT CERTAINLY SEEMED LIKE JACK HAD STOPPED TO HELP. THE DRIVER LOOKED VERY SHOOK UP.

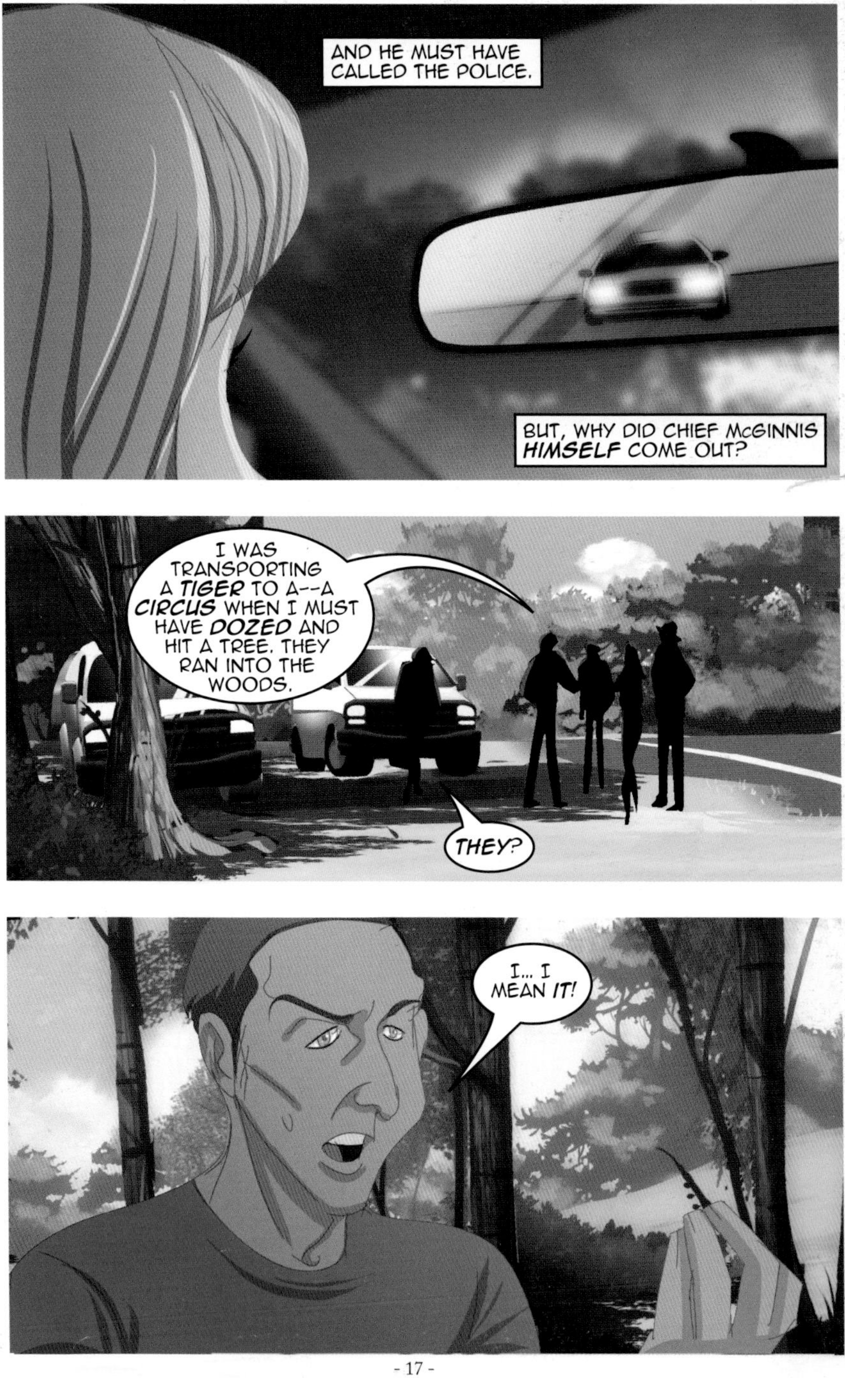
AND HE MUST HAVE CALLED THE POLICE.
BUT, WHY DID CHIEF McGINNIS HIMSELF COME OUT?
I WAS TRANSPORTING A TIGER TO A--A CIRCUS WHEN I MUST HAVE DOZED AND HIT A TREE. THEY RAN INTO THE WOODS.
THEY?
I... I MEAN IT!

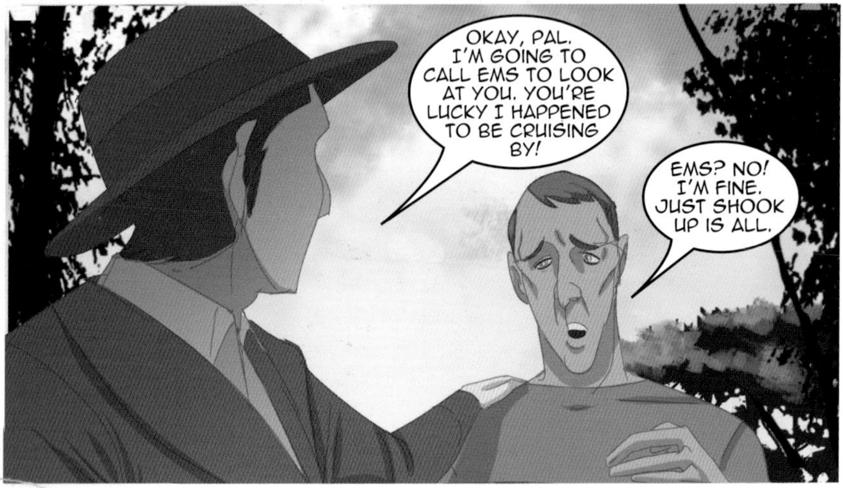
OKAY, PAL. I'M GOING TO CALL EMS TO LOOK AT YOU. YOU'RE LUCKY I HAPPENED TO BE CRUISING BY!
EMS? NO! I'M FINE. JUST SHOOK UP IS ALL.

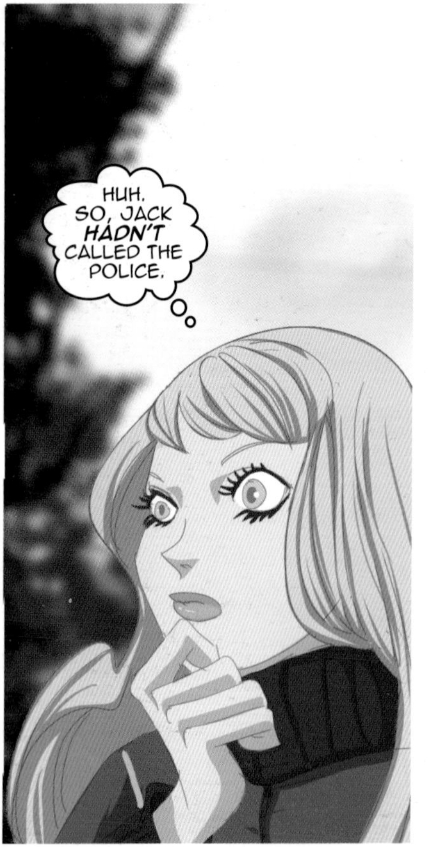
HUH. SO, JACK *HADN'T* CALLED THE POLICE.

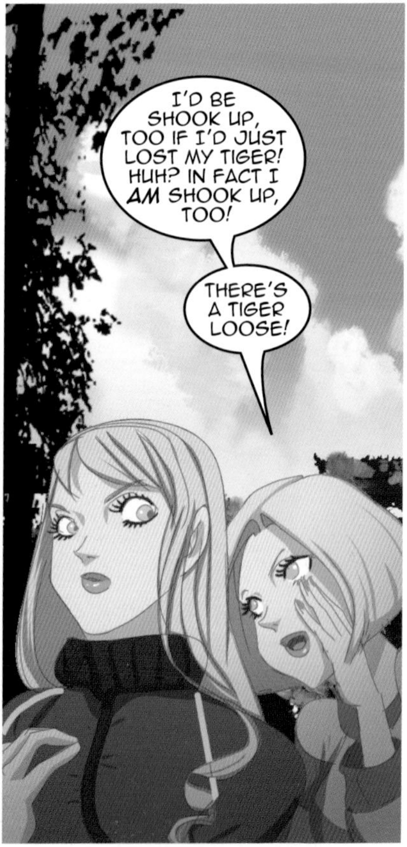
I'D BE SHOOK UP, TOO IF I'D JUST LOST MY TIGER! HUH? IN FACT I **AM** SHOOK UP, TOO!
THERE'S A TIGER LOOSE!

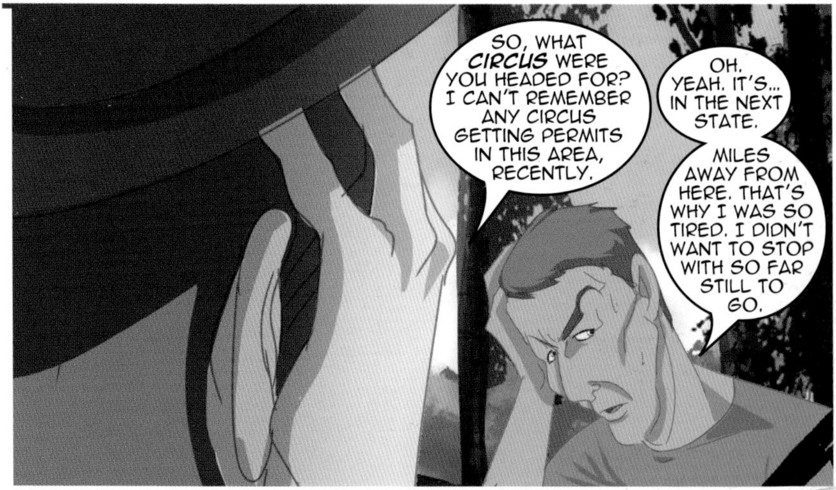
SO, WHAT CIRCUS WERE YOU HEADED FOR? I CAN'T REMEMBER ANY CIRCUS GETTING PERMITS IN THIS AREA, RECENTLY.
OH. YEAH. IT'S... IN THE NEXT STATE.
MILES AWAY FROM HERE. THAT'S WHY I WAS SO TIRED. I DIDN'T WANT TO STOP WITH SO FAR STILL TO GO.

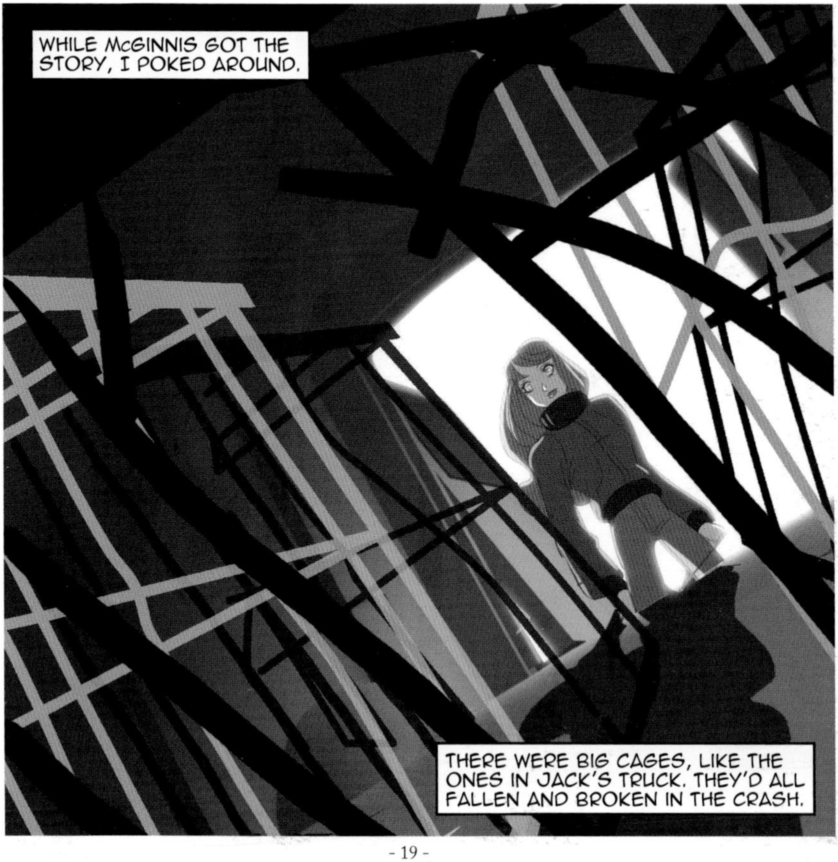
WHILE McGINNIS GOT THE STORY, I POKED AROUND.
THERE WERE BIG CAGES, LIKE THE ONES IN JACK'S TRUCK. THEY'D ALL FALLEN AND BROKEN IN THE CRASH.

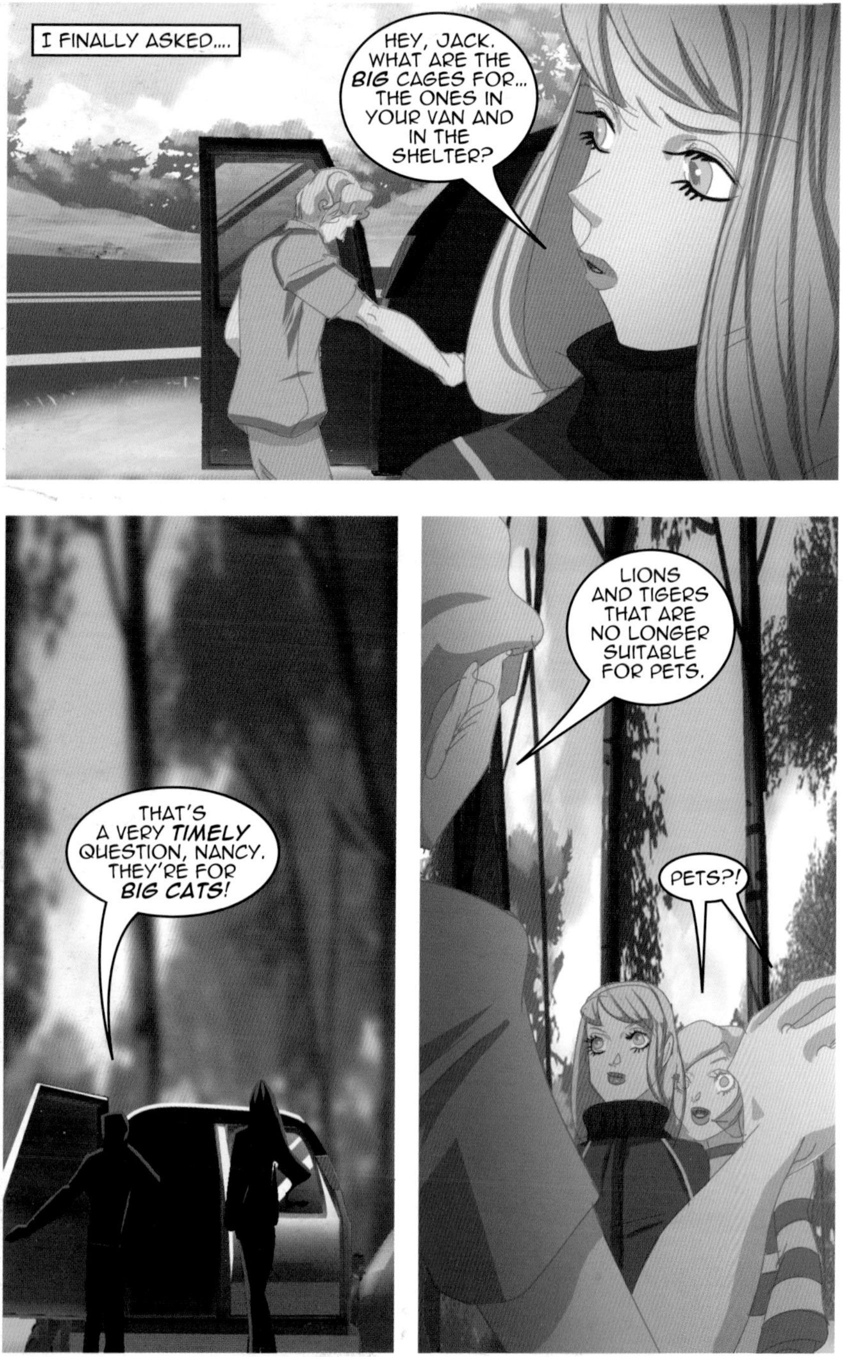
I FINALLY ASKED....
HEY, JACK. WHAT ARE THE BIG CAGES FOR... THE ONES IN YOUR VAN AND IN THE SHELTER?
THAT'S A VERY TIMELY QUESTION, NANCY. THEY'RE FOR BIG CATS!
LIONS AND TIGERS THAT ARE NO LONGER SUITABLE FOR PETS.
PETS?!

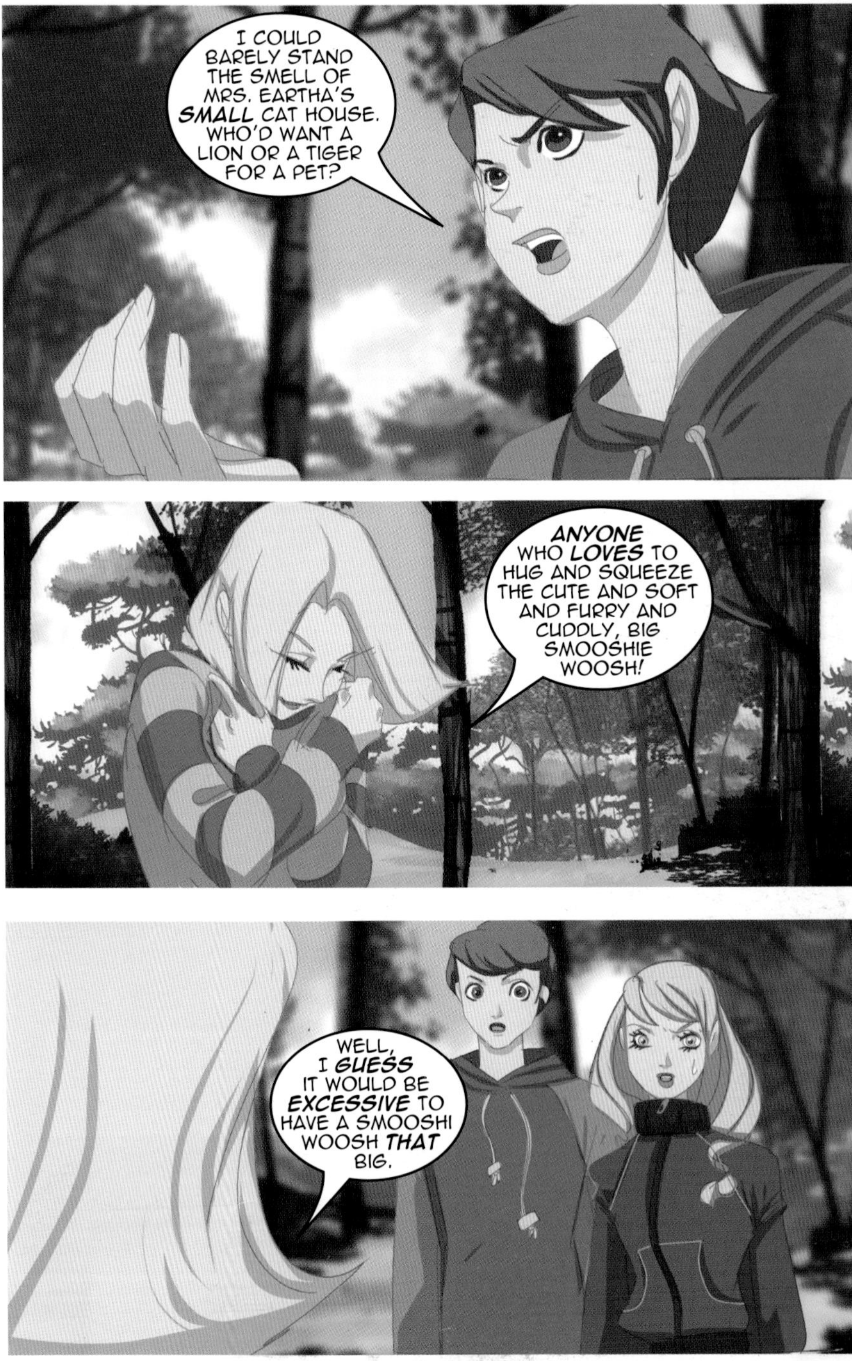
I COULD BARELY STAND THE SMELL OF MRS. EARTHA'S SMALL CAT HOUSE. WHO'D WANT A LION OR A TIGER FOR A PET?
ANYONE WHO LOVES TO HUG AND SQUEEZE THE CUTE AND SOFT AND FURRY AND CUDDLY, BIG SMOOSHIE WOOSH!
WELL, I GUESS IT WOULD BE EXCESSIVE TO HAVE A SMOOSHI WOOSH THAT BIG.

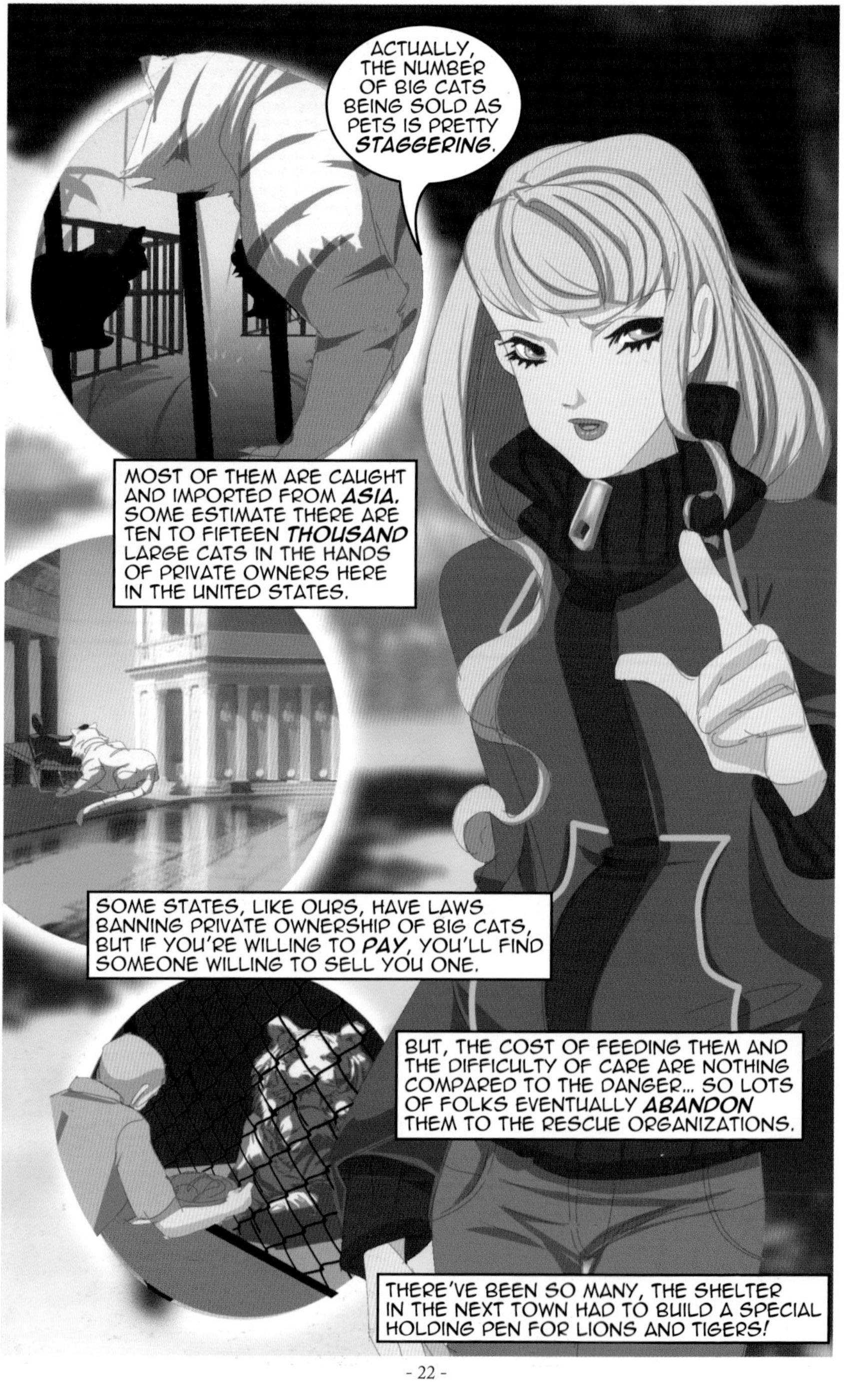
ACTUALLY, THE NUMBER OF BIG CATS BEING SOLD AS PETS IS PRETTY STAGGERING.
MOST OF THEM ARE CAUGHT AND IMPORTED FROM ASIA. SOME ESTIMATE THERE ARE TEN TO FIFTEEN THOUSAND LARGE CATS IN THE HANDS OF PRIVATE OWNERS HERE IN THE UNITED STATES.
SOME STATES, LIKE OURS, HAVE LAWS BANNING PRIVATE OWNERSHIP OF BIG CATS, BUT IF YOU'RE WILLING TO PAY, YOU'LL FIND SOMEONE WILLING TO SELL YOU ONE.
BUT, THE COST OF FEEDING THEM AND THE DIFFICULTY OF CARE ARE NOTHING COMPARED TO THE DANGER... SO LOTS OF FOLKS EVENTUALLY ABANDON THEM TO THE RESCUE ORGANIZATIONS.
THERE'VE BEEN SO MANY, THE SHELTER IN THE NEXT TOWN HAD TO BUILD A SPECIAL HOLDING PEN FOR LIONS AND TIGERS!

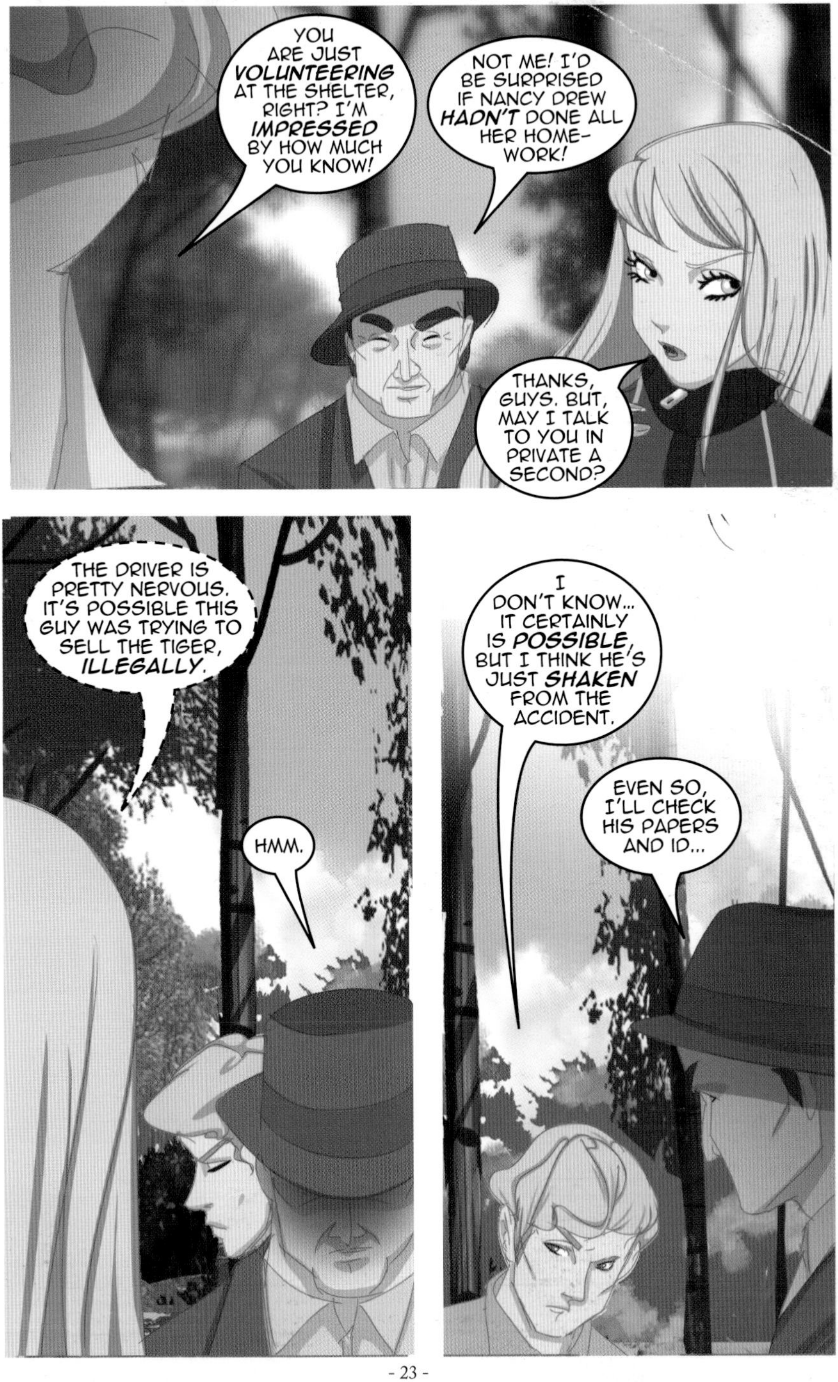
YOU ARE JUST VOLUNTEERING AT THE SHELTER, RIGHT? I'M IMPRESSED BY HOW MUCH YOU KNOW!
NOT ME! I'D BE SURPRISED IF NANCY DREW HADN'T DONE ALL HER HOME-WORK!
THANKS, GUYS. BUT, MAY I TALK TO YOU IN PRIVATE A SECOND?
THE DRIVER IS PRETTY NERVOUS. IT'S POSSIBLE THIS GUY WAS TRYING TO SELL THE TIGER, ILLEGALLY.
HMM.
I DON'T KNOW... IT CERTAINLY IS POSSIBLE, BUT I THINK HE'S JUST SHAKEN FROM THE ACCIDENT.
EVEN SO, I'LL CHECK HIS PAPERS AND ID...

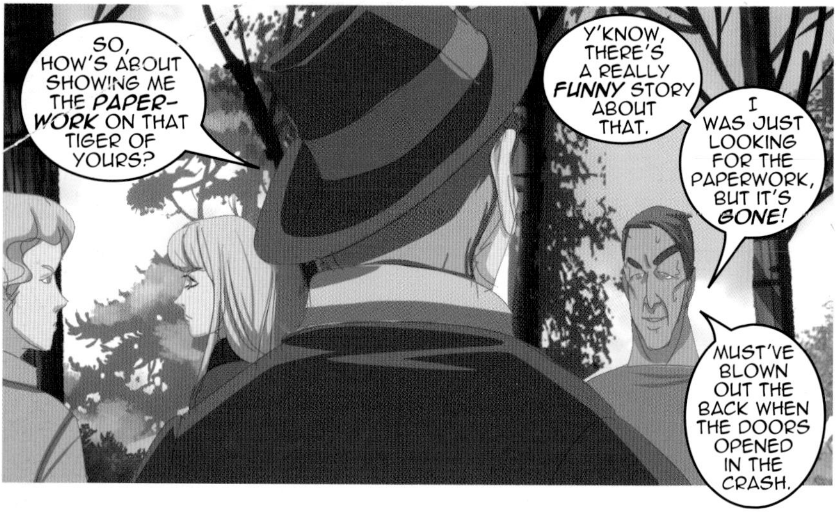
SO, HOW'S ABOUT SHOWING ME THE PAPER-WORK ON THAT TIGER OF YOURS?
Y'KNOW, THERE'S A REALLY FUNNY STORY ABOUT THAT.
I WAS JUST LOOKING FOR THE PAPERWORK, BUT IT'S GONE!
MUST'VE BLOWN OUT THE BACK WHEN THE DOORS OPENED IN THE CRASH.

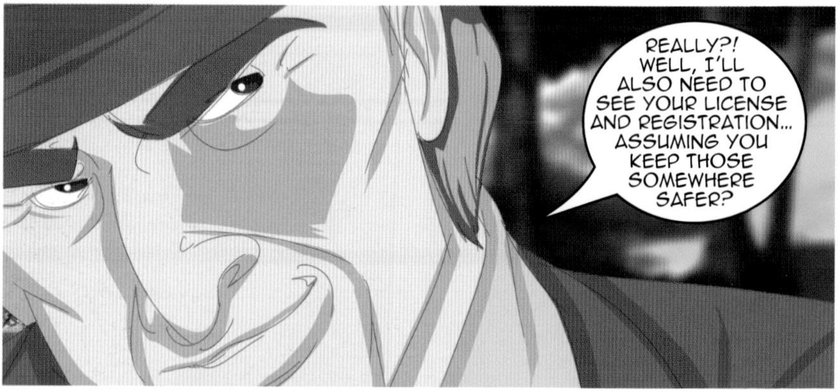
REALLY?! WELL, I'LL ALSO NEED TO SEE YOUR LICENSE AND REGISTRATION... ASSUMING YOU KEEP THOSE SOMEWHERE SAFER?

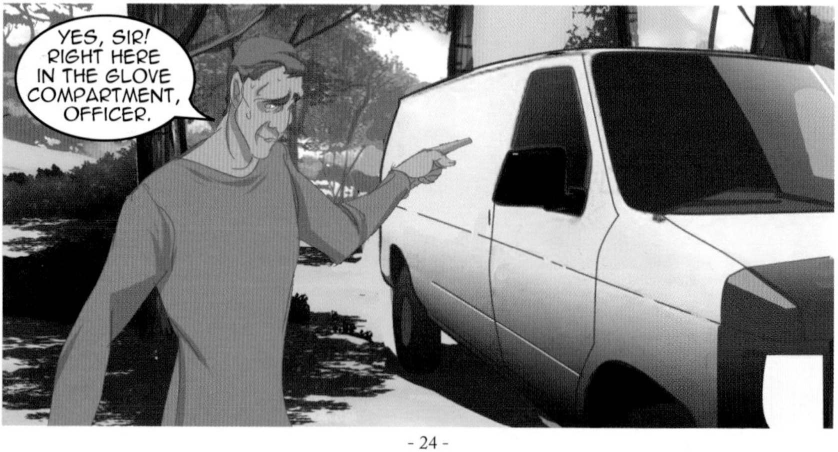
YES, SIR! RIGHT HERE IN THE GLOVE COMPARTMENT, OFFICER.

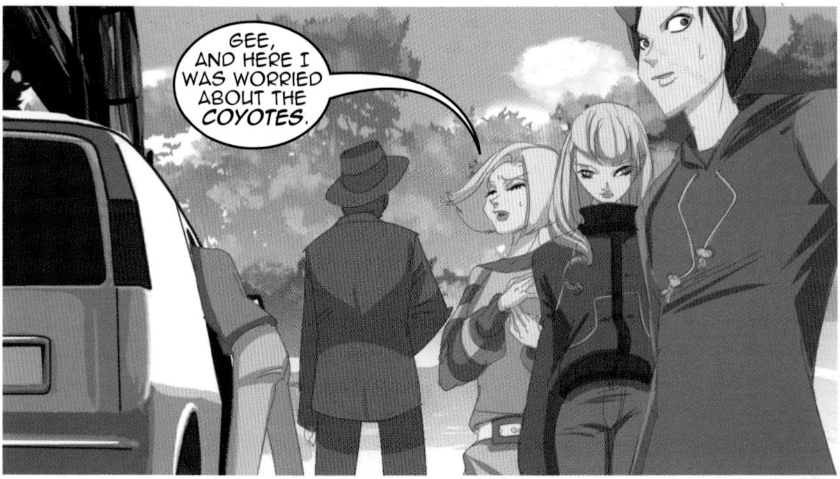
GEE, AND HERE I WAS WORRIED ABOUT THE COYOTES.

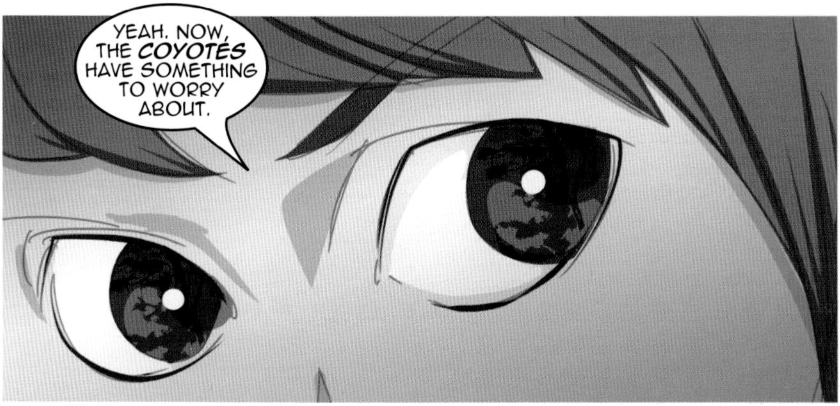
YEAH. NOW, THE COYOTES HAVE SOMETHING TO WORRY ABOUT.

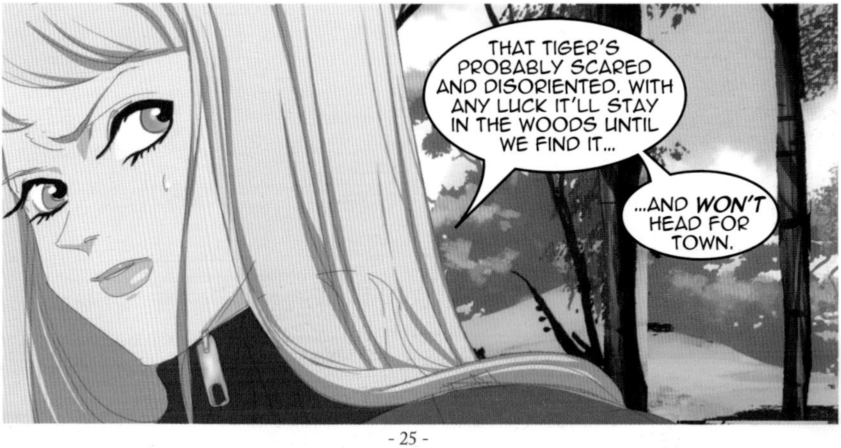
THAT TIGER'S PROBABLY SCARED AND DISORIENTED. WITH ANY LUCK IT'LL STAY IN THE WOODS UNTIL WE FIND IT...
...AND WON'T HEAD FOR TOWN.

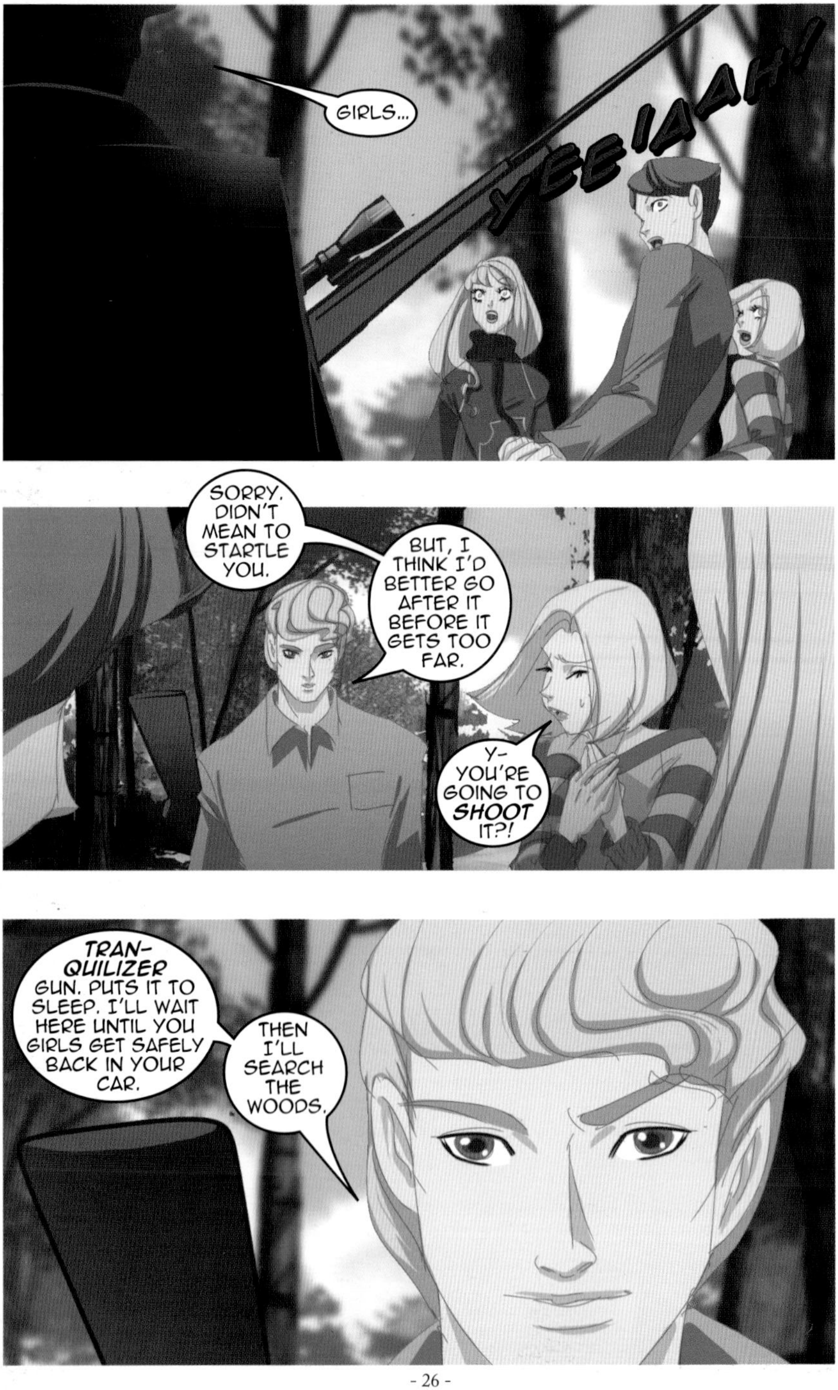
GIRLS...
YEE'IAAAH!
SORRY. DIDN'T MEAN TO STARTLE YOU.
BUT, I THINK I'D BETTER GO AFTER IT BEFORE IT GETS TOO FAR.
Y-YOU'RE GOING TO *SHOOT* IT?!
TRAN-QUILIZER GUN. PUTS IT TO SLEEP. I'LL WAIT HERE UNTIL YOU GIRLS GET SAFELY BACK IN YOUR CAR.
THEN I'LL SEARCH THE WOODS.

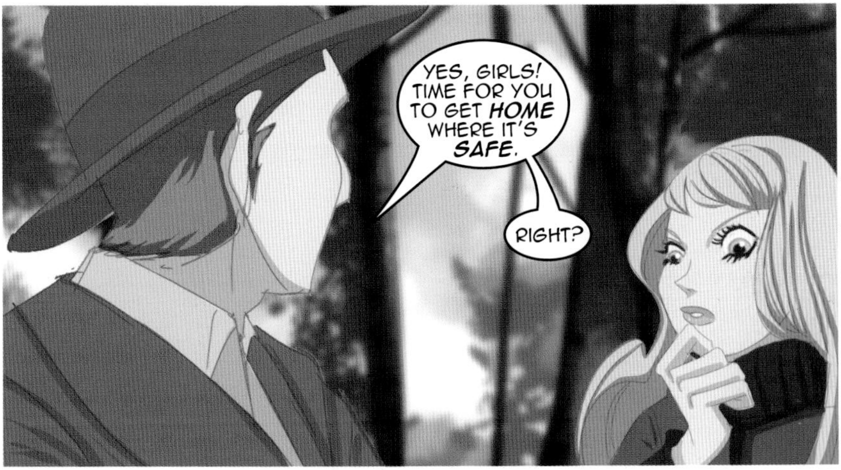
YES, GIRLS! TIME FOR YOU TO GET HOME WHERE IT'S SAFE.
RIGHT?

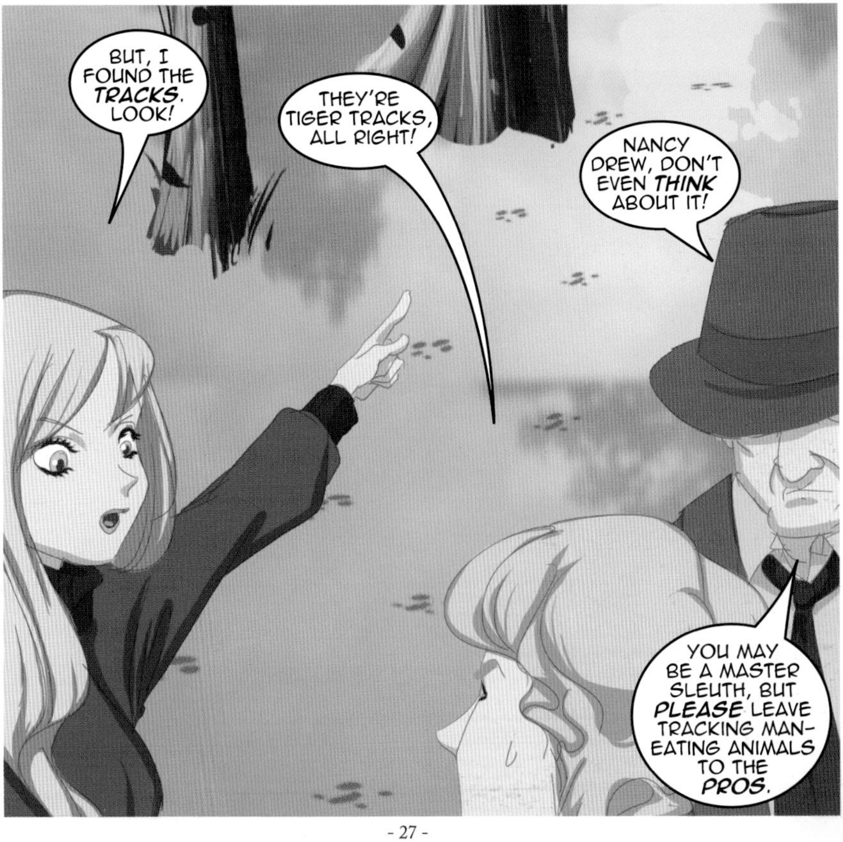
BUT, I FOUND THE TRACKS. LOOK!
THEY'RE TIGER TRACKS, ALL RIGHT!
NANCY DREW, DON'T EVEN THINK ABOUT IT!
YOU MAY BE A MASTER SLEUTH, BUT PLEASE LEAVE TRACKING MAN-EATING ANIMALS TO THE PROS.

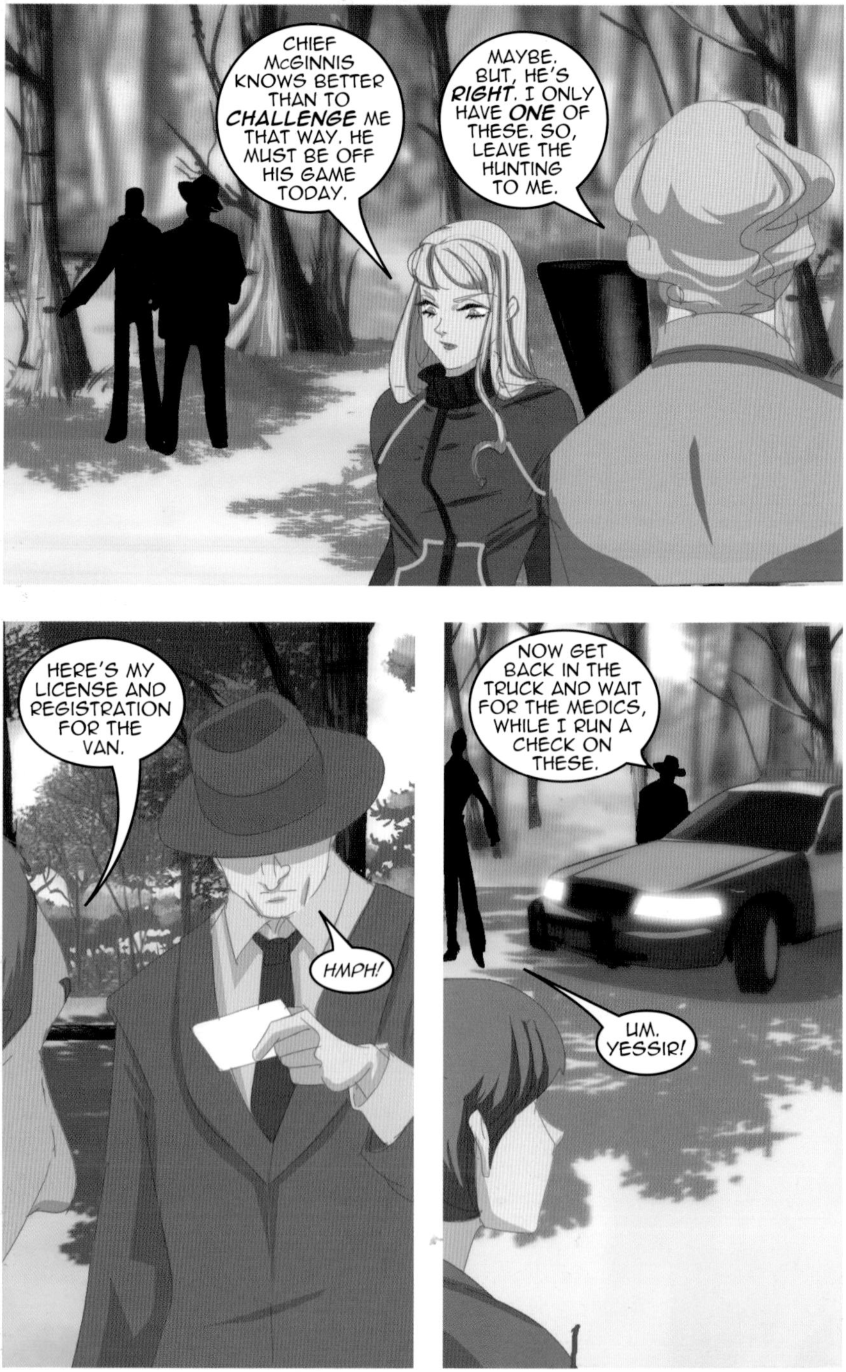
CHIEF McGINNIS KNOWS BETTER THAN TO **CHALLENGE** ME THAT WAY. HE MUST BE OFF HIS GAME TODAY.
MAYBE. BUT, HE'S **RIGHT**. I ONLY HAVE **ONE** OF THESE. SO, LEAVE THE HUNTING TO ME.
HERE'S MY LICENSE AND REGISTRATION FOR THE VAN.
HMPH!
NOW GET BACK IN THE TRUCK AND WAIT FOR THE MEDICS, WHILE I RUN A CHECK ON THESE.
UM. YESSIR!

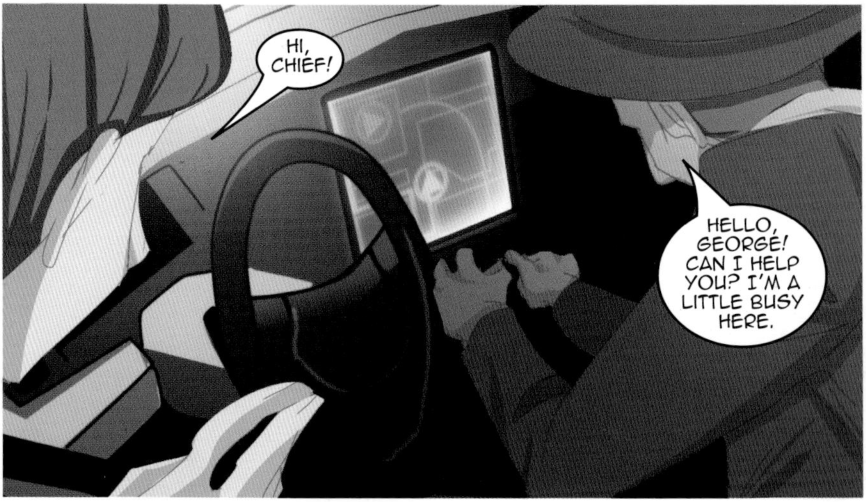
HI, CHIEF!
HELLO, GEORGE! CAN I HELP YOU? I'M A LITTLE BUSY HERE.

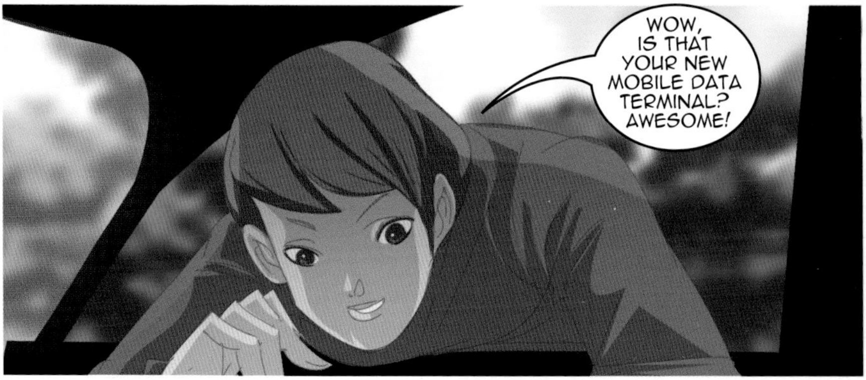
WOW, IS THAT YOUR NEW MOBILE DATA TERMINAL? AWESOME!

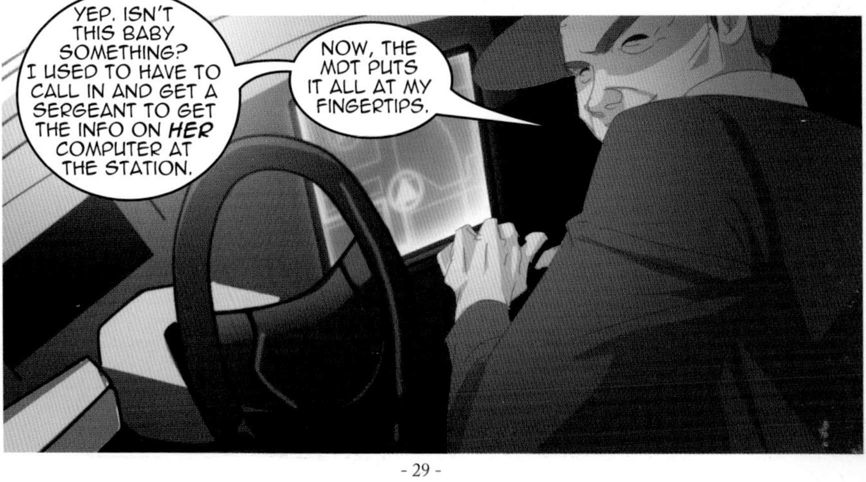
YEP. ISN'T THIS BABY SOMETHING? I USED TO HAVE TO CALL IN AND GET A SERGEANT TO GET THE INFO ON ***HER*** COMPUTER AT THE STATION.
NOW, THE MDT PUTS IT ALL AT MY FINGERTIPS.

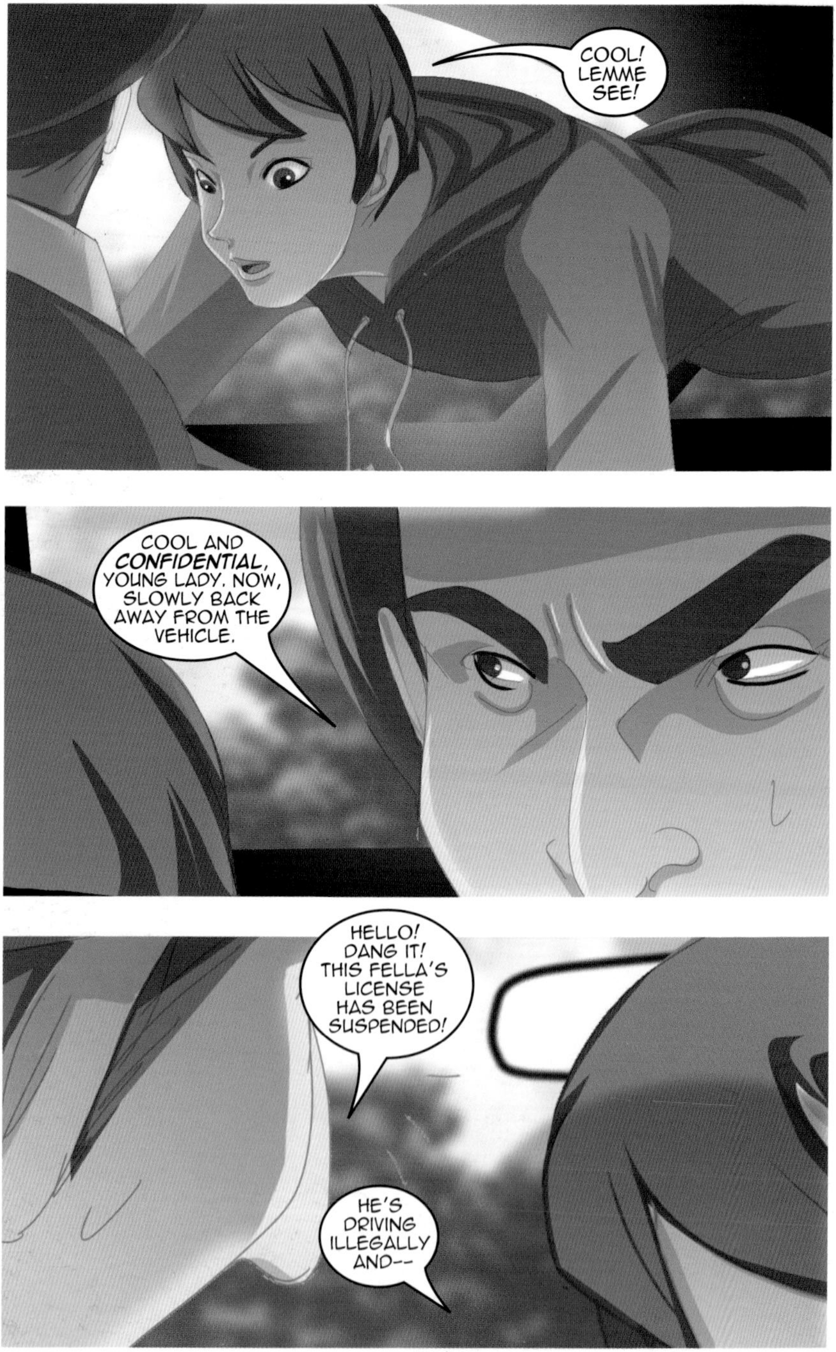

COOL! LEMME SEE!
COOL AND CONFIDENTIAL, YOUNG LADY. NOW, SLOWLY BACK AWAY FROM THE VEHICLE.
HELLO! DANG IT! THIS FELLA'S LICENSE HAS BEEN SUSPENDED!
HE'S DRIVING ILLEGALLY AND--

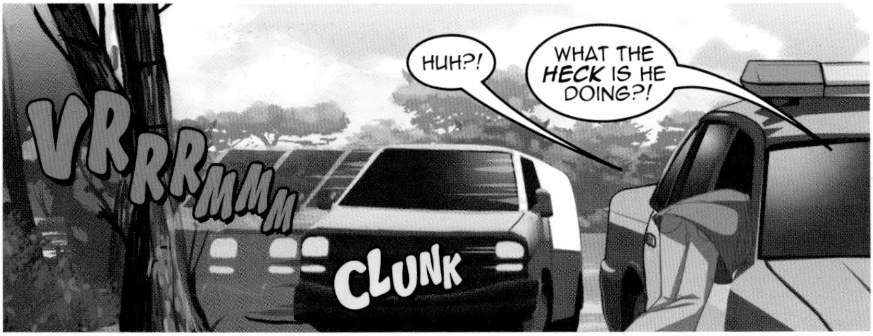
VRRRMMM
CLUNK
HUH?!
WHAT THE HECK IS HE DOING?!
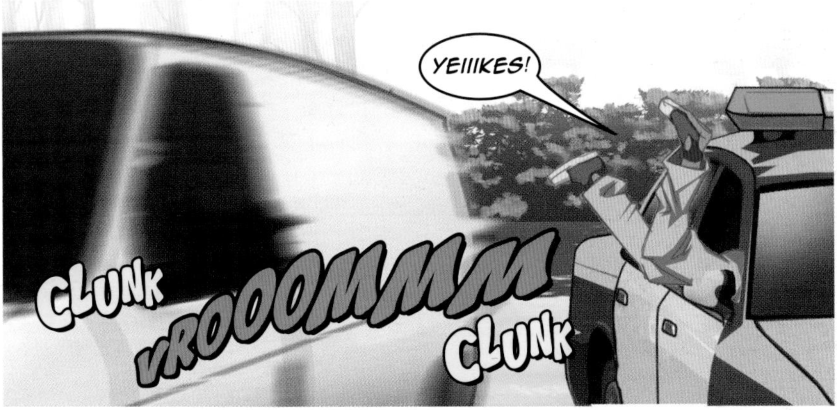
YEIIIKES!
CLUNK
VROOOMMMM
CLUNK
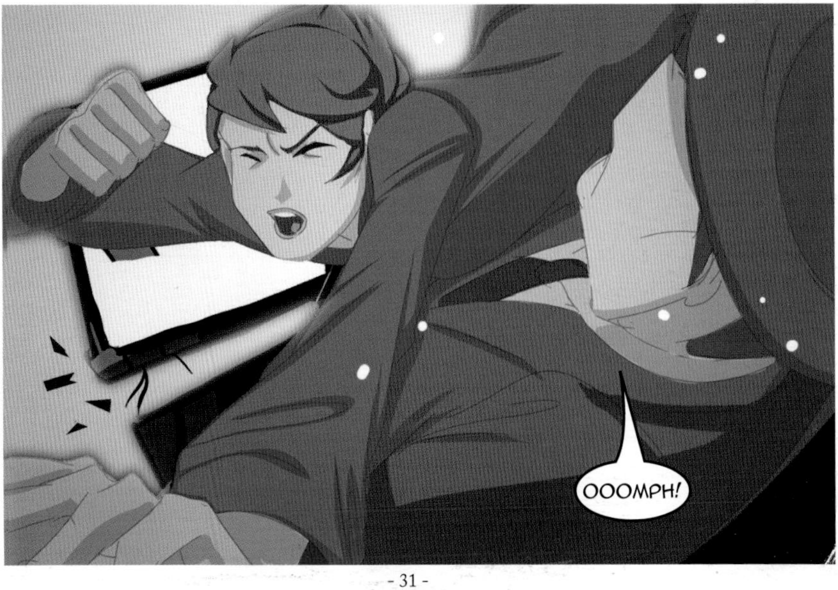
OOOMPH!

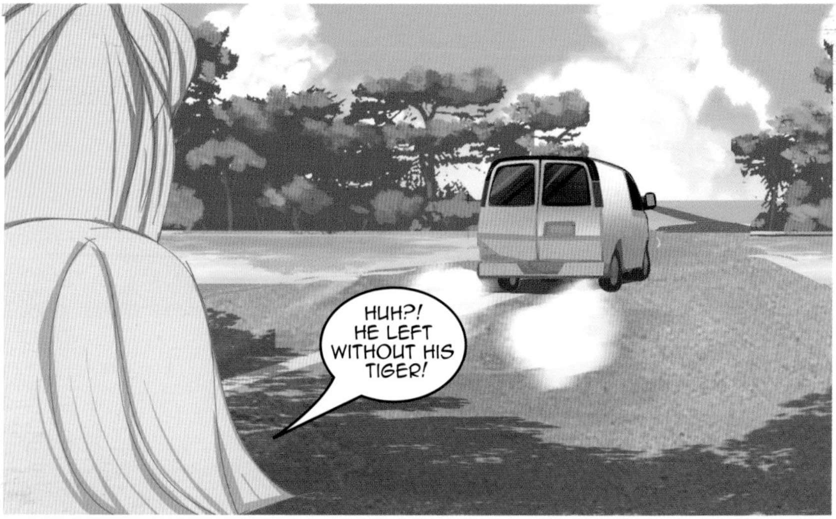
HUH?! HE LEFT WITHOUT HIS TIGER!

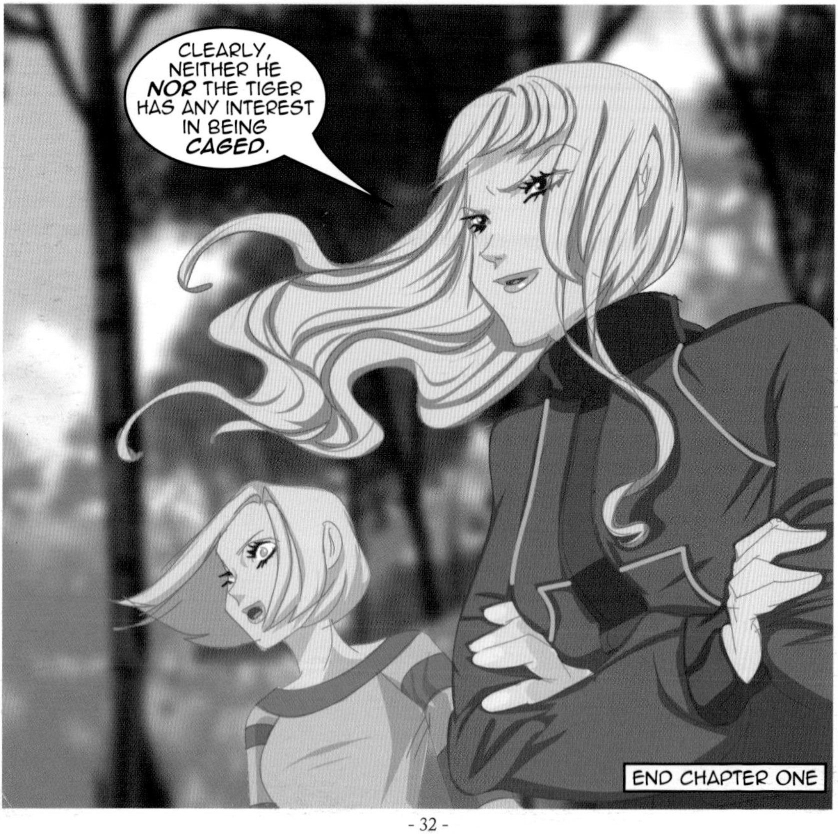
CLEARLY, NEITHER HE NOR THE TIGER HAS ANY INTEREST IN BEING CAGED.
END CHAPTER ONE

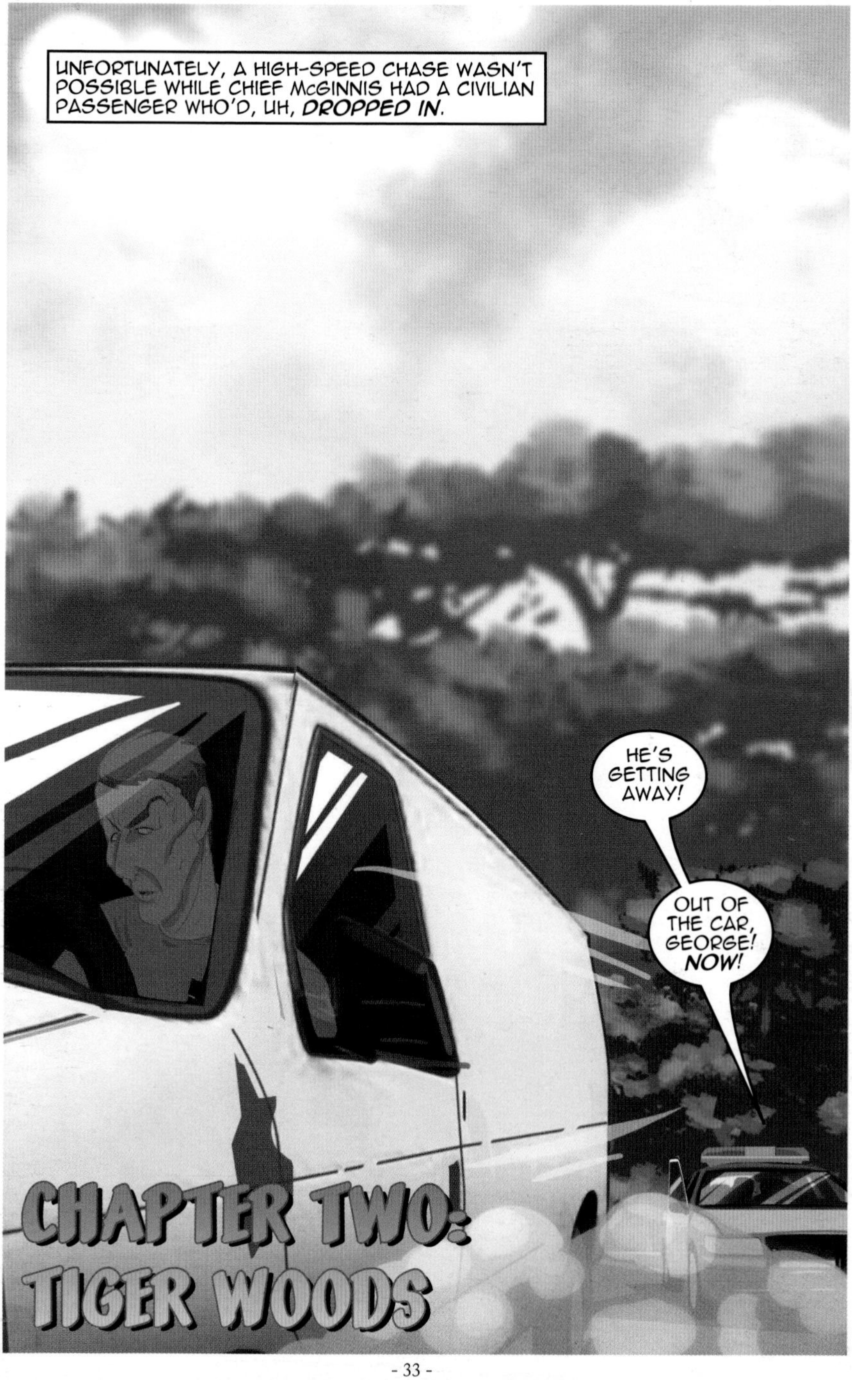
UNFORTUNATELY, A HIGH-SPEED CHASE WASN'T POSSIBLE WHILE CHIEF McGINNIS HAD A CIVILIAN PASSENGER WHO'D, UH, *DROPPED IN*.
HE'S GETTING AWAY!
OUT OF THE CAR, GEORGE! **NOW!**
CHAPTER TWO: TIGER WOODS

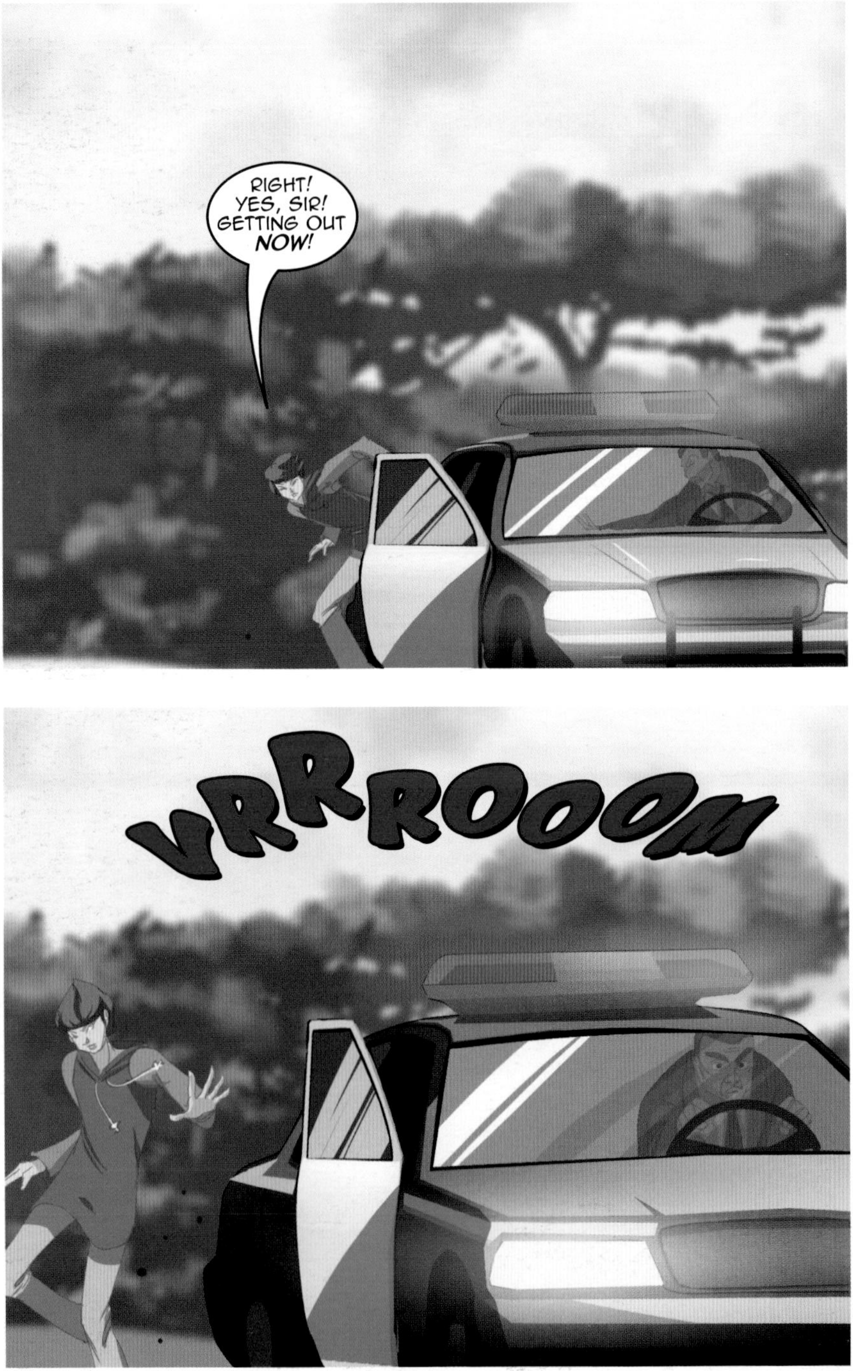
RIGHT! YES, SIR! GETTING OUT NOW!
VRRROOOM

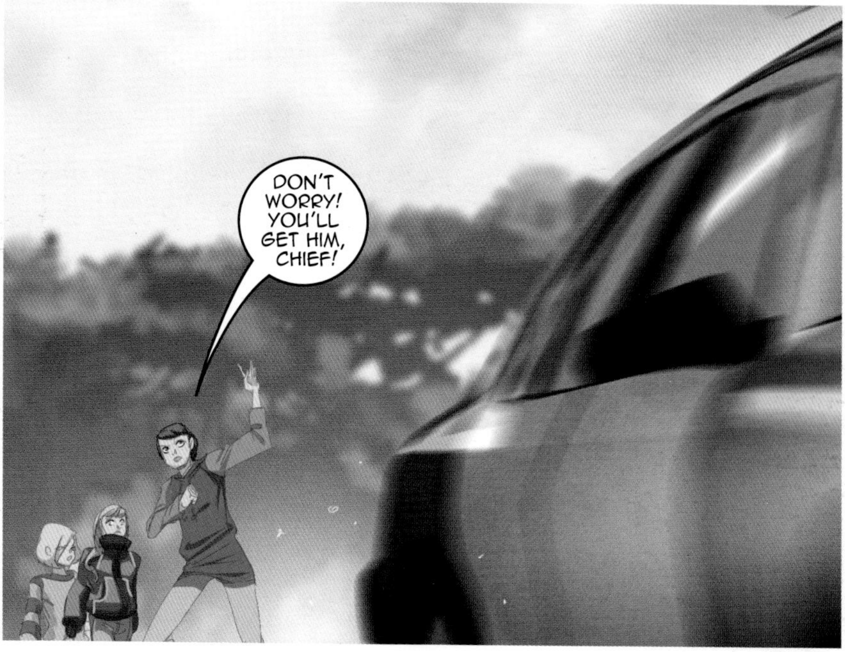
DON'T WORRY! YOU'LL GET HIM, CHIEF!

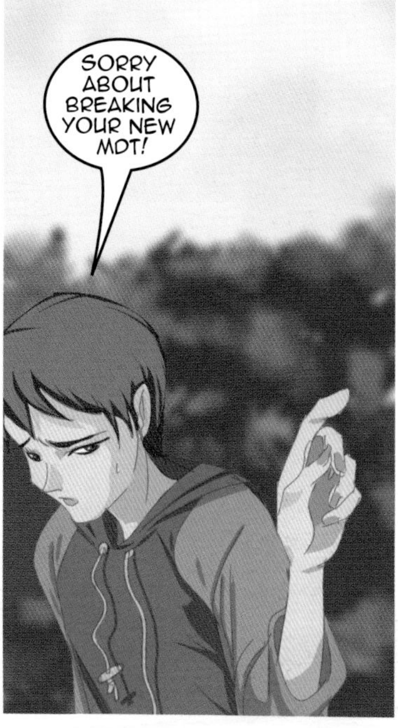
SORRY ABOUT BREAKING YOUR NEW MDT!

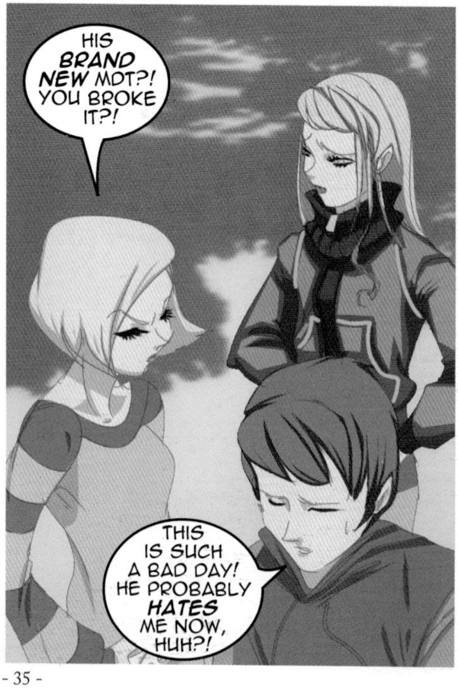
HIS BRAND NEW MDT?! YOU BROKE IT?!
THIS IS SUCH A BAD DAY! HE PROBABLY HATES ME NOW, HUH?!

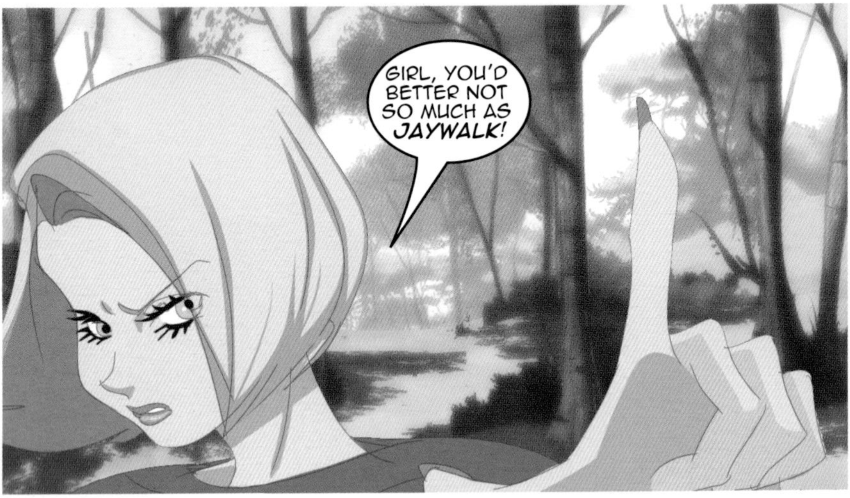
GIRL, YOU'D BETTER NOT SO MUCH AS JAYWALK!

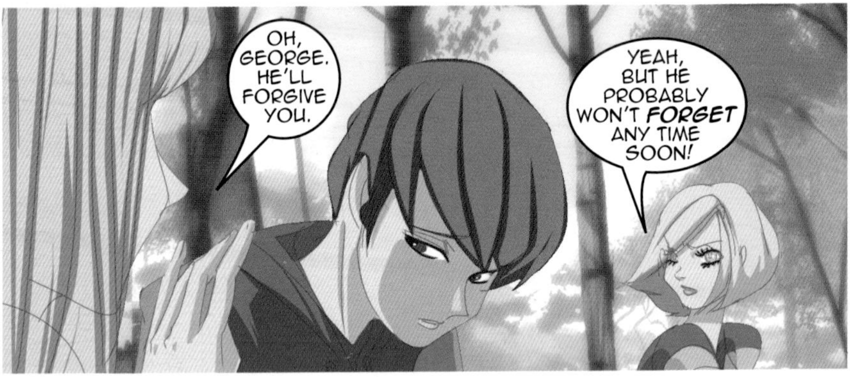
OH, GEORGE. HE'LL FORGIVE YOU.
YEAH, BUT HE PROBABLY WON'T FORGET ANY TIME SOON!

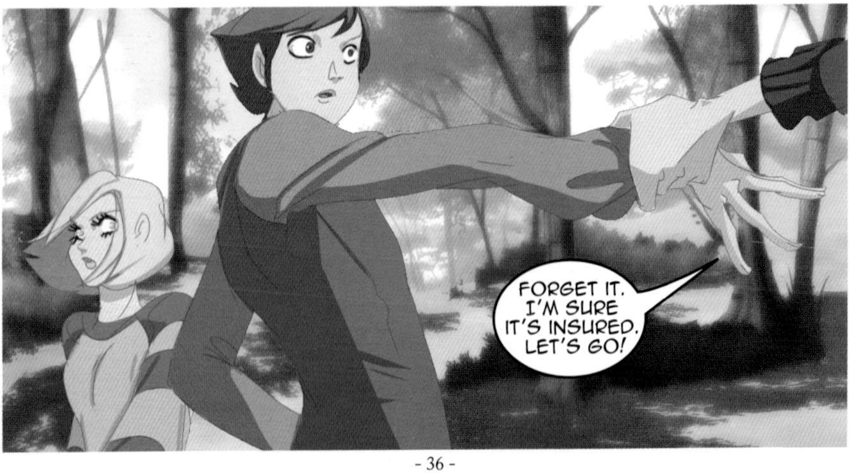
FORGET IT. I'M SURE IT'S INSURED. LET'S GO!

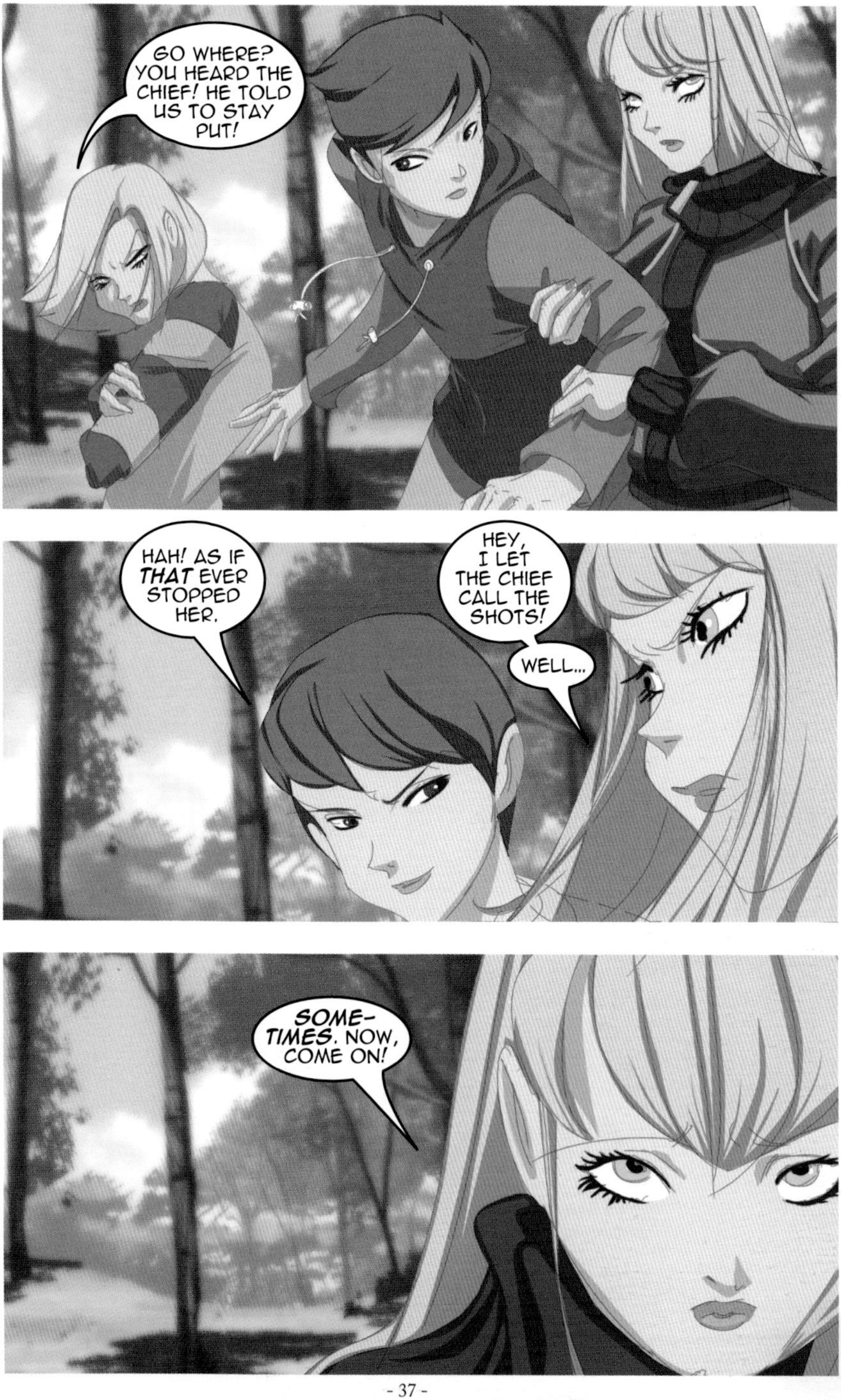
GO WHERE? YOU HEARD THE CHIEF! HE TOLD US TO STAY PUT!
HAH! AS IF *THAT* EVER STOPPED HER.
HEY, I LET THE CHIEF CALL THE SHOTS!
WELL...
SOME-TIMES. NOW, COME ON!

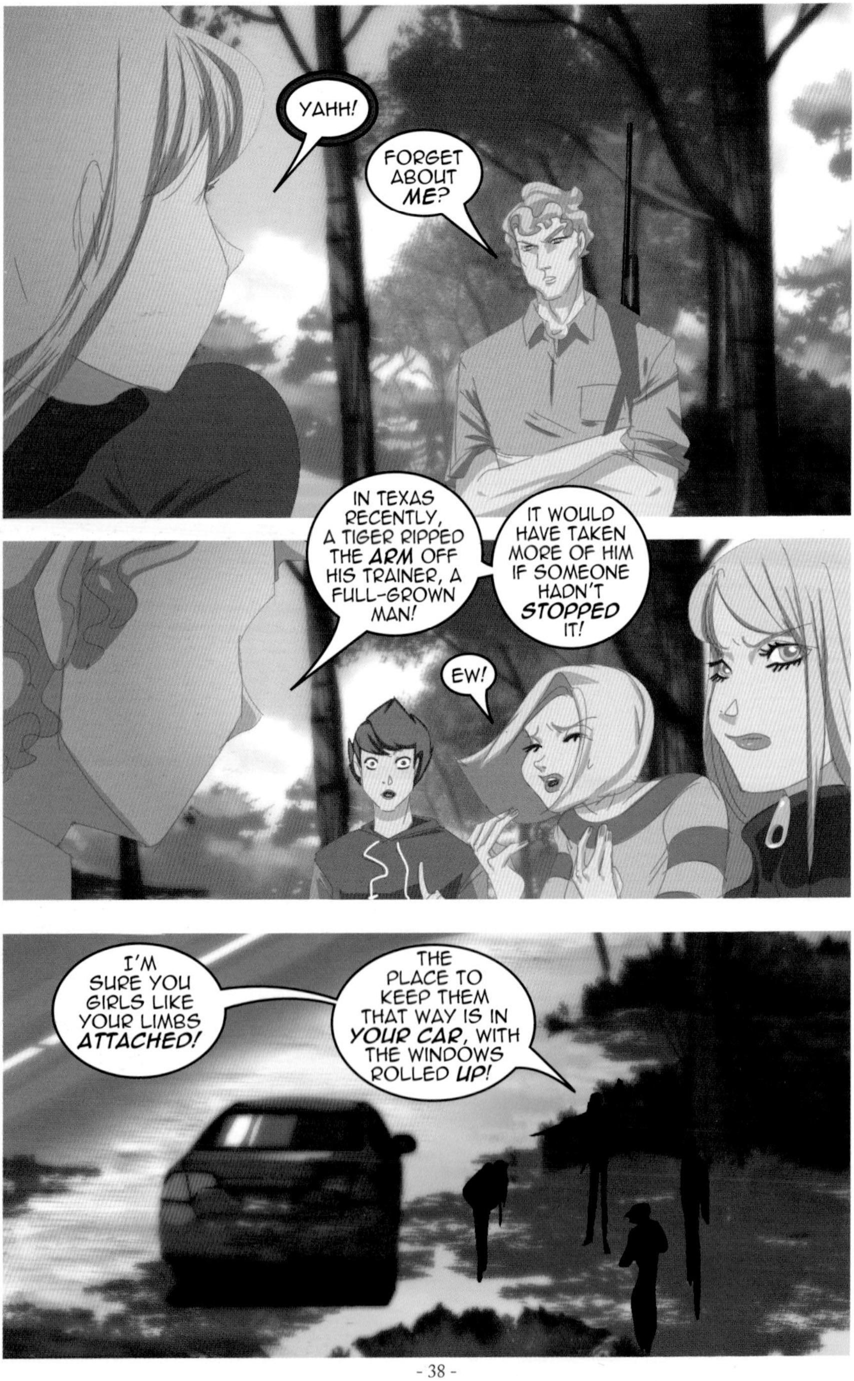
YAHH!
FORGET ABOUT ME?
IN TEXAS RECENTLY, A TIGER RIPPED THE ARM OFF HIS TRAINER, A FULL-GROWN MAN!
IT WOULD HAVE TAKEN MORE OF HIM IF SOMEONE HADN'T STOPPED IT!
EW!
I'M SURE YOU GIRLS LIKE YOUR LIMBS ATTACHED!
THE PLACE TO KEEP THEM THAT WAY IS IN YOUR CAR, WITH THE WINDOWS ROLLED UP!

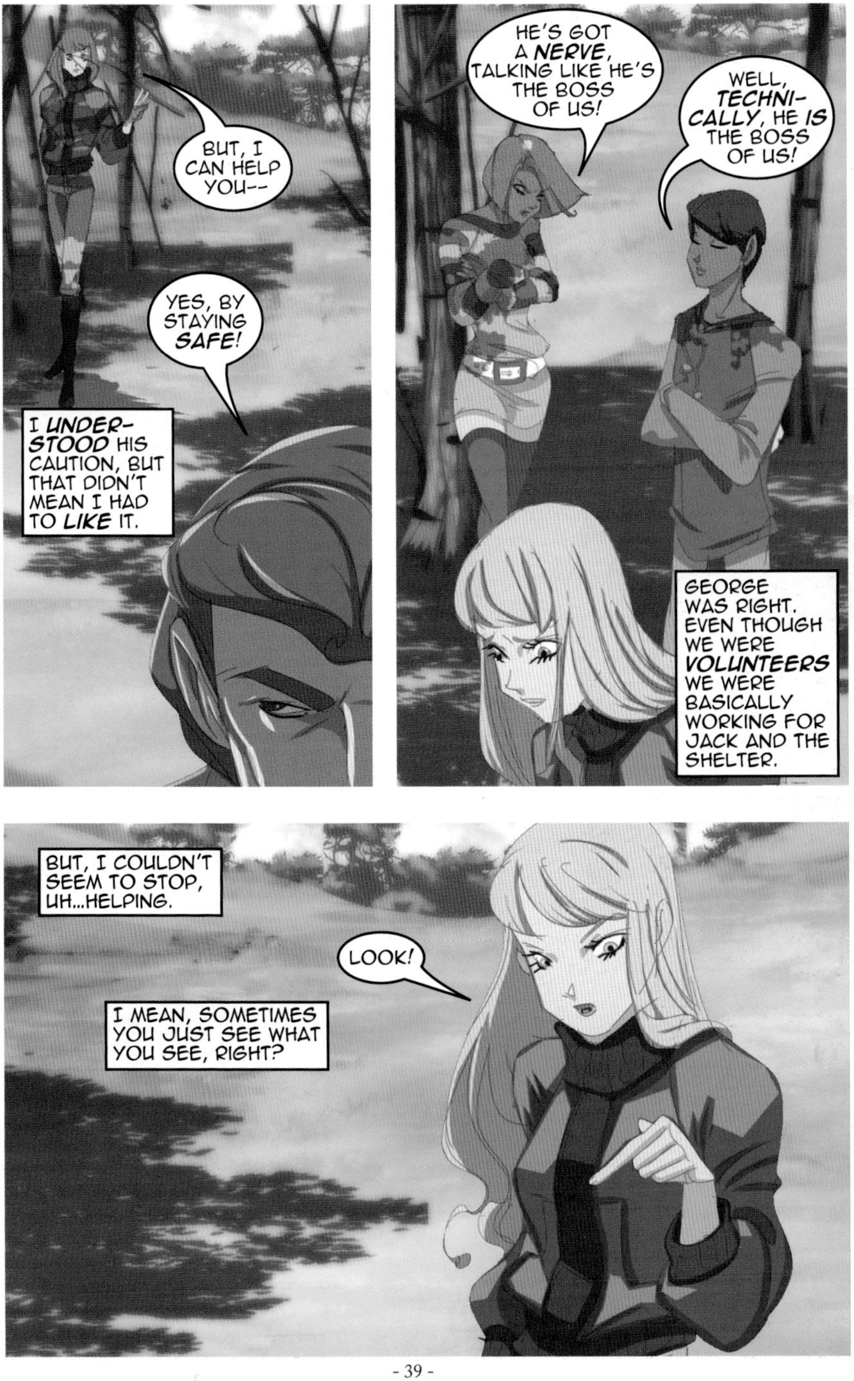
BUT, I CAN HELP YOU--
YES, BY STAYING SAFE!
I UNDERSTOOD HIS CAUTION, BUT THAT DIDN'T MEAN I HAD TO LIKE IT.
HE'S GOT A NERVE, TALKING LIKE HE'S THE BOSS OF US!
WELL, TECHNICALLY, HE IS THE BOSS OF US!
GEORGE WAS RIGHT. EVEN THOUGH WE WERE VOLUNTEERS WE WERE BASICALLY WORKING FOR JACK AND THE SHELTER.
BUT, I COULDN'T SEEM TO STOP, UH...HELPING.
LOOK!
I MEAN, SOMETIMES YOU JUST SEE WHAT YOU SEE, RIGHT?

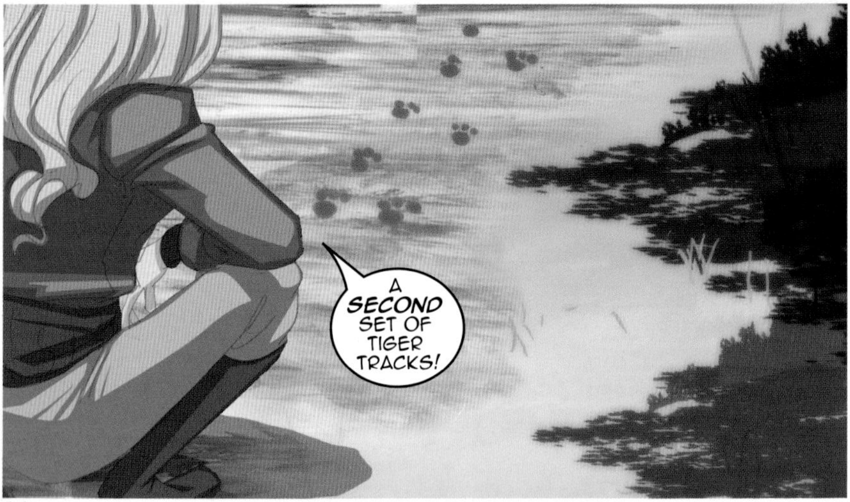
A SECOND SET OF TIGER TRACKS!

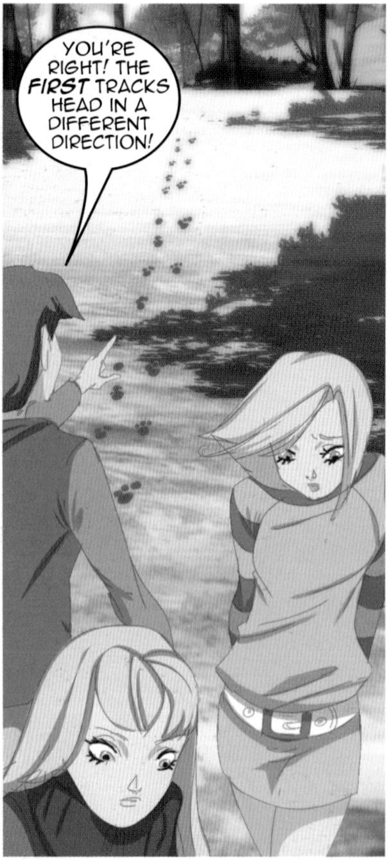
YOU'RE RIGHT! THE FIRST TRACKS HEAD IN A DIFFERENT DIRECTION!

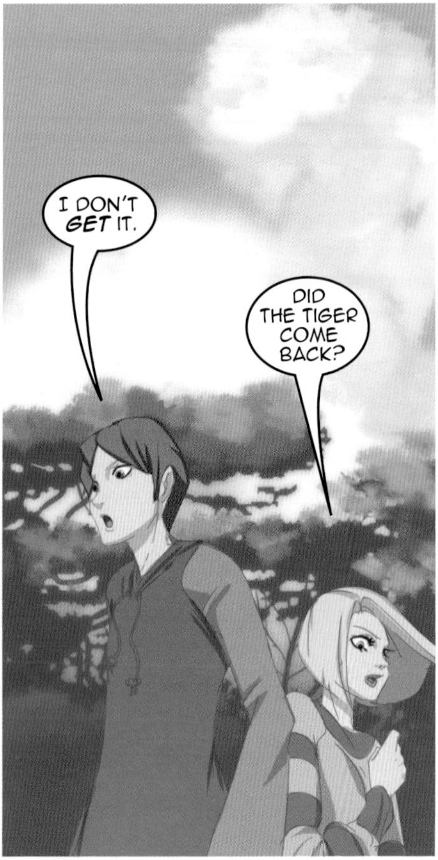
I DON'T GET IT.
DID THE TIGER COME BACK?

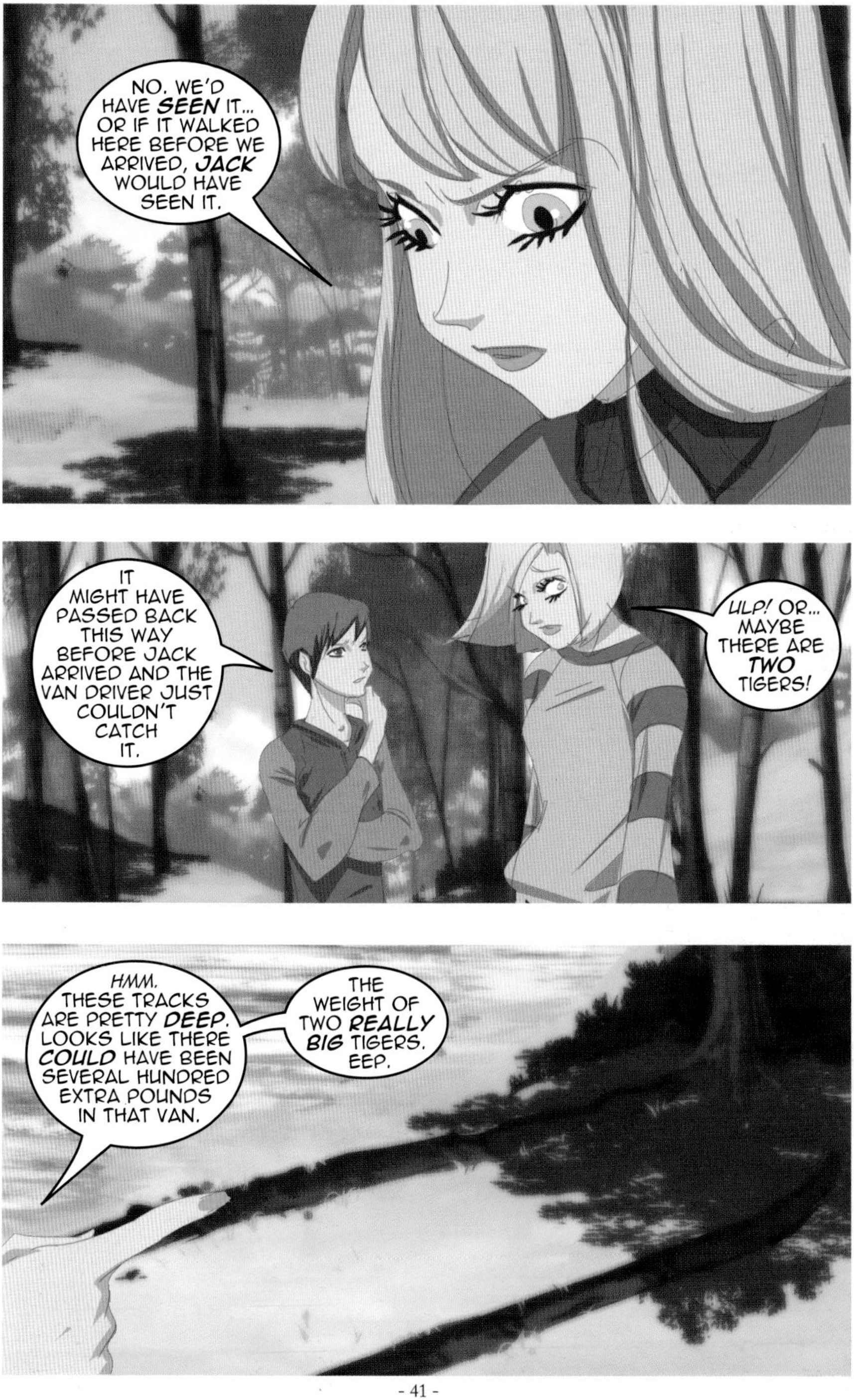
NO. WE'D HAVE SEEN IT... OR IF IT WALKED HERE BEFORE WE ARRIVED, JACK WOULD HAVE SEEN IT.
IT MIGHT HAVE PASSED BACK THIS WAY BEFORE JACK ARRIVED AND THE VAN DRIVER JUST COULDN'T CATCH IT.
ULP! OR... MAYBE THERE ARE TWO TIGERS!
HMM. THESE TRACKS ARE PRETTY DEEP. LOOKS LIKE THERE COULD HAVE BEEN SEVERAL HUNDRED EXTRA POUNDS IN THAT VAN.
THE WEIGHT OF TWO REALLY BIG TIGERS. EEP.

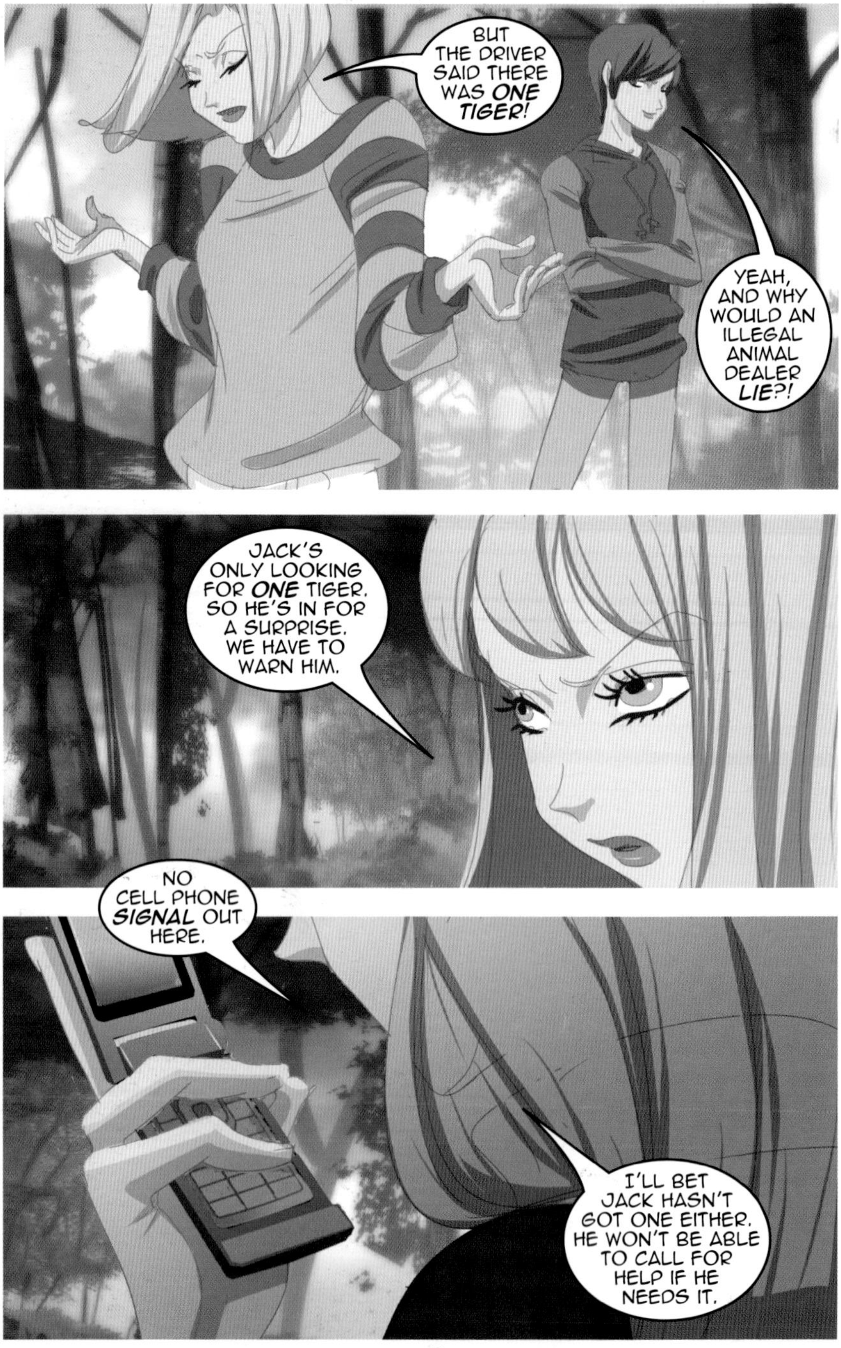
BUT THE DRIVER SAID THERE WAS ONE TIGER!
YEAH, AND WHY WOULD AN ILLEGAL ANIMAL DEALER LIE?!
JACK'S ONLY LOOKING FOR ONE TIGER. SO HE'S IN FOR A SURPRISE. WE HAVE TO WARN HIM.
NO CELL PHONE SIGNAL OUT HERE.
I'LL BET JACK HASN'T GOT ONE EITHER. HE WON'T BE ABLE TO CALL FOR HELP IF HE NEEDS IT.

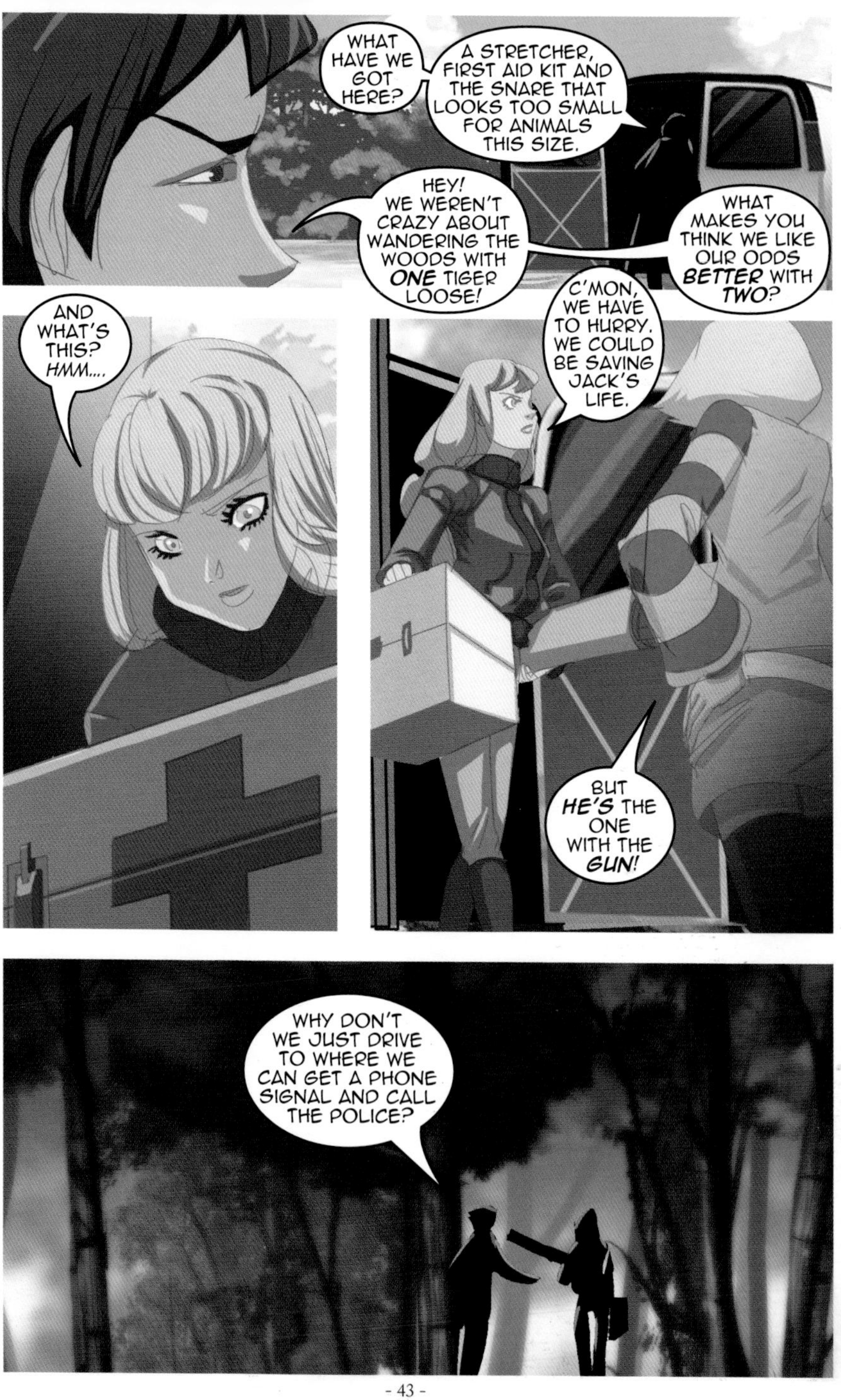
WHAT HAVE WE GOT HERE?
A STRETCHER, FIRST AID KIT AND THE SNARE THAT LOOKS TOO SMALL FOR ANIMALS THIS SIZE.
HEY! WE WEREN'T CRAZY ABOUT WANDERING THE WOODS WITH *ONE* TIGER LOOSE!
WHAT MAKES YOU THINK WE LIKE OUR ODDS *BETTER* WITH *TWO*?
AND WHAT'S THIS? *HMM....*
C'MON, WE HAVE TO HURRY. WE COULD BE SAVING JACK'S LIFE.
BUT *HE'S* THE ONE WITH THE *GUN*!
WHY DON'T WE JUST DRIVE TO WHERE WE CAN GET A PHONE SIGNAL AND CALL THE POLICE?

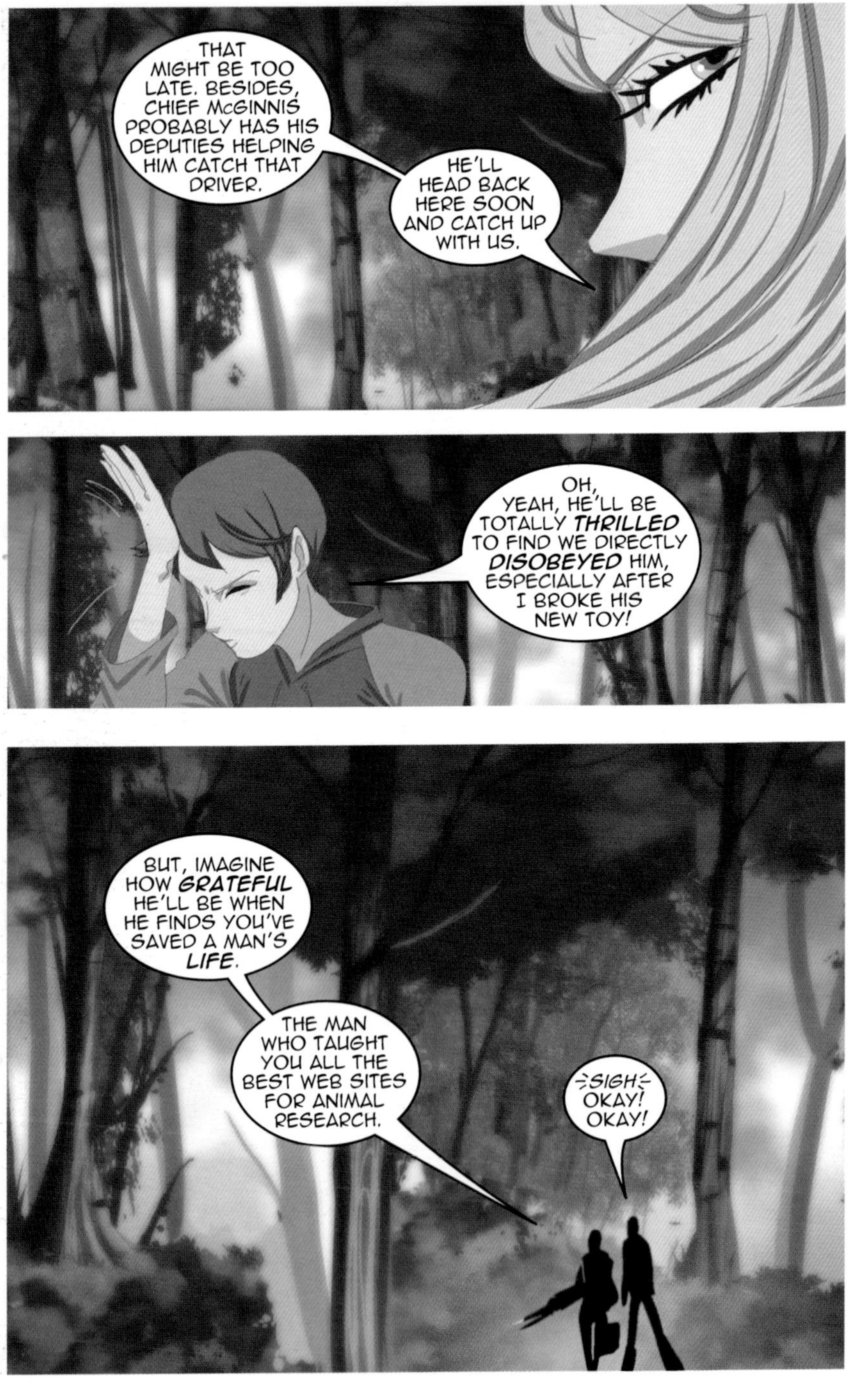
THAT MIGHT BE TOO LATE. BESIDES, CHIEF McGINNIS PROBABLY HAS HIS DEPUTIES HELPING HIM CATCH THAT DRIVER.
HE'LL HEAD BACK HERE SOON AND CATCH UP WITH US.
OH, YEAH, HE'LL BE TOTALLY THRILLED TO FIND WE DIRECTLY DISOBEYED HIM, ESPECIALLY AFTER I BROKE HIS NEW TOY!
BUT, IMAGINE HOW GRATEFUL HE'LL BE WHEN HE FINDS YOU'VE SAVED A MAN'S LIFE.
THE MAN WHO TAUGHT YOU ALL THE BEST WEB SITES FOR ANIMAL RESEARCH.
SIGH OKAY! OKAY!

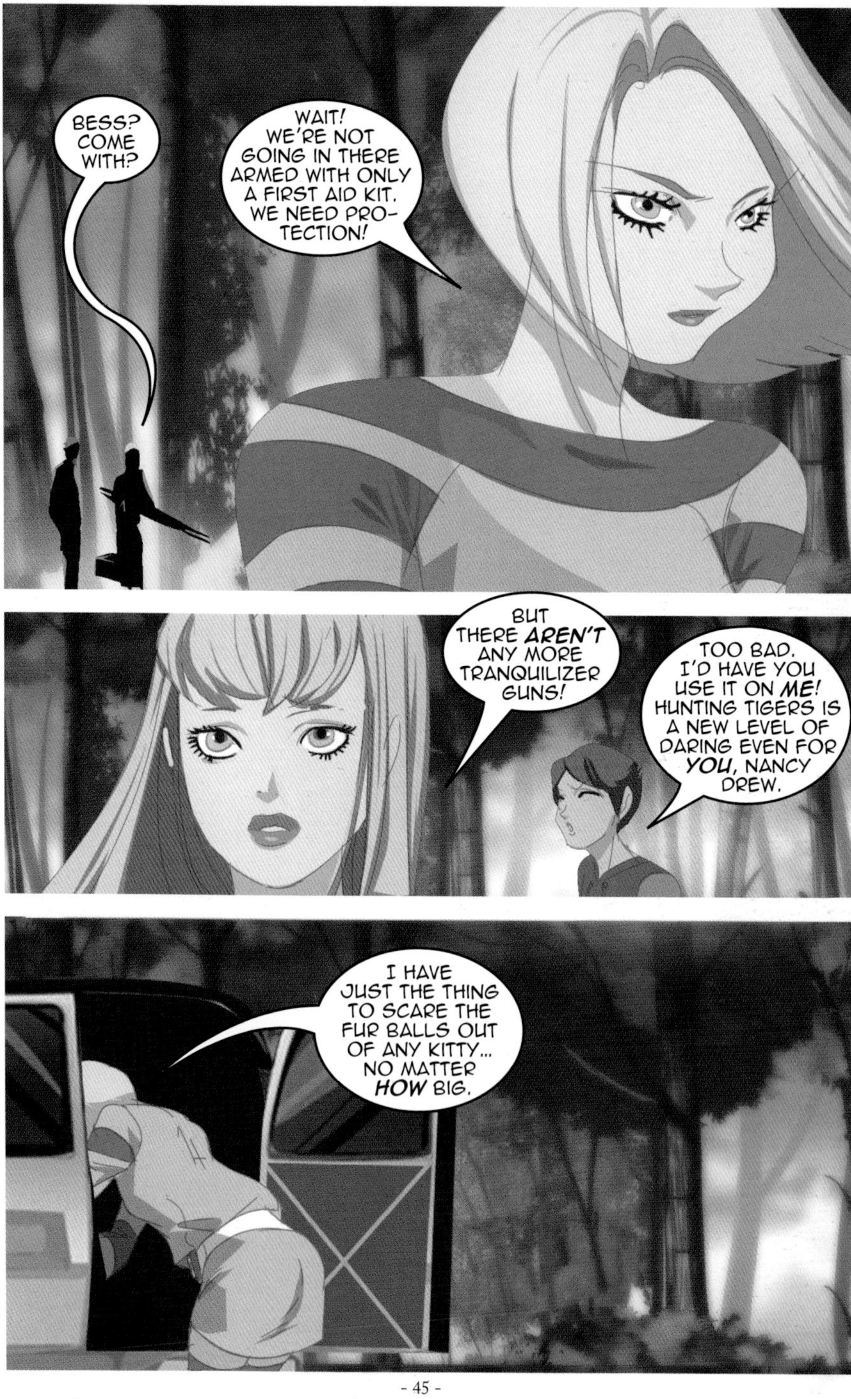
BESS? COME WITH?
WAIT! WE'RE NOT GOING IN THERE ARMED WITH ONLY A FIRST AID KIT. WE NEED PRO-TECTION!
BUT THERE AREN'T ANY MORE TRANQUILIZER GUNS!
TOO BAD. I'D HAVE YOU USE IT ON ME! HUNTING TIGERS IS A NEW LEVEL OF DARING EVEN FOR YOU, NANCY DREW.
I HAVE JUST THE THING TO SCARE THE FUR BALLS OUT OF ANY KITTY... NO MATTER HOW BIG.

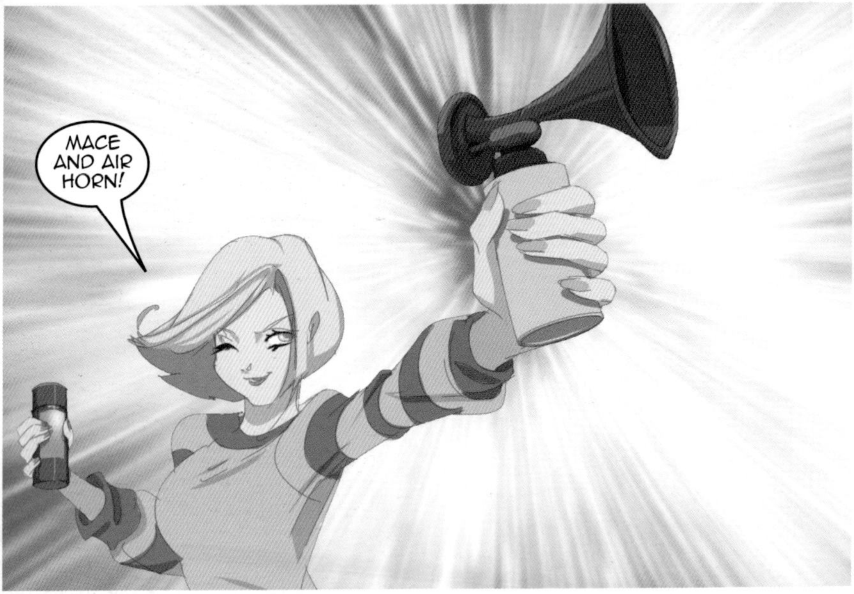
MACE AND AIR HORN!

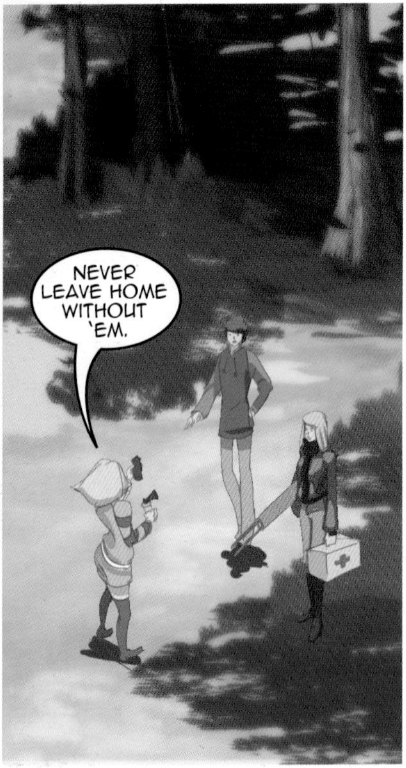
NEVER LEAVE HOME WITHOUT 'EM.

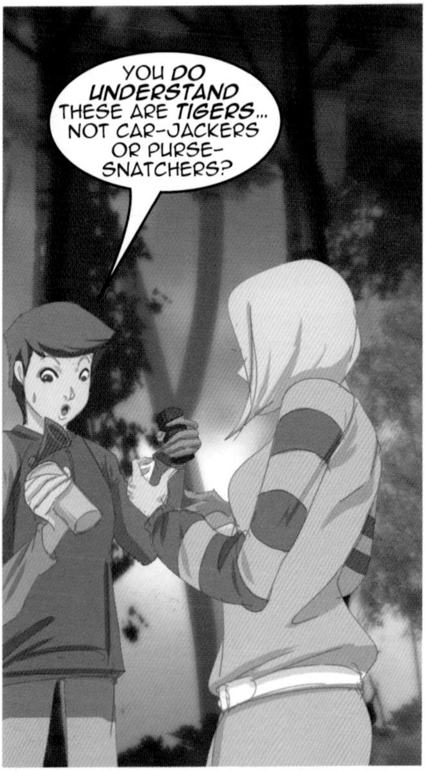
YOU *DO* ***UNDERSTAND*** THESE ARE ***TIGERS***... NOT CAR-JACKERS OR PURSE-SNATCHERS?

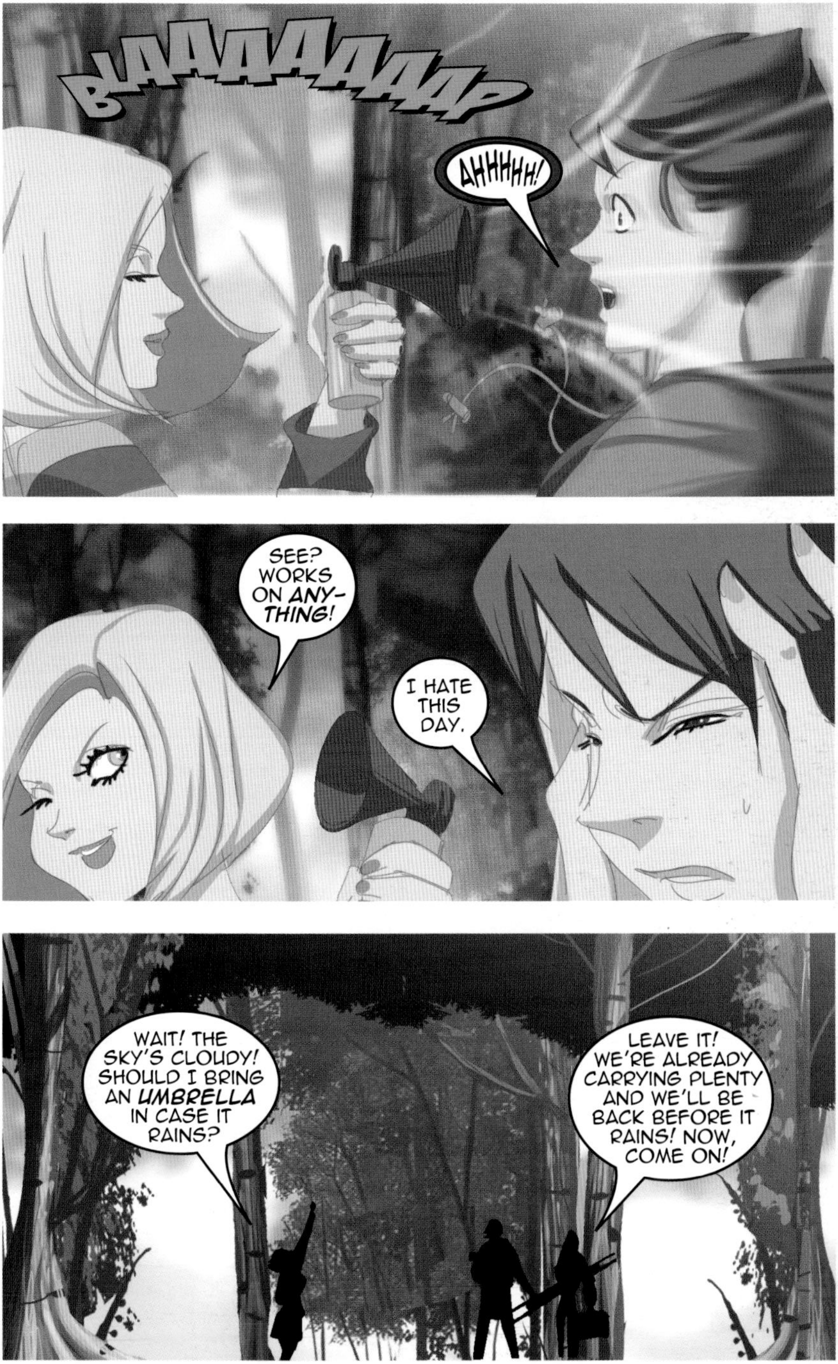

BLAAAAAAAAAP
AHHHHH!
SEE? WORKS ON ANY-THING!
I HATE THIS DAY.
WAIT! THE SKY'S CLOUDY! SHOULD I BRING AN UMBRELLA IN CASE IT RAINS?
LEAVE IT! WE'RE ALREADY CARRYING PLENTY AND WE'LL BE BACK BEFORE IT RAINS! NOW, COME ON!

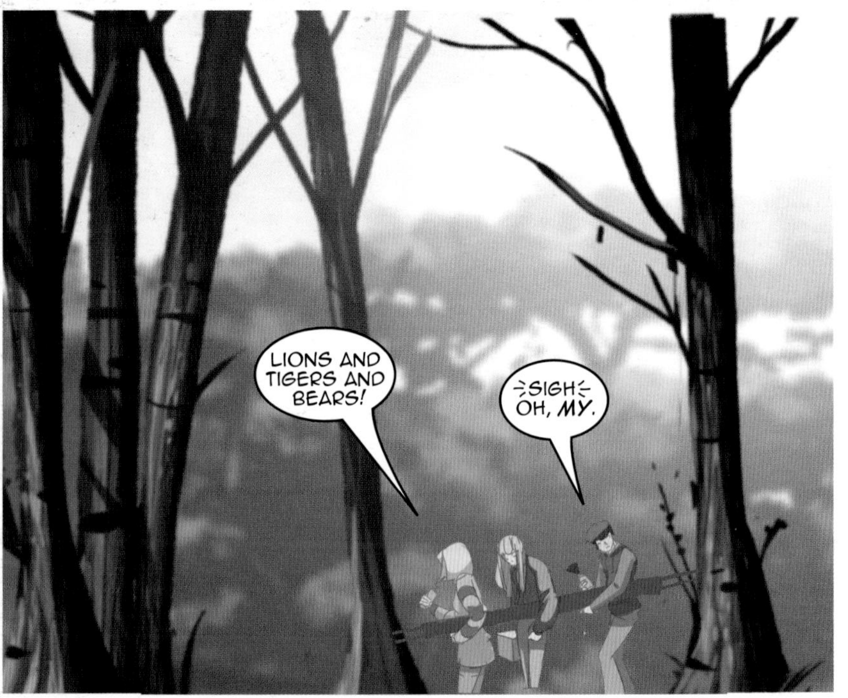
LIONS AND TIGERS AND BEARS!
=SIGH= OH, MY.

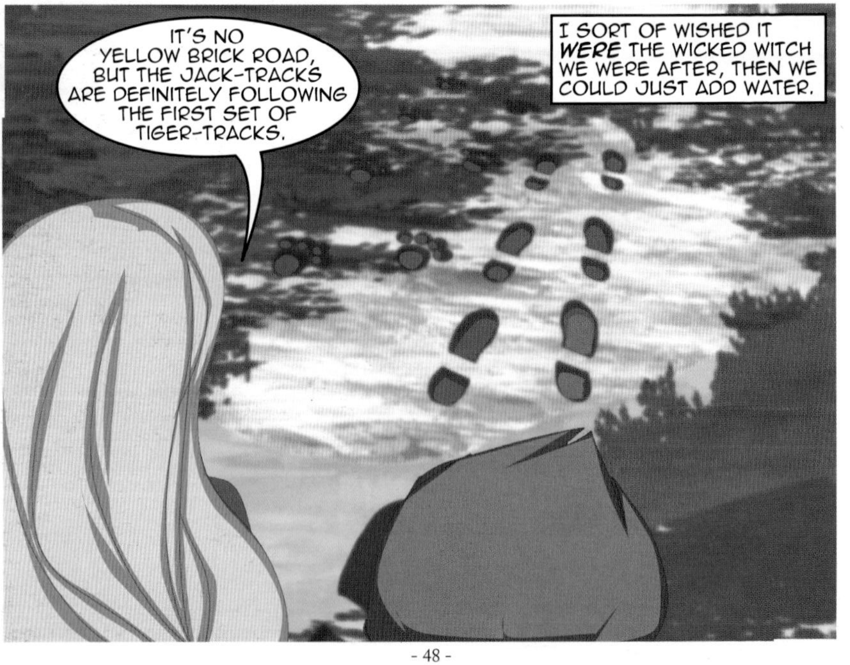
IT'S NO YELLOW BRICK ROAD, BUT THE JACK-TRACKS ARE DEFINITELY FOLLOWING THE FIRST SET OF TIGER-TRACKS.
I SORT OF WISHED IT WERE THE WICKED WITCH WE WERE AFTER, THEN WE COULD JUST ADD WATER.

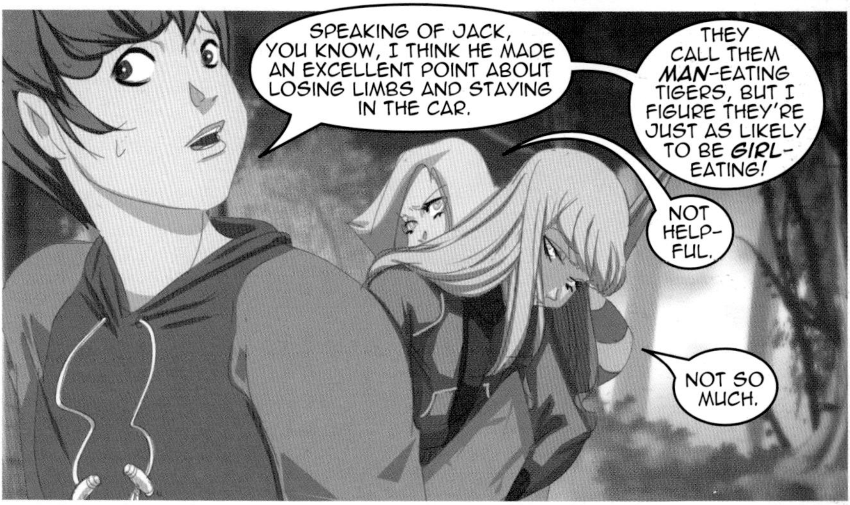
SPEAKING OF JACK, YOU KNOW, I THINK HE MADE AN EXCELLENT POINT ABOUT LOSING LIMBS AND STAYING IN THE CAR.
THEY CALL THEM MAN-EATING TIGERS, BUT I FIGURE THEY'RE JUST AS LIKELY TO BE GIRL-EATING!
NOT HELPFUL.
NOT SO MUCH.

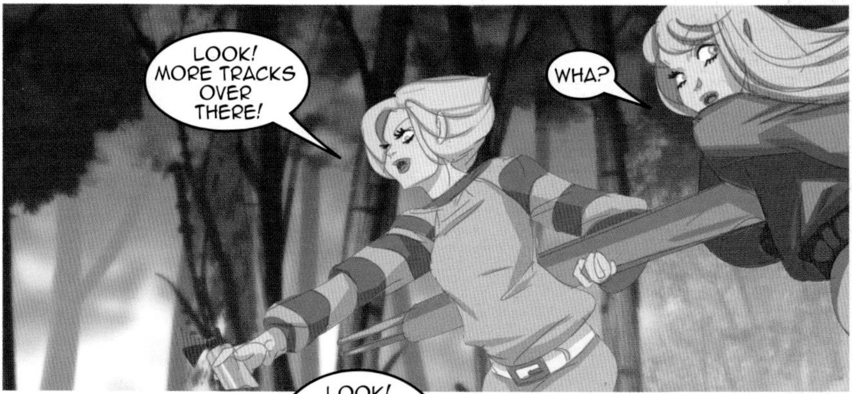
LOOK! MORE TRACKS OVER THERE!
WHA?

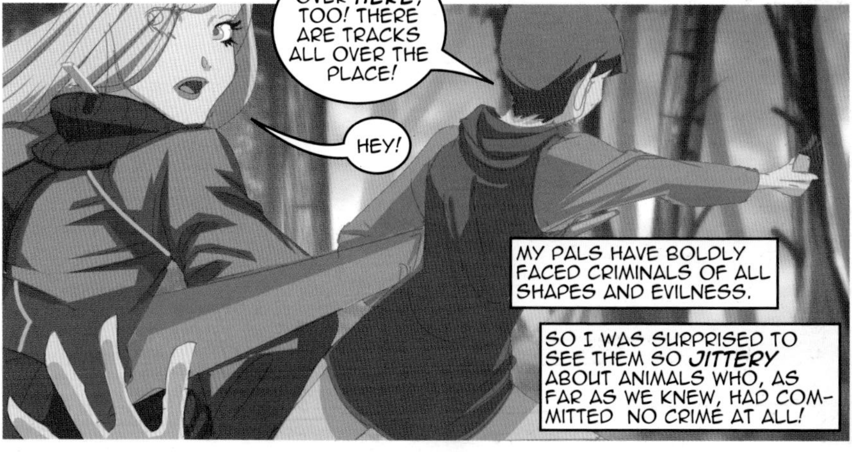
LOOK! OVER HERE, TOO! THERE ARE TRACKS ALL OVER THE PLACE!
HEY!
MY PALS HAVE BOLDLY FACED CRIMINALS OF ALL SHAPES AND EVILNESS.
SO I WAS SURPRISED TO SEE THEM SO JITTERY ABOUT ANIMALS WHO, AS FAR AS WE KNEW, HAD COMMITTED NO CRIME AT ALL!

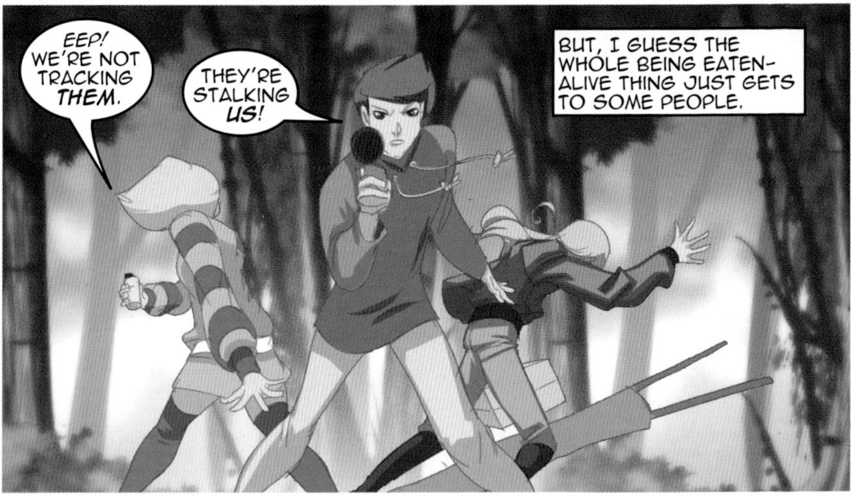
EEP! WE'RE NOT TRACKING THEM.
THEY'RE STALKING US!
BUT, I GUESS THE WHOLE BEING EATEN-ALIVE THING JUST GETS TO SOME PEOPLE.

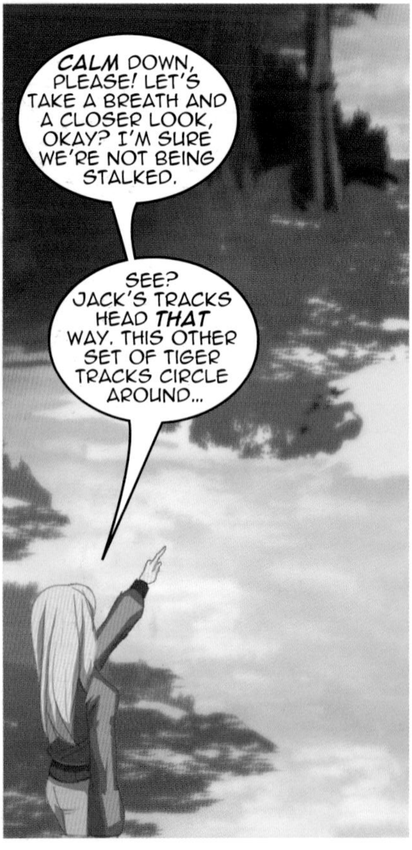
CALM DOWN, PLEASE! LET'S TAKE A BREATH AND A CLOSER LOOK, OKAY? I'M SURE WE'RE NOT BEING STALKED.
SEE? JACK'S TRACKS HEAD THAT WAY. THIS OTHER SET OF TIGER TRACKS CIRCLE AROUND...

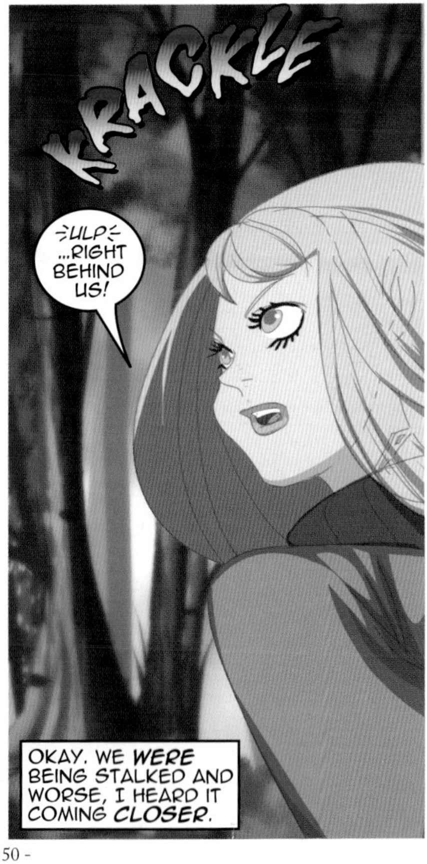
KRACKLE
ULP
...RIGHT BEHIND US!
OKAY. WE WERE BEING STALKED AND WORSE, I HEARD IT COMING CLOSER.

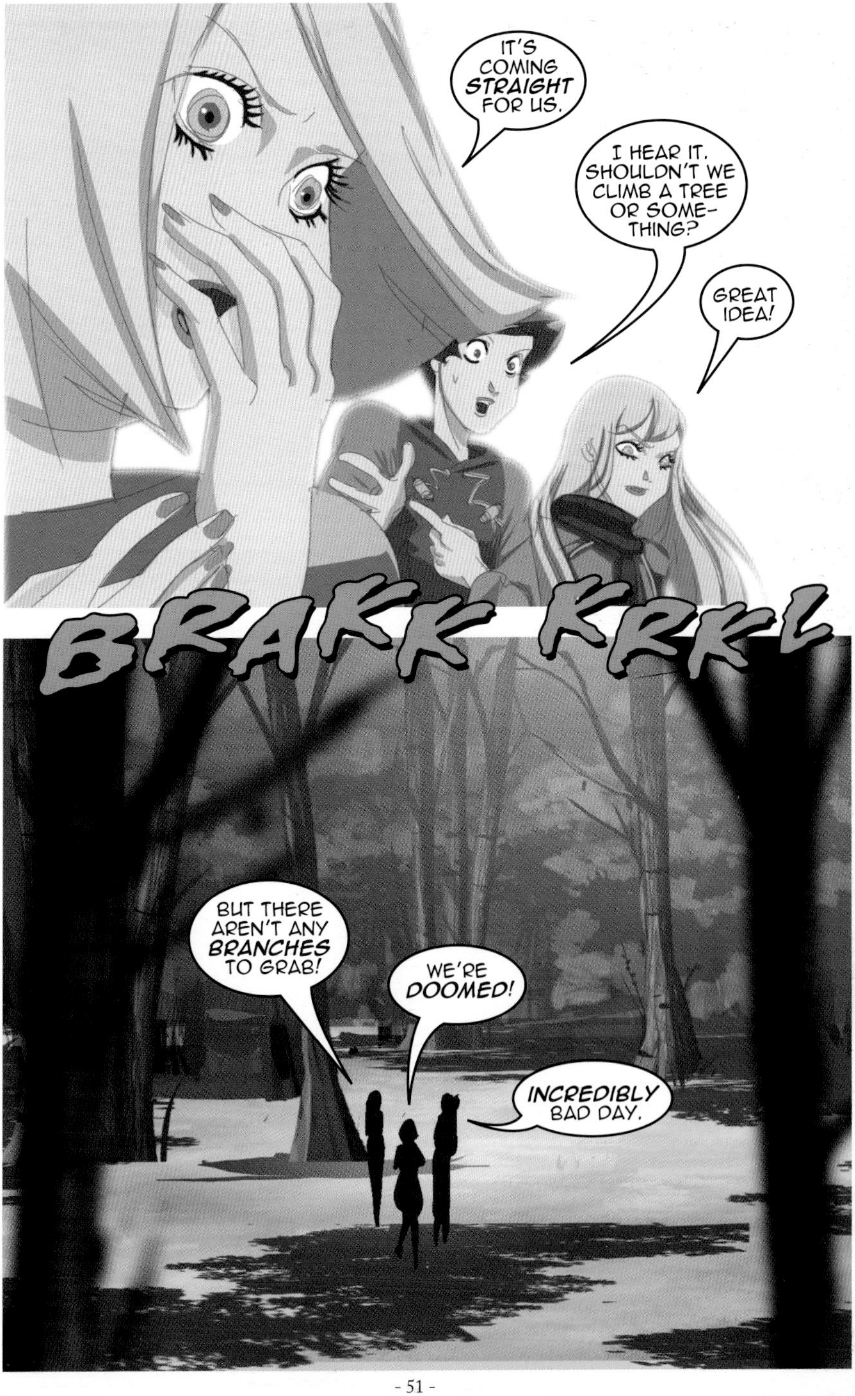
IT'S COMING STRAIGHT FOR US.
I HEAR IT. SHOULDN'T WE CLIMB A TREE OR SOME-THING?
GREAT IDEA!
BRAKK KRKL
BUT THERE AREN'T ANY BRANCHES TO GRAB!
WE'RE DOOMED!
INCREDIBLY BAD DAY.

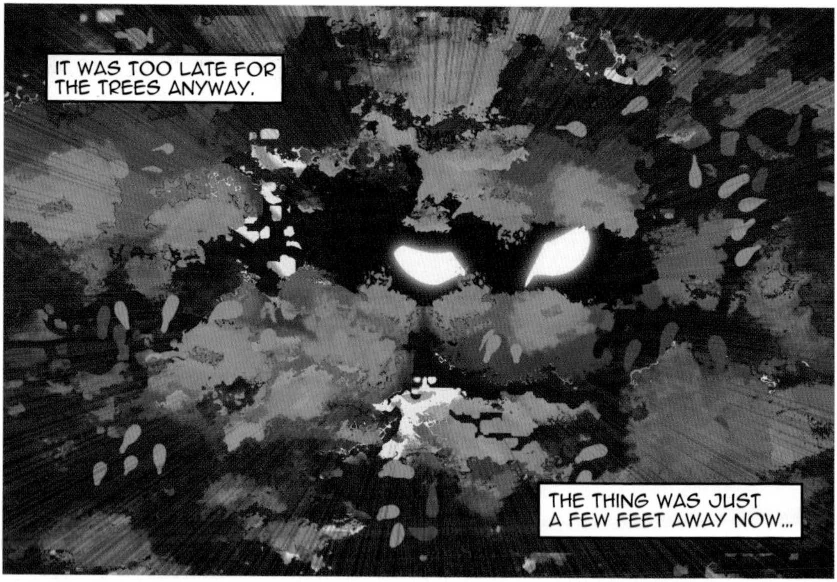
IT WAS TOO LATE FOR THE TREES ANYWAY.
THE THING WAS JUST A FEW FEET AWAY NOW...

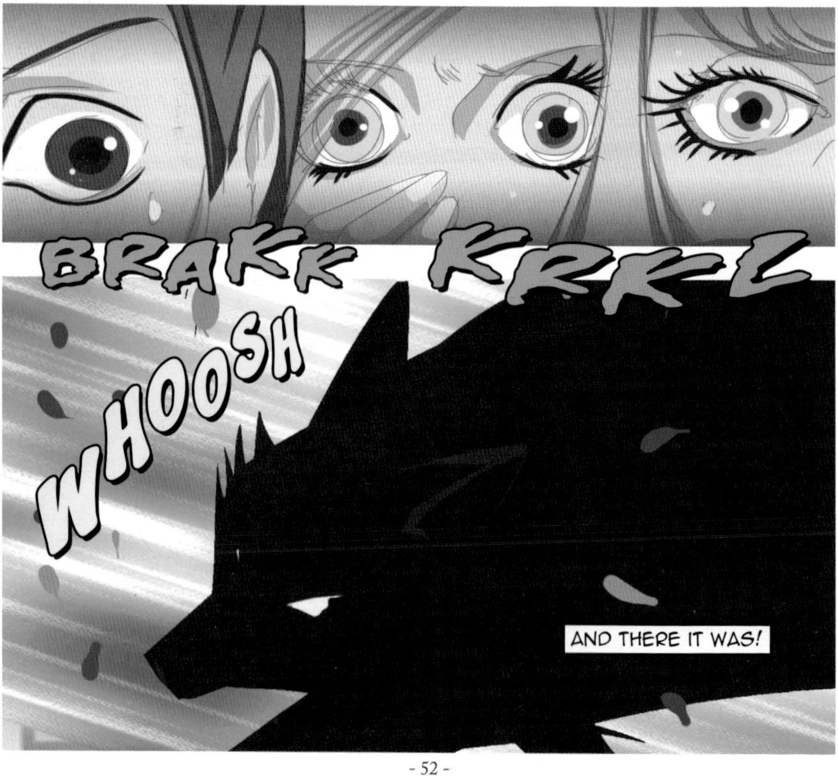
BRAKK
KRKKL
WHOOSH
AND THERE IT WAS!

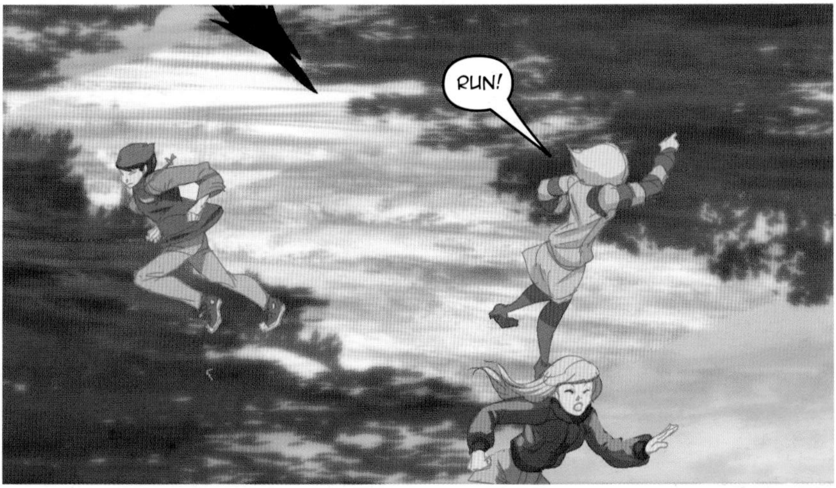
RUN!

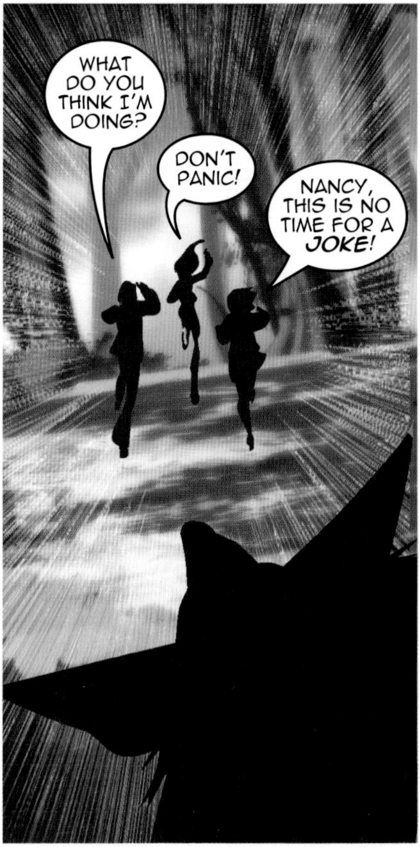
WHAT DO YOU THINK I'M DOING?
DON'T PANIC!
NANCY, THIS IS NO TIME FOR A JOKE!

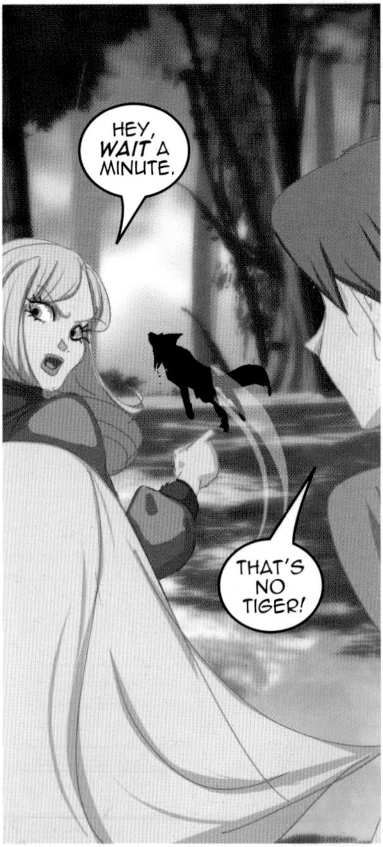
HEY, WAIT A MINUTE.
THAT'S NO TIGER!

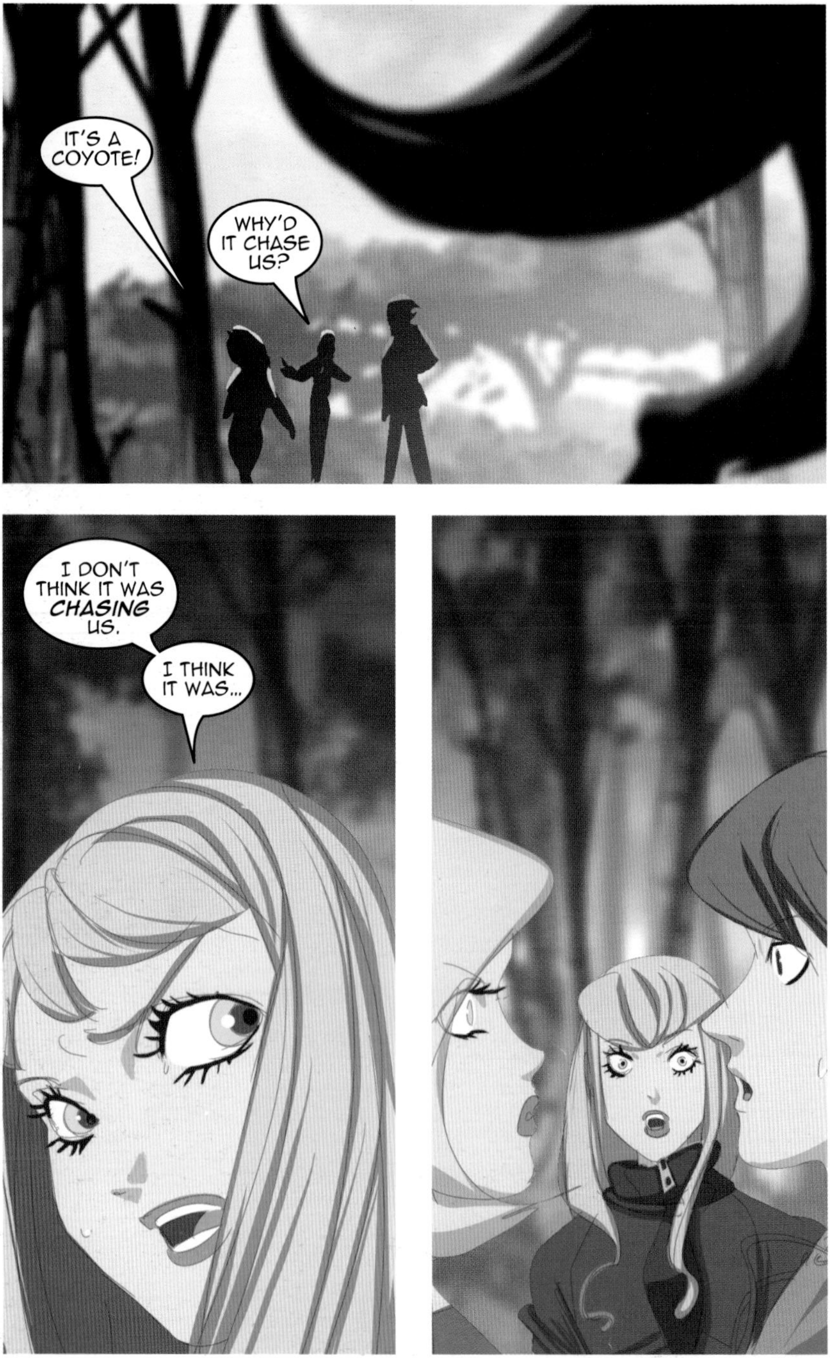
IT'S A COYOTE!
WHY'D IT CHASE US?
I DON'T THINK IT WAS **CHASING** US.
I THINK IT WAS...

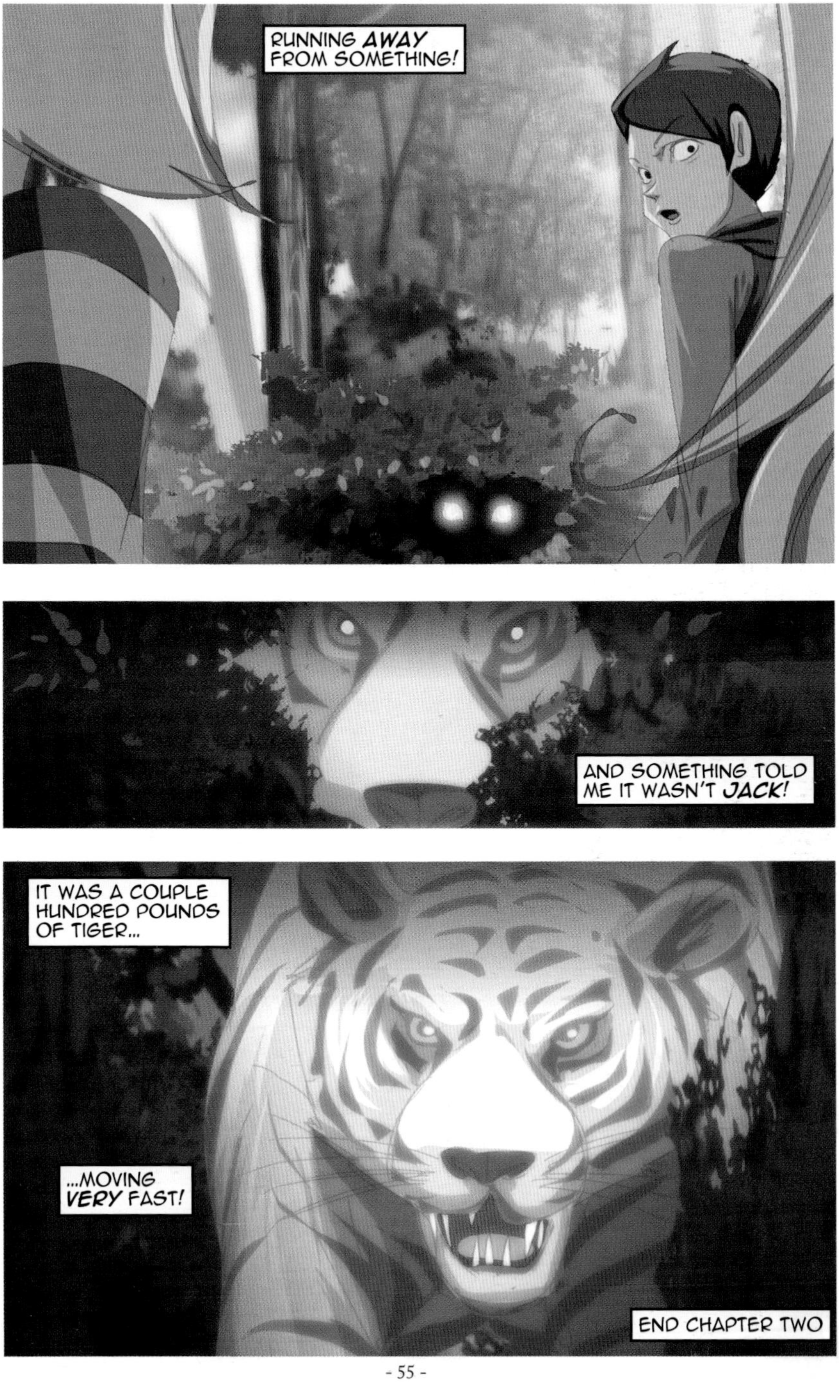
RUNNING AWAY FROM SOMETHING!
AND SOMETHING TOLD ME IT WASN'T JACK!
IT WAS A COUPLE HUNDRED POUNDS OF TIGER...
...MOVING VERY FAST!
END CHAPTER TWO

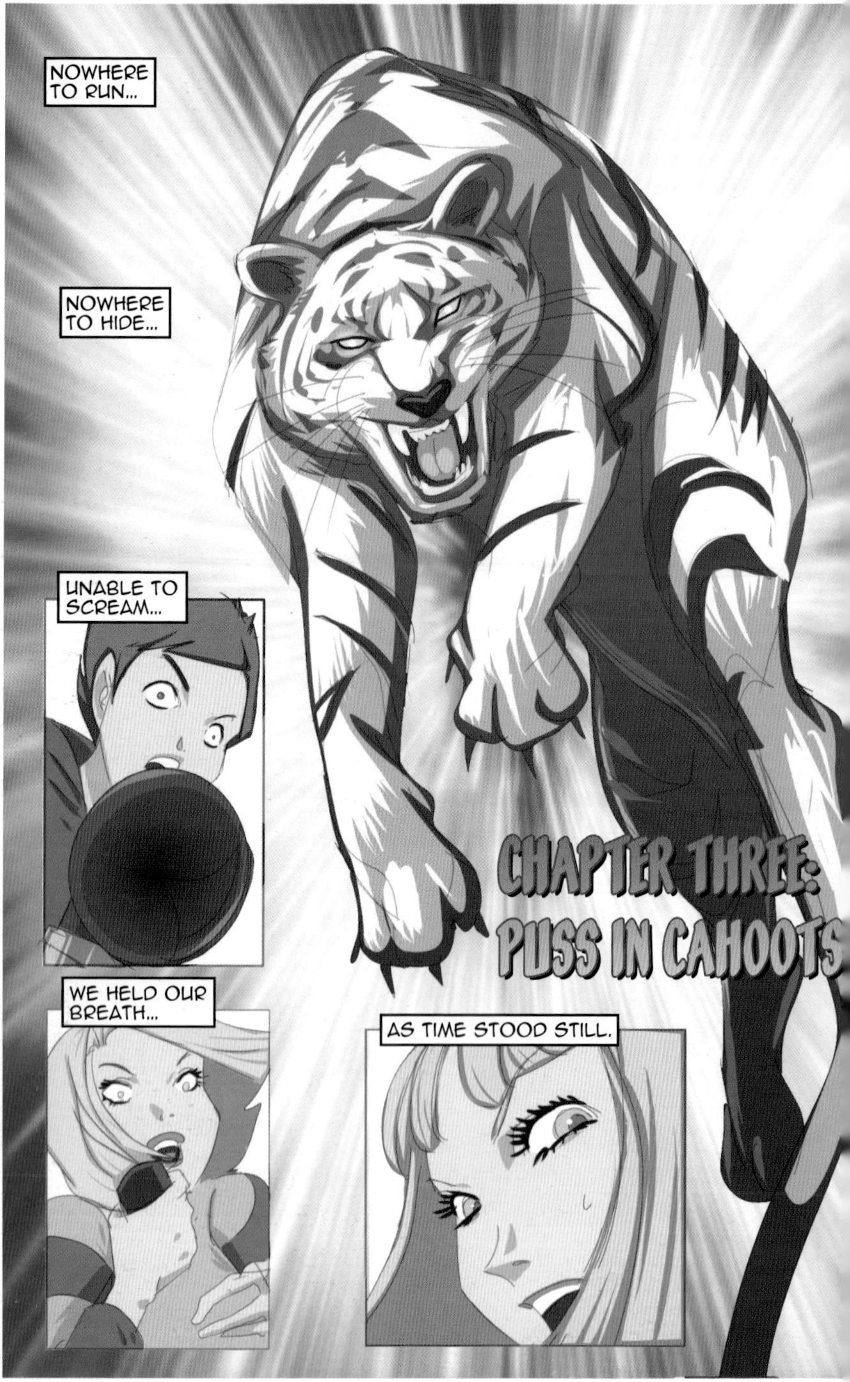
NOWHERE TO RUN...
NOWHERE TO HIDE...
UNABLE TO SCREAM...
CHAPTER THREE: PUSS IN CAHOOTS
WE HELD OUR BREATH...
AS TIME STOOD STILL.

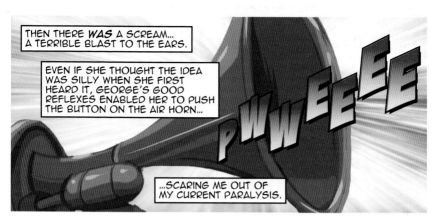

THEN THERE *WAS* A SCREAM... A TERRIBLE BLAST TO THE EARS.

EVEN IF SHE THOUGHT THE IDEA WAS SILLY WHEN SHE FIRST HEARD IT, GEORGE'S GOOD REFLEXES ENABLED HER TO PUSH THE BUTTON ON THE AIR HORN...

PWWEEEE

...SCARING ME OUT OF MY CURRENT PARALYSIS.

THE PAINFUL BLAST *DISTRACTED* THE TIGER...

...FOR A SECOND.

RROOAR

BUT, RATHER THAN SCARING IT *AWAY*...

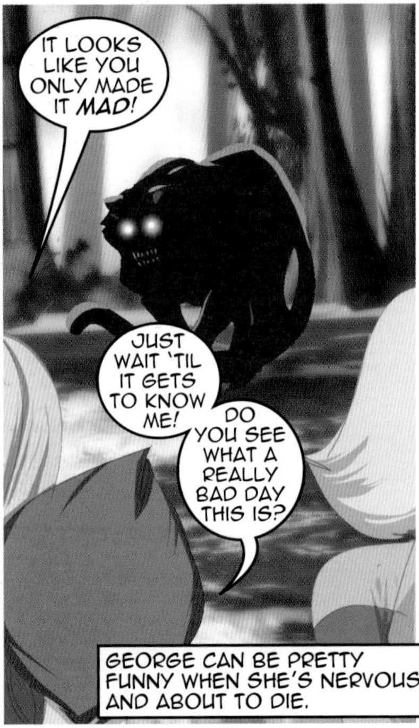
IT LOOKS LIKE YOU ONLY MADE IT MAD!
JUST WAIT 'TIL IT GETS TO KNOW ME!
DO YOU SEE WHAT A REALLY BAD DAY THIS IS?
GEORGE CAN BE PRETTY FUNNY WHEN SHE'S NERVOUS AND ABOUT TO DIE.

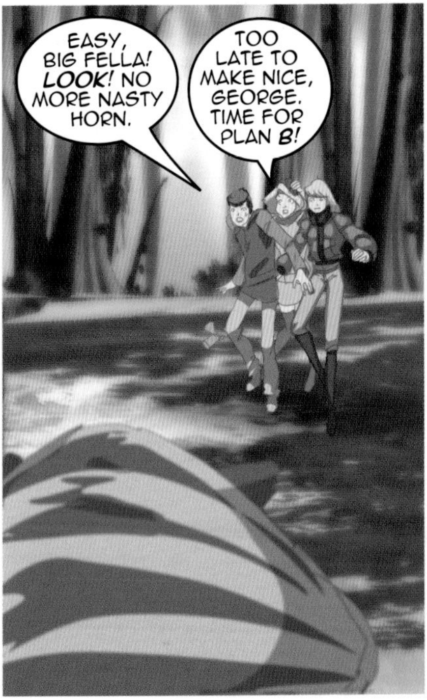
EASY, BIG FELLA! LOOK! NO MORE NASTY HORN.
TOO LATE TO MAKE NICE, GEORGE. TIME FOR PLAN B!

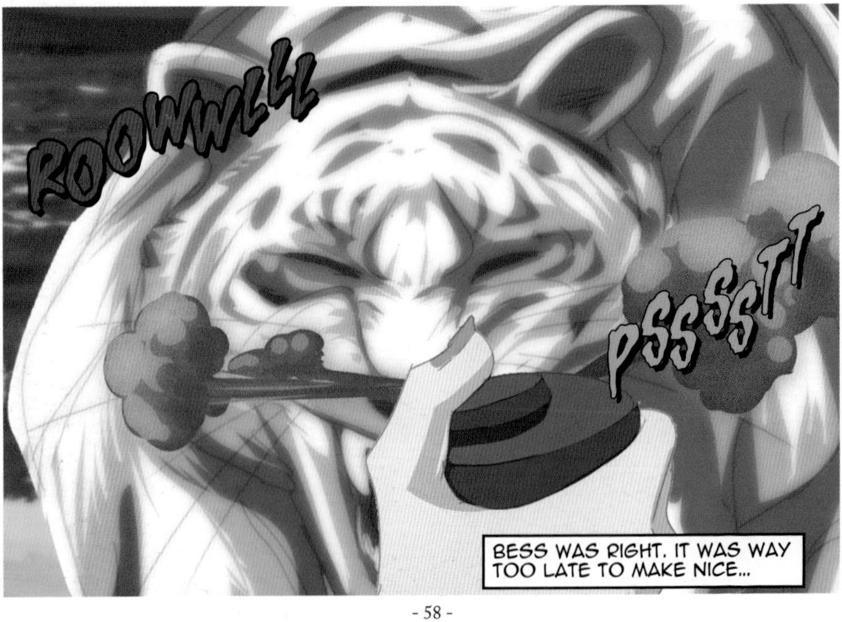
ROOWWLLL
PSSSSTT
BESS WAS RIGHT. IT WAS WAY TOO LATE TO MAKE NICE...

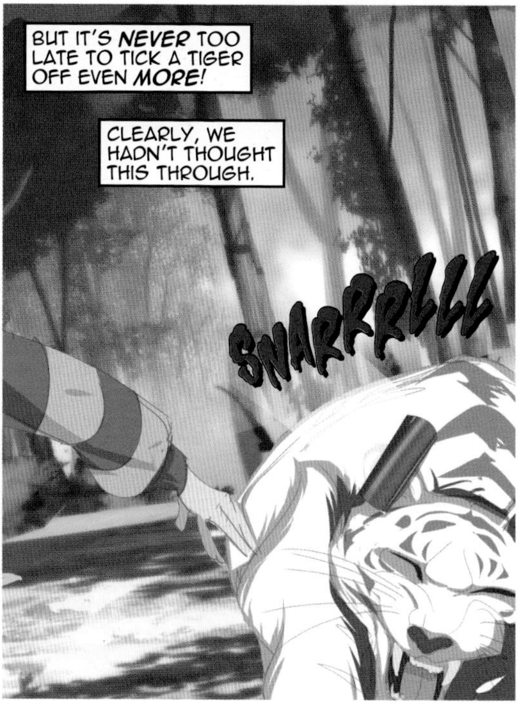
BUT IT'S **NEVER** TOO LATE TO TICK A TIGER OFF EVEN **MORE**!
CLEARLY, WE HADN'T THOUGHT THIS THROUGH.
SNARRRLLL

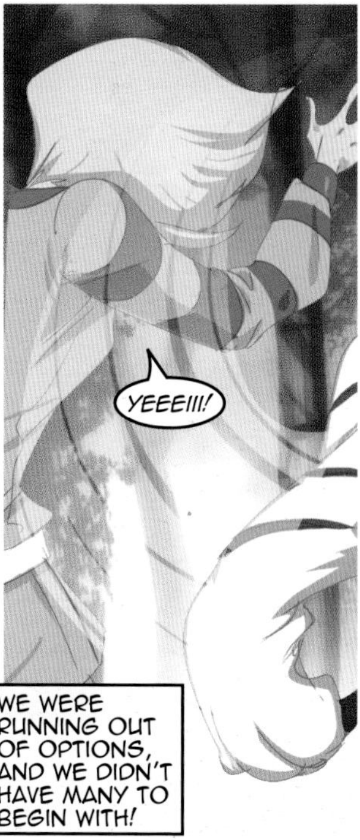
YEEEIII!
WE WERE RUNNING OUT OF OPTIONS, AND WE DIDN'T HAVE MANY TO BEGIN WITH!

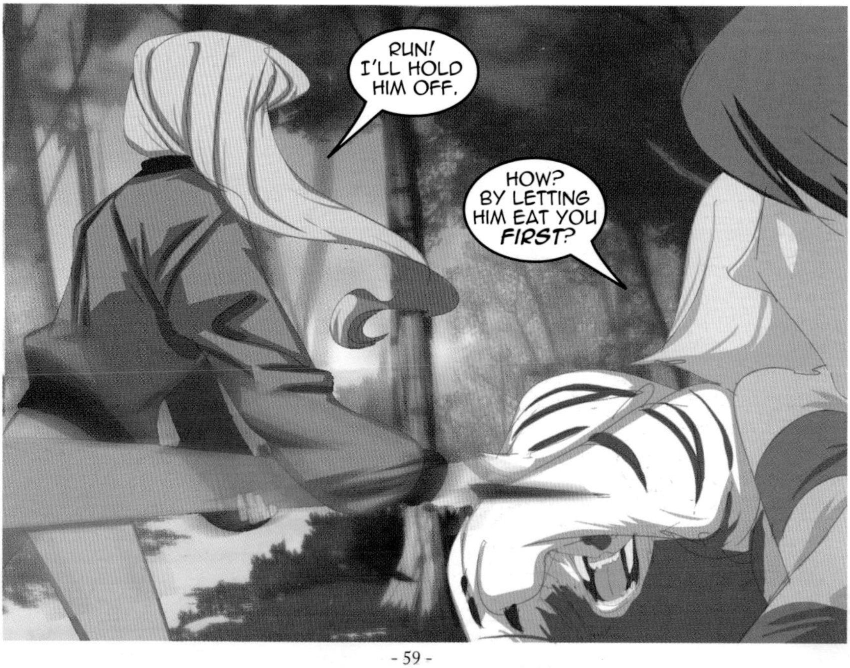
RUN! I'LL HOLD HIM OFF.
HOW? BY LETTING HIM EAT YOU ***FIRST***?

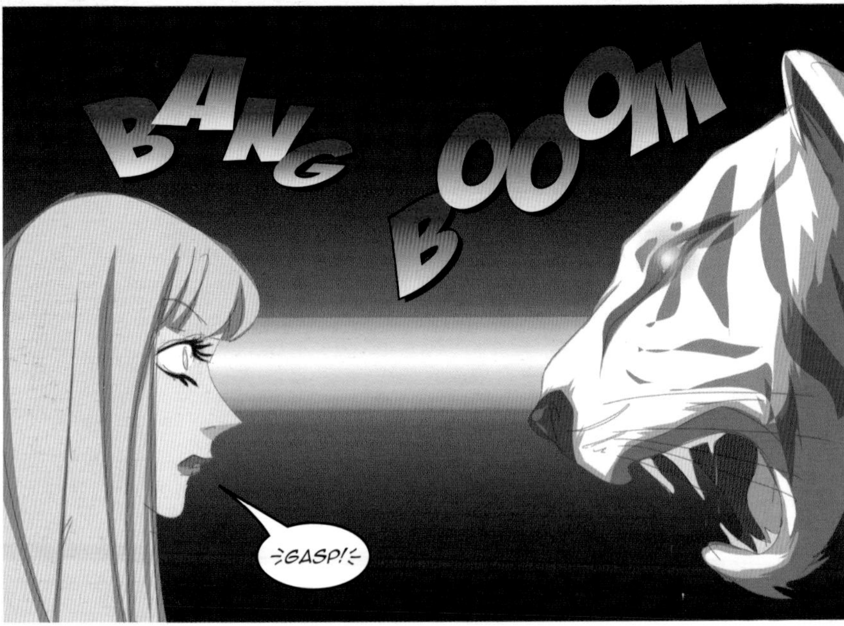
BANG
BOOOOM
GASP!

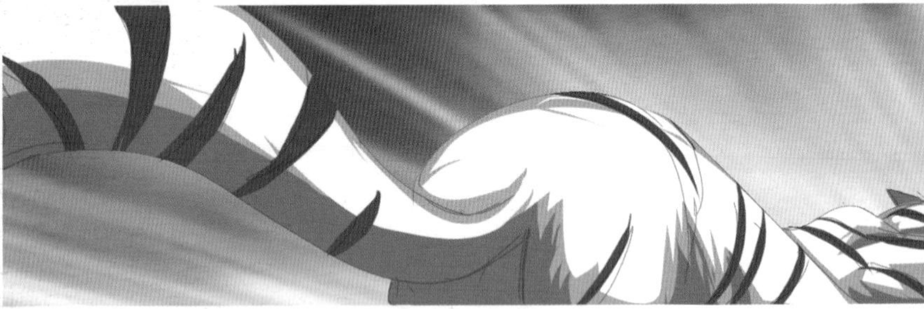

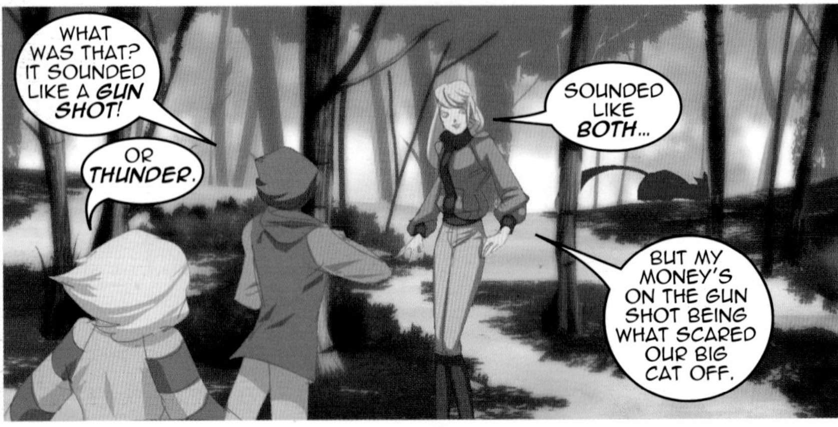
WHAT WAS THAT? IT SOUNDED LIKE A GUN SHOT!
OR THUNDER.
SOUNDED LIKE BOTH...
BUT MY MONEY'S ON THE GUN SHOT BEING WHAT SCARED OUR BIG CAT OFF.

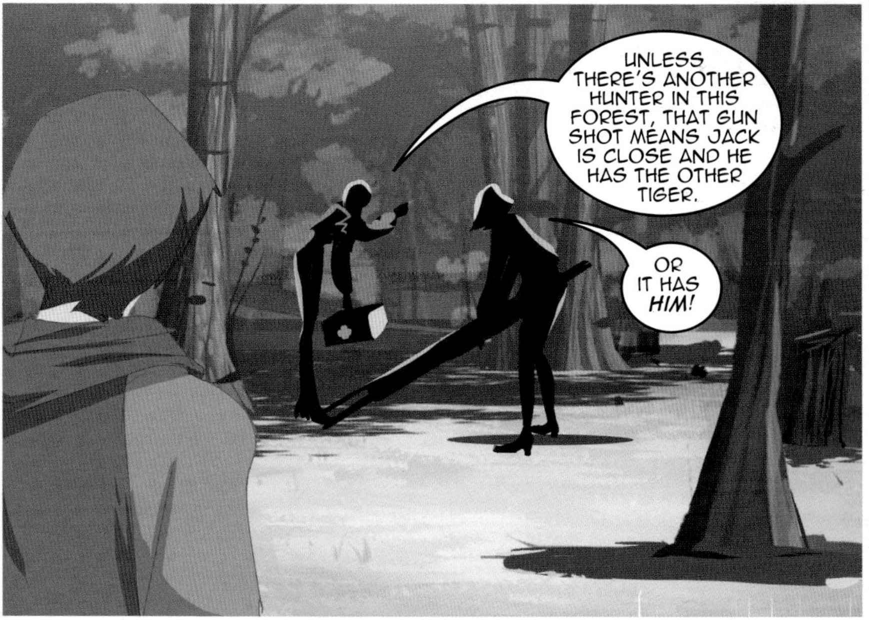
UNLESS THERE'S ANOTHER HUNTER IN THIS FOREST, THAT GUN SHOT MEANS JACK IS CLOSE AND HE HAS THE OTHER TIGER.
OR IT HAS *HIM!*

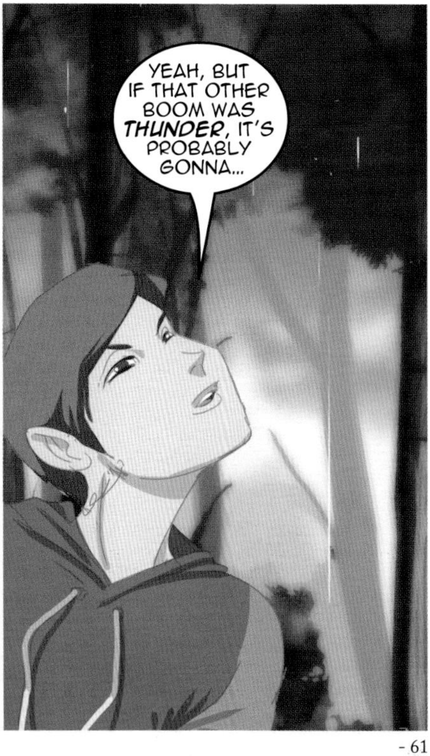
YEAH, BUT IF THAT OTHER BOOM WAS *THUNDER*, IT'S PROBABLY GONNA...

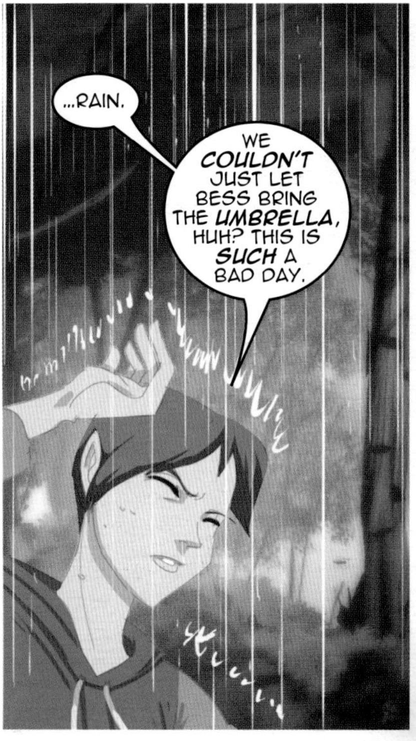
...RAIN.
WE *COULDN'T* JUST LET BESS BRING THE *UMBRELLA*, HUH? THIS IS *SUCH* A BAD DAY.

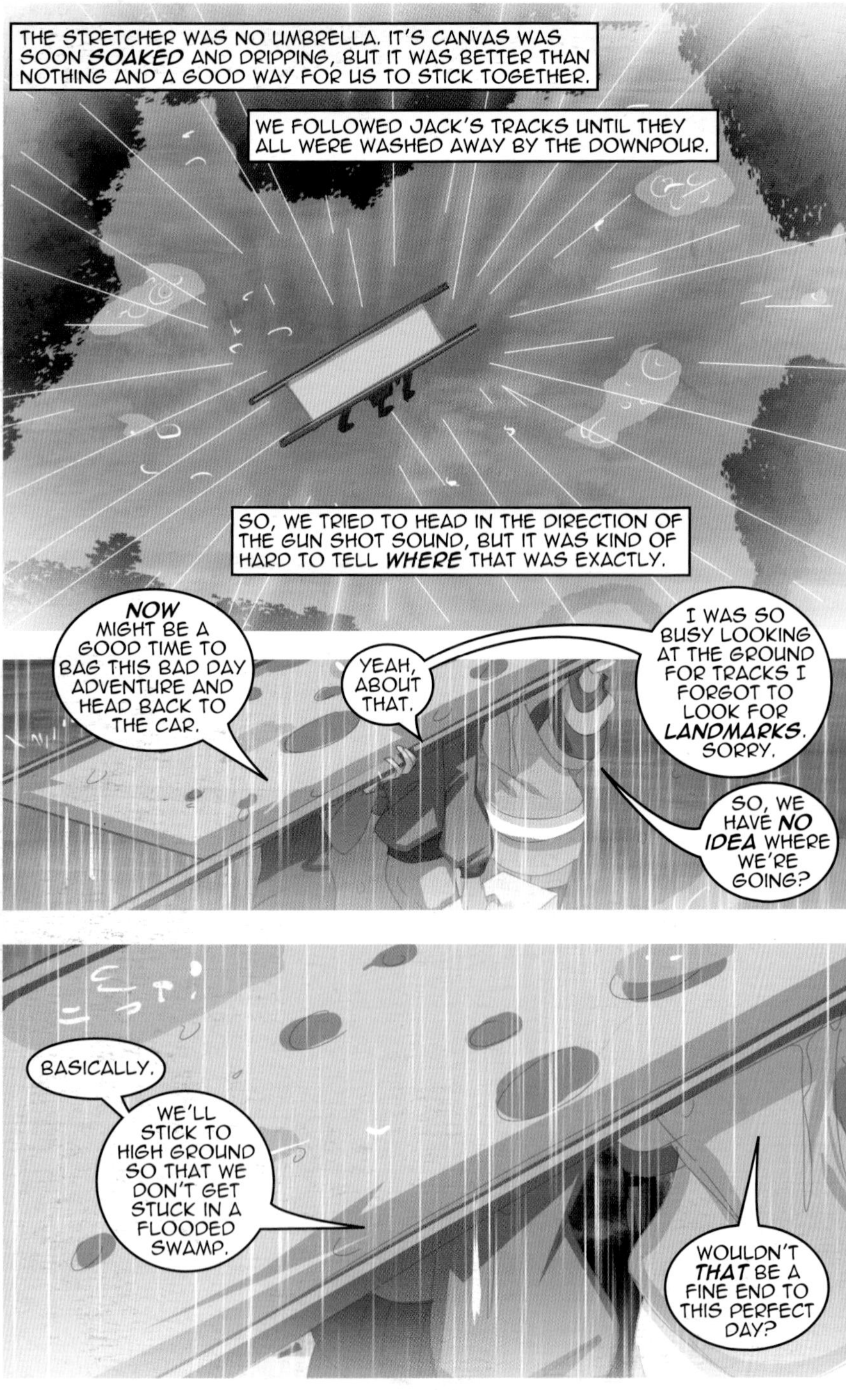
THE STRETCHER WAS NO UMBRELLA. IT'S CANVAS WAS SOON SOAKED AND DRIPPING, BUT IT WAS BETTER THAN NOTHING AND A GOOD WAY FOR US TO STICK TOGETHER.
WE FOLLOWED JACK'S TRACKS UNTIL THEY ALL WERE WASHED AWAY BY THE DOWNPOUR.
SO, WE TRIED TO HEAD IN THE DIRECTION OF THE GUN SHOT SOUND, BUT IT WAS KIND OF HARD TO TELL WHERE THAT WAS EXACTLY.
NOW MIGHT BE A GOOD TIME TO BAG THIS BAD DAY ADVENTURE AND HEAD BACK TO THE CAR.
YEAH, ABOUT THAT.
I WAS SO BUSY LOOKING AT THE GROUND FOR TRACKS I FORGOT TO LOOK FOR LANDMARKS. SORRY.
SO, WE HAVE NO IDEA WHERE WE'RE GOING?
BASICALLY.
WE'LL STICK TO HIGH GROUND SO THAT WE DON'T GET STUCK IN A FLOODED SWAMP.
WOULDN'T THAT BE A FINE END TO THIS PERFECT DAY?

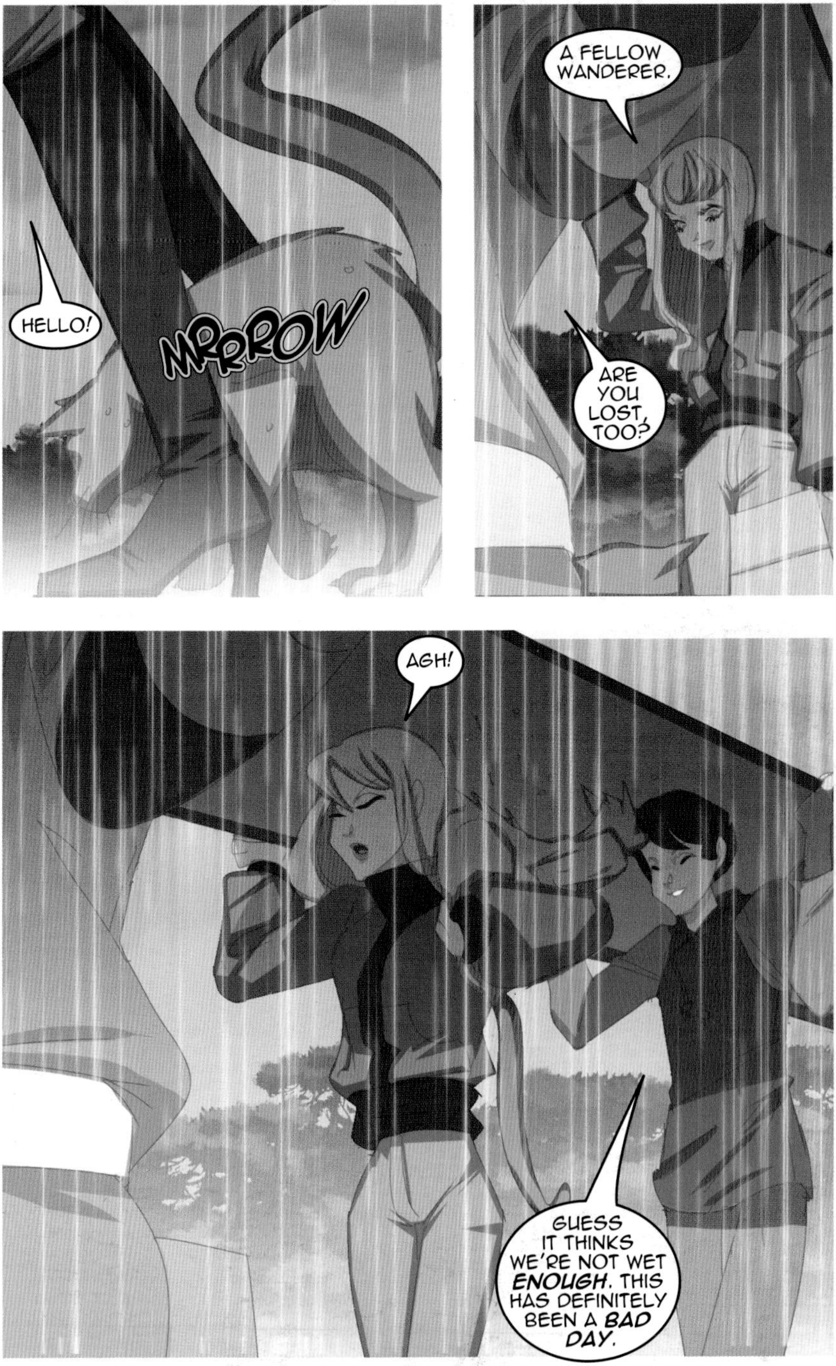
HELLO!
MRRROW
A FELLOW WANDERER.
ARE YOU LOST, TOO?
AGH!
GUESS IT THINKS WE'RE NOT WET ENOUGH. THIS HAS DEFINITELY BEEN A BAD DAY.

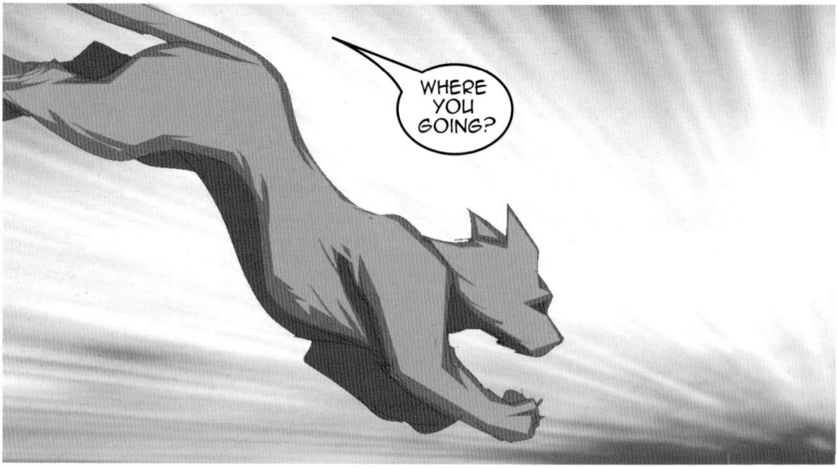
WHERE YOU GOING?

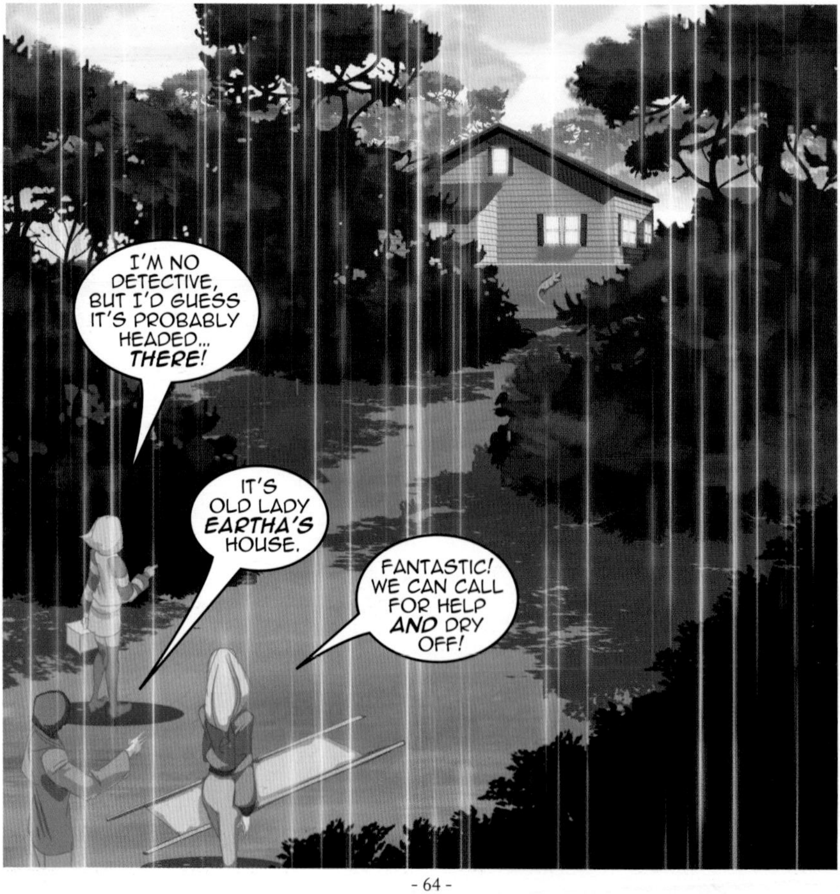
I'M NO DETECTIVE, BUT I'D GUESS IT'S PROBABLY HEADED... *THERE!*
IT'S OLD LADY *EARTHA'S* HOUSE.
FANTASTIC! WE CAN CALL FOR HELP *AND* DRY OFF!

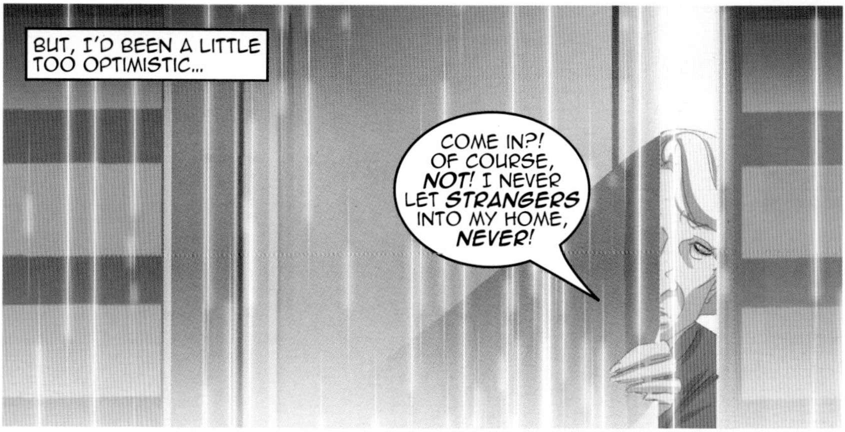
BUT, I'D BEEN A LITTLE TOO OPTIMISTIC...
COME IN?! OF COURSE, NOT! I NEVER LET STRANGERS INTO MY HOME, NEVER!

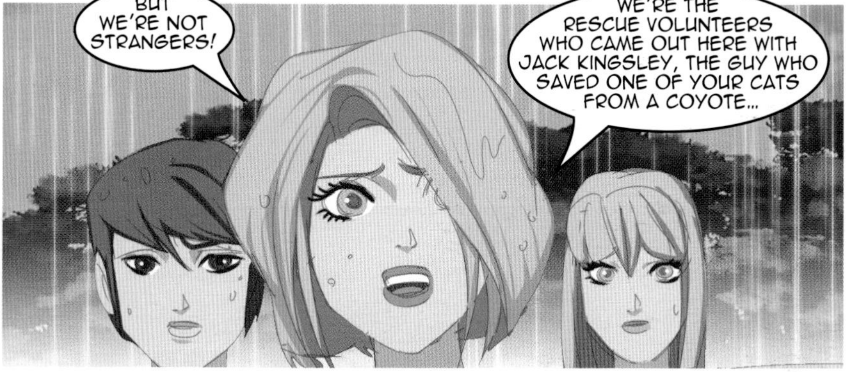
BUT WE'RE NOT STRANGERS!
WE'RE THE RESCUE VOLUNTEERS WHO CAME OUT HERE WITH JACK KINGSLEY, THE GUY WHO SAVED ONE OF YOUR CATS FROM A COYOTE...

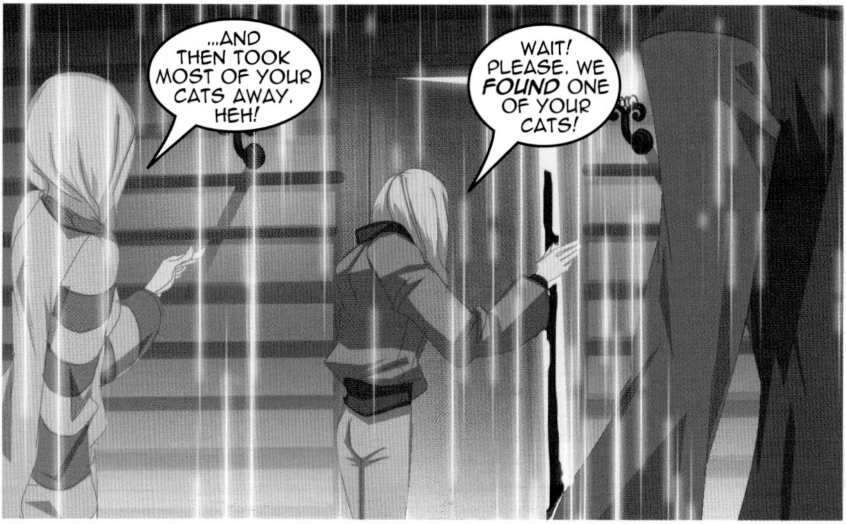
...AND THEN TOOK MOST OF YOUR CATS AWAY. HEH!
WAIT! PLEASE. WE FOUND ONE OF YOUR CATS!

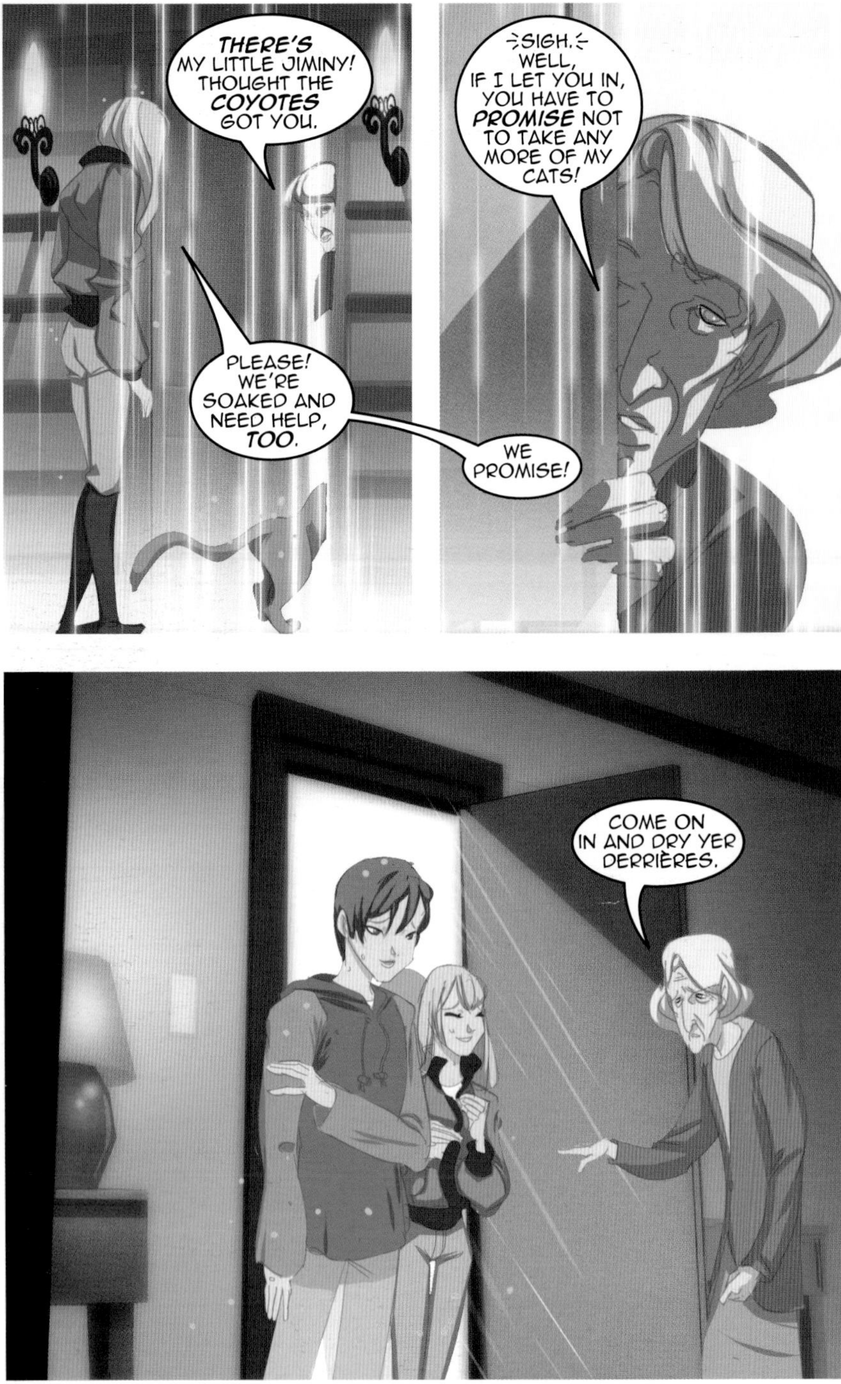
THERE'S MY LITTLE JIMINY! THOUGHT THE COYOTES GOT YOU.
PLEASE! WE'RE SOAKED AND NEED HELP, TOO.
SIGH. WELL, IF I LET YOU IN, YOU HAVE TO PROMISE NOT TO TAKE ANY MORE OF MY CATS!
WE PROMISE!
COME ON IN AND DRY YER DERRIÈRES.

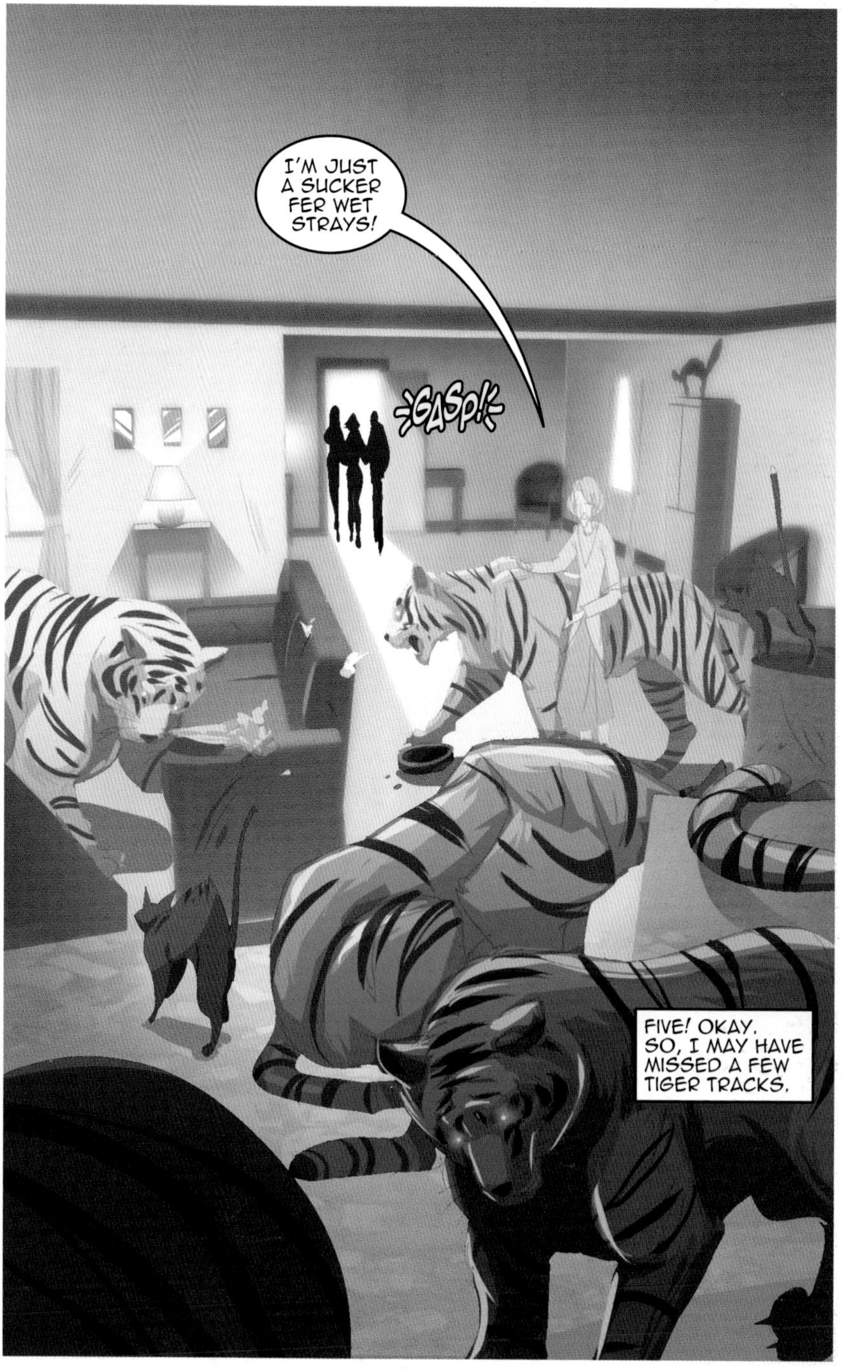
I'M JUST A SUCKER FER WET STRAYS!
GASP!
FIVE! OKAY. SO, I MAY HAVE MISSED A FEW TIGER TRACKS.

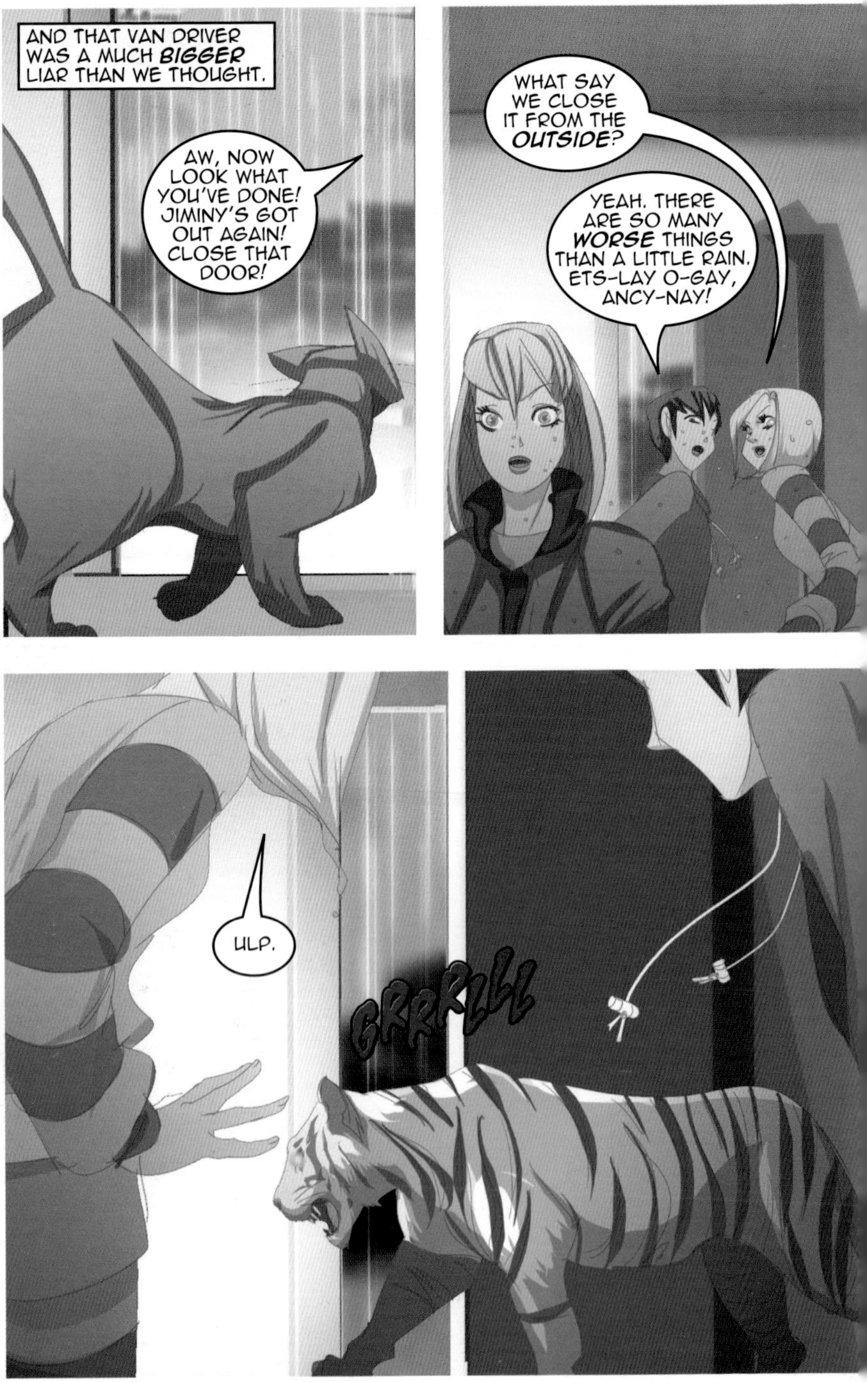
AND THAT VAN DRIVER WAS A MUCH BIGGER LIAR THAN WE THOUGHT.
AW, NOW LOOK WHAT YOU'VE DONE! JIMINY'S GOT OUT AGAIN! CLOSE THAT DOOR!
WHAT SAY WE CLOSE IT FROM THE OUTSIDE?
YEAH. THERE ARE SO MANY WORSE THINGS THAN A LITTLE RAIN. ETS-LAY O-GAY, ANCY-NAY!
ULP.
GRRRLLL

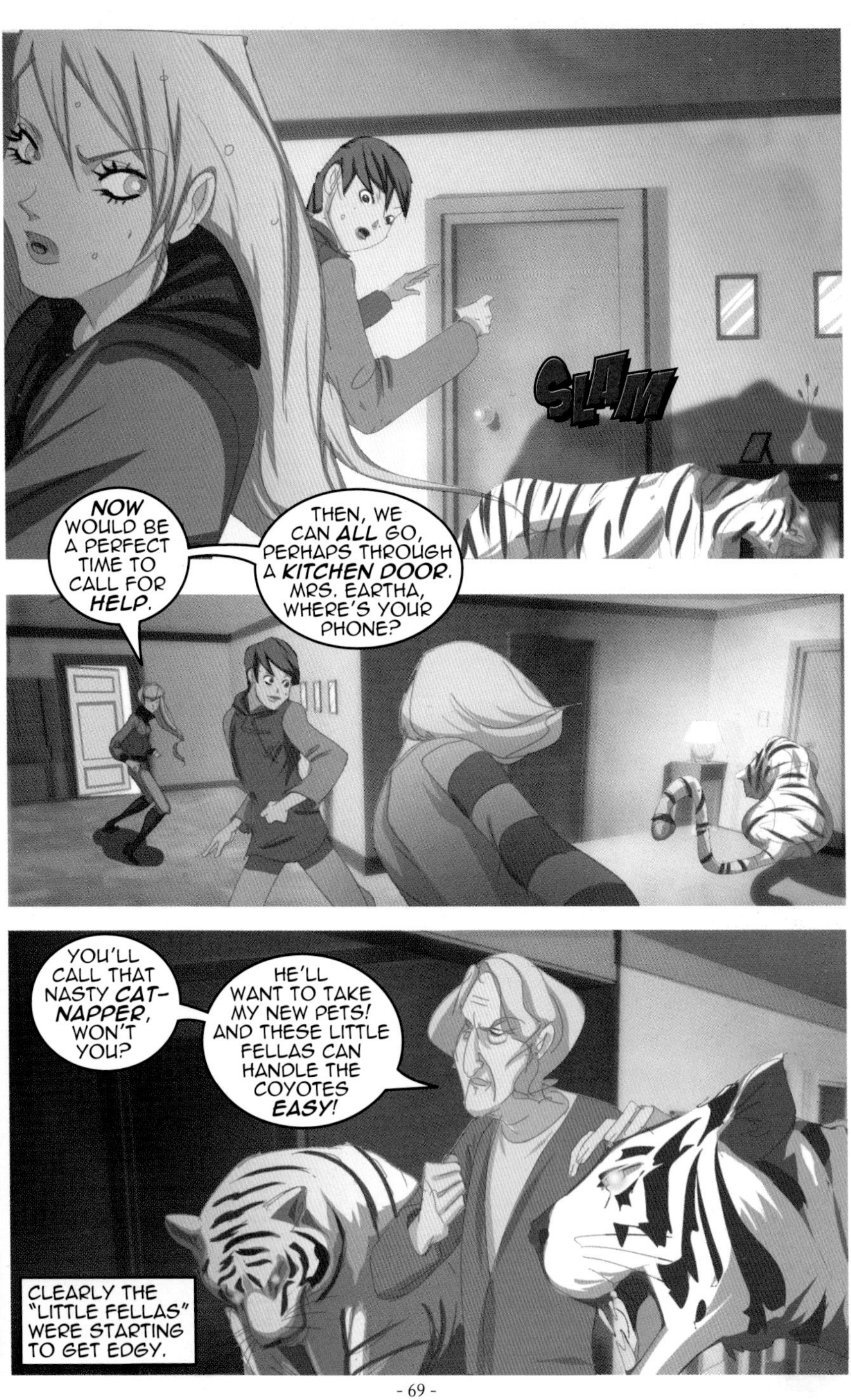
SLAM
NOW WOULD BE A PERFECT TIME TO CALL FOR HELP.
THEN, WE CAN ALL GO, PERHAPS THROUGH A KITCHEN DOOR. MRS. EARTHA, WHERE'S YOUR PHONE?
YOU'LL CALL THAT NASTY CAT-NAPPER, WON'T YOU?
HE'LL WANT TO TAKE MY NEW PETS! AND THESE LITTLE FELLAS CAN HANDLE THE COYOTES EASY!
CLEARLY THE "LITTLE FELLAS" WERE STARTING TO GET EDGY.

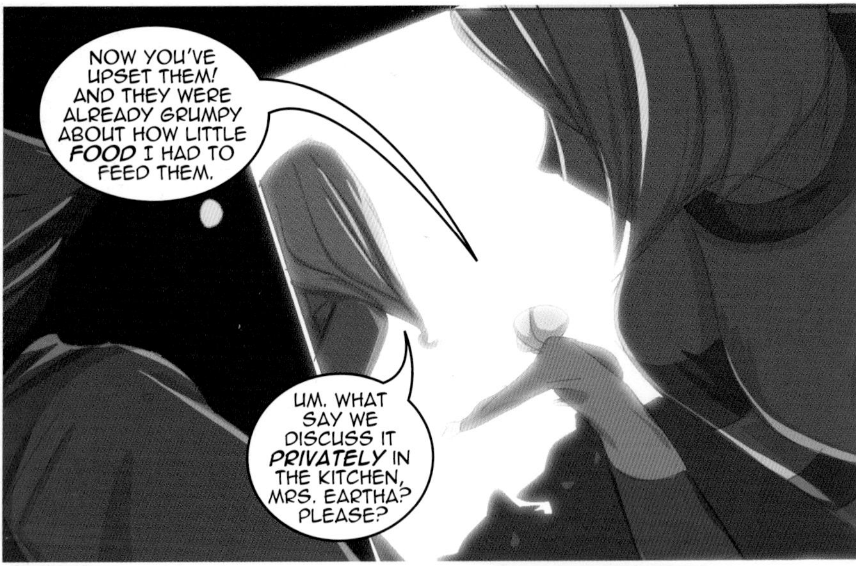
NOW YOU'VE UPSET THEM! AND THEY WERE ALREADY GRUMPY ABOUT HOW LITTLE FOOD I HAD TO FEED THEM.
UM. WHAT SAY WE DISCUSS IT PRIVATELY IN THE KITCHEN, MRS. EARTHA? PLEASE?

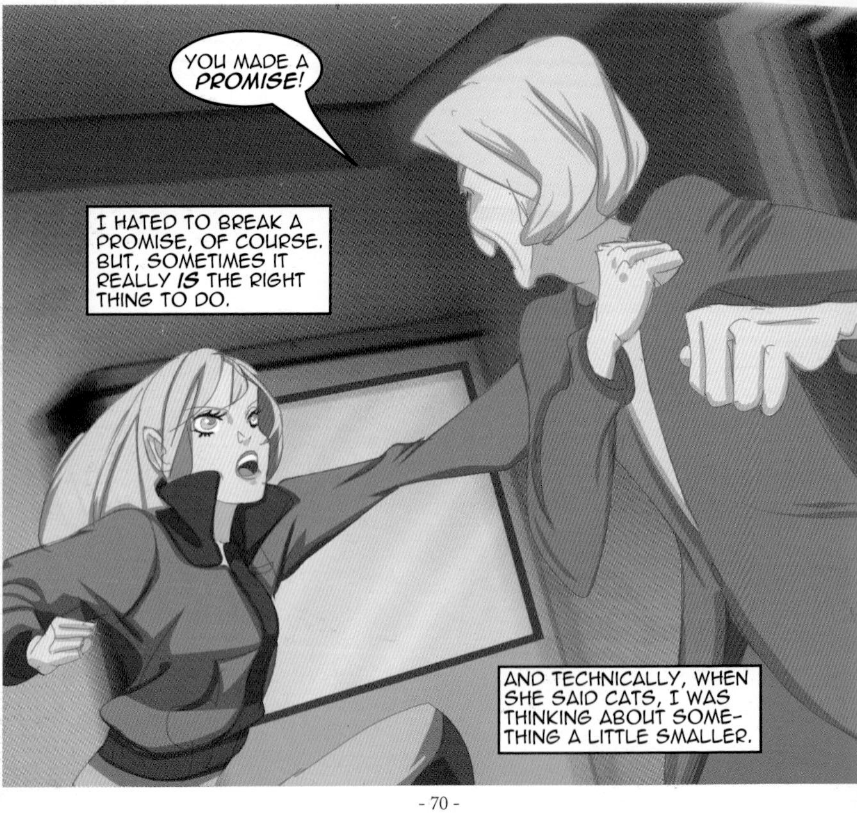
YOU MADE A PROMISE!
I HATED TO BREAK A PROMISE, OF COURSE. BUT, SOMETIMES IT REALLY IS THE RIGHT THING TO DO.
AND TECHNICALLY, WHEN SHE SAID CATS, I WAS THINKING ABOUT SOME-THING A LITTLE SMALLER.

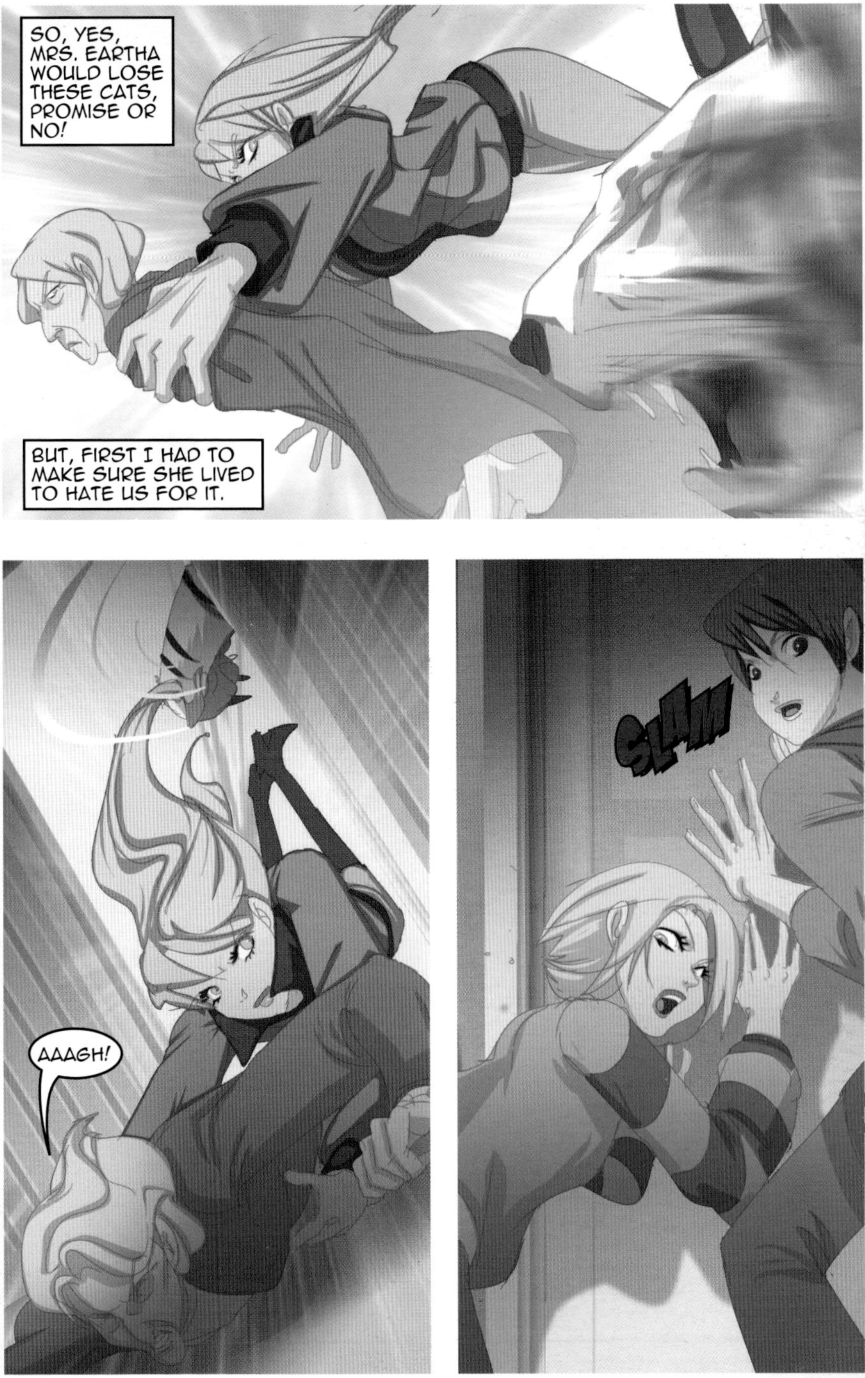
SO, YES, MRS. EARTHA WOULD LOSE THESE CATS, PROMISE OR NO!
BUT, FIRST I HAD TO MAKE SURE SHE LIVED TO HATE US FOR IT.
AAAGH!
SLAM

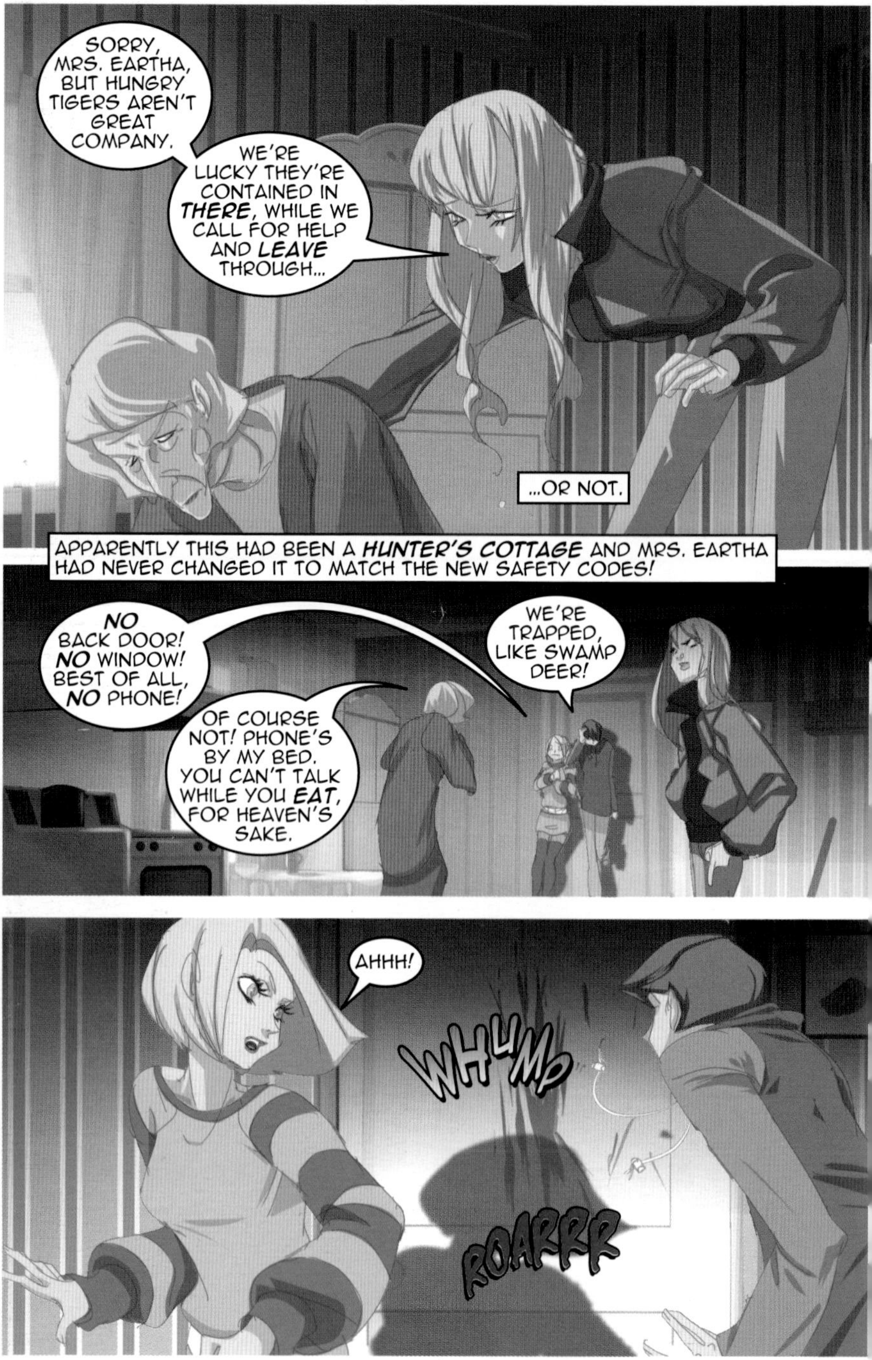
SORRY, MRS. EARTHA, BUT HUNGRY TIGERS AREN'T GREAT COMPANY.
WE'RE LUCKY THEY'RE CONTAINED IN THERE, WHILE WE CALL FOR HELP AND LEAVE THROUGH...
...OR NOT.
APPARENTLY THIS HAD BEEN A HUNTER'S COTTAGE AND MRS. EARTHA HAD NEVER CHANGED IT TO MATCH THE NEW SAFETY CODES!
NO BACK DOOR! NO WINDOW! BEST OF ALL, NO PHONE!
WE'RE TRAPPED, LIKE SWAMP DEER!
OF COURSE NOT! PHONE'S BY MY BED. YOU CAN'T TALK WHILE YOU EAT, FOR HEAVEN'S SAKE.
AHHH!
WHUMP
ROARRR

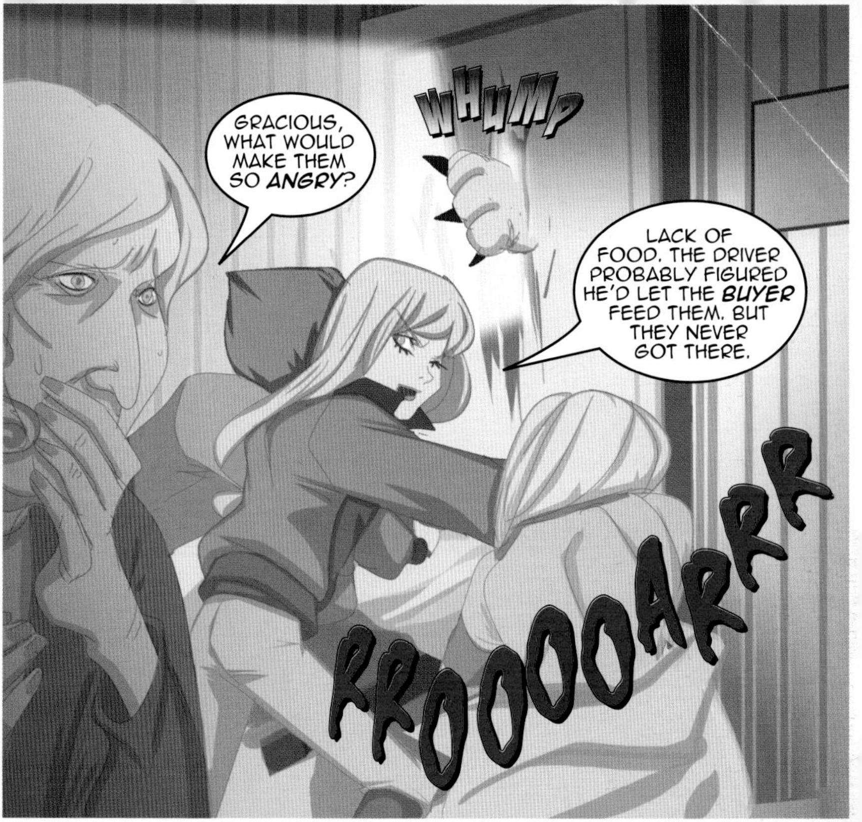
WHUMP
GRACIOUS, WHAT WOULD MAKE THEM SO ANGRY?
LACK OF FOOD. THE DRIVER PROBABLY FIGURED HE'D LET THE BUYER FEED THEM. BUT THEY NEVER GOT THERE.
RROOOOARRR

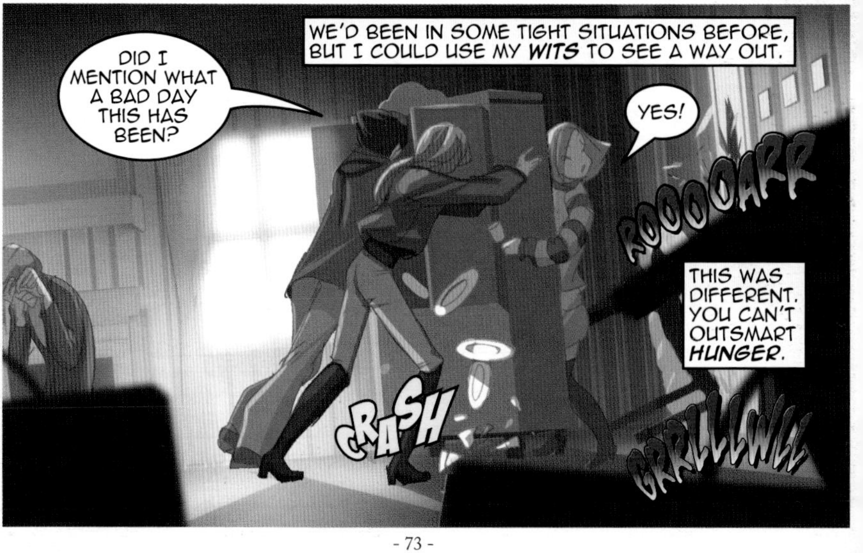
WE'D BEEN IN SOME TIGHT SITUATIONS BEFORE, BUT I COULD USE MY WITS TO SEE A WAY OUT.
DID I MENTION WHAT A BAD DAY THIS HAS BEEN?
YES!
ROOOOARR
THIS WAS DIFFERENT. YOU CAN'T OUTSMART HUNGER.
CRASH
GRRLLLWLL

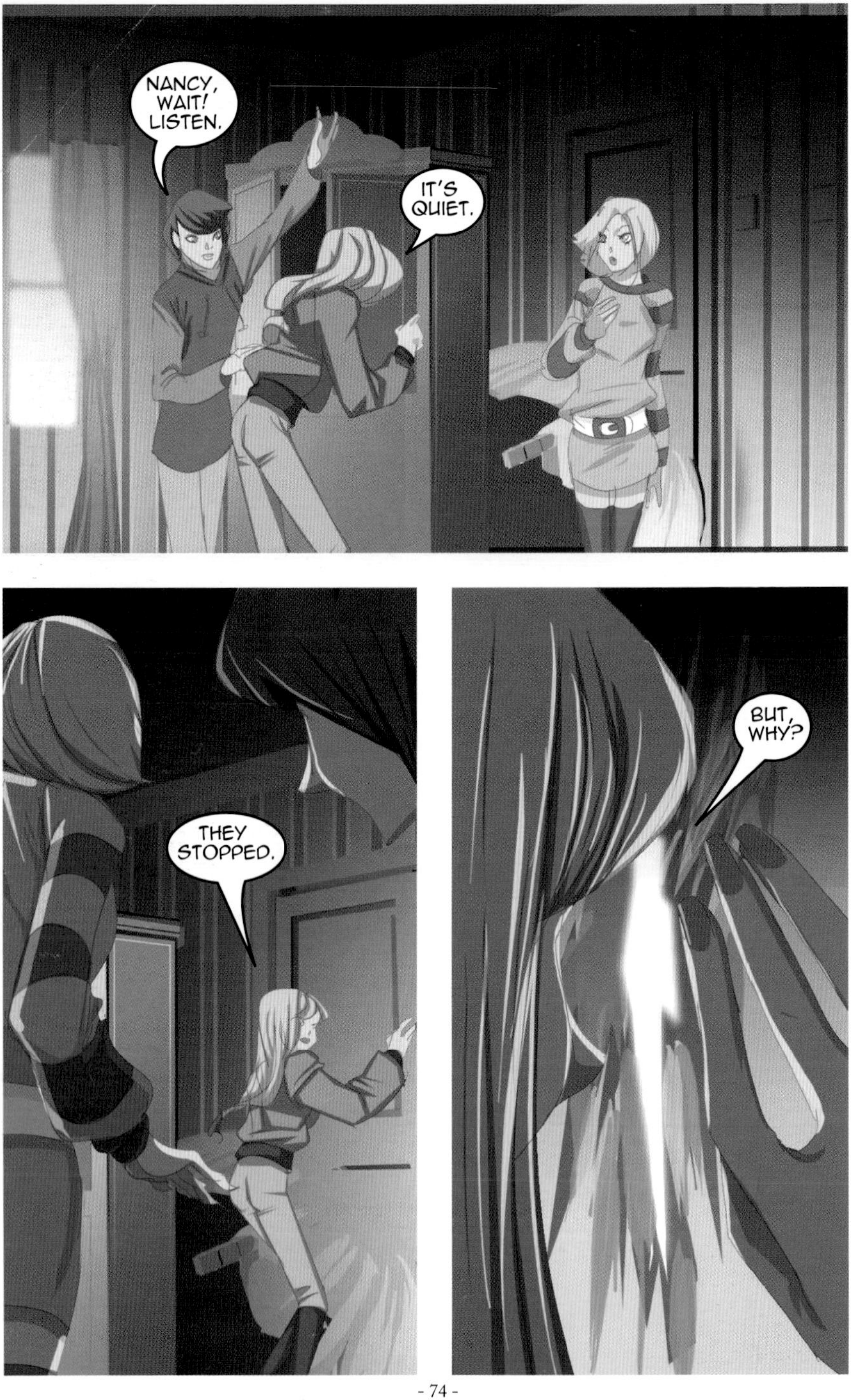
NANCY, WAIT! LISTEN.
IT'S QUIET.
THEY STOPPED.
BUT, WHY?

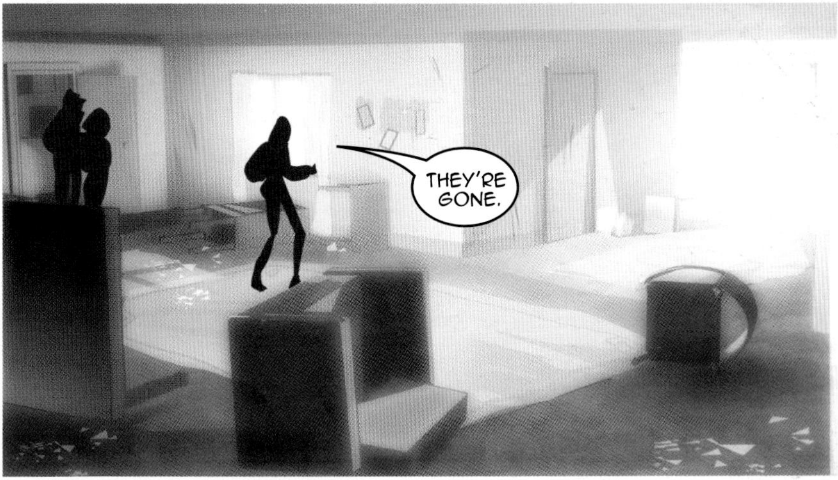
THEY'RE GONE.

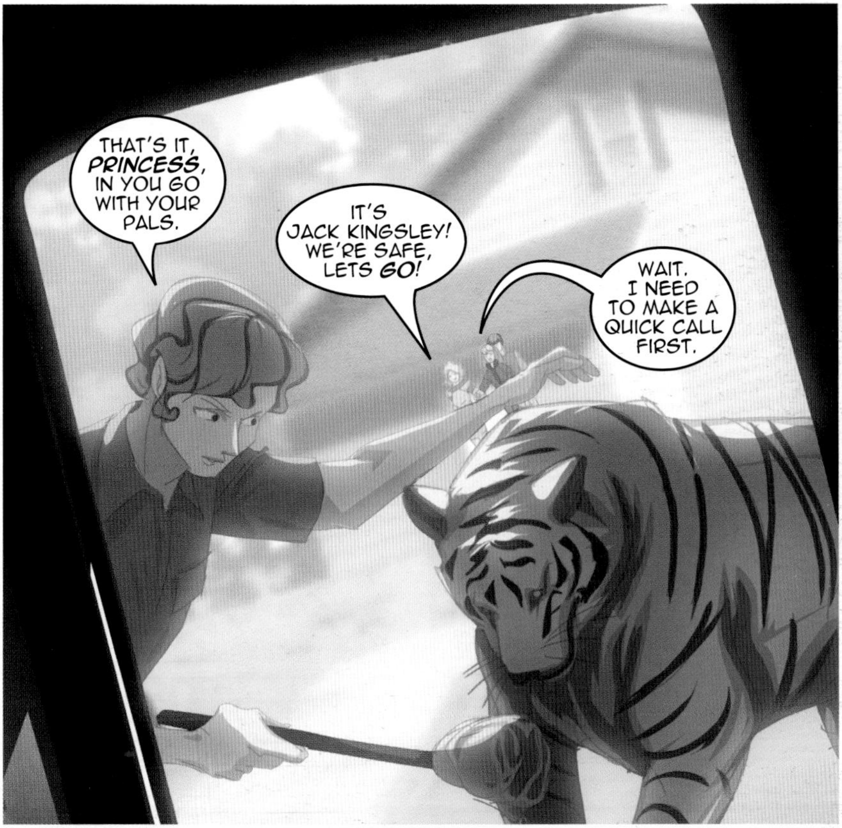
THAT'S IT, *PRINCESS*, IN YOU GO WITH YOUR PALS.
IT'S JACK KINGSLEY! WE'RE SAFE, LETS *GO*!
WAIT. I NEED TO MAKE A QUICK CALL FIRST.

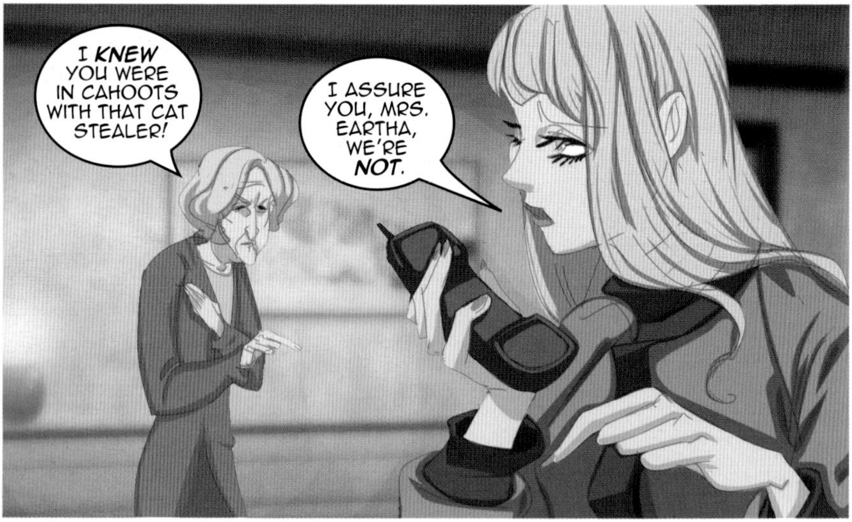
I KNEW YOU WERE IN CAHOOTS WITH THAT CAT STEALER!
I ASSURE YOU, MRS. EARTHA, WE'RE NOT.

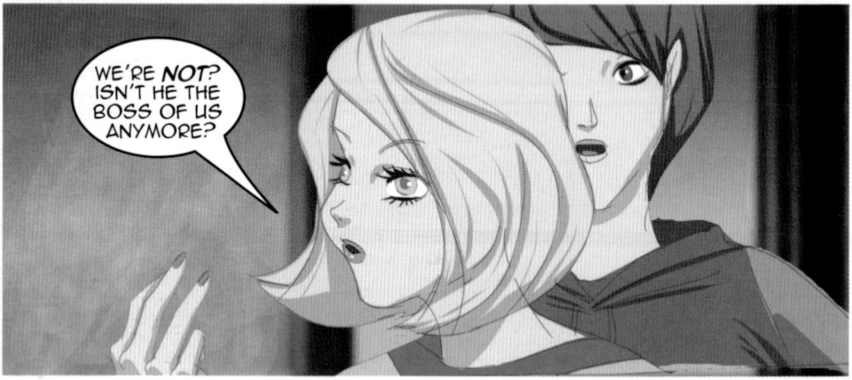
WE'RE NOT? ISN'T HE THE BOSS OF US ANYMORE?

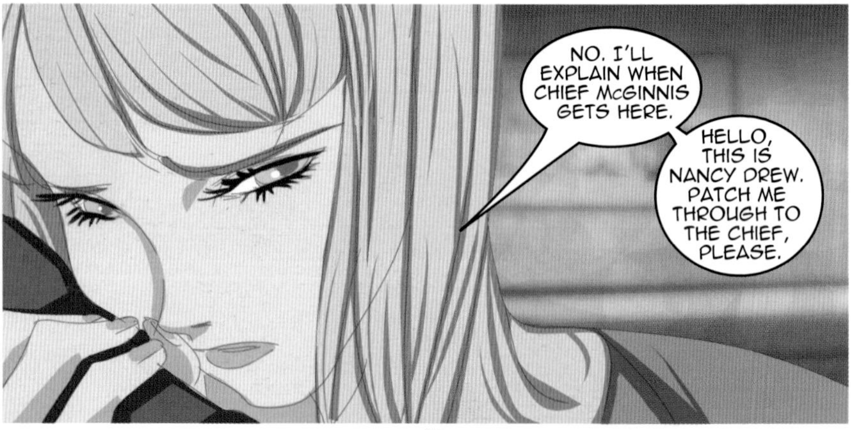
NO. I'LL EXPLAIN WHEN CHIEF McGINNIS GETS HERE.
HELLO, THIS IS NANCY DREW. PATCH ME THROUGH TO THE CHIEF, PLEASE.

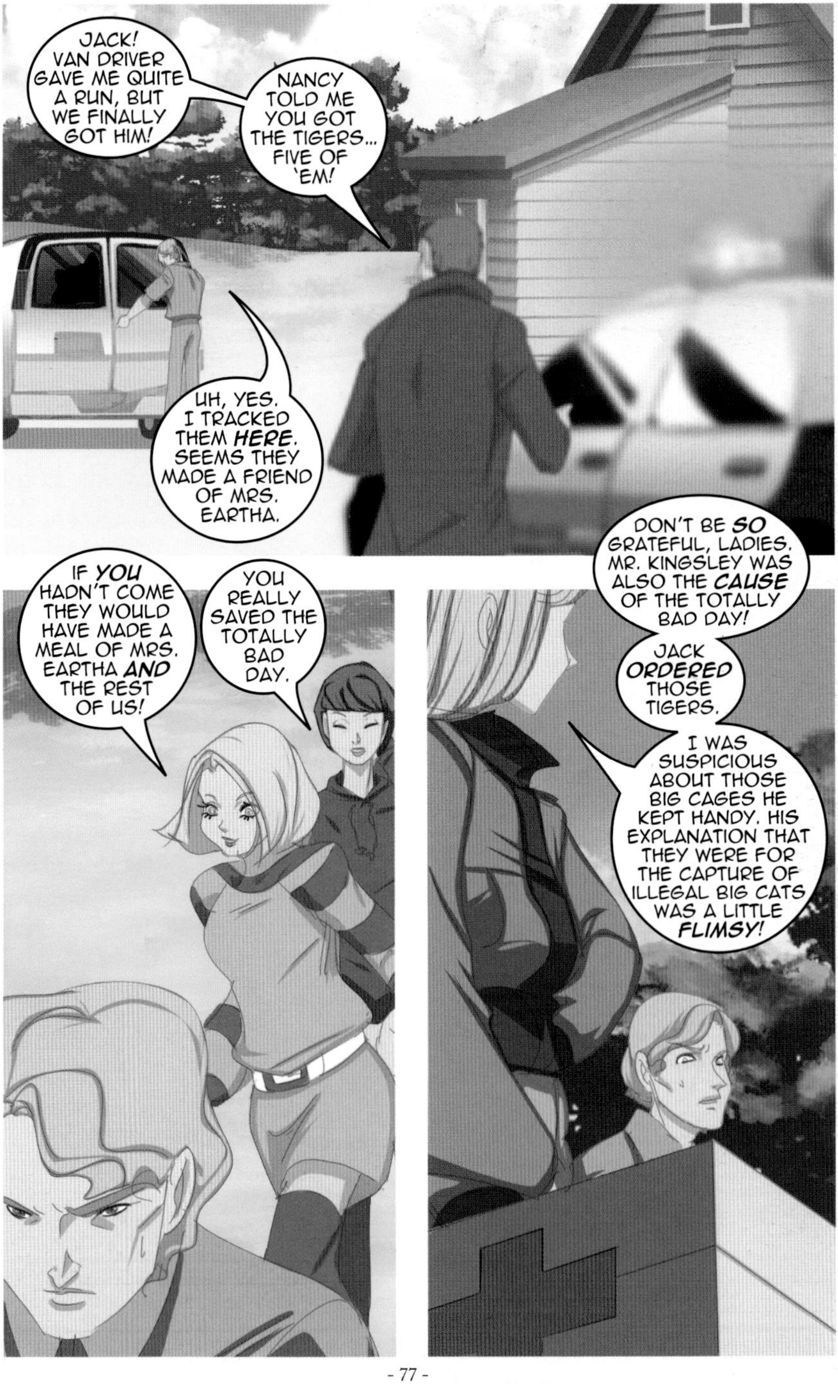
JACK! VAN DRIVER GAVE ME QUITE A RUN, BUT WE FINALLY GOT HIM!
NANCY TOLD ME YOU GOT THE TIGERS... FIVE OF 'EM!
UH, YES. I TRACKED THEM HERE. SEEMS THEY MADE A FRIEND OF MRS. EARTHA.
IF YOU HADN'T COME THEY WOULD HAVE MADE A MEAL OF MRS. EARTHA AND THE REST OF US!
YOU REALLY SAVED THE TOTALLY BAD DAY.
DON'T BE SO GRATEFUL, LADIES. MR. KINGSLEY WAS ALSO THE CAUSE OF THE TOTALLY BAD DAY!
JACK ORDERED THOSE TIGERS.
I WAS SUSPICIOUS ABOUT THOSE BIG CAGES HE KEPT HANDY. HIS EXPLANATION THAT THEY WERE FOR THE CAPTURE OF ILLEGAL BIG CATS WAS A LITTLE FLIMSY!

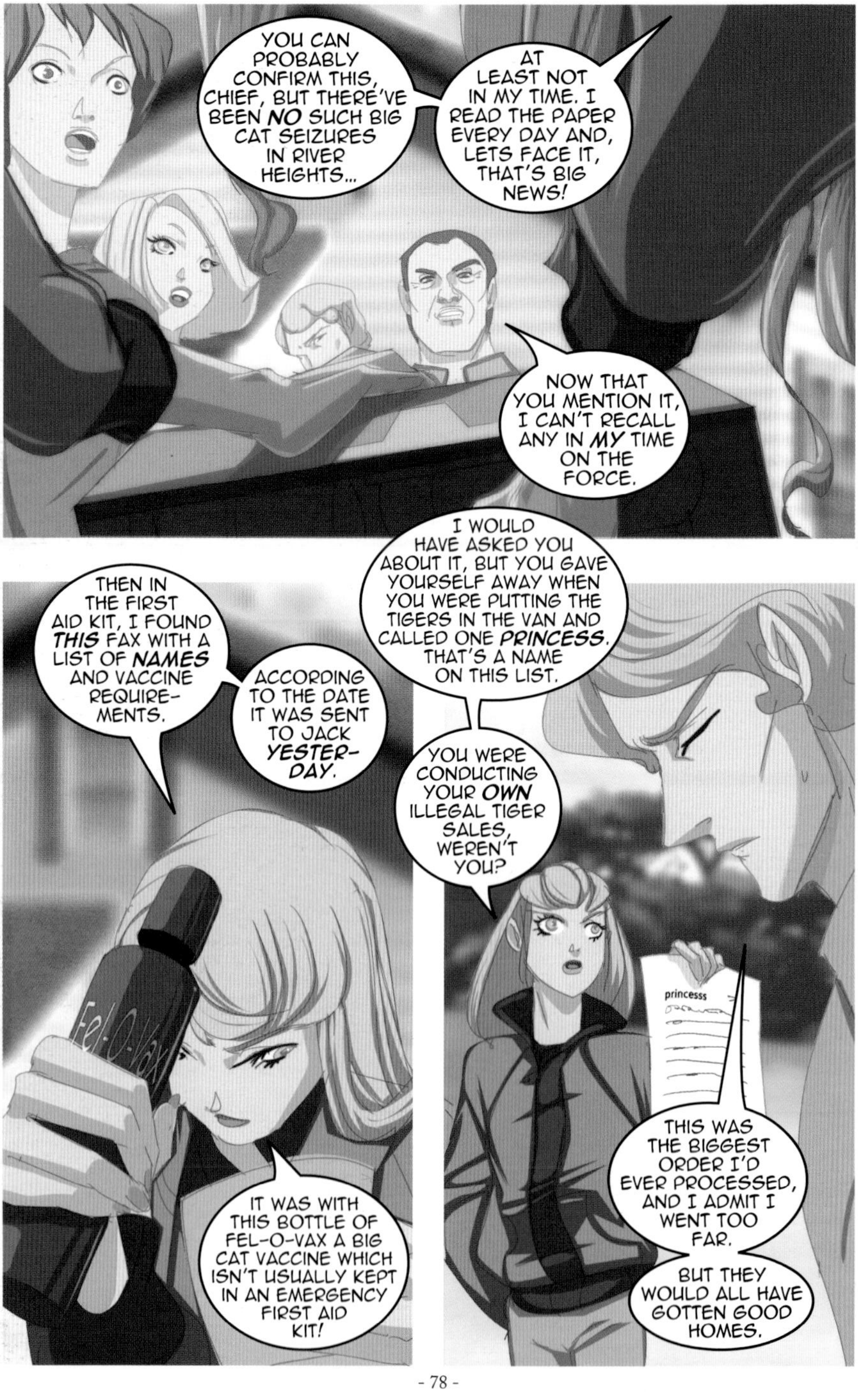
YOU CAN PROBABLY CONFIRM THIS, CHIEF, BUT THERE'VE BEEN ***NO*** SUCH BIG CAT SEIZURES IN RIVER HEIGHTS...
AT LEAST NOT IN MY TIME. I READ THE PAPER EVERY DAY AND, LETS FACE IT, THAT'S BIG NEWS!
NOW THAT YOU MENTION IT, I CAN'T RECALL ANY IN ***MY*** TIME ON THE FORCE.
THEN IN THE FIRST AID KIT, I FOUND ***THIS*** FAX WITH A LIST OF ***NAMES*** AND VACCINE REQUIRE-MENTS.
ACCORDING TO THE DATE IT WAS SENT TO JACK ***YESTER-DAY***.
Fel-O-Vax
IT WAS WITH THIS BOTTLE OF FEL-O-VAX A BIG CAT VACCINE WHICH ISN'T USUALLY KEPT IN AN EMERGENCY FIRST AID KIT!
I WOULD HAVE ASKED YOU ABOUT IT, BUT YOU GAVE YOURSELF AWAY WHEN YOU WERE PUTTING THE TIGERS IN THE VAN AND CALLED ONE ***PRINCESS***. THAT'S A NAME ON THIS LIST.
YOU WERE CONDUCTING YOUR ***OWN*** ILLEGAL TIGER SALES, WEREN'T YOU?
princesss
THIS WAS THE BIGGEST ORDER I'D EVER PROCESSED, AND I ADMIT I WENT TOO FAR.
BUT THEY WOULD ALL HAVE GOTTEN GOOD HOMES.

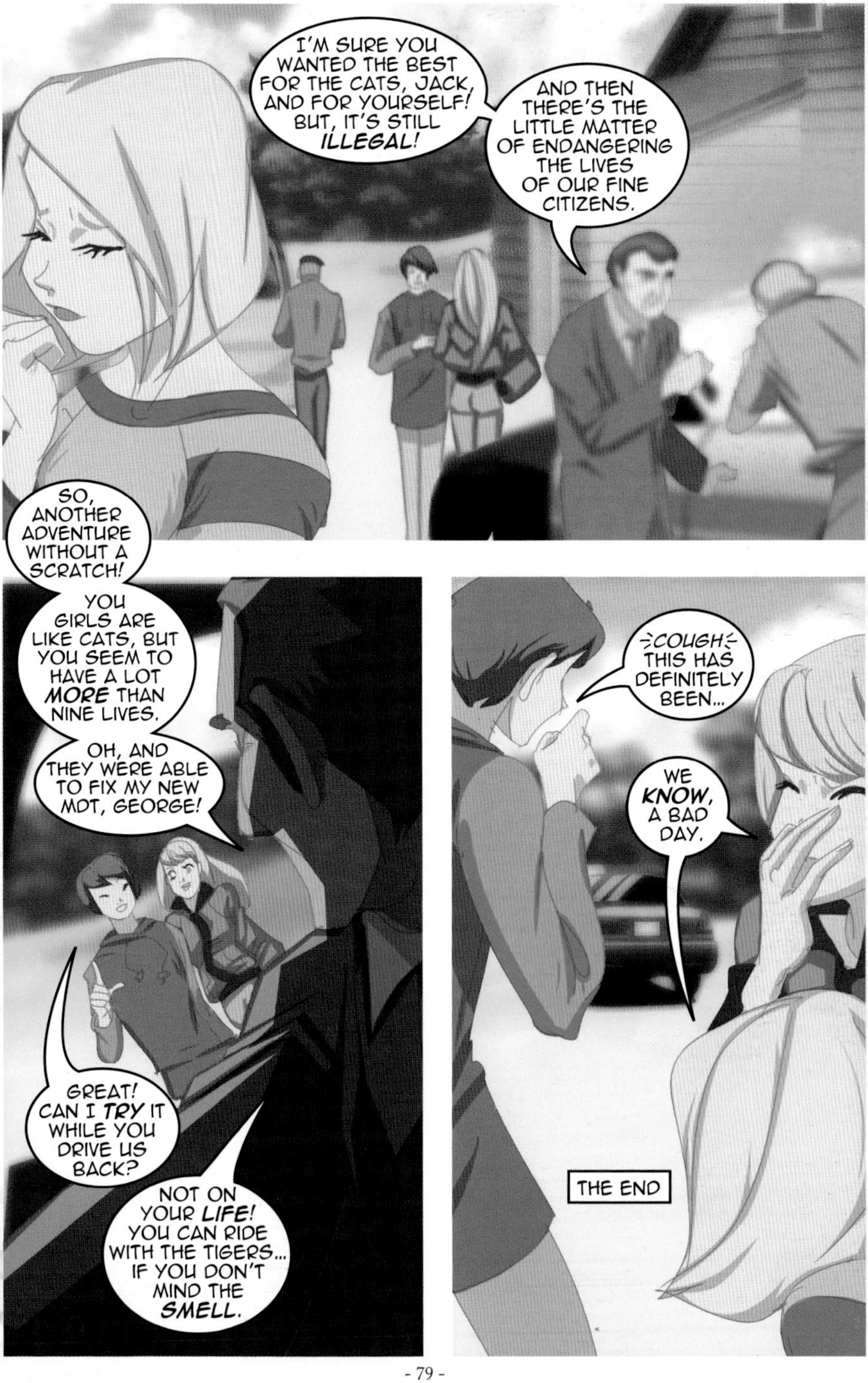

I'M SURE YOU WANTED THE BEST FOR THE CATS, JACK, AND FOR YOURSELF! BUT, IT'S STILL ILLEGAL!
AND THEN THERE'S THE LITTLE MATTER OF ENDANGERING THE LIVES OF OUR FINE CITIZENS.
SO, ANOTHER ADVENTURE WITHOUT A SCRATCH!
YOU GIRLS ARE LIKE CATS, BUT YOU SEEM TO HAVE A LOT MORE THAN NINE LIVES.
OH, AND THEY WERE ABLE TO FIX MY NEW MDT, GEORGE!
GREAT! CAN I TRY IT WHILE YOU DRIVE US BACK?
NOT ON YOUR LIFE! YOU CAN RIDE WITH THE TIGERS... IF YOU DON'T MIND THE SMELL.
COUGH THIS HAS DEFINITELY BEEN...
WE KNOW, A BAD DAY.
THE END

WATCH OUT FOR PAPERCUTZ

Hi, mystery-lovers! Welcome to the eighth electrifying, extra-exciting NANCY DREW DIARIES graphic novel by Stefan Petrucha, Sarah Kinney, Sho Murase, and Carlos Jose Guzman from Papercutz—those animal-loving, pet detectives dedicated to publishing great graphic novels for all ages. I'm Jim Salicrup, the Editor-in-Chief and Life Coach for the Cowardly Lion.

As much as I love and respect our favorite Girl Detective, I'm a bit concerned that she may have crossed a line in both "Tiger Counter" and "What Goes Up…" When warned not to go into the woods to search for tigers—Nancy should have listened. When warned not to go up the the mountain after the bad guys—Nancy should have listened. In both cases, Nancy not only needlessly endangered herself but her two best friends, George and Bess. While we all know that Nancy only has the very best intentions, and that she simply can't resist a mystery, she does need to be realistic. Fortunately in these two cases she was very lucky and no one was hurt.

Speaking of mysteries, for those of you new to the world of Nancy Drew you may wonder what's up with "George." The answer is that her real name is Georgia Fayne, but she prefers to be called "George." Bess Marvin is her cousin, and both George and Bess are not only Nancy's BFFs, but they also work with her to help solve mysteries. Mystery solved!

For those of you who might think that the idea of regular people keeping such animals as tigers for pets is a little far-fetched, know that there are people who really do try to do exactly that! When reality finally sets in, the authorities have to step in and take the animals away. Years ago, I was invited to the home of legenday movie star Tippie Hendren, most famous for starring in Alfred Hitchcock's *The Birds*. Unfortunately, I had to decline the gracious invitation because her home served as part of her non-profit organization, The Roar Foundation, which is dedicated to the care of lions and tigers. At the time, I was hobbling about on crutches because I was recovering from a broken ankle. I was informed that the animals, when seeing me on crutches, would possibly charge at me. I decided that maybe I'd see Ms. Hendren some other time.

As some of you may know, the stories that we're presenting in the NANCY DREW DIARIES were previously published some years back as separate graphic novels, many of which are long out-of-print. We're thrilled to be able to bring those terrific tales back into print as part of this series, but for those of you fans who may already have those NANCY DREW graphic novels and are looking for all-new tales of the teen sleuth, we've got good news for you! It was just announced that Dynamite, the comics and graphic novel publishers will be doing all-new comics starring Nancy Drew (as well as THE HARDY BOYS). We'll have more details on the exciting development in NANCY DREW DIARIES #9.

In the meantime, Papercutz recently launched a new series that may just be the next big hit in the all-ages graphic novel market—THE SISTERS by Cazenove and William. Originally published in French, THE SISTERS is all about the adventures of big sister Wendy and little sister Maureen. Rather than me describe exactly what the series is about, just check out the preview pages following the next Nancy Drew story. And on that note, time for me to stop emitting hot air and let you move on to "What Goes Up…" on the following pages…

Thanks,

Jim

Cazenove
William
The Sisters
1. Just Like Family
PAPERCUTZ

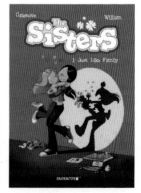

STAY IN TOUCH!

EMAIL:	salicrup@papercutz.com
WEB:	www.papercutz.com
TWITTER:	@papercutzgn
FACEBOOK:	PAPERCUTZGRAPHICNOVELS
REGULAR MAIL:	Papercutz, 160 Broadway, Suite 700, East Wing, New York, NY 10038

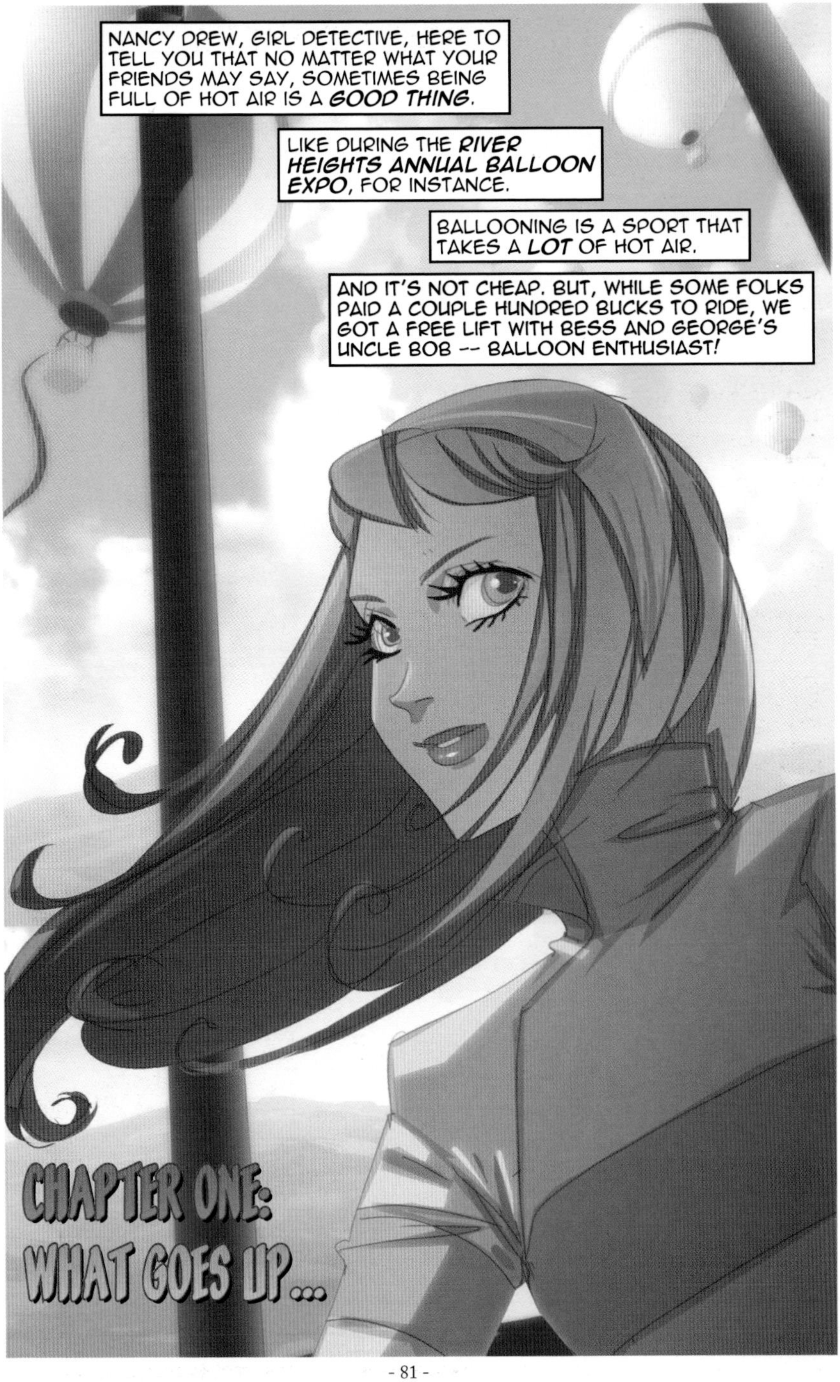
NANCY DREW, GIRL DETECTIVE, HERE TO TELL YOU THAT NO MATTER WHAT YOUR FRIENDS MAY SAY, SOMETIMES BEING FULL OF HOT AIR IS A *GOOD THING*.
LIKE DURING THE *RIVER HEIGHTS ANNUAL BALLOON EXPO*, FOR INSTANCE.
BALLOONING IS A SPORT THAT TAKES A *LOT* OF HOT AIR.
AND IT'S NOT CHEAP. BUT, WHILE SOME FOLKS PAID A COUPLE HUNDRED BUCKS TO RIDE, WE GOT A FREE LIFT WITH BESS AND GEORGE'S UNCLE BOB -- BALLOON ENTHUSIAST!
CHAPTER ONE:
WHAT GOES UP...

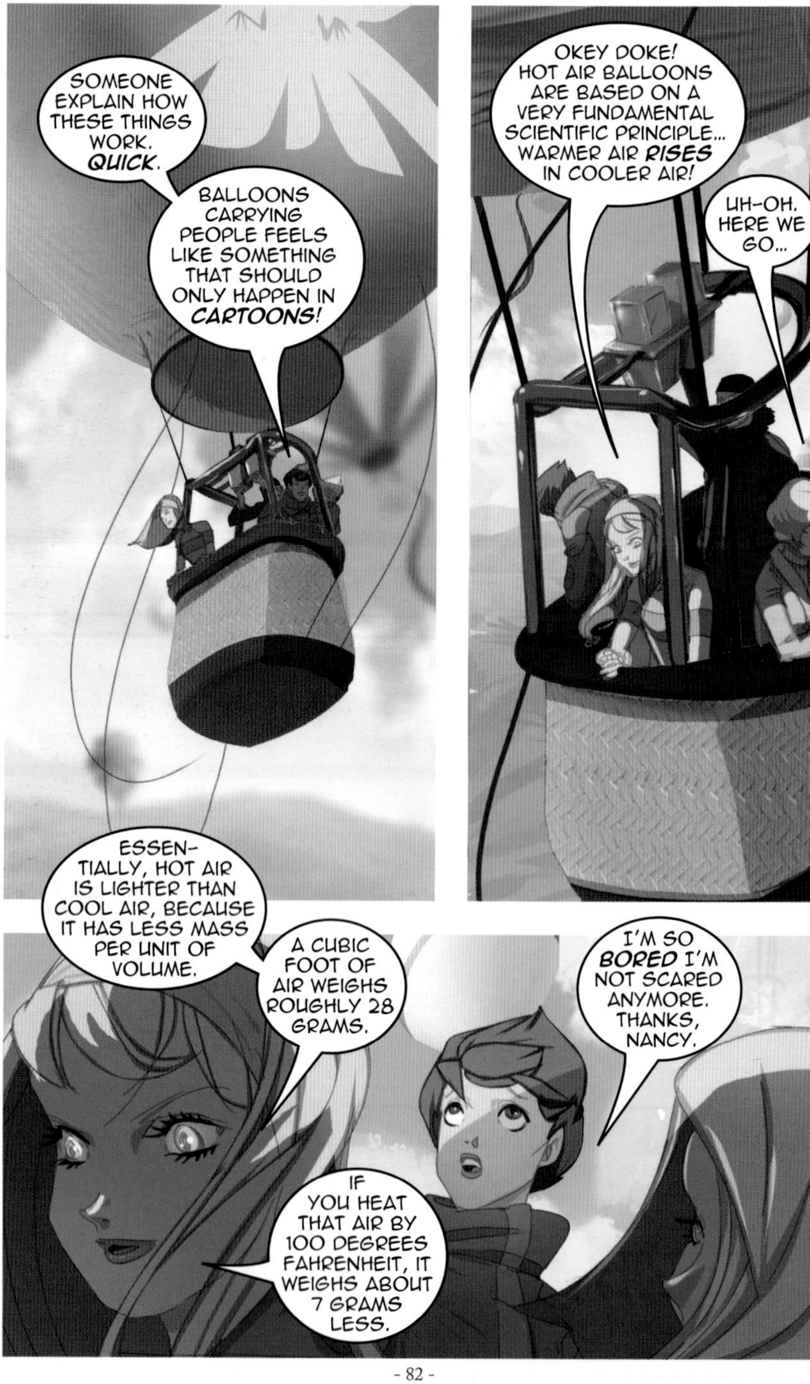
SOMEONE EXPLAIN HOW THESE THINGS WORK. **QUICK**.
BALLOONS CARRYING PEOPLE FEELS LIKE SOMETHING THAT SHOULD ONLY HAPPEN IN **CARTOONS**!
OKEY DOKE! HOT AIR BALLOONS ARE BASED ON A VERY FUNDAMENTAL SCIENTIFIC PRINCIPLE... WARMER AIR **RISES** IN COOLER AIR!
UH-OH. HERE WE GO...
ESSEN-TIALLY, HOT AIR IS LIGHTER THAN COOL AIR, BECAUSE IT HAS LESS MASS PER UNIT OF VOLUME.
A CUBIC FOOT OF AIR WEIGHS ROUGHLY 28 GRAMS.
IF YOU HEAT THAT AIR BY 100 DEGREES FAHRENHEIT, IT WEIGHS ABOUT 7 GRAMS LESS.
I'M SO **BORED** I'M NOT SCARED ANYMORE. THANKS, NANCY.

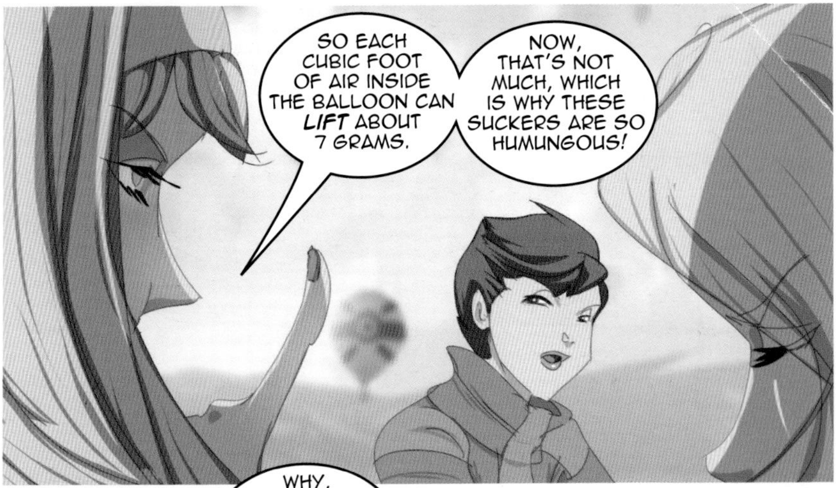
SO EACH CUBIC FOOT OF AIR INSIDE THE BALLOON CAN **LIFT** ABOUT 7 GRAMS.
NOW, THAT'S NOT MUCH, WHICH IS WHY THESE SUCKERS ARE SO HUMUNGOUS!

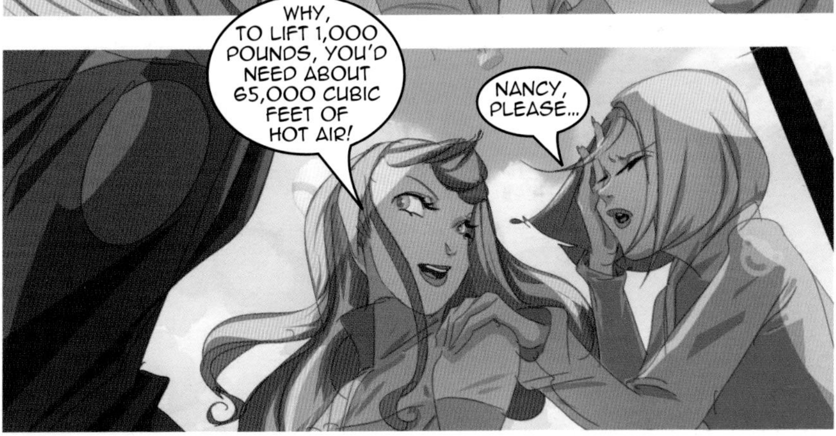
WHY, TO LIFT 1,000 POUNDS, YOU'D NEED ABOUT 65,000 CUBIC FEET OF HOT AIR!
NANCY, PLEASE...

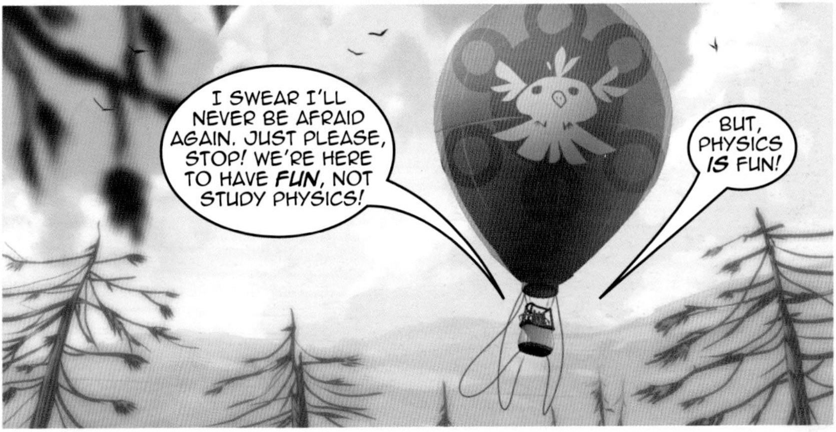
I SWEAR I'LL NEVER BE AFRAID AGAIN. JUST PLEASE, STOP! WE'RE HERE TO HAVE **FUN**, NOT STUDY PHYSICS!
BUT, PHYSICS **IS** FUN!

BESIDES... YOU *DID* ASK!

MY MISTAKE. I MEANT TO ASK SIMPLY HOW *WELL* DOES IT WORK!

AND AS YOU CAN SEE, LADIES, IT WORKS *JUST FINE!* SORRY THE RIDE DIDN'T LAST LONG...

I IMAGINE THE PRICE OF PROPANE MUST LIMIT THE FUN.

THAT BURNER OF YOURS PUTS OUT ENOUGH BTU'S PER HOUR TO HEAT OVER 100 HOUSES COMFORT-ABLY.

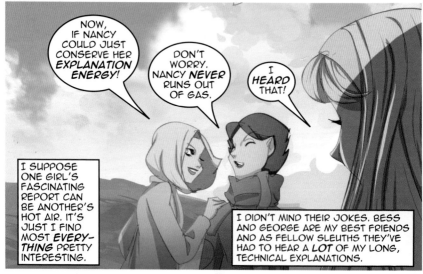

NOW, IF NANCY COULD JUST CONSERVE HER *EXPLANATION ENERGY!*

DON'T WORRY. NANCY *NEVER* RUNS OUT OF GAS.

I *HEARD* THAT!

I SUPPOSE ONE GIRL'S FASCINATING REPORT CAN BE ANOTHER'S HOT AIR. IT'S JUST I FIND MOST *EVERYTHING* PRETTY INTERESTING.

I DIDN'T MIND THEIR JOKES. BESS AND GEORGE ARE MY BEST FRIENDS AND AS FELLOW SLEUTHS THEY'VE HAD TO HEAR A *LOT* OF MY LONG, TECHNICAL EXPLANATIONS.

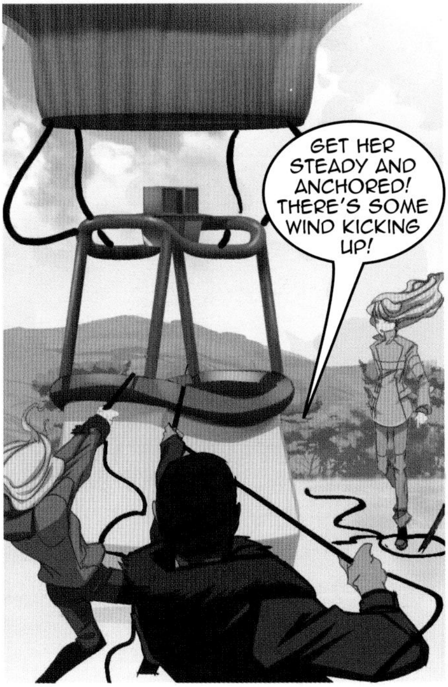
GET HER STEADY AND ANCHORED! THERE'S SOME WIND KICKING UP!

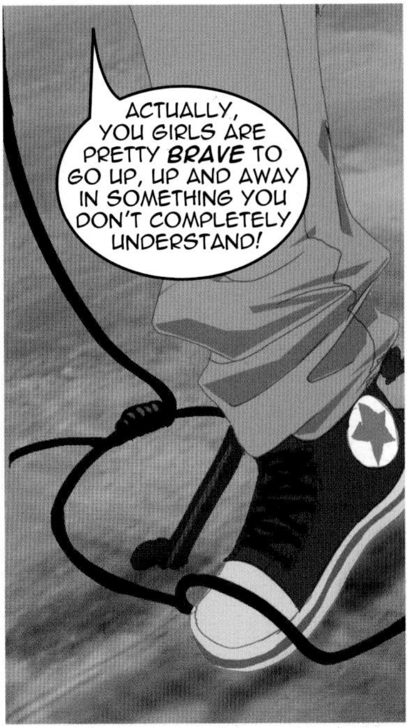
ACTUALLY, YOU GIRLS ARE PRETTY BRAVE TO GO UP, UP AND AWAY IN SOMETHING YOU DON'T COMPLETELY UNDERSTAND!

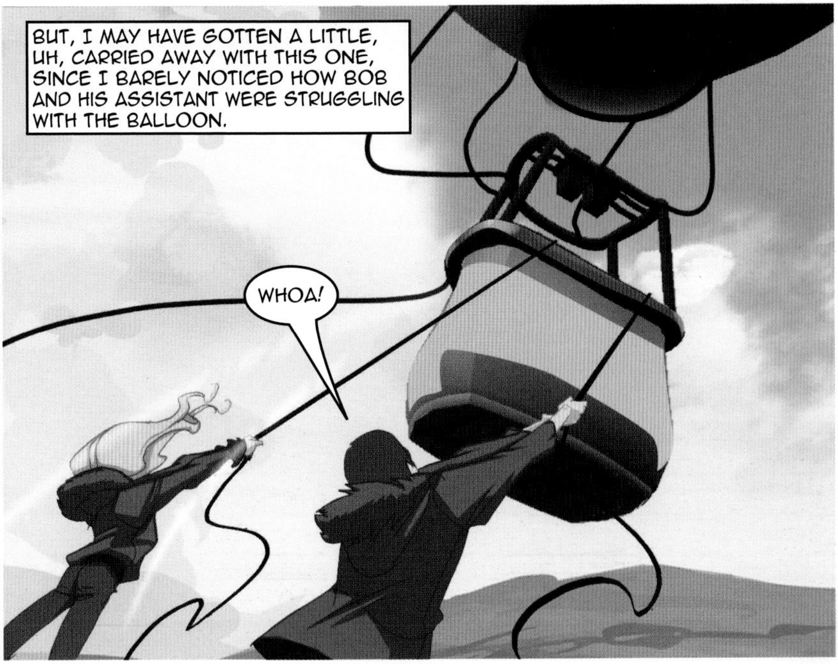
BUT, I MAY HAVE GOTTEN A LITTLE, UH, CARRIED AWAY WITH THIS ONE, SINCE I BARELY NOTICED HOW BOB AND HIS ASSISTANT WERE STRUGGLING WITH THE BALLOON.
WHOA!

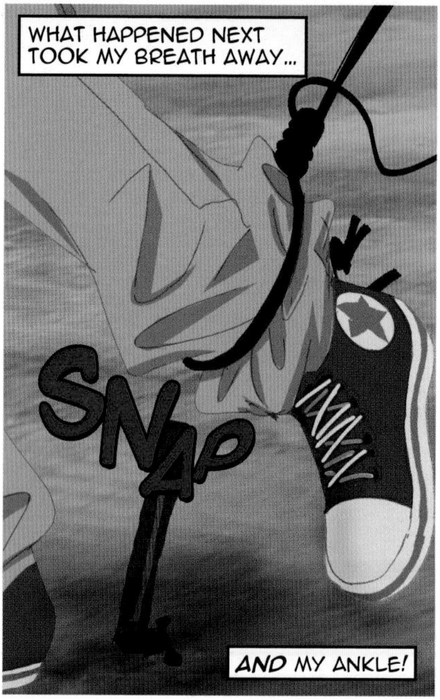
WHAT HAPPENED NEXT
TOOK MY BREATH AWAY...
SNAP
AND MY ANKLE!

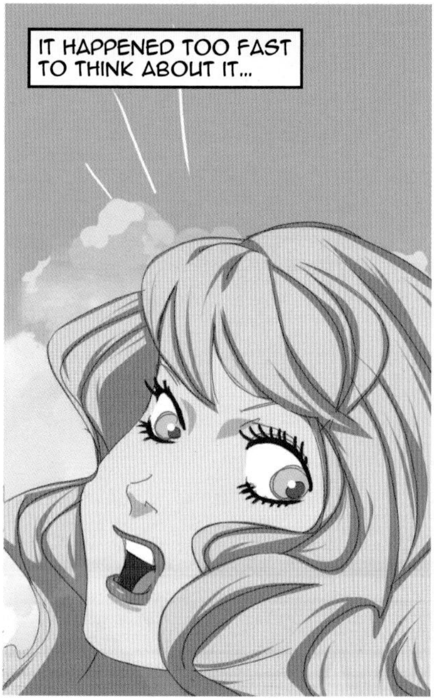
IT HAPPENED TOO FAST
TO THINK ABOUT IT...

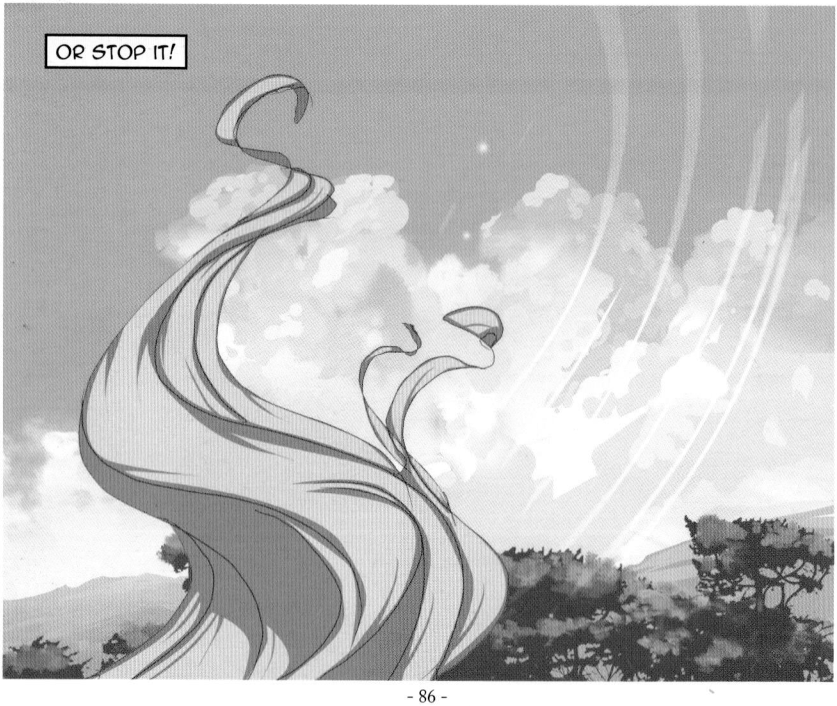
OR STOP IT!

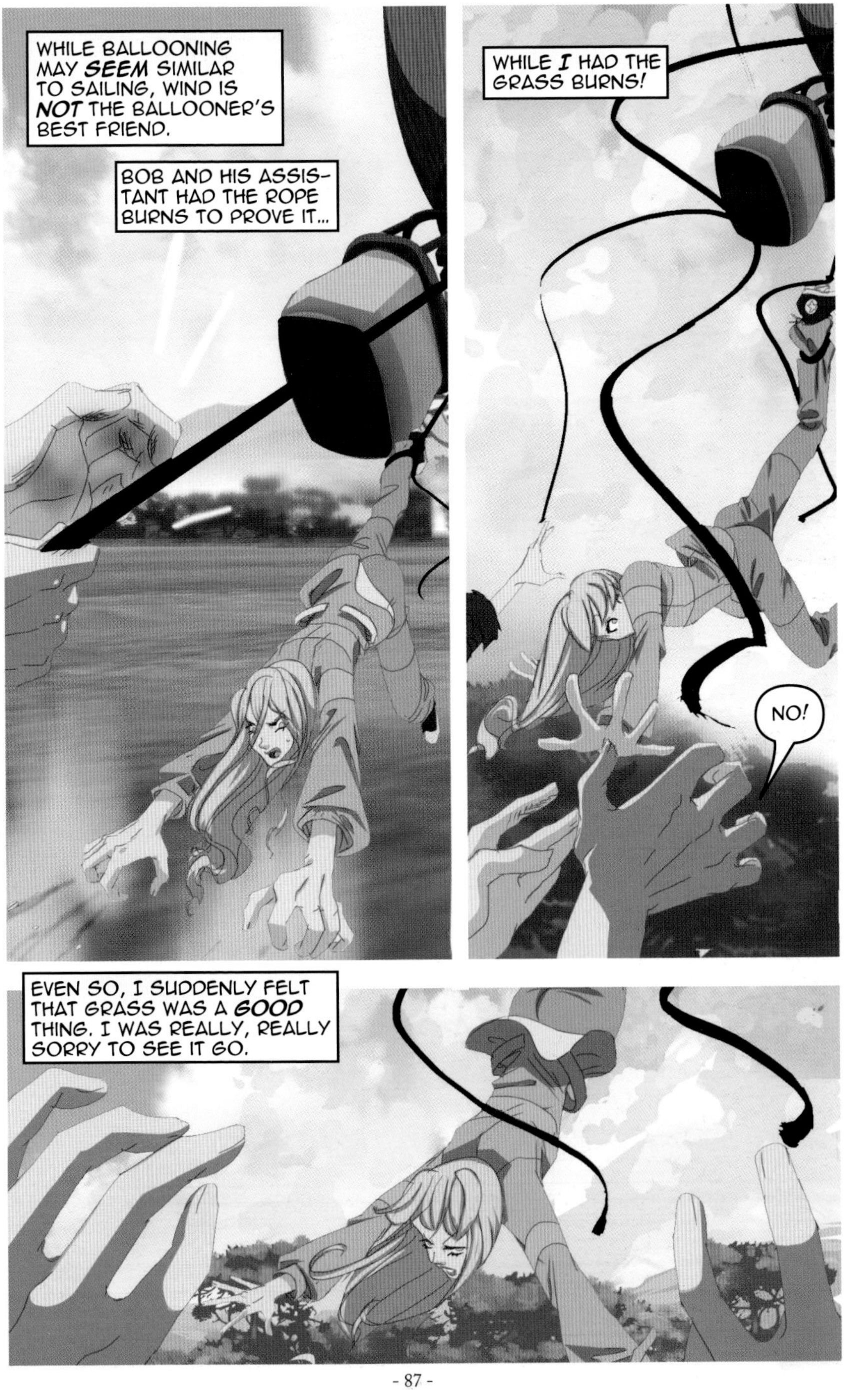
WHILE BALLOONING MAY SEEM SIMILAR TO SAILING, WIND IS NOT THE BALLOONER'S BEST FRIEND.
BOB AND HIS ASSIS-TANT HAD THE ROPE BURNS TO PROVE IT...
WHILE I HAD THE GRASS BURNS!
NO!
EVEN SO, I SUDDENLY FELT THAT GRASS WAS A GOOD THING. I WAS REALLY, REALLY SORRY TO SEE IT GO.

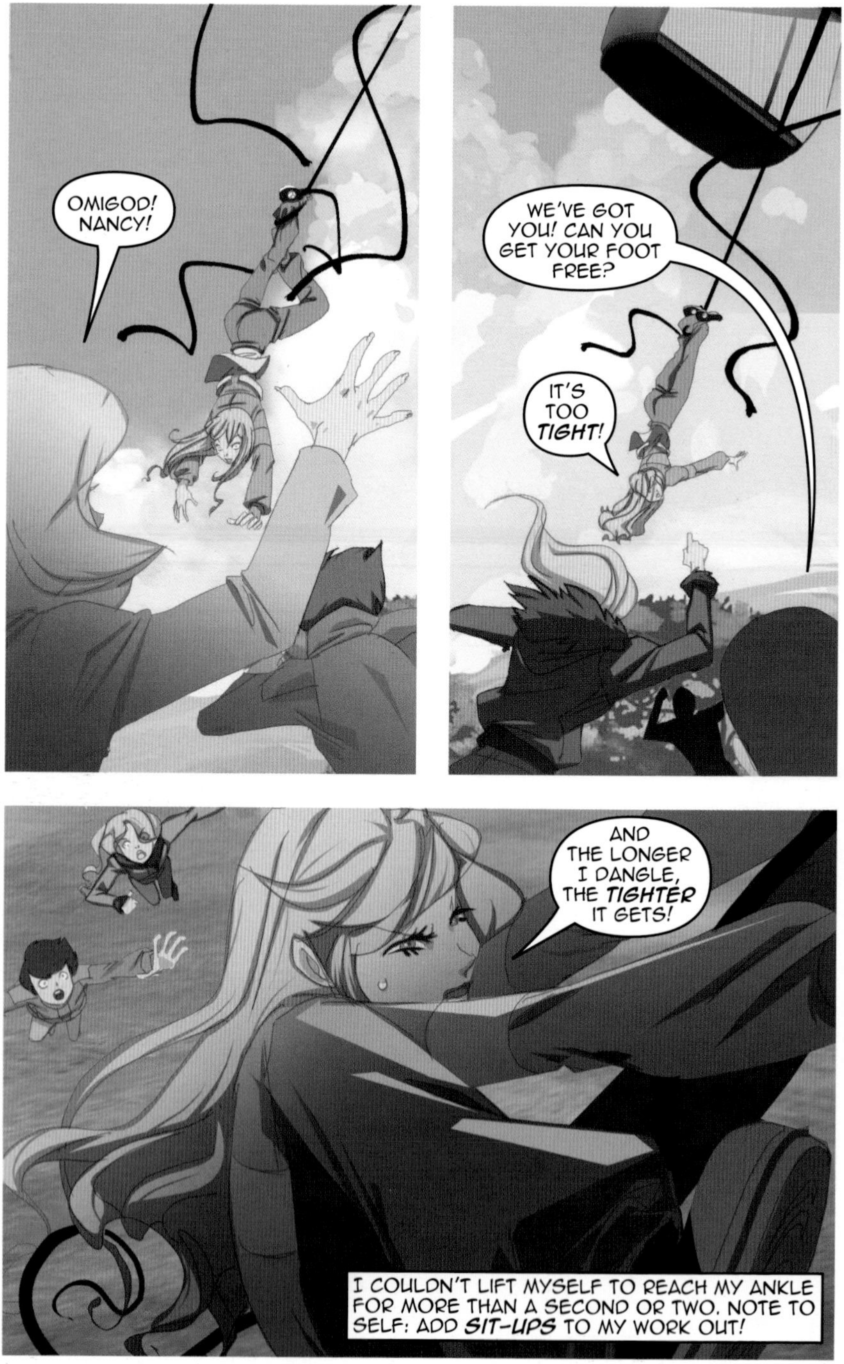
OMIGOD! NANCY!
WE'VE GOT YOU! CAN YOU GET YOUR FOOT FREE?
IT'S TOO ***TIGHT***!
AND THE LONGER I DANGLE, THE ***TIGHTER*** IT GETS!
I COULDN'T LIFT MYSELF TO REACH MY ANKLE FOR MORE THAN A SECOND OR TWO. NOTE TO SELF: ADD ***SIT-UPS*** TO MY WORK OUT!

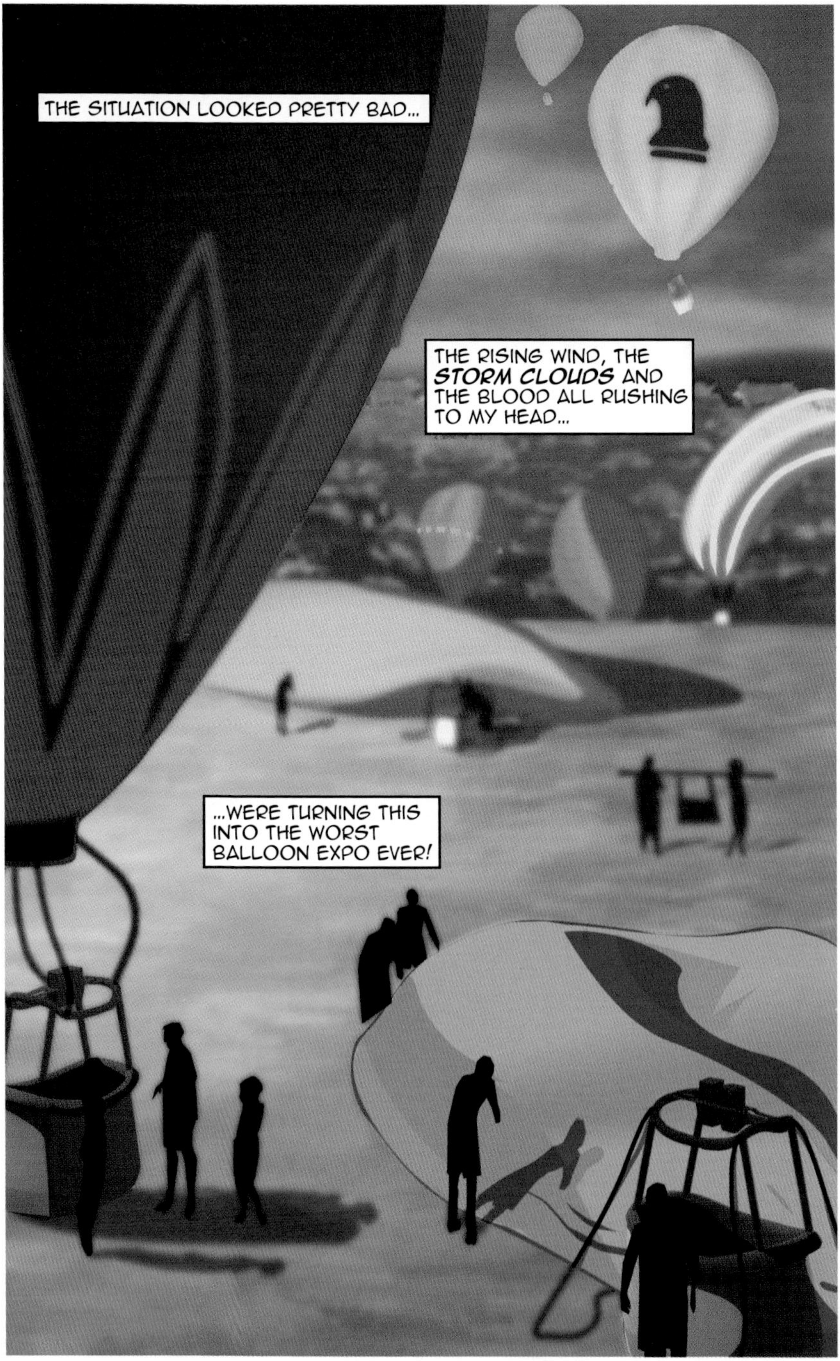
THE SITUATION LOOKED PRETTY BAD...
THE RISING WIND, THE *STORM CLOUDS* AND THE BLOOD ALL RUSHING TO MY HEAD...
...WERE TURNING THIS INTO THE WORST BALLOON EXPO EVER!

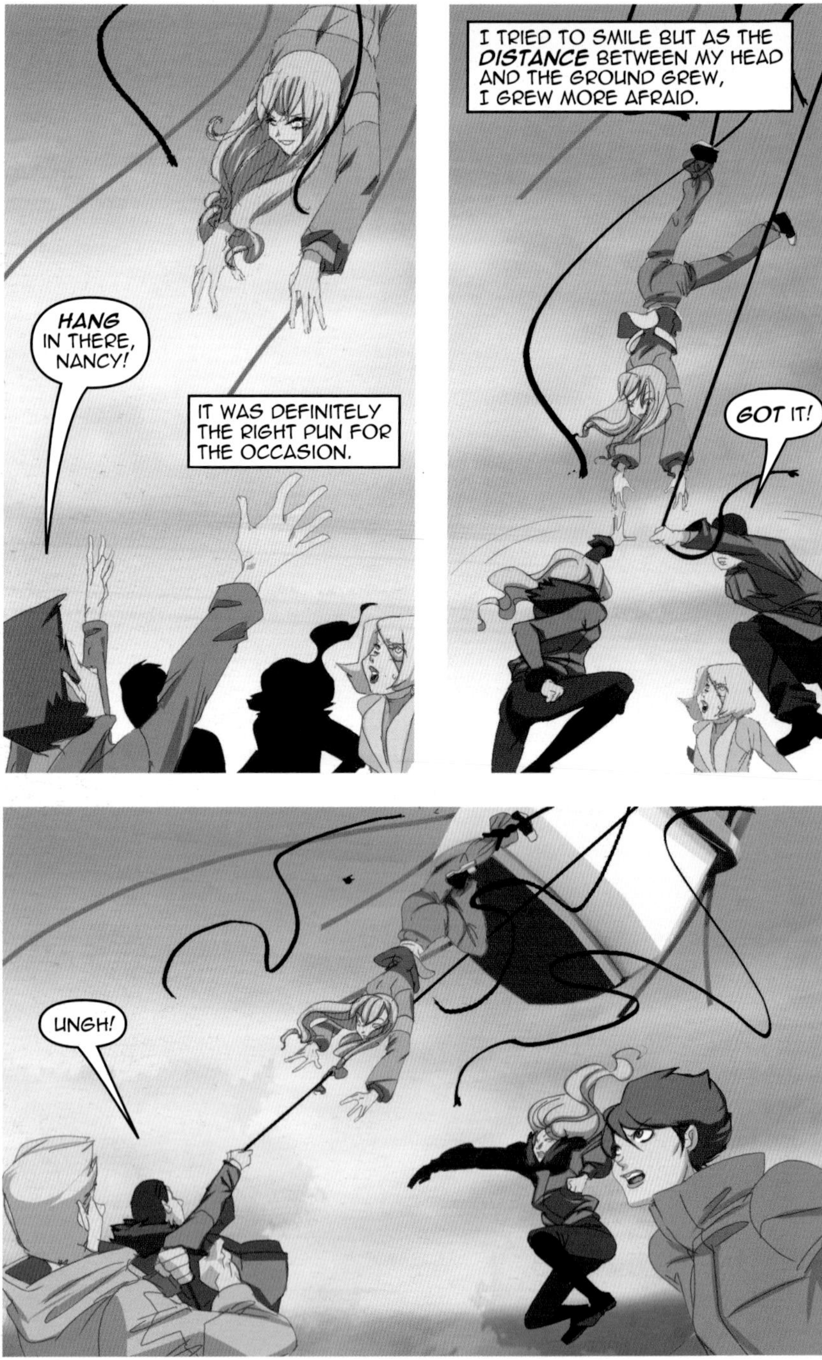
HANG IN THERE, NANCY!
IT WAS DEFINITELY THE RIGHT PUN FOR THE OCCASION.
I TRIED TO SMILE BUT AS THE DISTANCE BETWEEN MY HEAD AND THE GROUND GREW, I GREW MORE AFRAID.
GOT IT!
UNGH!

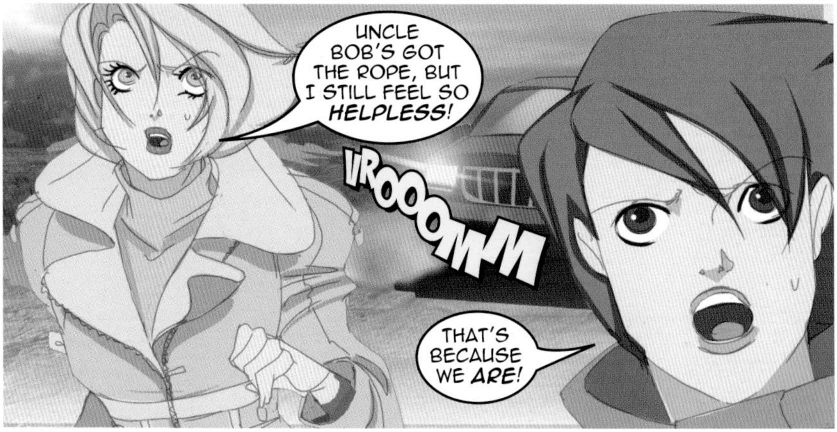
UNCLE BOB'S GOT THE ROPE, BUT I STILL FEEL SO HELPLESS!
VROOOOMMM
THAT'S BECAUSE WE ARE!

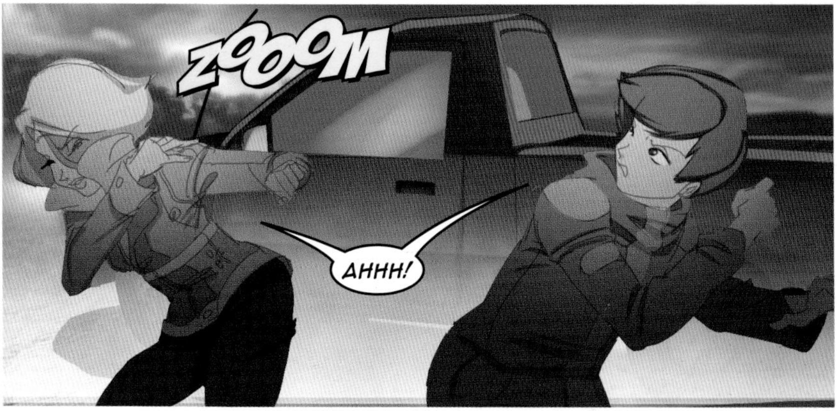
ZOOOM
AHHH!

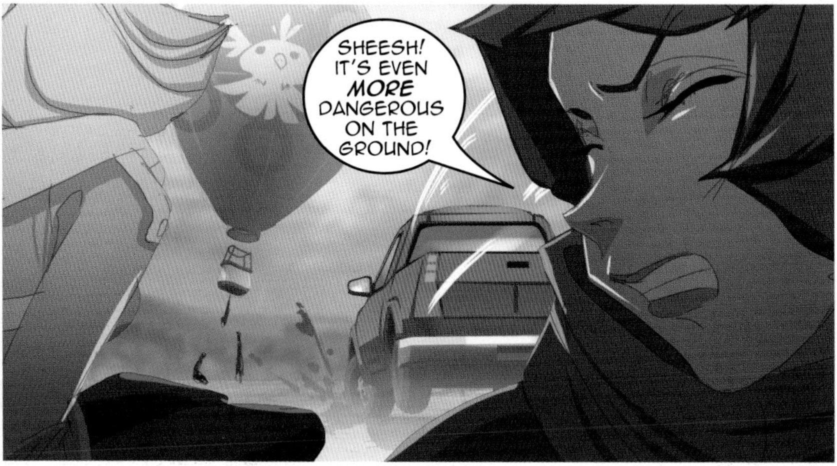
SHEESH! IT'S EVEN MORE DANGEROUS ON THE GROUND!

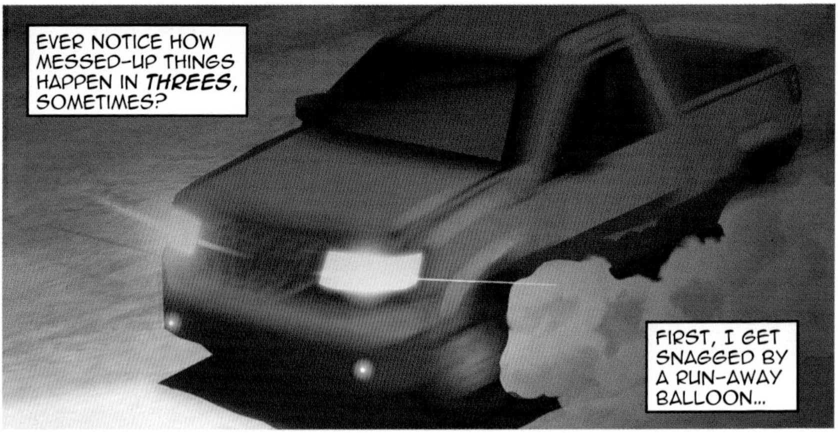
EVER NOTICE HOW MESSED-UP THINGS HAPPEN IN THREES, SOMETIMES?
FIRST, I GET SNAGGED BY A RUN-AWAY BALLOON...

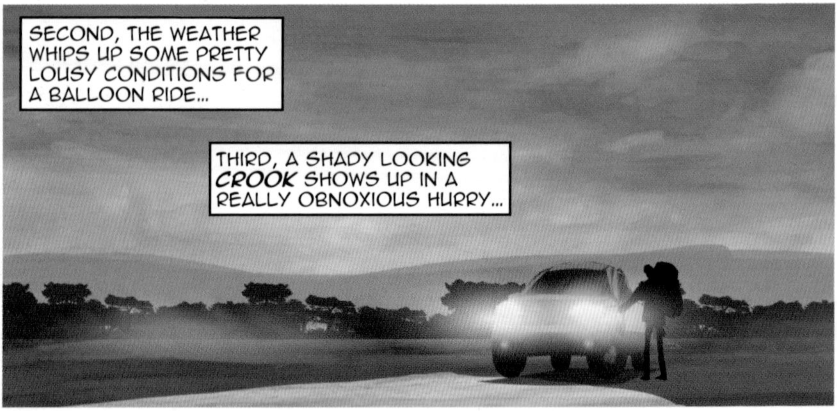
SECOND, THE WEATHER WHIPS UP SOME PRETTY LOUSY CONDITIONS FOR A BALLOON RIDE...
THIRD, A SHADY LOOKING CROOK SHOWS UP IN A REALLY OBNOXIOUS HURRY...

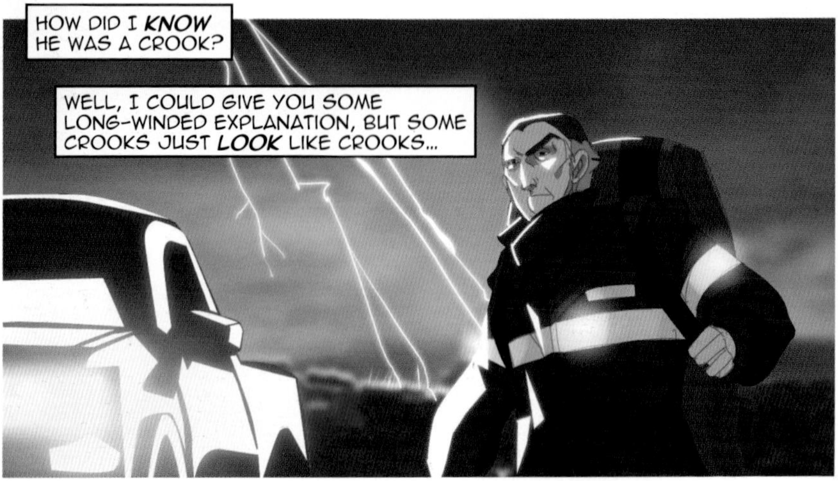
HOW DID I KNOW HE WAS A CROOK?
WELL, I COULD GIVE YOU SOME LONG-WINDED EXPLANATION, BUT SOME CROOKS JUST LOOK LIKE CROOKS...

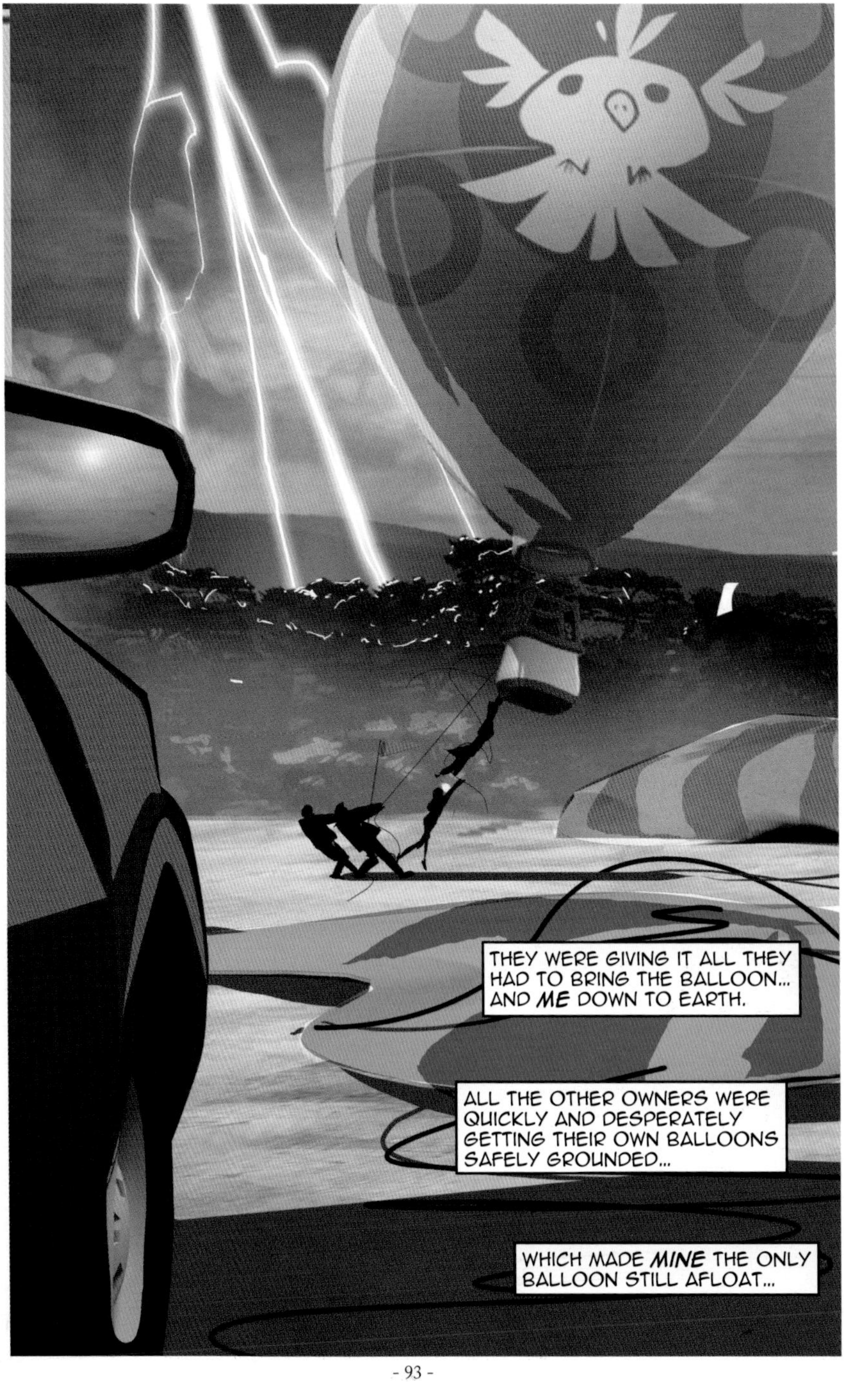
THEY WERE GIVING IT ALL THEY HAD TO BRING THE BALLOON... AND ME DOWN TO EARTH.
ALL THE OTHER OWNERS WERE QUICKLY AND DESPERATELY GETTING THEIR OWN BALLOONS SAFELY GROUNDED...
WHICH MADE MINE THE ONLY BALLOON STILL AFLOAT...

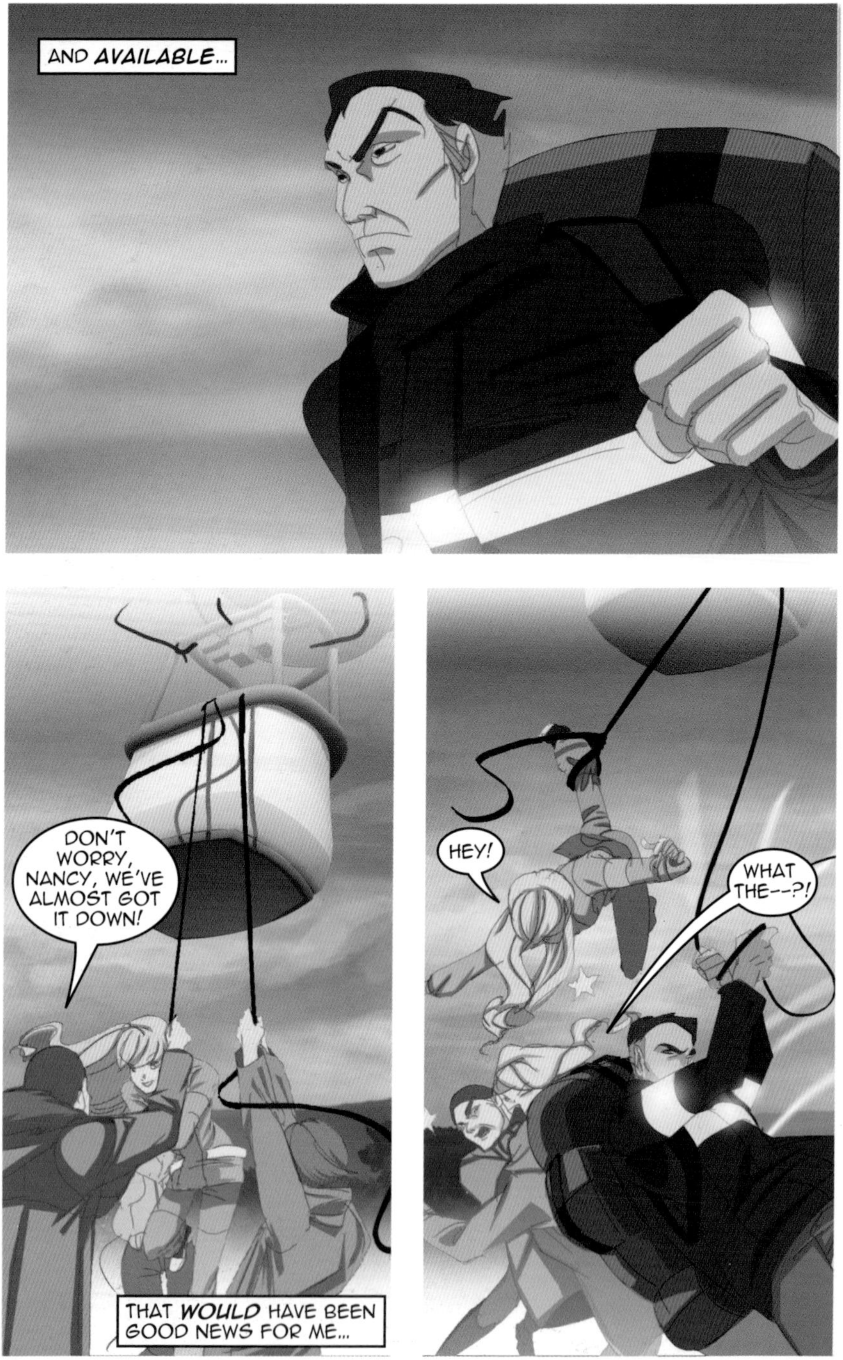
AND AVAILABLE...
DON'T WORRY, NANCY, WE'VE ALMOST GOT IT DOWN!
THAT WOULD HAVE BEEN GOOD NEWS FOR ME...
HEY!
WHAT THE--?!

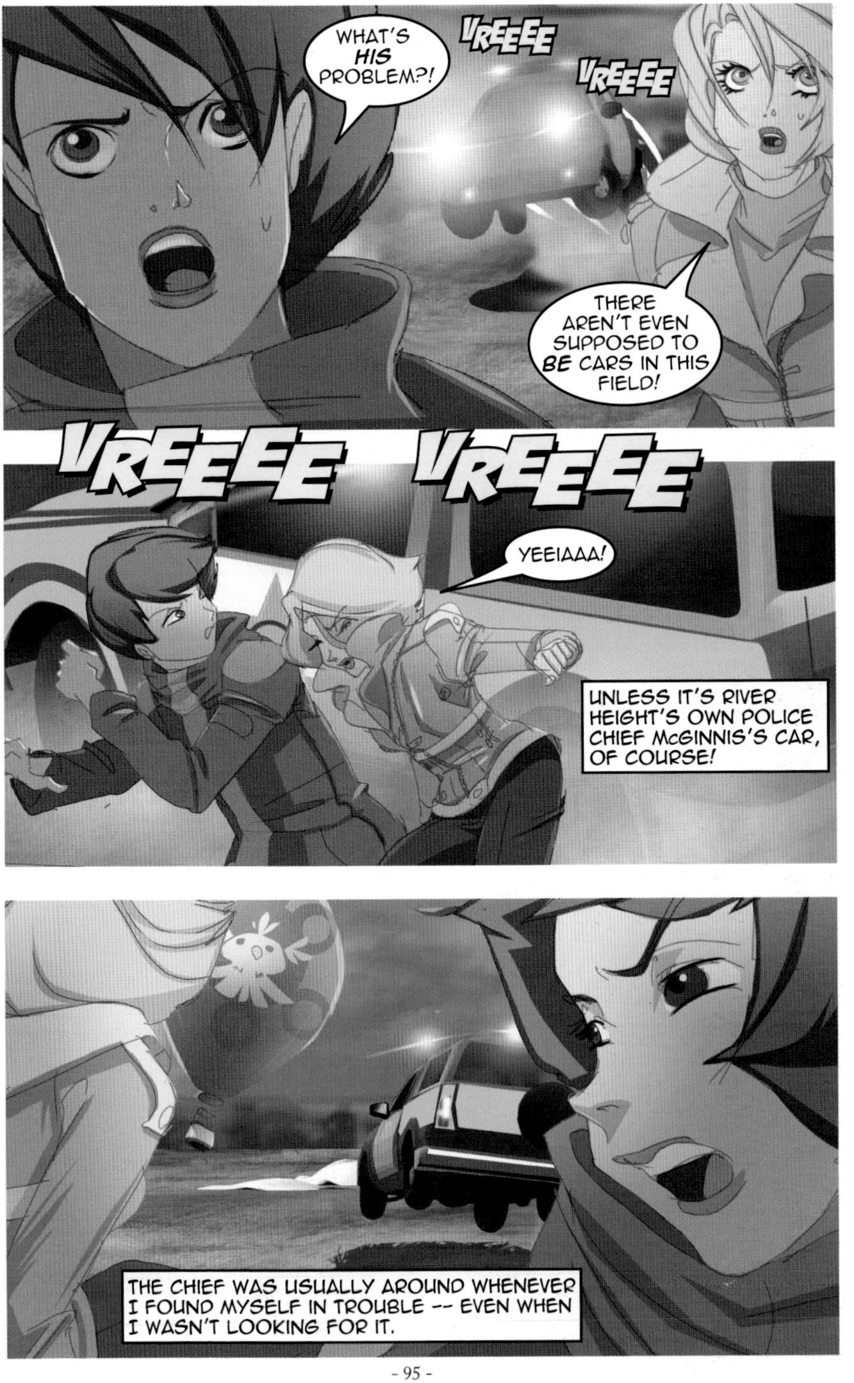
WHAT'S HIS PROBLEM?!
VREEEE
VREEEE
THERE AREN'T EVEN SUPPOSED TO BE CARS IN THIS FIELD!
VREEEE VREEEE
YEEIAAA!
UNLESS IT'S RIVER HEIGHT'S OWN POLICE CHIEF McGINNIS'S CAR, OF COURSE!
THE CHIEF WAS USUALLY AROUND WHENEVER I FOUND MYSELF IN TROUBLE -- EVEN WHEN I WASN'T LOOKING FOR IT.

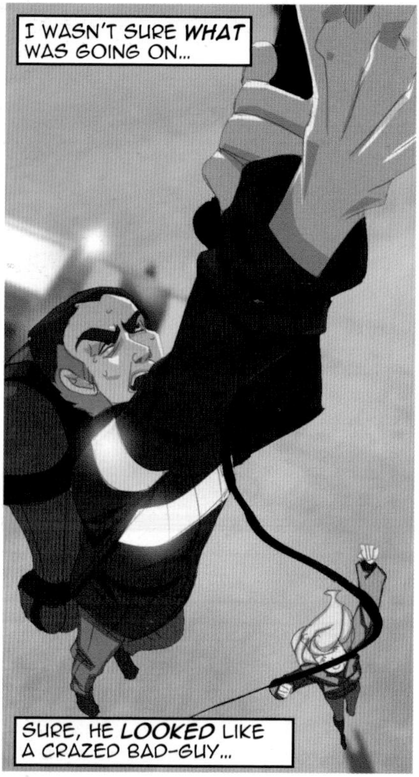
I WASN'T SURE ***WHAT*** WAS GOING ON...
SURE, HE ***LOOKED*** LIKE A CRAZED BAD-GUY...

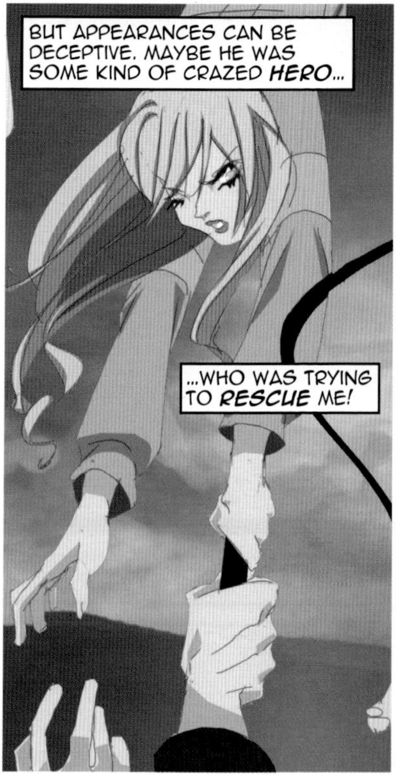
BUT APPEARANCES CAN BE DECEPTIVE. MAYBE HE WAS SOME KIND OF CRAZED ***HERO***...
...WHO WAS TRYING TO ***RESCUE*** ME!

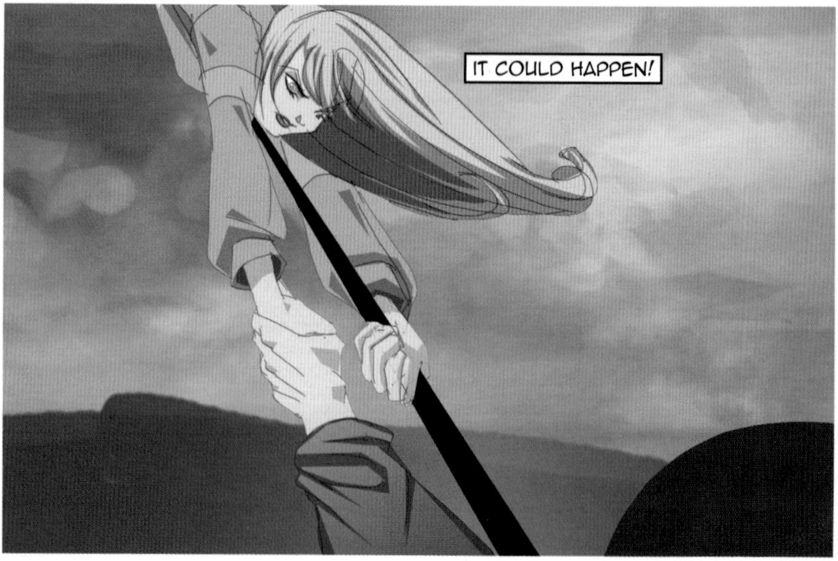
IT COULD HAPPEN!

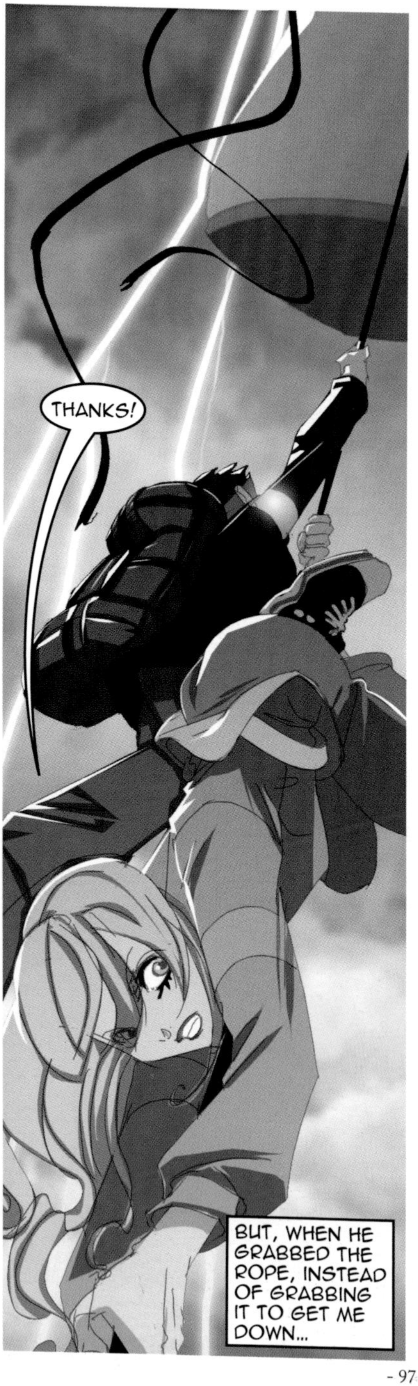
THANKS!
BUT, WHEN HE GRABBED THE ROPE, INSTEAD OF GRABBING IT TO GET ME DOWN...

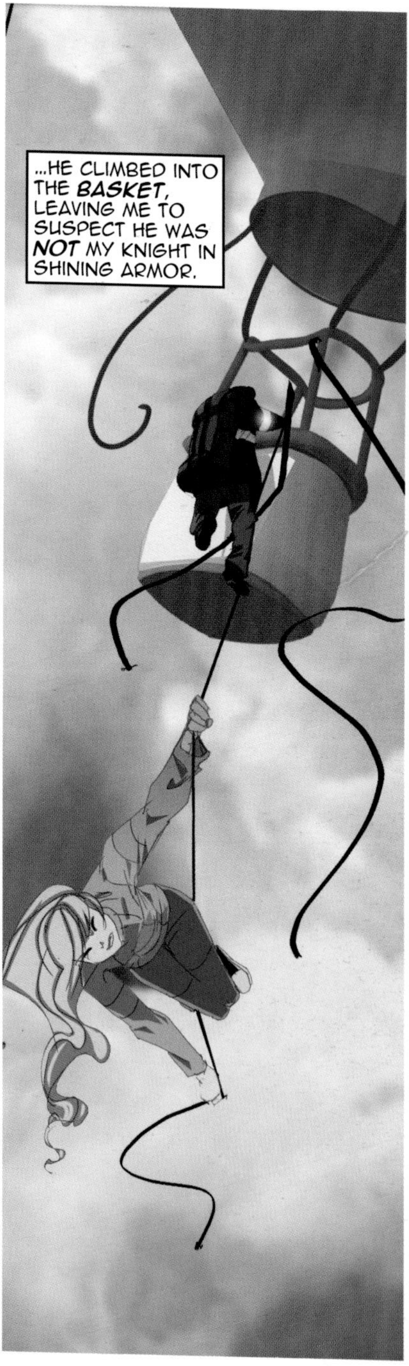
...HE CLIMBED INTO THE BASKET, LEAVING ME TO SUSPECT HE WAS NOT MY KNIGHT IN SHINING ARMOR.

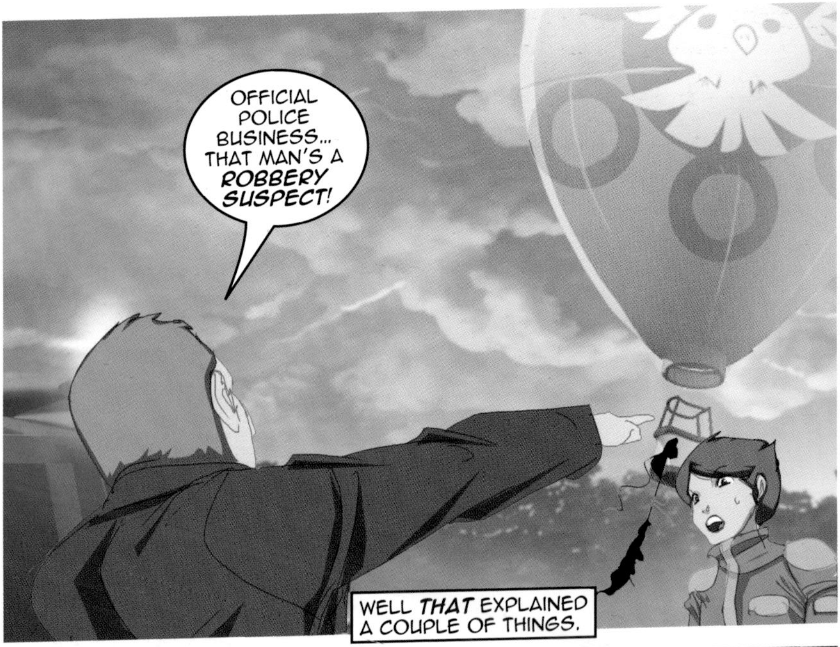
OFFICIAL POLICE BUSINESS... THAT MAN'S A ROBBERY SUSPECT!
WELL THAT EXPLAINED A COUPLE OF THINGS.

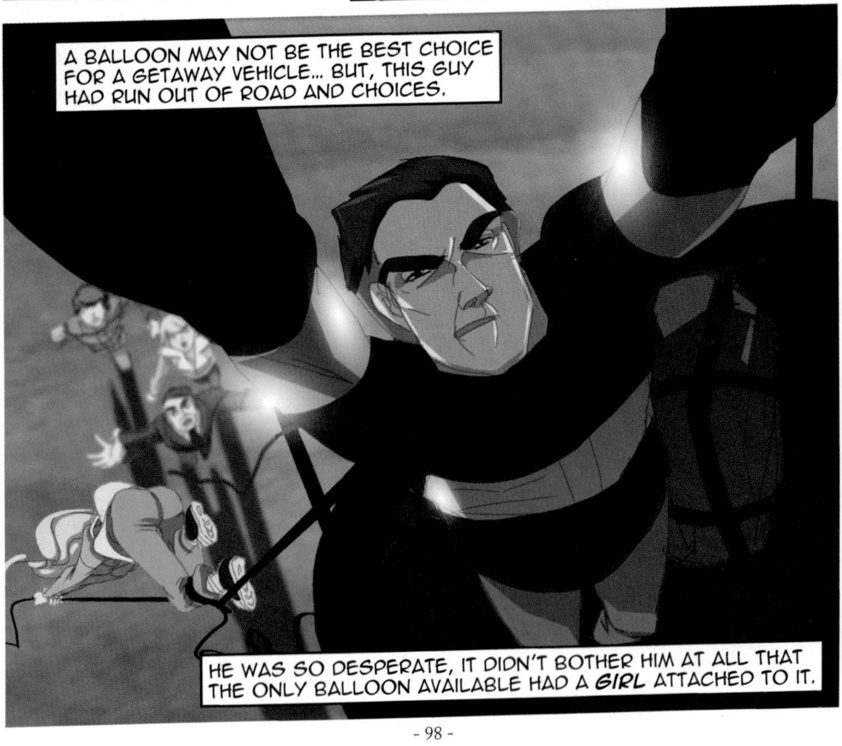
A BALLOON MAY NOT BE THE BEST CHOICE FOR A GETAWAY VEHICLE... BUT, THIS GUY HAD RUN OUT OF ROAD AND CHOICES.
HE WAS SO DESPERATE, IT DIDN'T BOTHER HIM AT ALL THAT THE ONLY BALLOON AVAILABLE HAD A GIRL ATTACHED TO IT.

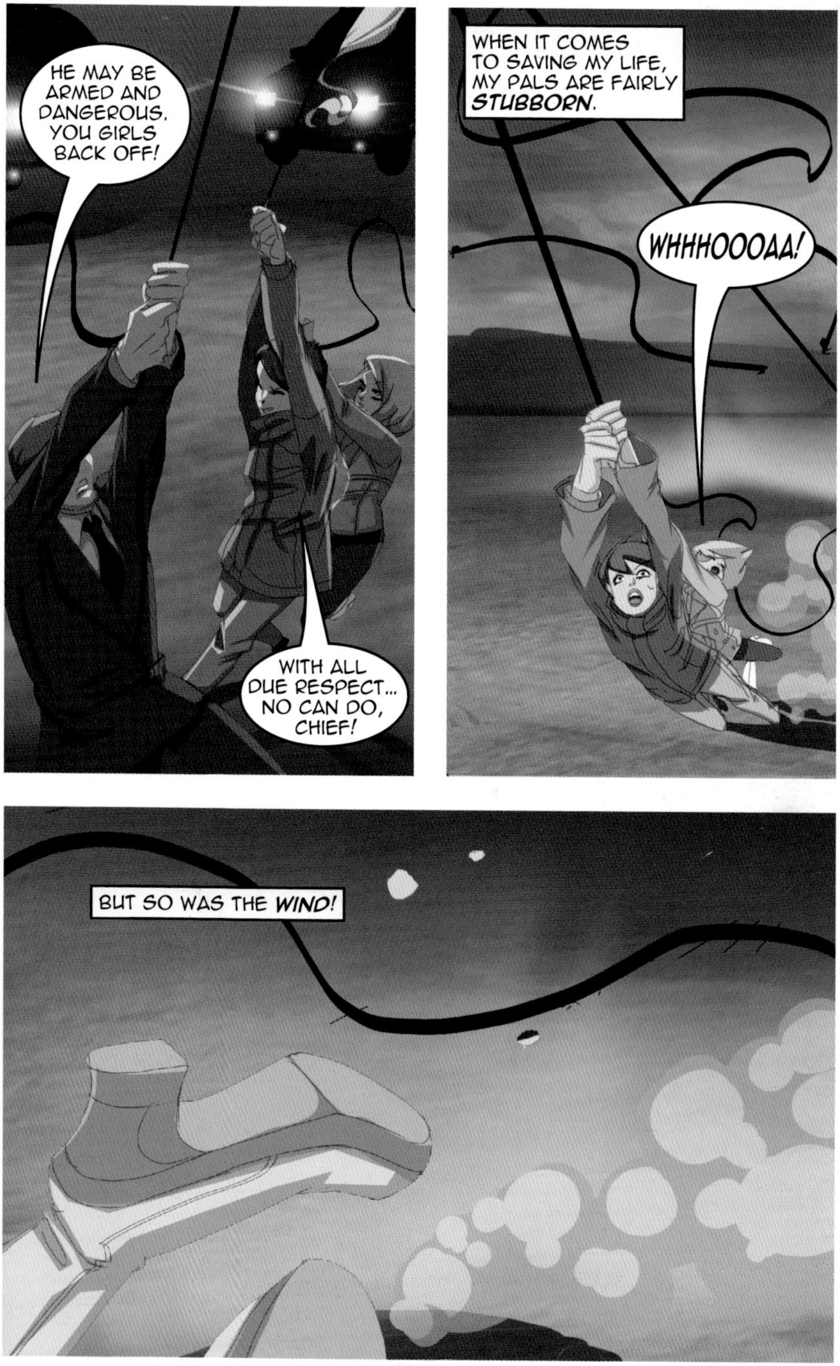
HE MAY BE ARMED AND DANGEROUS. YOU GIRLS BACK OFF!
WITH ALL DUE RESPECT... NO CAN DO, CHIEF!
WHEN IT COMES TO SAVING MY LIFE, MY PALS ARE FAIRLY STUBBORN.
WHHHOOOAA!
BUT SO WAS THE WIND!

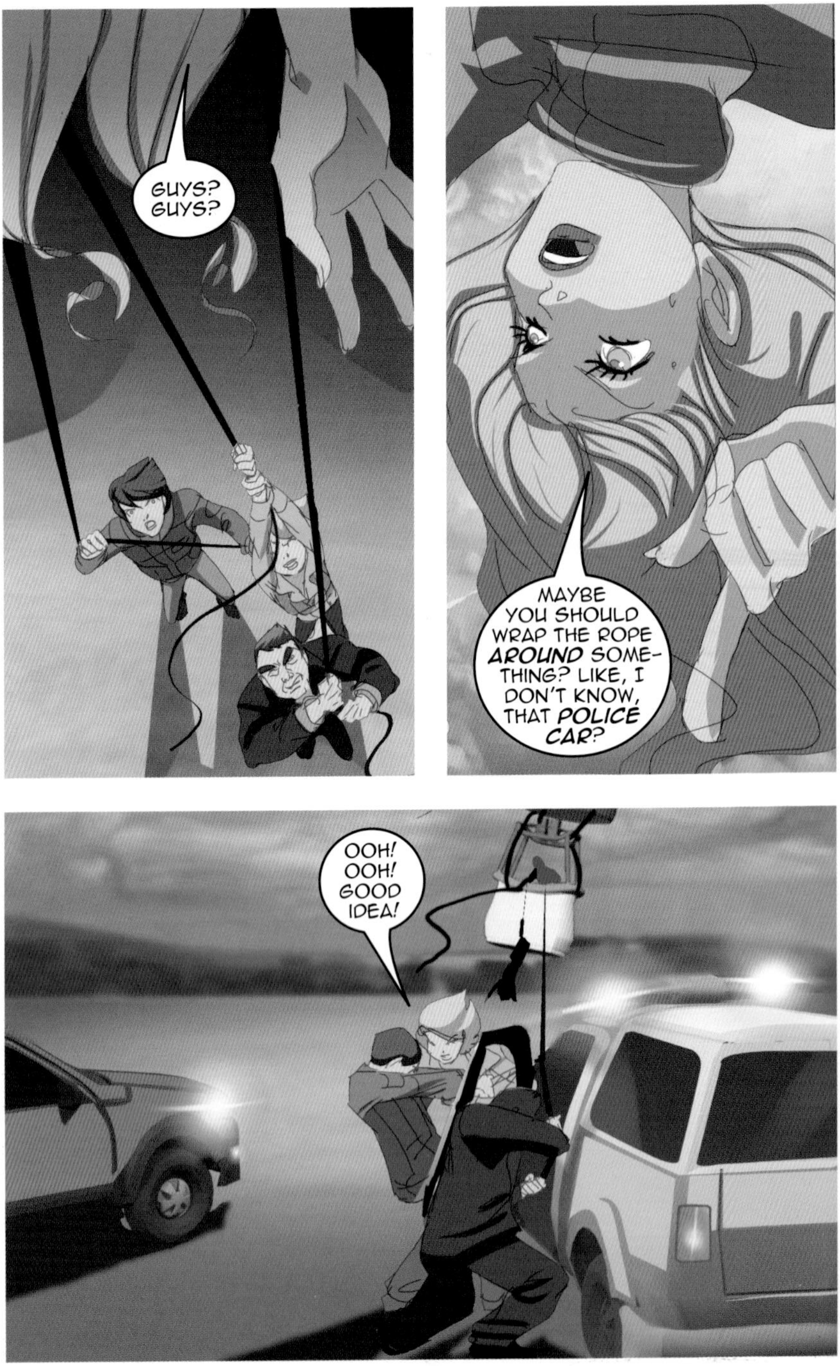
GUYS? GUYS?
MAYBE YOU SHOULD WRAP THE ROPE **AROUND** SOME-THING? LIKE, I DON'T KNOW, THAT **POLICE CAR**?
OOH! OOH! GOOD IDEA!

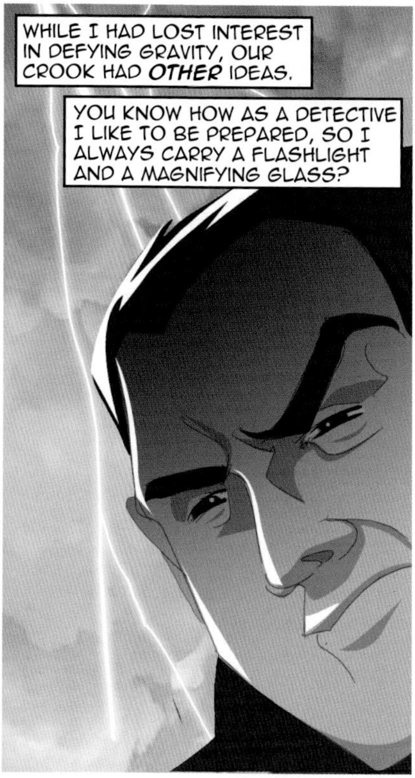
WHILE I HAD LOST INTEREST IN DEFYING GRAVITY, OUR CROOK HAD ***OTHER*** IDEAS.
YOU KNOW HOW AS A DETECTIVE I LIKE TO BE PREPARED, SO I ALWAYS CARRY A FLASHLIGHT AND A MAGNIFYING GLASS?

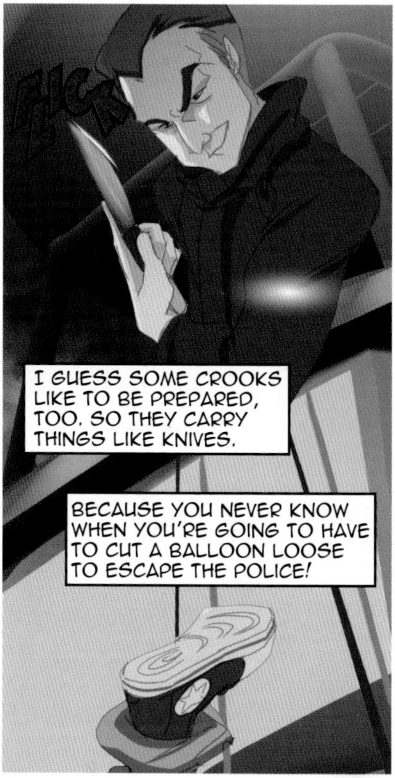
I GUESS SOME CROOKS LIKE TO BE PREPARED, TOO. SO THEY CARRY THINGS LIKE KNIVES.
BECAUSE YOU NEVER KNOW WHEN YOU'RE GOING TO HAVE TO CUT A BALLOON LOOSE TO ESCAPE THE POLICE!

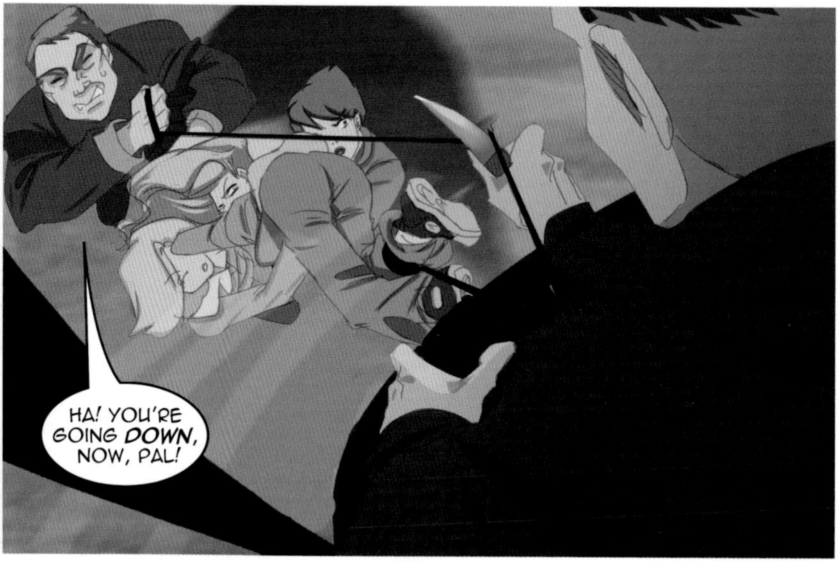
HA! YOU'RE GOING ***DOWN***, NOW, PAL!

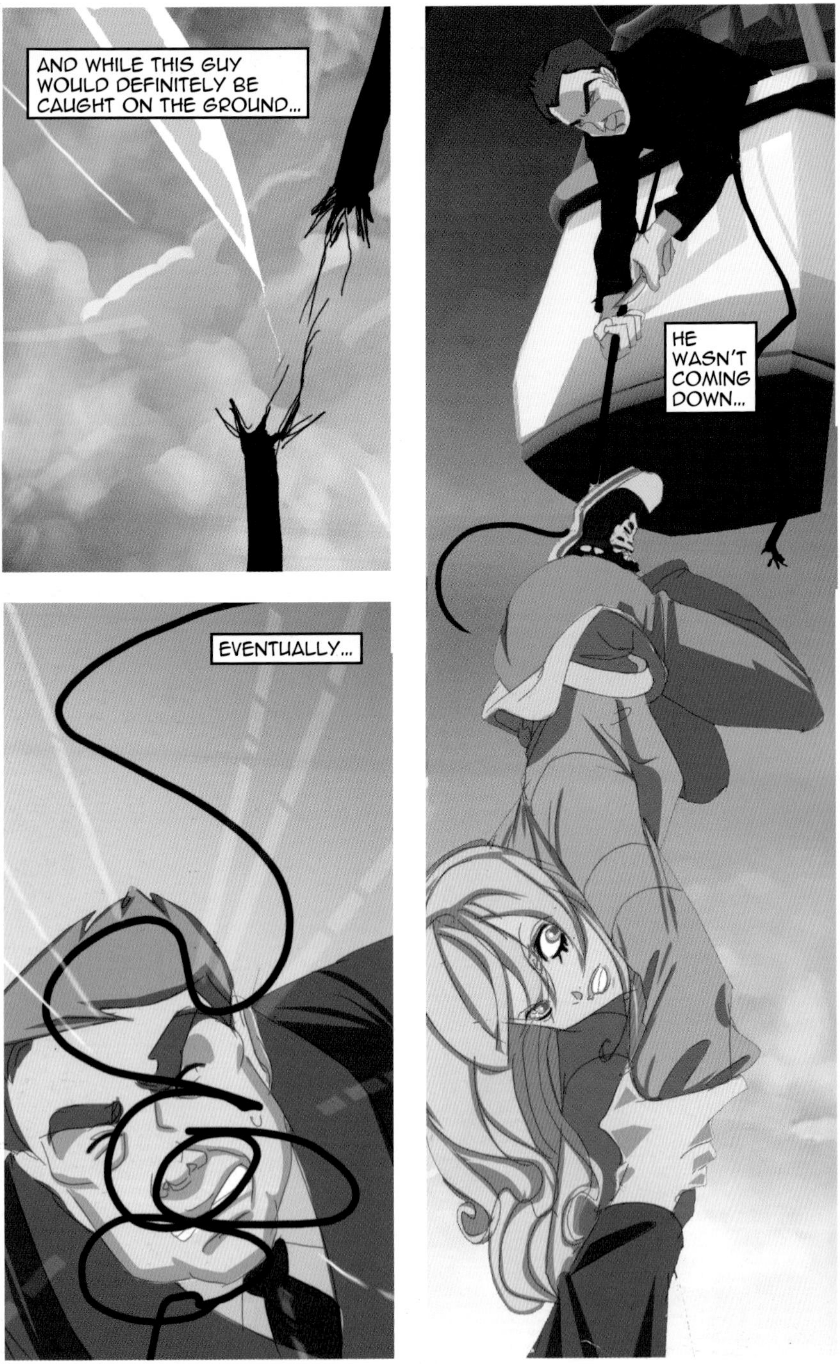
AND WHILE THIS GUY WOULD DEFINITELY BE CAUGHT ON THE GROUND...
HE WASN'T COMING DOWN...
EVENTUALLY...

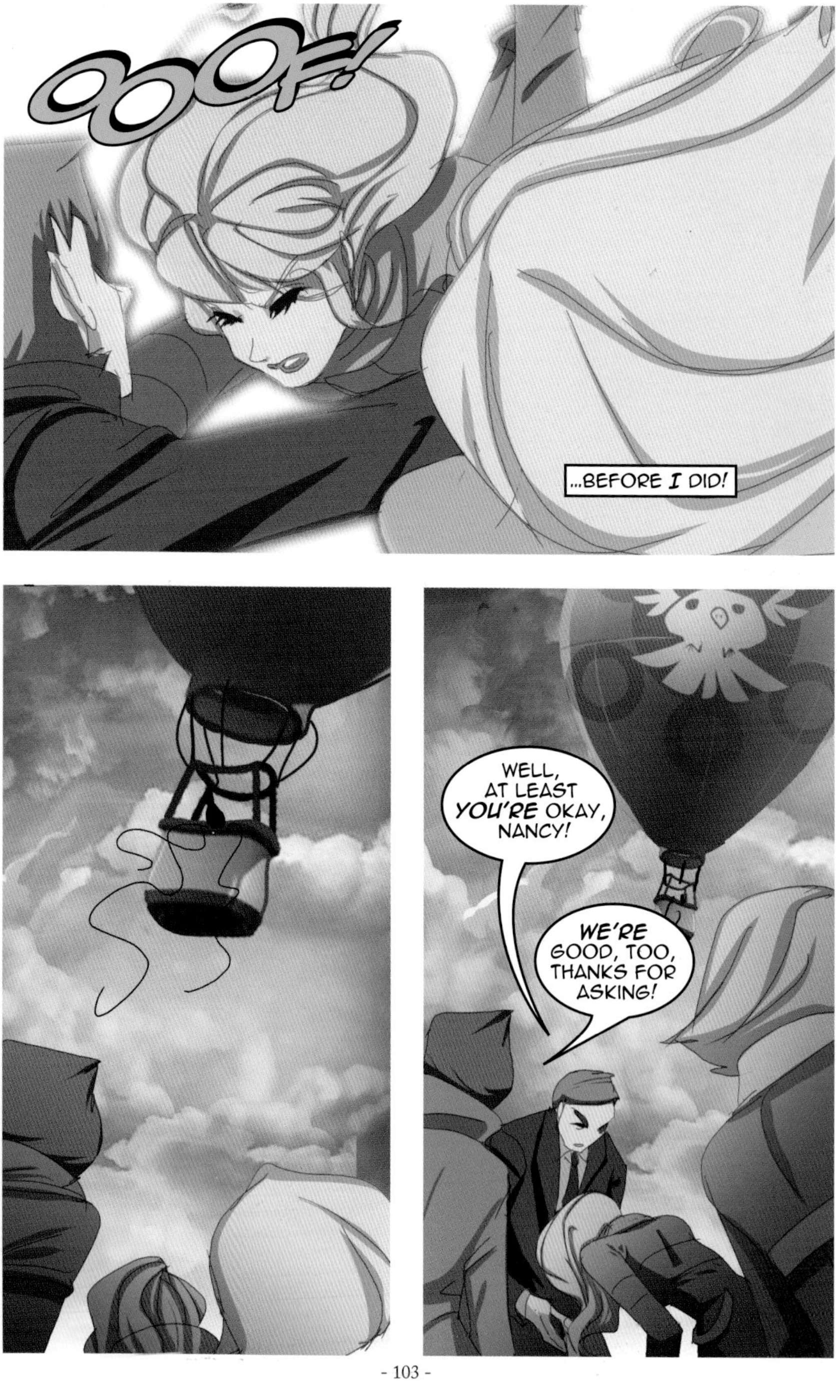
OOOF!
...BEFORE I DID!
WELL, AT LEAST YOU'RE OKAY, NANCY!
WE'RE GOOD, TOO, THANKS FOR ASKING!

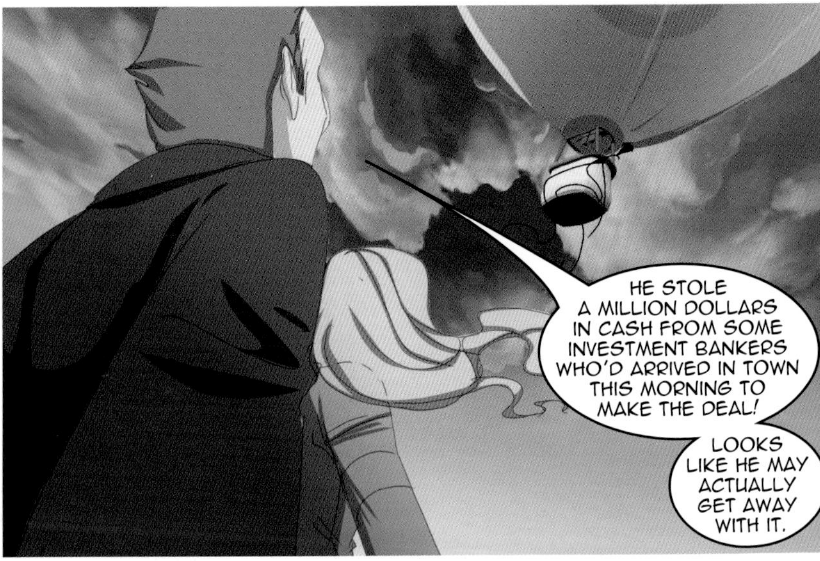
HE STOLE A MILLION DOLLARS IN CASH FROM SOME INVESTMENT BANKERS WHO'D ARRIVED IN TOWN THIS MORNING TO MAKE THE DEAL!
LOOKS LIKE HE MAY ACTUALLY GET AWAY WITH IT.

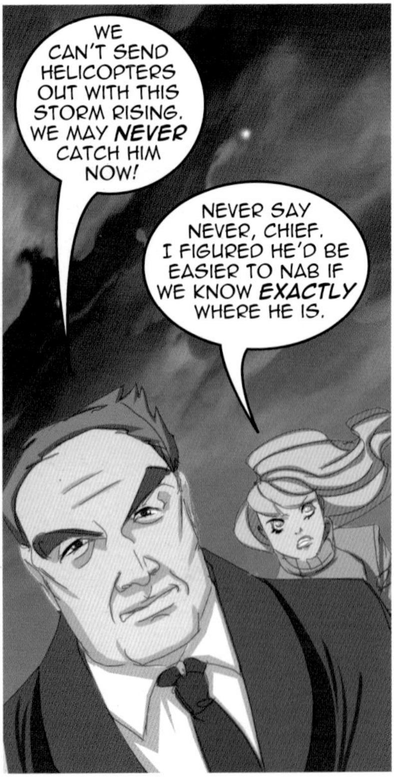
WE CAN'T SEND HELICOPTERS OUT WITH THIS STORM RISING. WE MAY **NEVER** CATCH HIM NOW!
NEVER SAY NEVER, CHIEF. I FIGURED HE'D BE EASIER TO NAB IF WE KNOW **EXACTLY** WHERE HE IS.

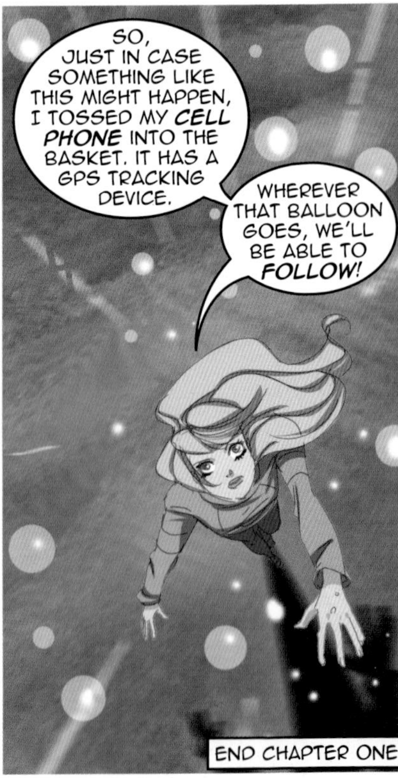
SO, JUST IN CASE SOMETHING LIKE THIS MIGHT HAPPEN, I TOSSED MY **CELL PHONE** INTO THE BASKET. IT HAS A GPS TRACKING DEVICE.
WHEREVER THAT BALLOON GOES, WE'LL BE ABLE TO **FOLLOW!**
END CHAPTER ONE

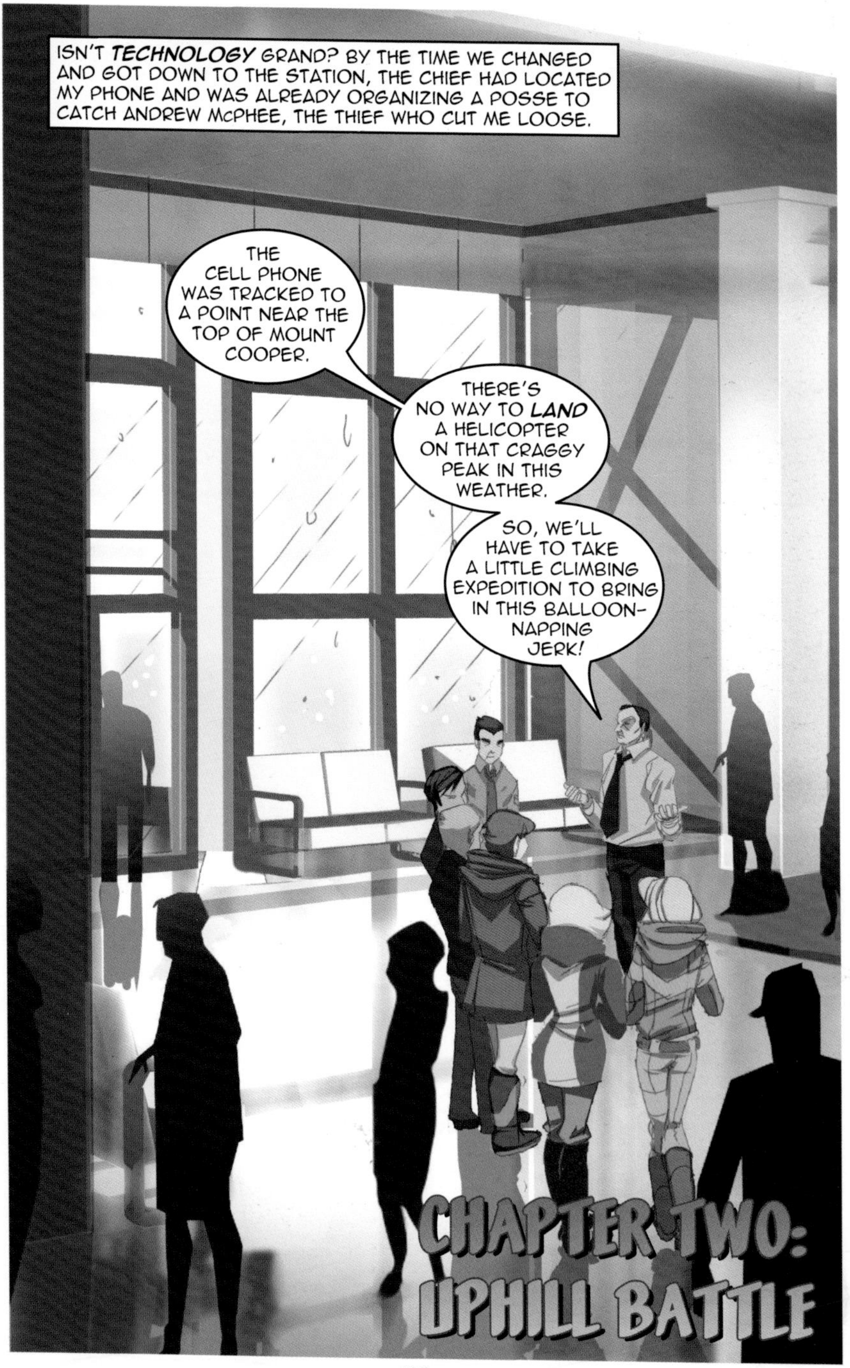
ISN'T *TECHNOLOGY* GRAND? BY THE TIME WE CHANGED AND GOT DOWN TO THE STATION, THE CHIEF HAD LOCATED MY PHONE AND WAS ALREADY ORGANIZING A POSSE TO CATCH ANDREW McPHEE, THE THIEF WHO CUT ME LOOSE.
THE CELL PHONE WAS TRACKED TO A POINT NEAR THE TOP OF MOUNT COOPER.
THERE'S NO WAY TO *LAND* A HELICOPTER ON THAT CRAGGY PEAK IN THIS WEATHER.
SO, WE'LL HAVE TO TAKE A LITTLE CLIMBING EXPEDITION TO BRING IN THIS BALLOON-NAPPING JERK!
CHAPTER TWO: UPHILL BATTLE

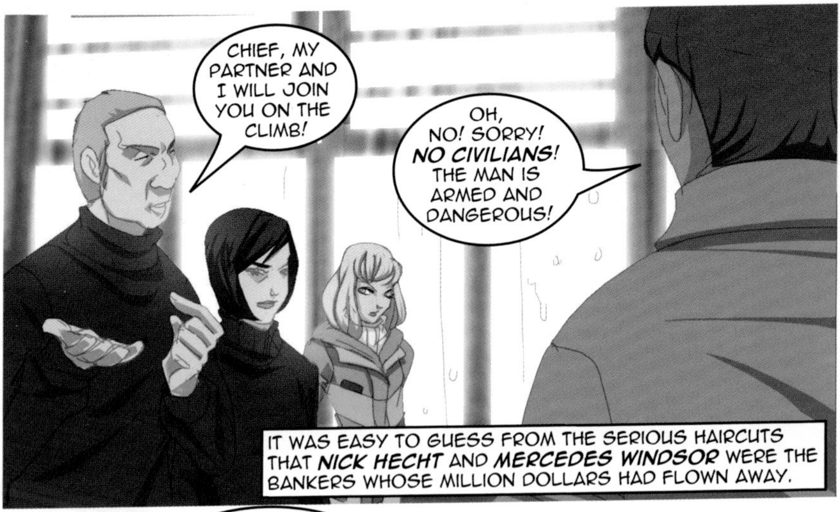

CHIEF, MY PARTNER AND I WILL JOIN YOU ON THE CLIMB!
OH, NO! SORRY! NO CIVILIANS! THE MAN IS ARMED AND DANGEROUS!
IT WAS EASY TO GUESS FROM THE SERIOUS HAIRCUTS THAT NICK HECHT AND MERCEDES WINDSOR WERE THE BANKERS WHOSE MILLION DOLLARS HAD FLOWN AWAY.

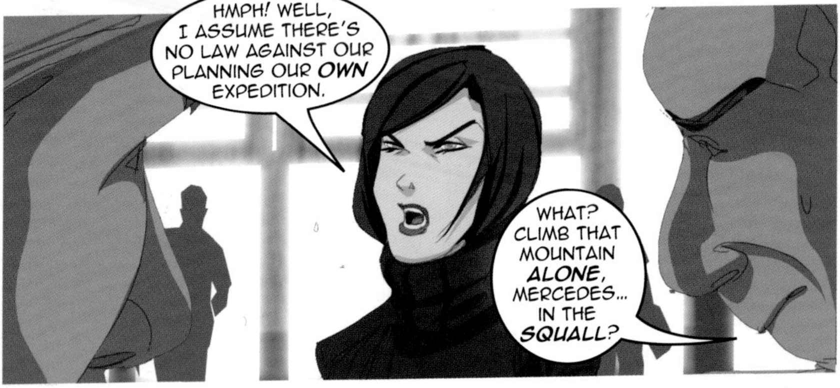

HMPH! WELL, I ASSUME THERE'S NO LAW AGAINST OUR PLANNING OUR OWN EXPEDITION.
WHAT? CLIMB THAT MOUNTAIN ALONE, MERCEDES... IN THE SQUALL?

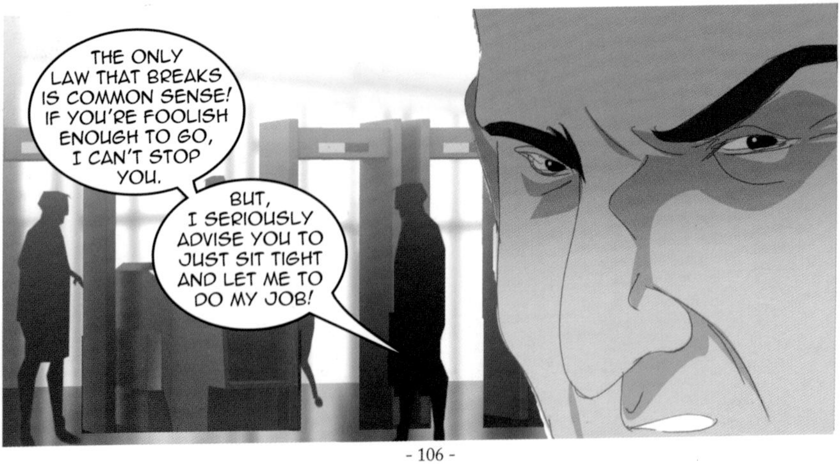

THE ONLY LAW THAT BREAKS IS COMMON SENSE! IF YOU'RE FOOLISH ENOUGH TO GO, I CAN'T STOP YOU.
BUT, I SERIOUSLY ADVISE YOU TO JUST SIT TIGHT AND LET ME TO DO MY JOB!

IT'S A **BIG** MOUNTAIN. WE'LL TRY TO STAY OUT OF YOUR WAY, CHIEF.

THAT "NO CIVILIANS" RULE DIDN'T APPLY TO **ME**, RIGHT?

ESPECIALLY YOU, NANCY! THERE'S **NO** WAY YOU'RE COMING ALONG AND THAT'S **FINAL**.

I **KNEW** HE'D SAY THAT. BUT, I TRY NEVER TO LET KNOWING THE ANSWER STOP ME FROM ASKING A QUESTION.

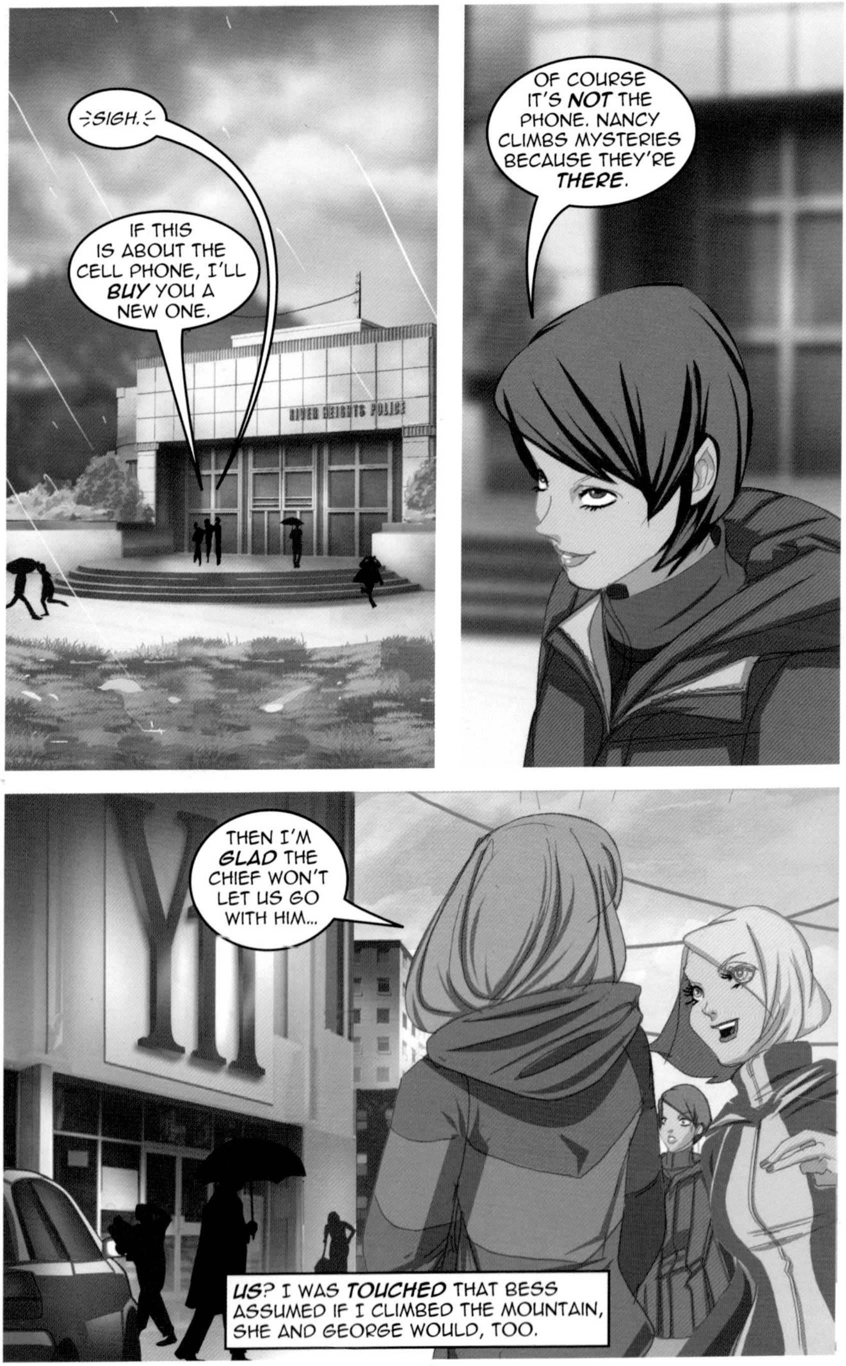

SIGH.
IF THIS IS ABOUT THE CELL PHONE, I'LL *BUY* YOU A NEW ONE.
RIVER HEIGHTS POLICE
OF COURSE IT'S *NOT* THE PHONE. NANCY CLIMBS MYSTERIES BECAUSE THEY'RE *THERE*.
THEN I'M *GLAD* THE CHIEF WON'T LET US GO WITH HIM...
US? I WAS *TOUCHED* THAT BESS ASSUMED IF I CLIMBED THE MOUNTAIN, SHE AND GEORGE WOULD, TOO.

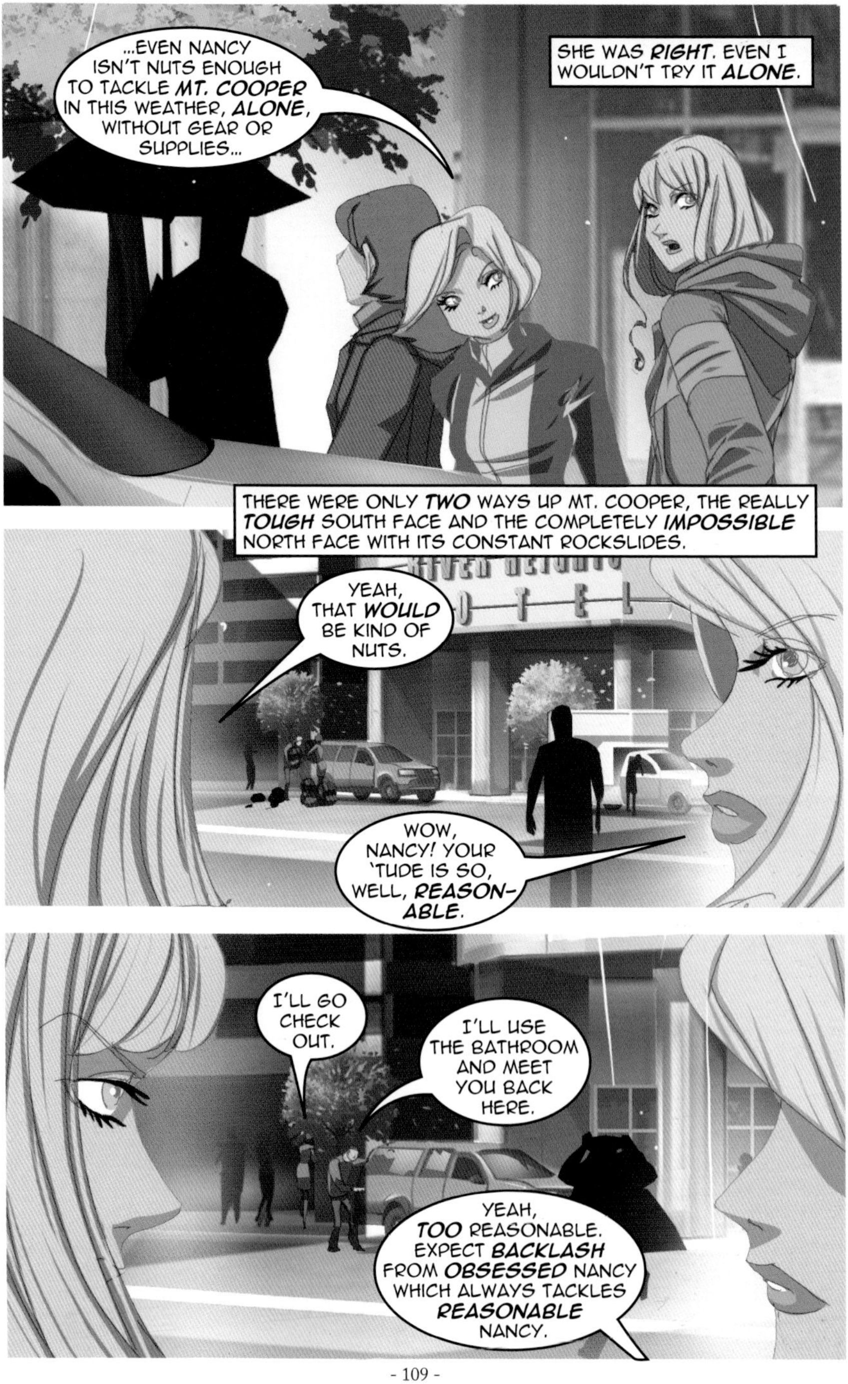
...EVEN NANCY ISN'T NUTS ENOUGH TO TACKLE MT. COOPER IN THIS WEATHER, ALONE, WITHOUT GEAR OR SUPPLIES...
SHE WAS RIGHT. EVEN I WOULDN'T TRY IT ALONE.
THERE WERE ONLY TWO WAYS UP MT. COOPER, THE REALLY TOUGH SOUTH FACE AND THE COMPLETELY IMPOSSIBLE NORTH FACE WITH ITS CONSTANT ROCKSLIDES.
YEAH, THAT WOULD BE KIND OF NUTS.
WOW, NANCY! YOUR 'TUDE IS SO, WELL, REASON-ABLE.
I'LL GO CHECK OUT.
I'LL USE THE BATHROOM AND MEET YOU BACK HERE.
YEAH, TOO REASONABLE. EXPECT BACKLASH FROM OBSESSED NANCY WHICH ALWAYS TACKLES REASONABLE NANCY.

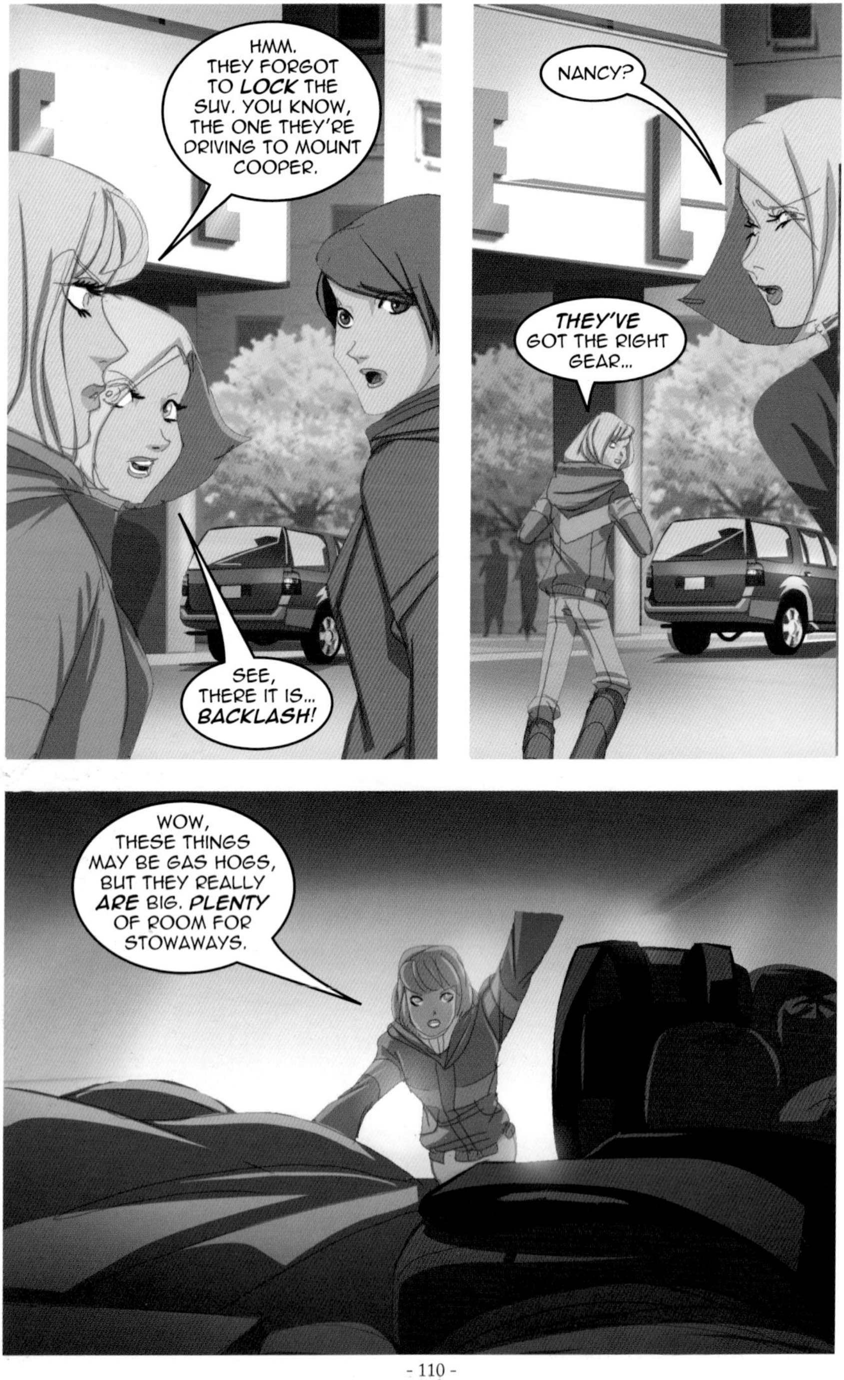
HMM. THEY FORGOT TO LOCK THE SUV. YOU KNOW, THE ONE THEY'RE DRIVING TO MOUNT COOPER.
SEE, THERE IT IS... BACKLASH!
NANCY?
THEY'VE GOT THE RIGHT GEAR...
WOW, THESE THINGS MAY BE GAS HOGS, BUT THEY REALLY ARE BIG. PLENTY OF ROOM FOR STOWAWAYS.

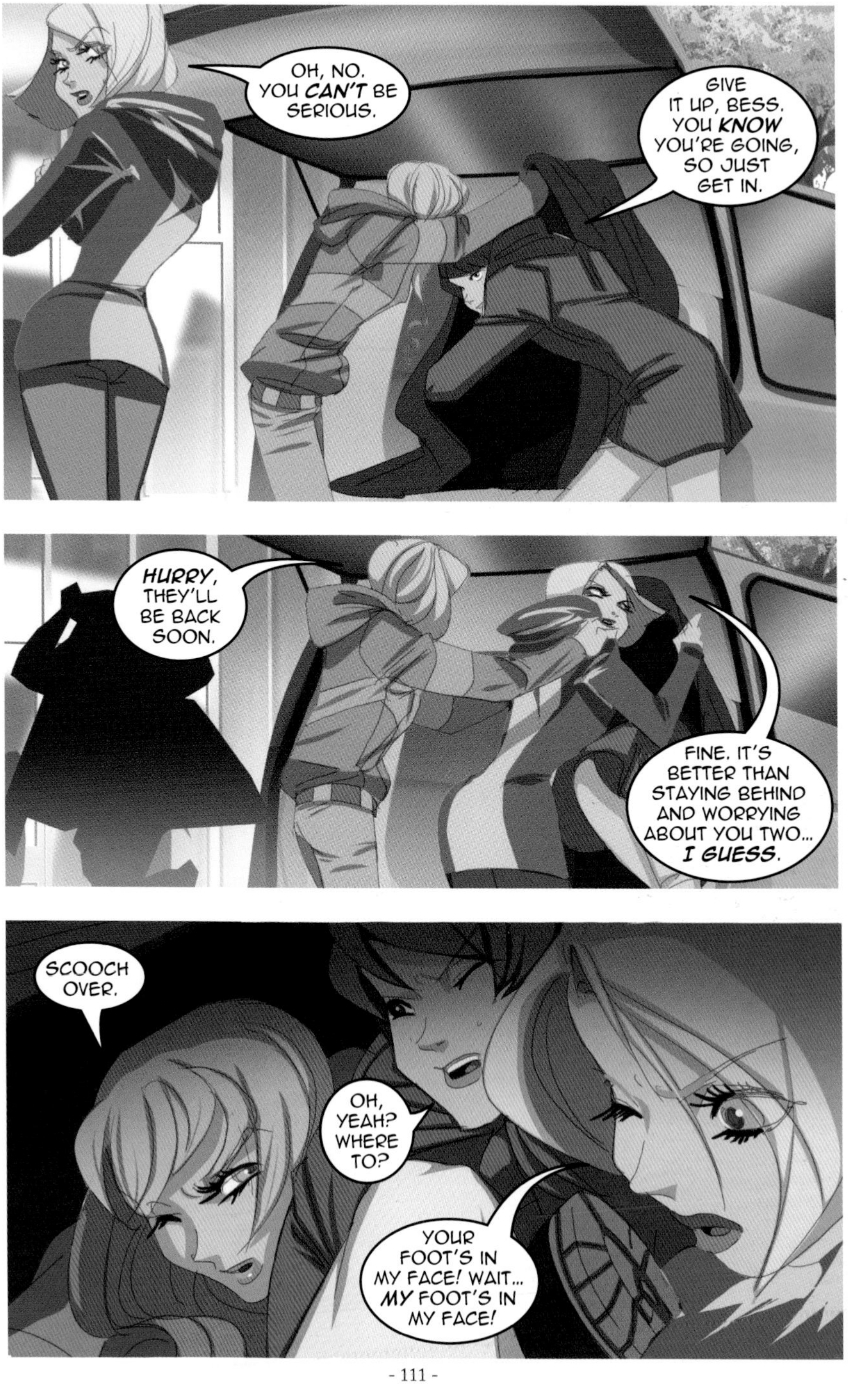
OH, NO. YOU *CAN'T* BE SERIOUS.
GIVE IT UP, BESS. YOU *KNOW* YOU'RE GOING, SO JUST GET IN.
HURRY, THEY'LL BE BACK SOON.
FINE. IT'S BETTER THAN STAYING BEHIND AND WORRYING ABOUT YOU TWO... *I GUESS*.
SCOOCH OVER.
OH, YEAH? WHERE TO?
YOUR FOOT'S IN MY FACE! WAIT... *MY* FOOT'S IN MY FACE!

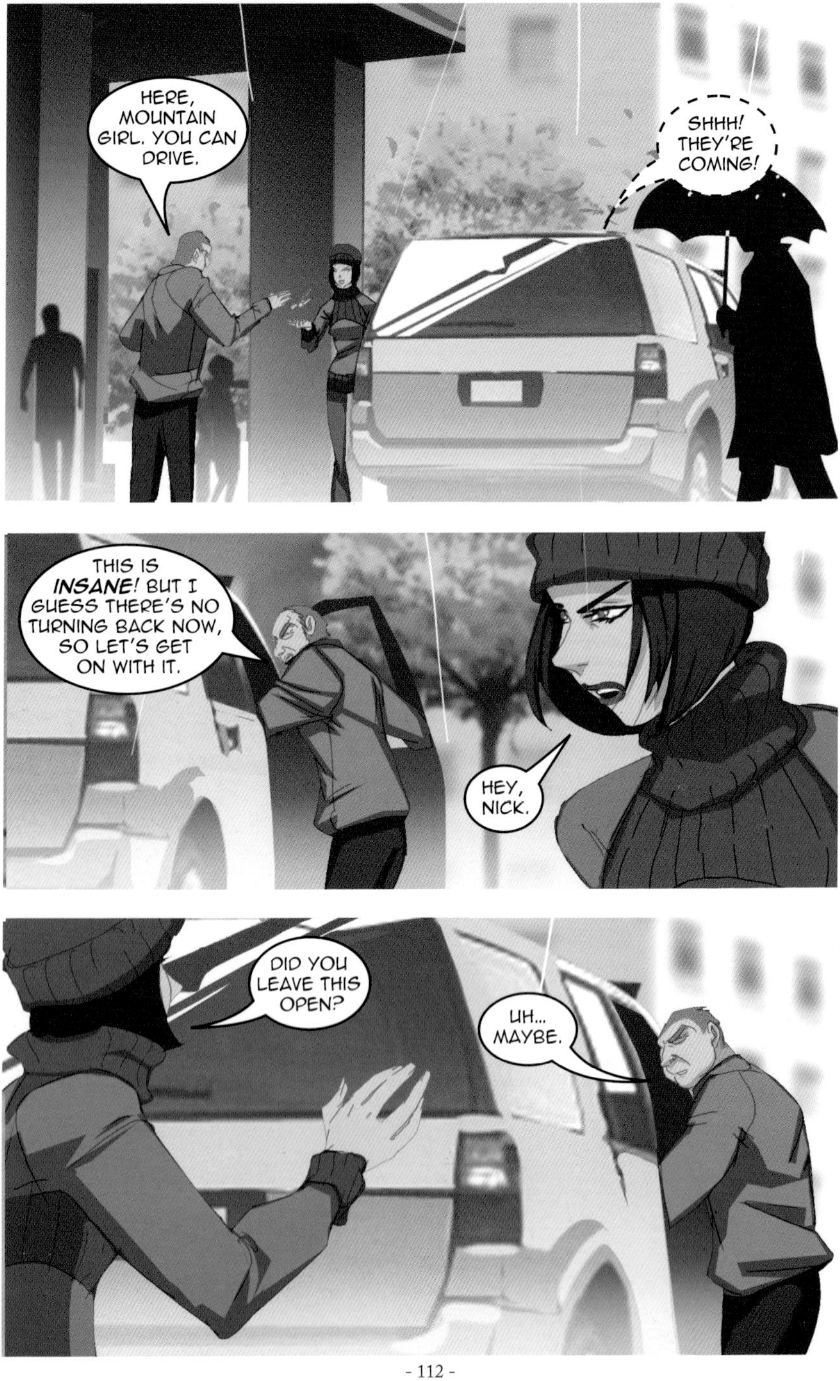
HERE, MOUNTAIN GIRL. YOU CAN DRIVE.
SHHH! THEY'RE COMING!
THIS IS *INSANE*! BUT I GUESS THERE'S NO TURNING BACK NOW, SO LET'S GET ON WITH IT.
HEY, NICK.
DID YOU LEAVE THIS OPEN?
UH... MAYBE.

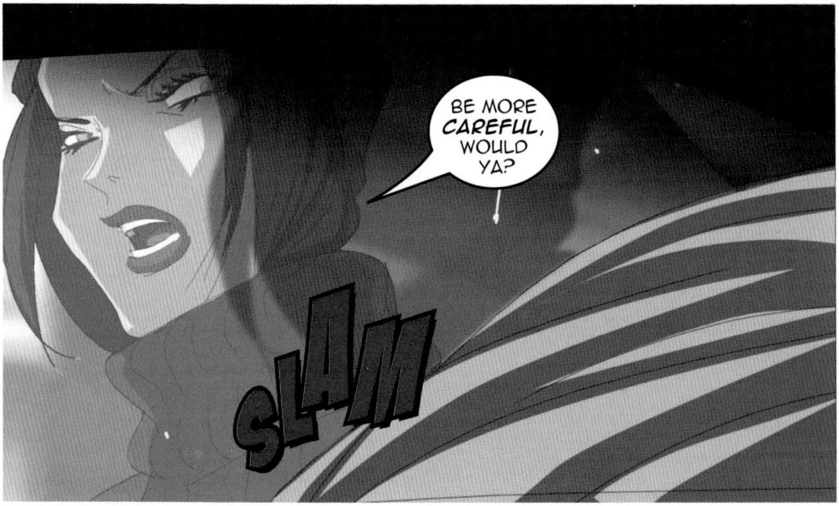
BE MORE CAREFUL, WOULD YA?
SLAM

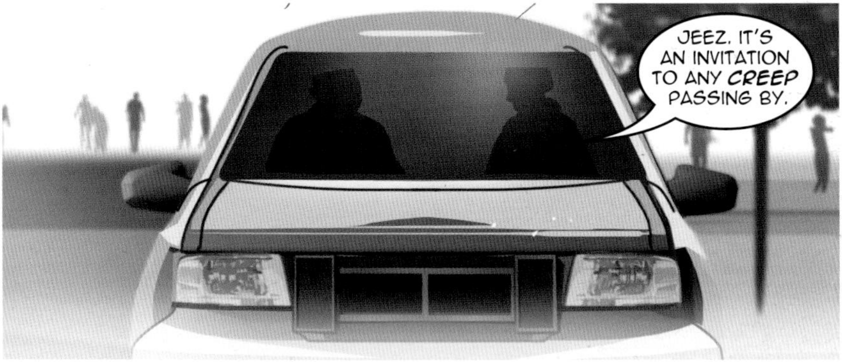
JEEZ. IT'S AN INVITATION TO ANY CREEP PASSING BY.

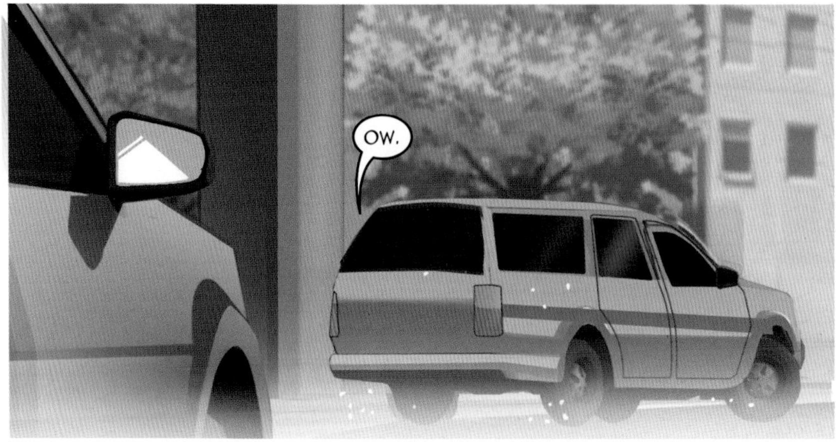
OW.

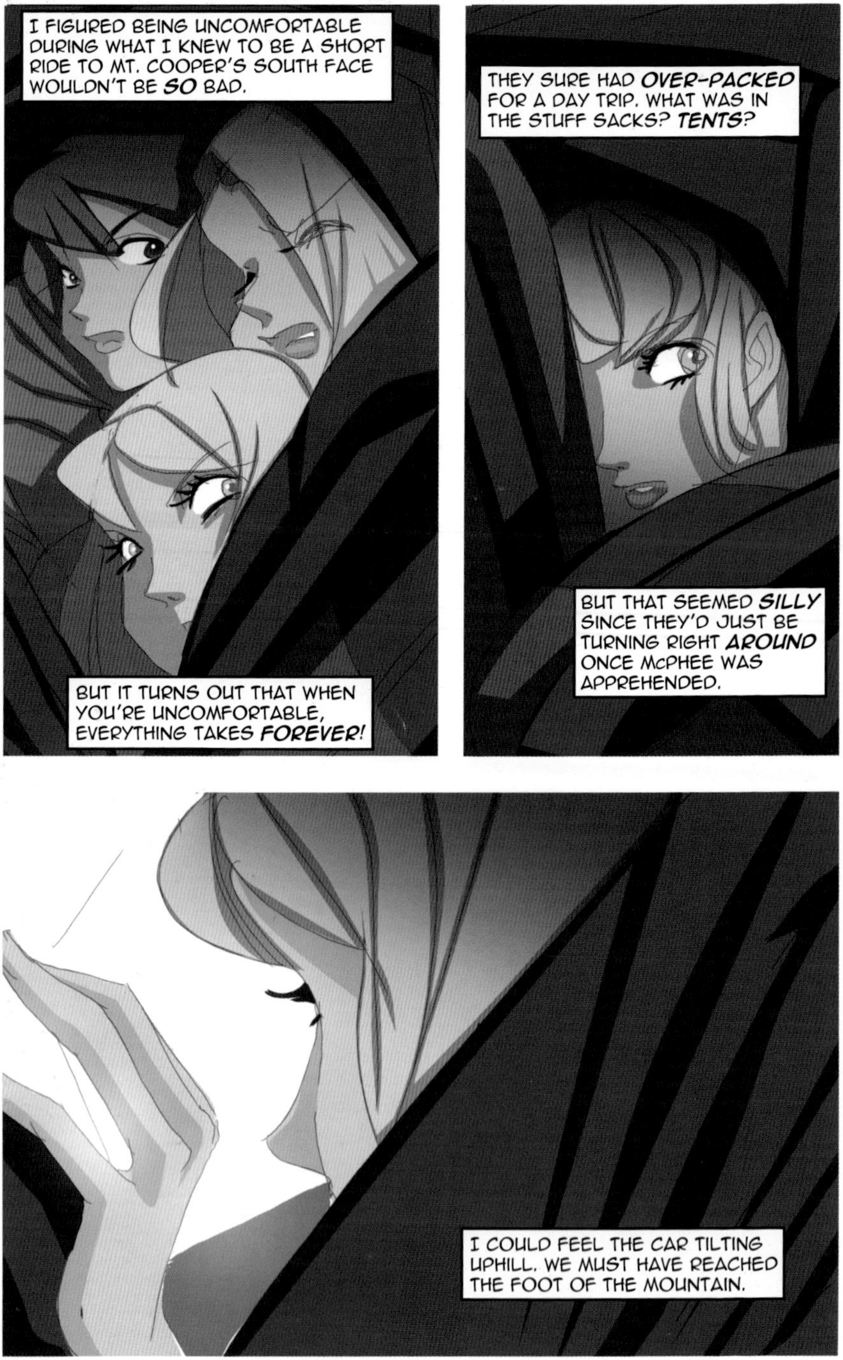
I FIGURED BEING UNCOMFORTABLE DURING WHAT I KNEW TO BE A SHORT RIDE TO MT. COOPER'S SOUTH FACE WOULDN'T BE *SO* BAD.
BUT IT TURNS OUT THAT WHEN YOU'RE UNCOMFORTABLE, EVERYTHING TAKES *FOREVER*!
THEY SURE HAD *OVER-PACKED* FOR A DAY TRIP. WHAT WAS IN THE STUFF SACKS? *TENTS*?
BUT THAT SEEMED *SILLY* SINCE THEY'D JUST BE TURNING RIGHT *AROUND* ONCE McPHEE WAS APPREHENDED.
I COULD FEEL THE CAR TILTING UPHILL. WE MUST HAVE REACHED THE FOOT OF THE MOUNTAIN.

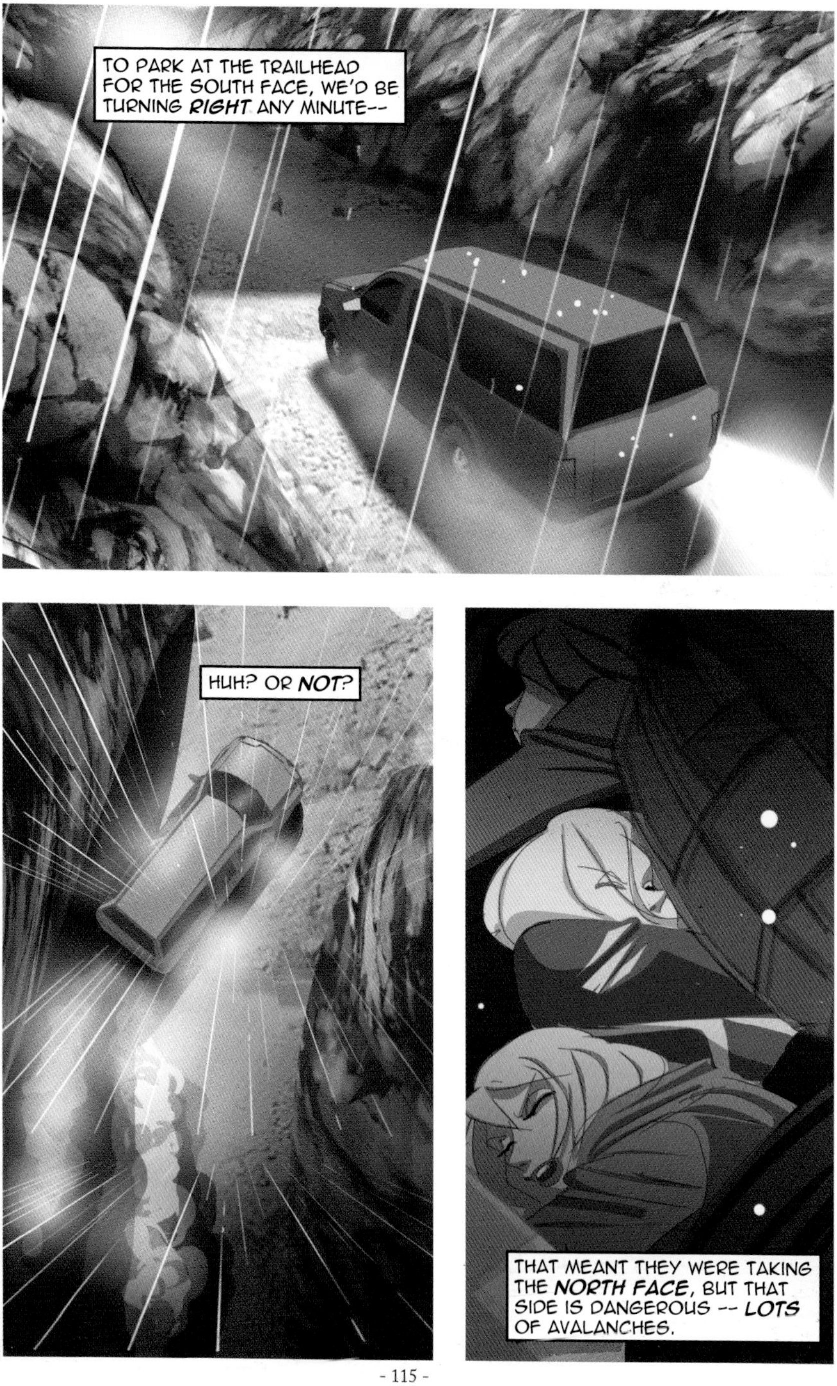

TO PARK AT THE TRAILHEAD FOR THE SOUTH FACE, WE'D BE TURNING RIGHT ANY MINUTE--
HUH? OR NOT?
THAT MEANT THEY WERE TAKING THE NORTH FACE, BUT THAT SIDE IS DANGEROUS -- LOTS OF AVALANCHES.

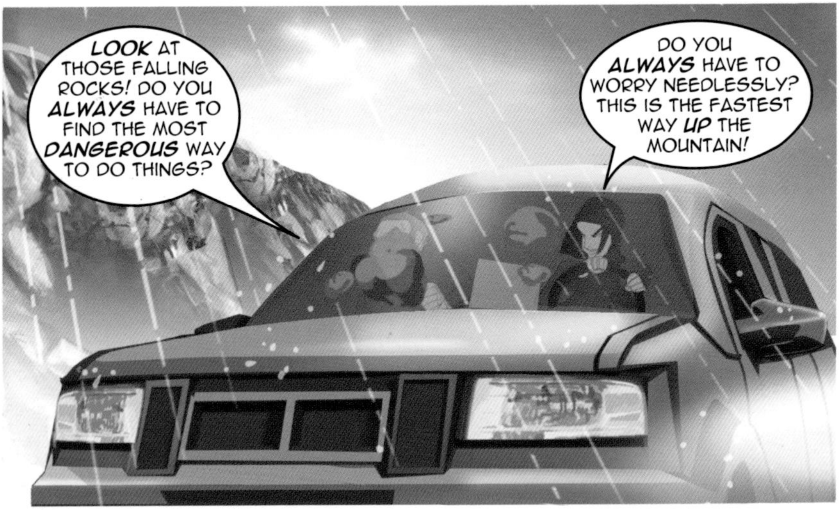
LOOK AT THOSE FALLING ROCKS! DO YOU ALWAYS HAVE TO FIND THE MOST DANGEROUS WAY TO DO THINGS?
DO YOU ALWAYS HAVE TO WORRY NEEDLESSLY? THIS IS THE FASTEST WAY UP THE MOUNTAIN!

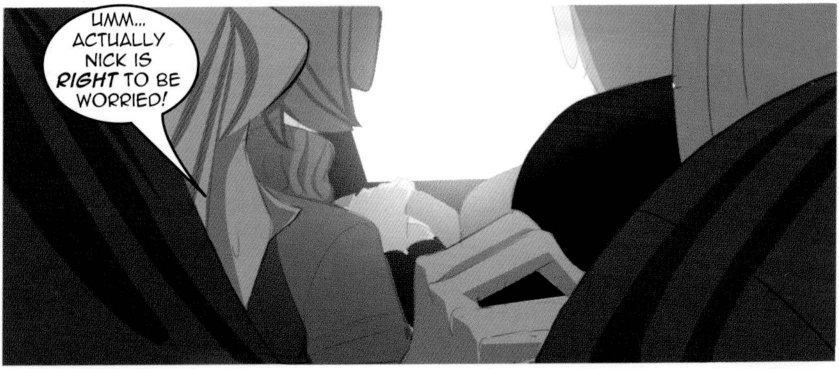
UMM... ACTUALLY NICK IS RIGHT TO BE WORRIED!

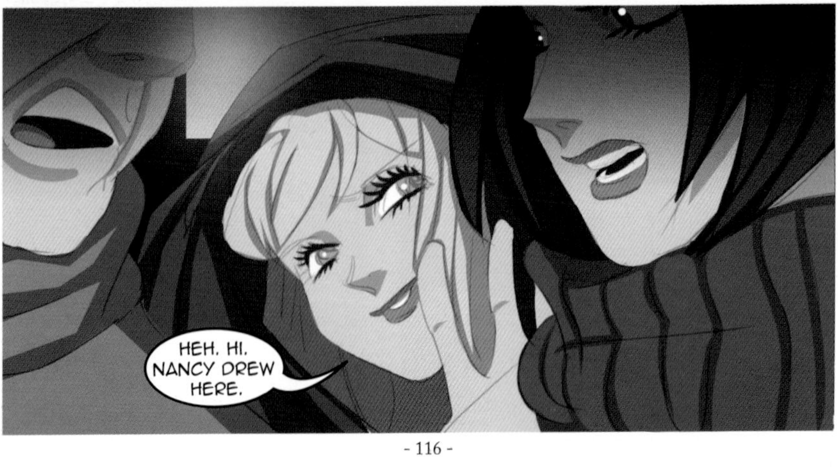
HEH. HI. NANCY DREW HERE.

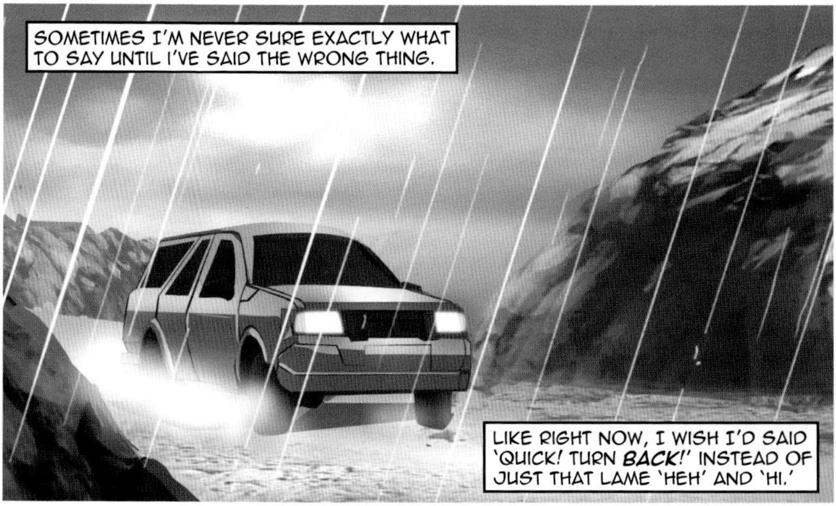
SOMETIMES I'M NEVER SURE EXACTLY WHAT TO SAY UNTIL I'VE SAID THE WRONG THING.
LIKE RIGHT NOW, I WISH I'D SAID 'QUICK! TURN *BACK*!' INSTEAD OF JUST THAT LAME 'HEH' AND 'HI.'

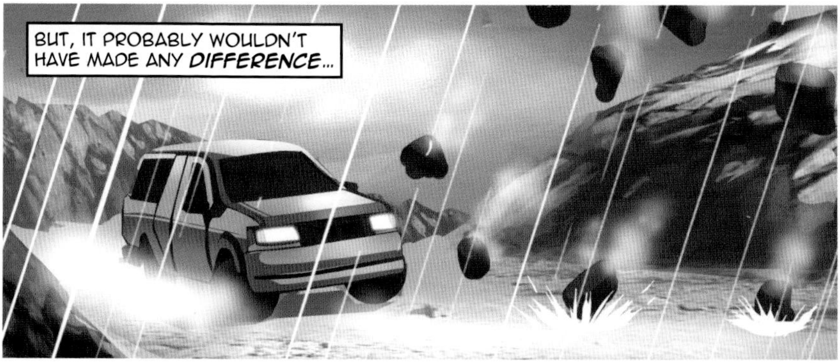
BUT, IT PROBABLY WOULDN'T HAVE MADE ANY *DIFFERENCE*...

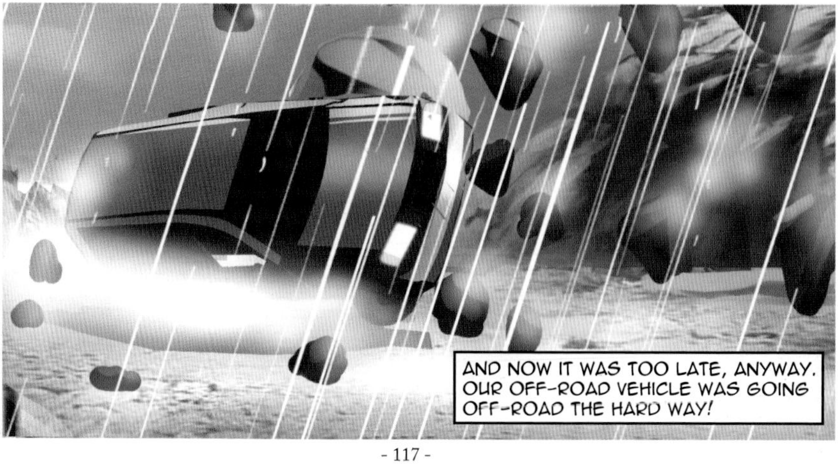
AND NOW IT WAS TOO LATE, ANYWAY. OUR OFF-ROAD VEHICLE WAS GOING OFF-ROAD THE HARD WAY!

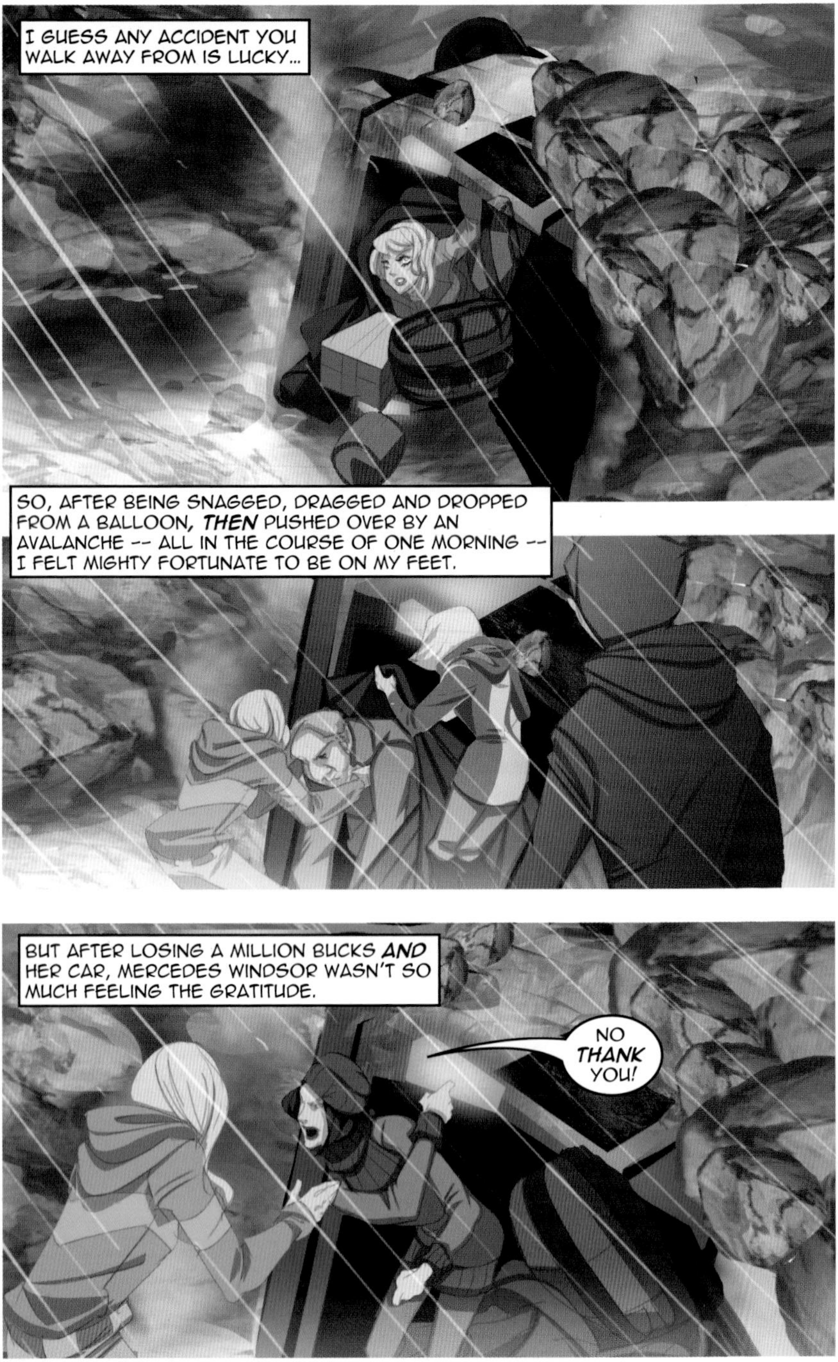
I GUESS ANY ACCIDENT YOU WALK AWAY FROM IS LUCKY...
SO, AFTER BEING SNAGGED, DRAGGED AND DROPPED FROM A BALLOON, ***THEN*** PUSHED OVER BY AN AVALANCHE -- ALL IN THE COURSE OF ONE MORNING -- I FELT MIGHTY FORTUNATE TO BE ON MY FEET.
BUT AFTER LOSING A MILLION BUCKS ***AND*** HER CAR, MERCEDES WINDSOR WASN'T SO MUCH FEELING THE GRATITUDE.
NO ***THANK*** YOU!

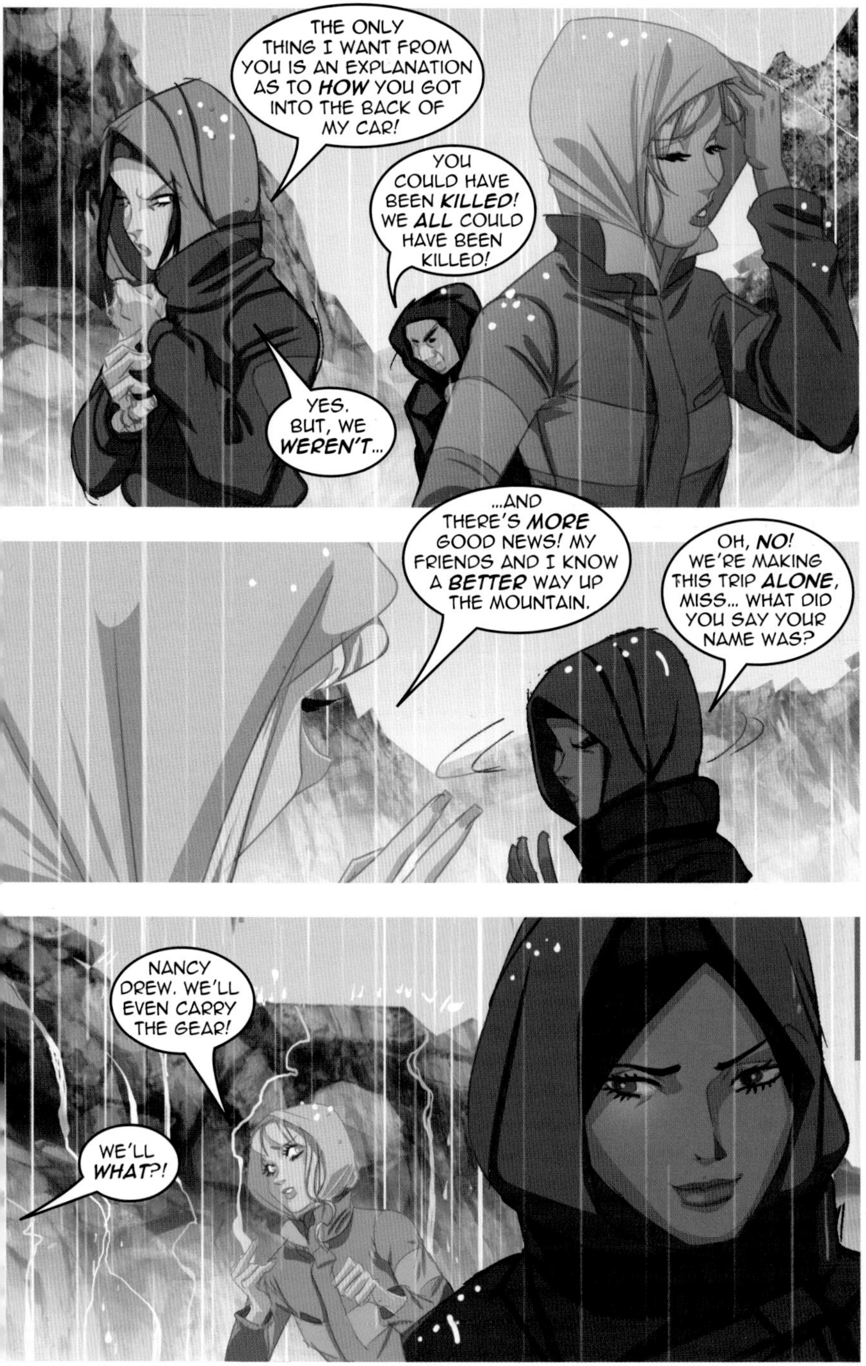
THE ONLY THING I WANT FROM YOU IS AN EXPLANATION AS TO *HOW* YOU GOT INTO THE BACK OF MY CAR!
YOU COULD HAVE BEEN *KILLED*! WE *ALL* COULD HAVE BEEN KILLED!
YES. BUT, WE *WEREN'T*...
...AND THERE'S *MORE* GOOD NEWS! MY FRIENDS AND I KNOW A *BETTER* WAY UP THE MOUNTAIN.
OH, *NO*! WE'RE MAKING THIS TRIP *ALONE*, MISS... WHAT DID YOU SAY YOUR NAME WAS?
NANCY DREW. WE'LL EVEN CARRY THE GEAR!
WE'LL *WHAT*?!

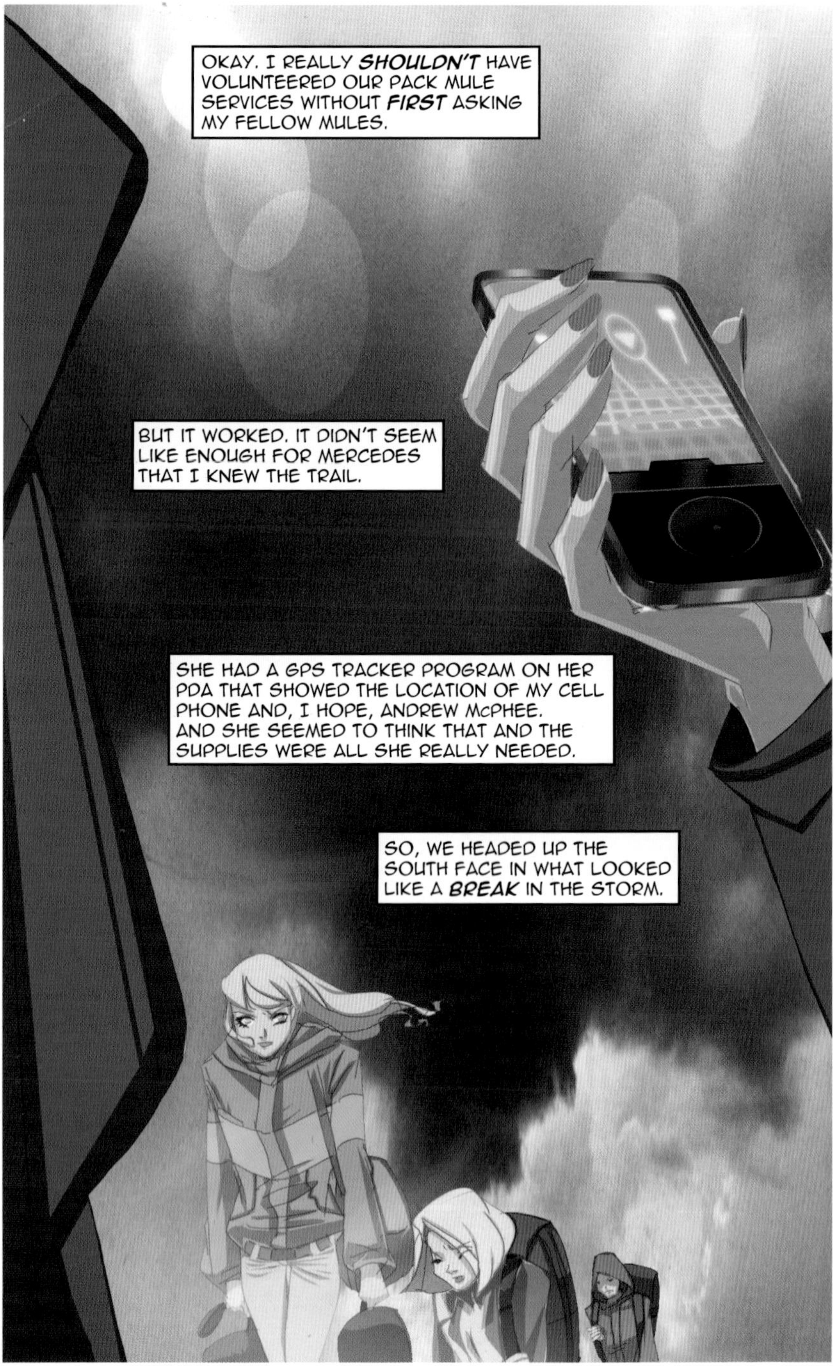
OKAY. I REALLY **SHOULDN'T** HAVE VOLUNTEERED OUR PACK MULE SERVICES WITHOUT **FIRST** ASKING MY FELLOW MULES.
BUT IT WORKED. IT DIDN'T SEEM LIKE ENOUGH FOR MERCEDES THAT I KNEW THE TRAIL.
SHE HAD A GPS TRACKER PROGRAM ON HER PDA THAT SHOWED THE LOCATION OF MY CELL PHONE AND, I HOPE, ANDREW McPHEE. AND SHE SEEMED TO THINK THAT AND THE SUPPLIES WERE ALL SHE REALLY NEEDED.
SO, WE HEADED UP THE SOUTH FACE IN WHAT LOOKED LIKE A **BREAK** IN THE STORM.

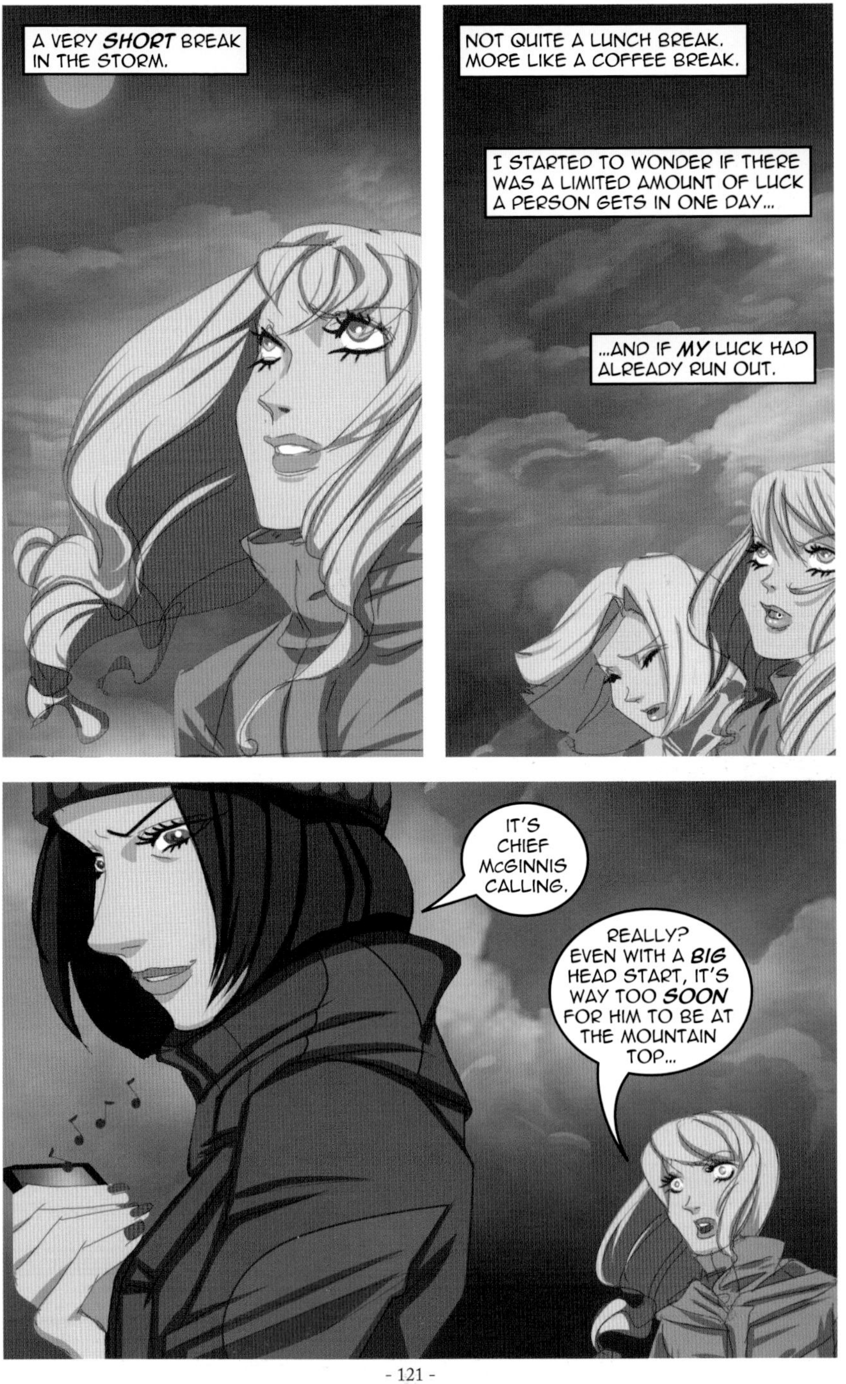
A VERY SHORT BREAK IN THE STORM.
NOT QUITE A LUNCH BREAK. MORE LIKE A COFFEE BREAK.
I STARTED TO WONDER IF THERE WAS A LIMITED AMOUNT OF LUCK A PERSON GETS IN ONE DAY...
...AND IF MY LUCK HAD ALREADY RUN OUT.
IT'S CHIEF McGINNIS CALLING.
REALLY? EVEN WITH A BIG HEAD START, IT'S WAY TOO SOON FOR HIM TO BE AT THE MOUNTAIN TOP...

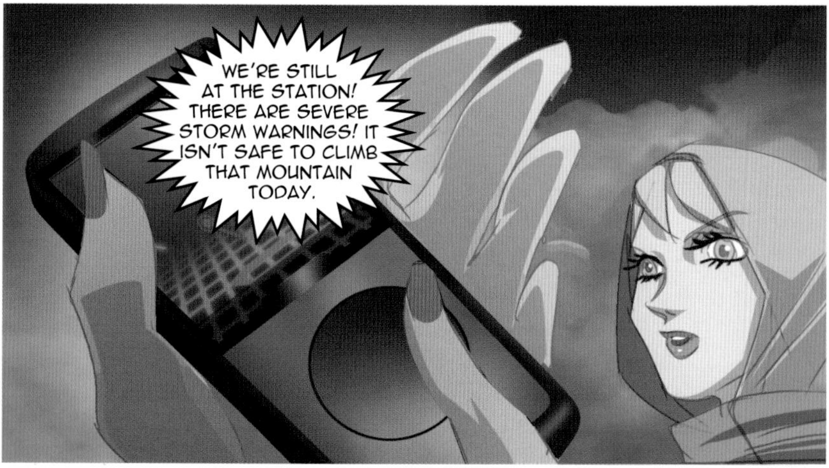
WE'RE STILL AT THE STATION! THERE ARE SEVERE STORM WARNINGS! IT ISN'T SAFE TO CLIMB THAT MOUNTAIN TODAY.

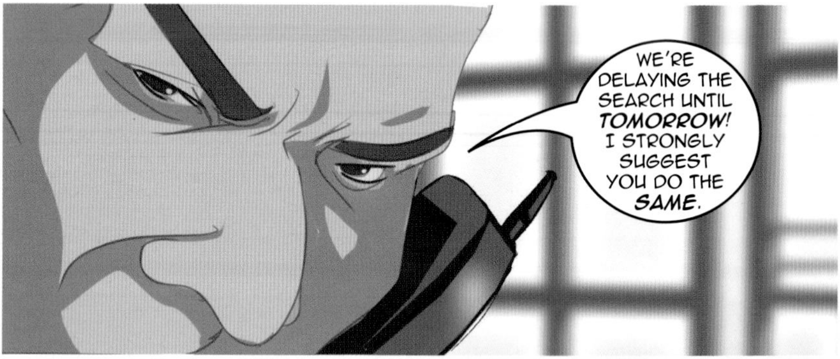
WE'RE DELAYING THE SEARCH UNTIL ***TOMORROW***! I STRONGLY SUGGEST YOU DO THE ***SAME***.

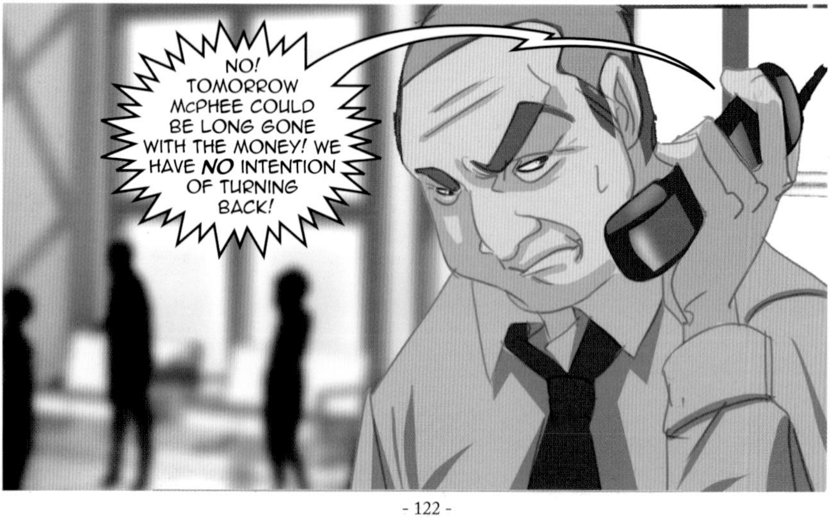
NO! TOMORROW McPHEE COULD BE LONG GONE WITH THE MONEY! WE HAVE ***NO*** INTENTION OF TURNING BACK!

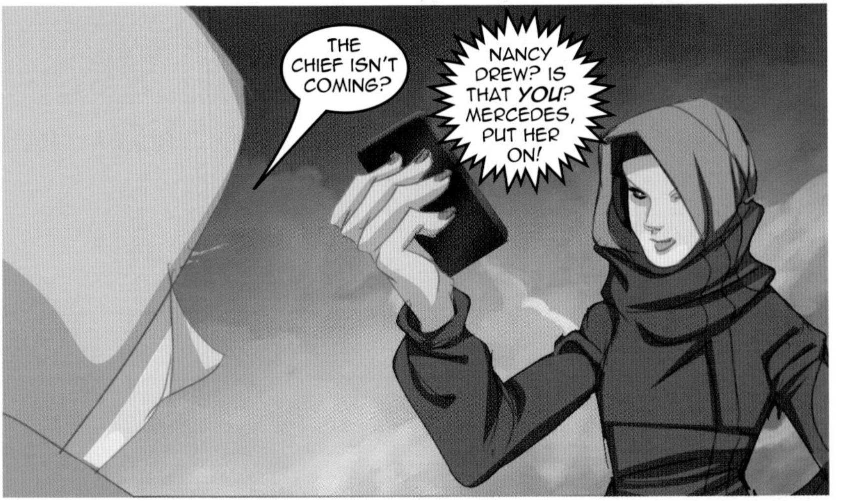
THE CHIEF ISN'T COMING?
NANCY DREW? IS THAT YOU? MERCEDES, PUT HER ON!

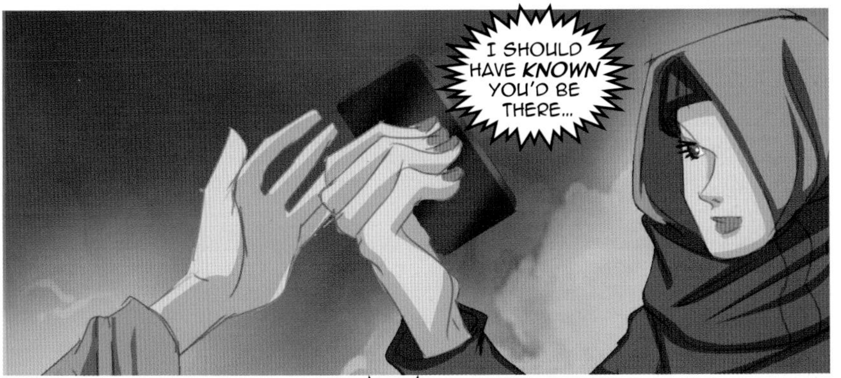
I SHOULD HAVE KNOWN YOU'D BE THERE...

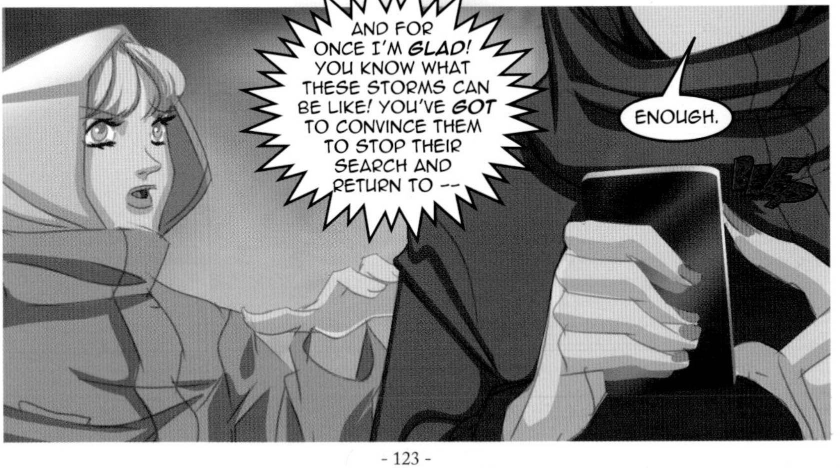
AND FOR ONCE I'M GLAD! YOU KNOW WHAT THESE STORMS CAN BE LIKE! YOU'VE GOT TO CONVINCE THEM TO STOP THEIR SEARCH AND RETURN TO --
ENOUGH.

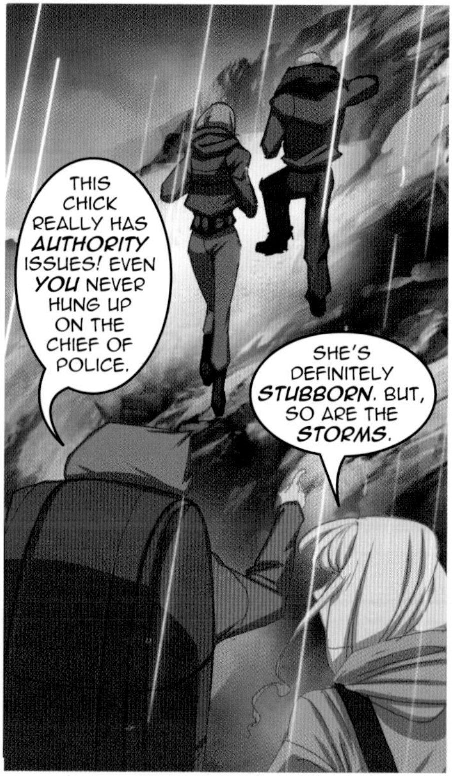
THIS CHICK REALLY HAS AUTHORITY ISSUES! EVEN YOU NEVER HUNG UP ON THE CHIEF OF POLICE.
SHE'S DEFINITELY STUBBORN. BUT, SO ARE THE STORMS.

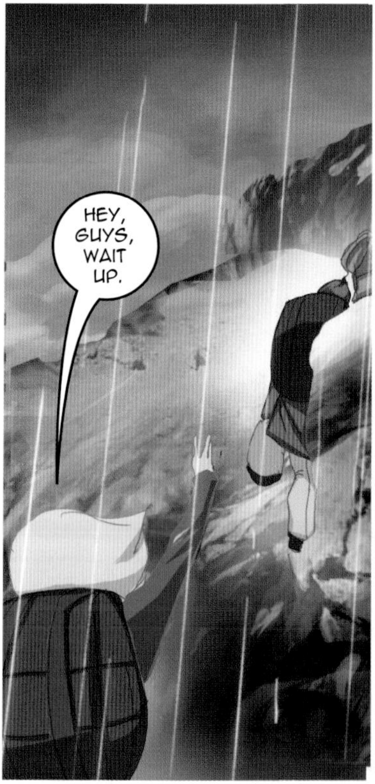
HEY, GUYS, WAIT UP.

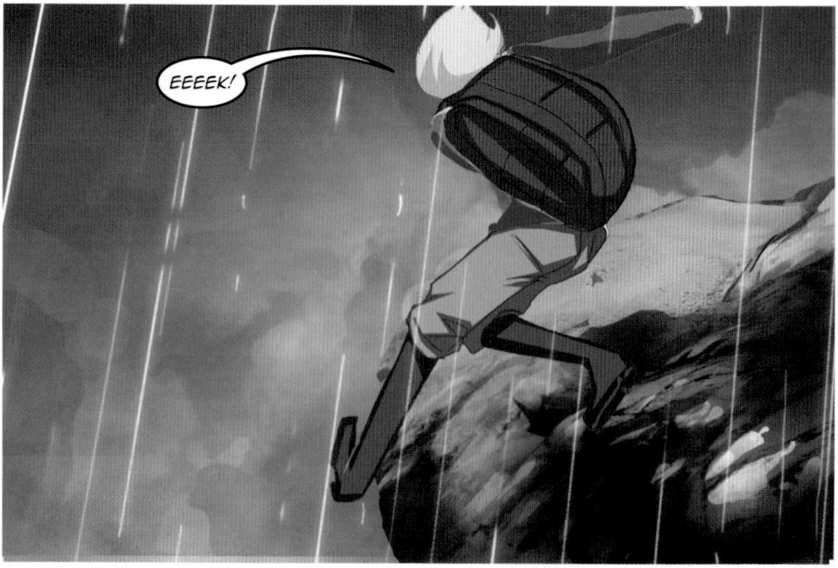
EEEEK!

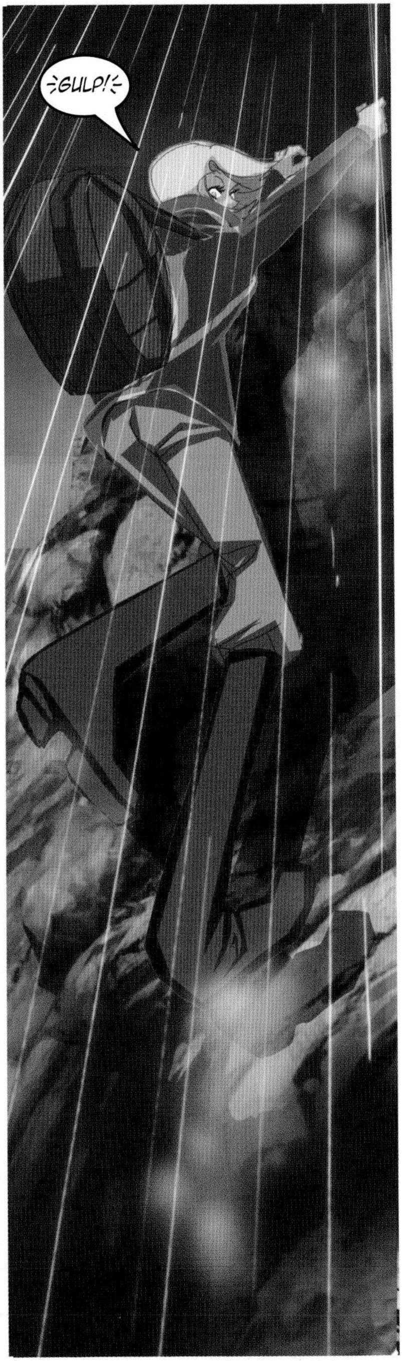
GULP!

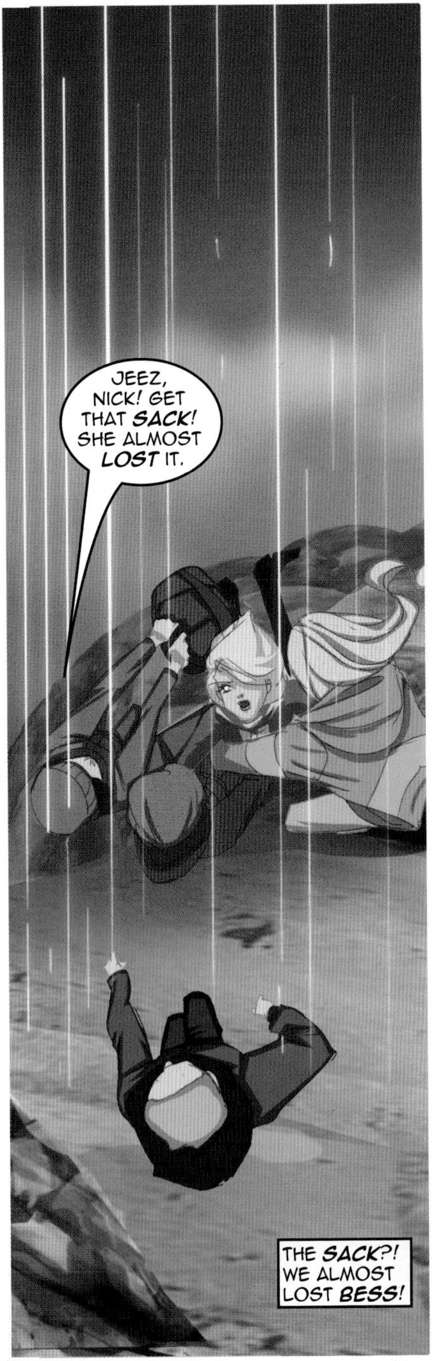
JEEZ, NICK! GET THAT SACK! SHE ALMOST LOST IT.
THE SACK?! WE ALMOST LOST BESS!

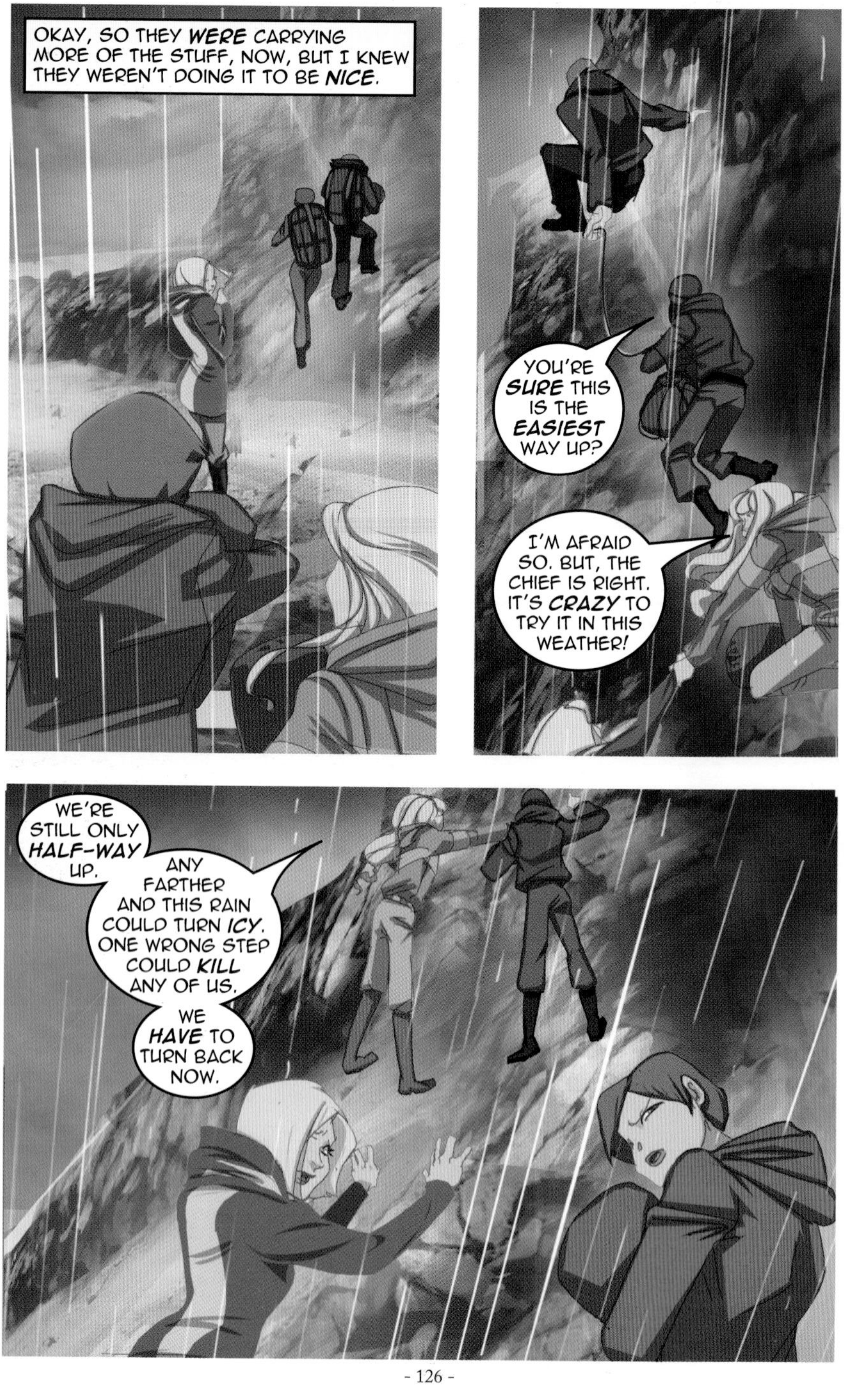
OKAY, SO THEY *WERE* CARRYING MORE OF THE STUFF, NOW, BUT I KNEW THEY WEREN'T DOING IT TO BE *NICE*.
YOU'RE *SURE* THIS IS THE *EASIEST* WAY UP?
I'M AFRAID SO. BUT, THE CHIEF IS RIGHT. IT'S *CRAZY* TO TRY IT IN THIS WEATHER!
WE'RE STILL ONLY *HALF-WAY* UP.
ANY FARTHER AND THIS RAIN COULD TURN *ICY*. ONE WRONG STEP COULD *KILL* ANY OF US.
WE *HAVE* TO TURN BACK NOW.

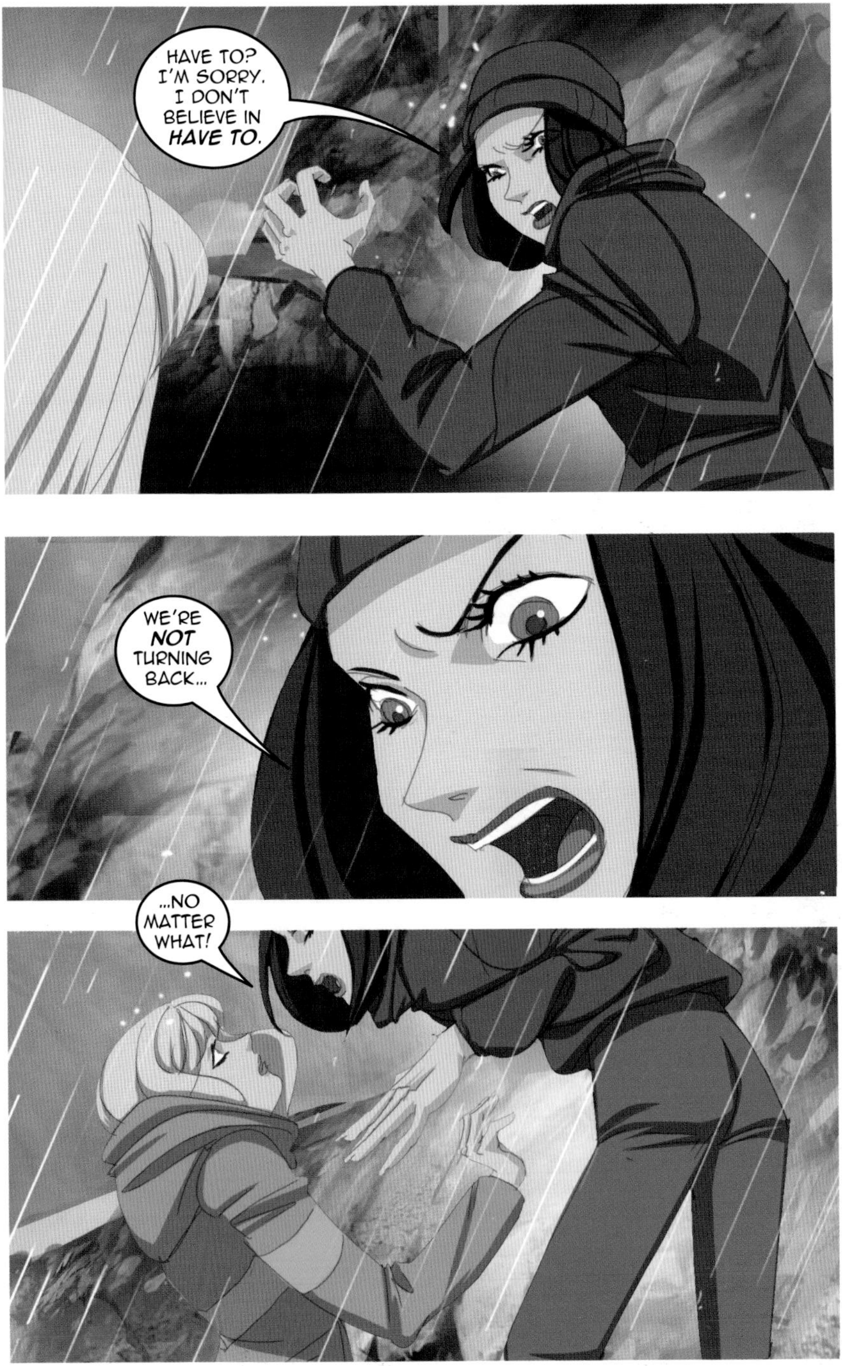
HAVE TO? I'M SORRY. I DON'T BELIEVE IN HAVE TO.
WE'RE NOT TURNING BACK...
...NO MATTER WHAT!

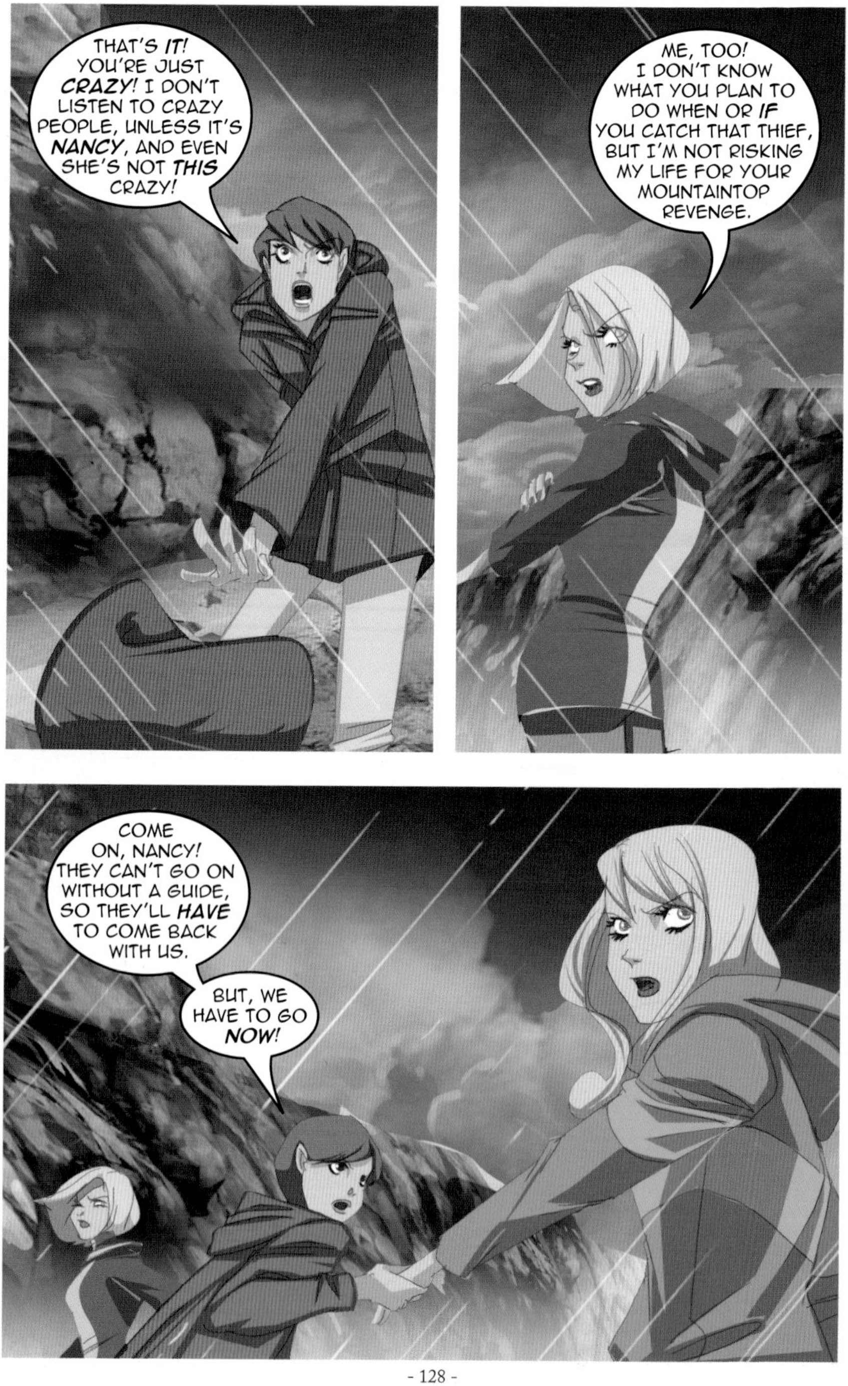
THAT'S *IT*! YOU'RE JUST *CRAZY*! I DON'T LISTEN TO CRAZY PEOPLE, UNLESS IT'S *NANCY*, AND EVEN SHE'S NOT *THIS* CRAZY!
ME, TOO! I DON'T KNOW WHAT YOU PLAN TO DO WHEN OR *IF* YOU CATCH THAT THIEF, BUT I'M NOT RISKING MY LIFE FOR YOUR MOUNTAINTOP REVENGE.
COME ON, NANCY! THEY CAN'T GO ON WITHOUT A GUIDE, SO THEY'LL *HAVE* TO COME BACK WITH US.
BUT, WE HAVE TO GO *NOW*!

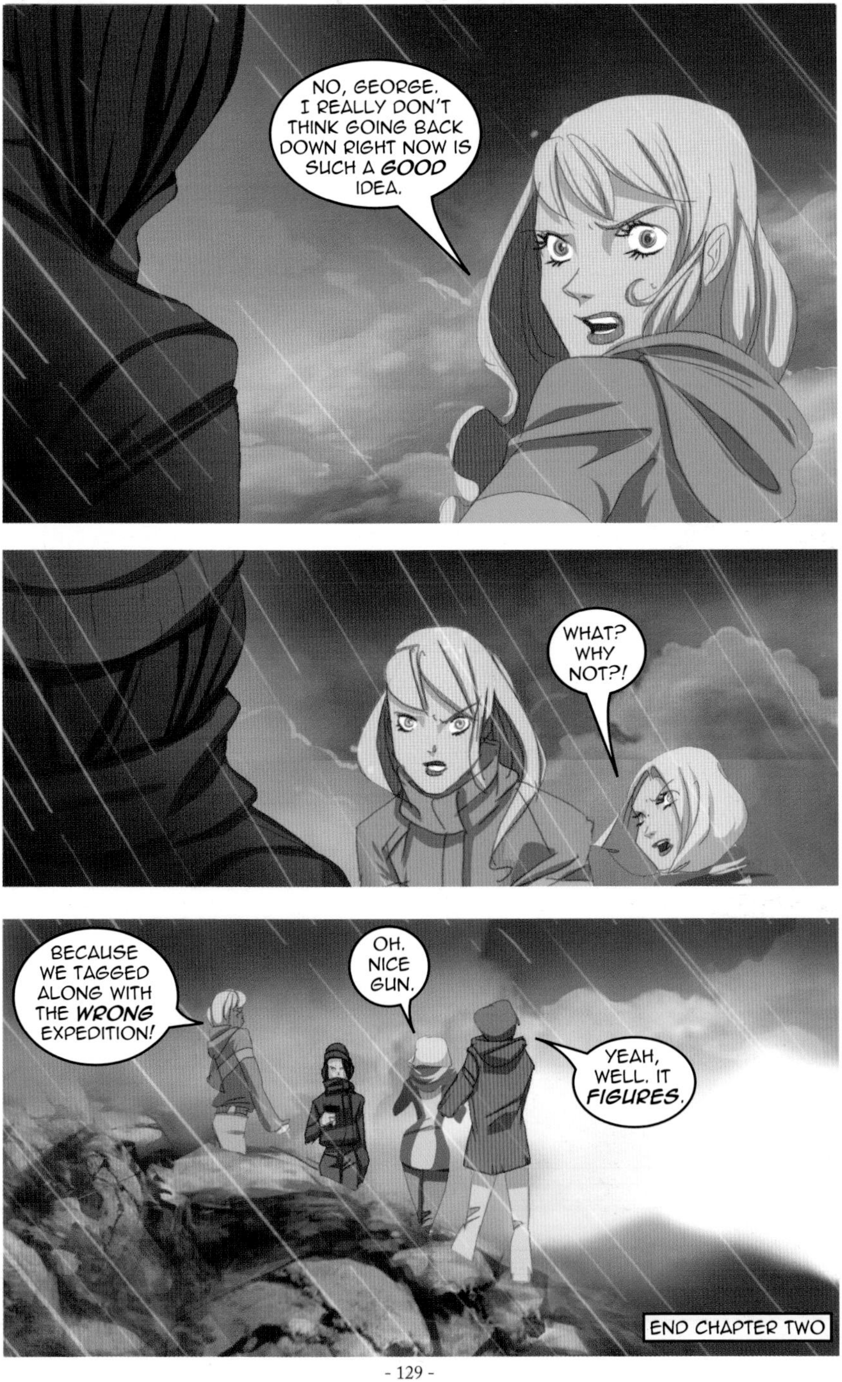
NO, GEORGE. I REALLY DON'T THINK GOING BACK DOWN RIGHT NOW IS SUCH A **GOOD** IDEA.
WHAT? WHY NOT?!
BECAUSE WE TAGGED ALONG WITH THE **WRONG** EXPEDITION!
OH. NICE GUN.
YEAH, WELL. IT **FIGURES**.
END CHAPTER TWO

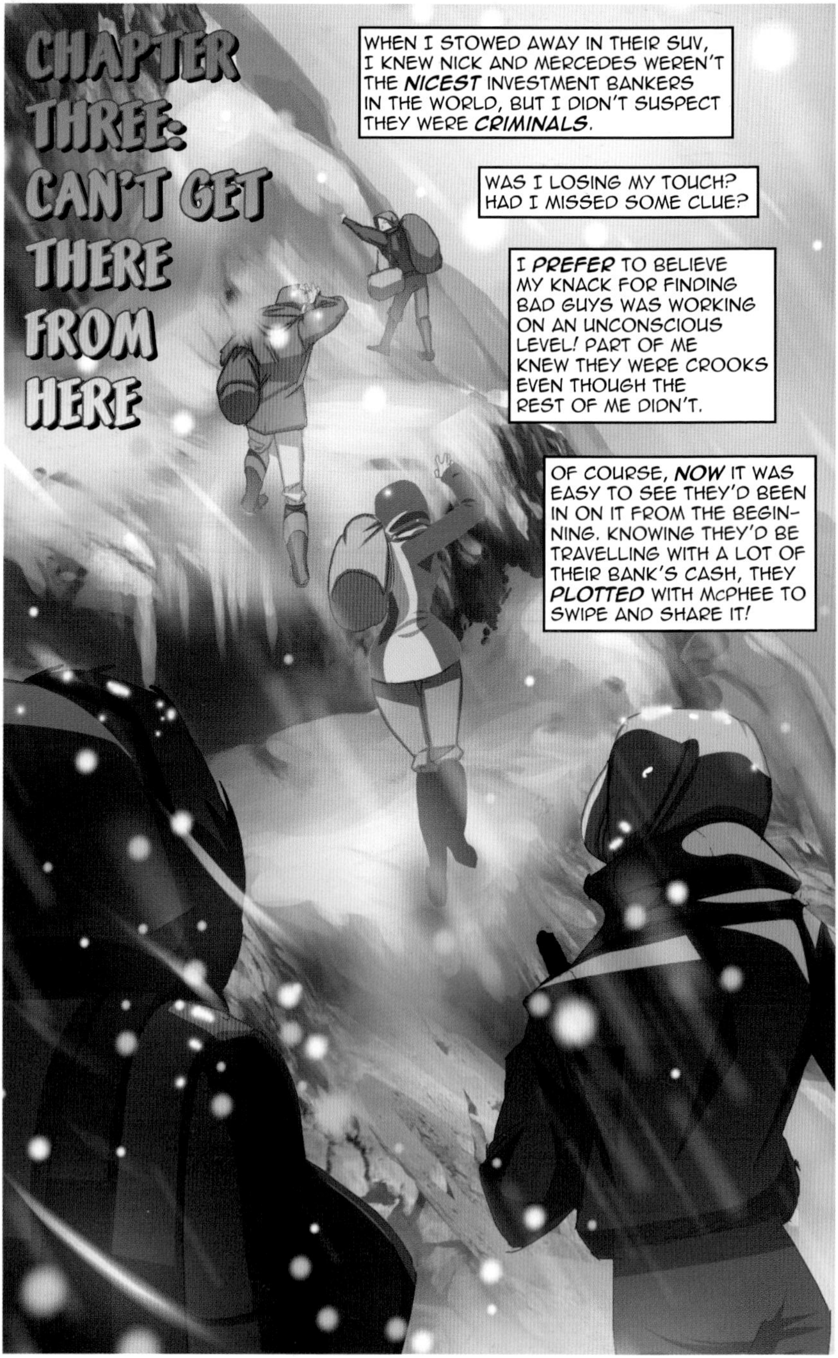
CHAPTER THREE: CAN'T GET THERE FROM HERE
WHEN I STOWED AWAY IN THEIR SUV, I KNEW NICK AND MERCEDES WEREN'T THE *NICEST* INVESTMENT BANKERS IN THE WORLD, BUT I DIDN'T SUSPECT THEY WERE *CRIMINALS*.
WAS I LOSING MY TOUCH? HAD I MISSED SOME CLUE?
I *PREFER* TO BELIEVE MY KNACK FOR FINDING BAD GUYS WAS WORKING ON AN UNCONSCIOUS LEVEL! PART OF ME KNEW THEY WERE CROOKS EVEN THOUGH THE REST OF ME DIDN'T.
OF COURSE, *NOW* IT WAS EASY TO SEE THEY'D BEEN IN ON IT FROM THE BEGINNING. KNOWING THEY'D BE TRAVELLING WITH A LOT OF THEIR BANK'S CASH, THEY *PLOTTED* WITH McPHEE TO SWIPE AND SHARE IT!

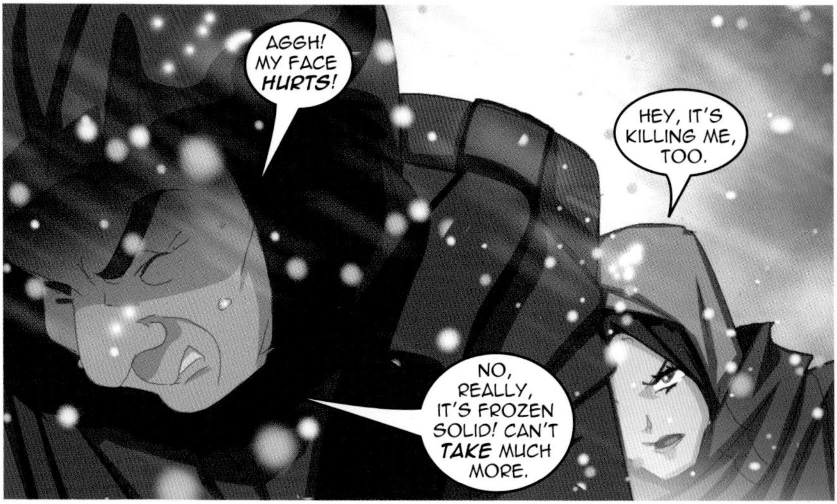
AGGH! MY FACE HURTS!
HEY, IT'S KILLING ME, TOO.
NO, REALLY, IT'S FROZEN SOLID! CAN'T TAKE MUCH MORE.

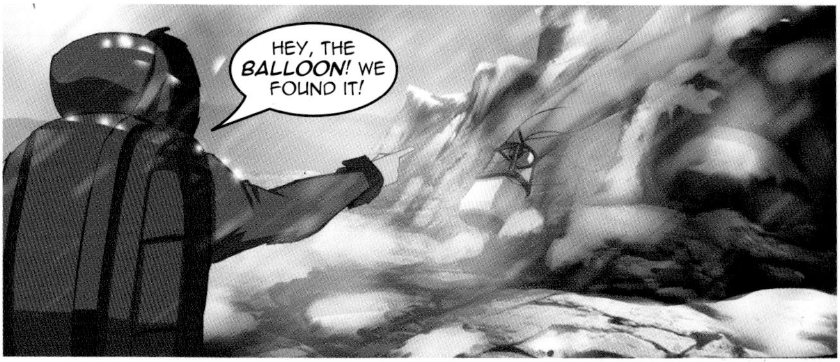
HEY, THE BALLOON! WE FOUND IT!

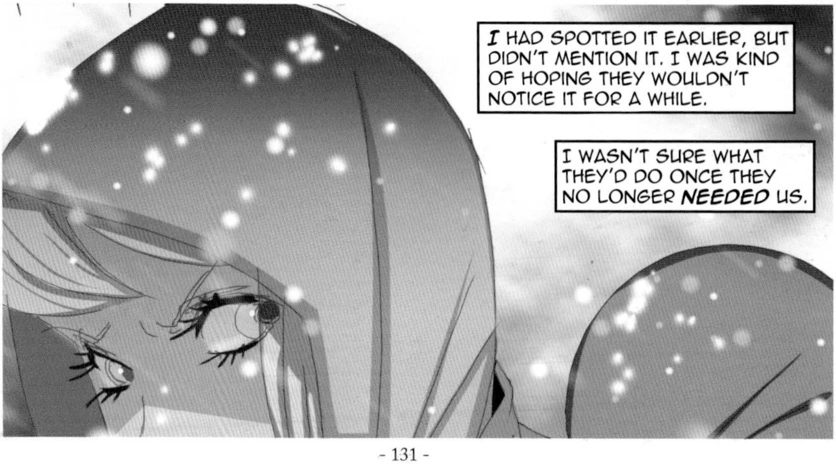
I HAD SPOTTED IT EARLIER, BUT DIDN'T MENTION IT. I WAS KIND OF HOPING THEY WOULDN'T NOTICE IT FOR A WHILE.
I WASN'T SURE WHAT THEY'D DO ONCE THEY NO LONGER NEEDED US.

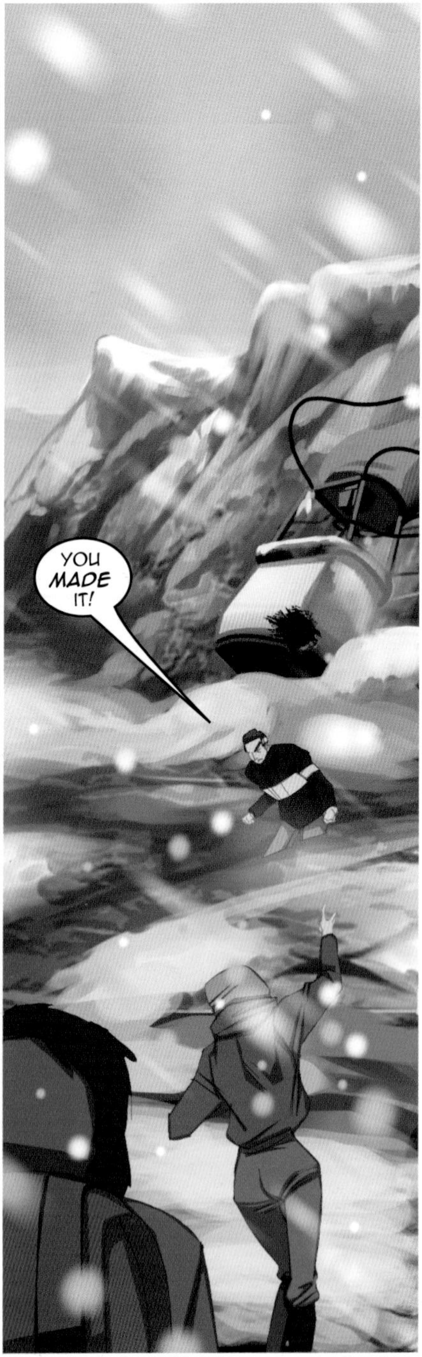
YOU MADE IT!

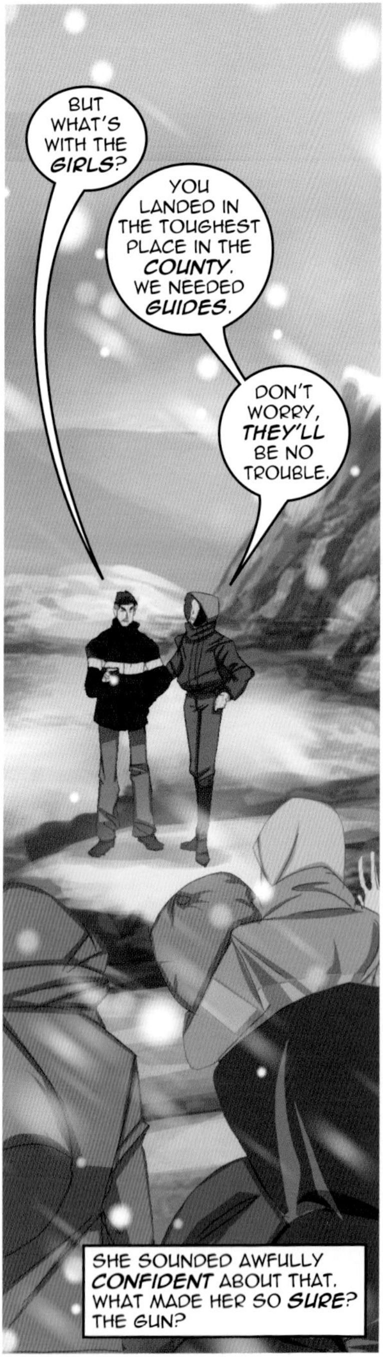
BUT WHAT'S WITH THE GIRLS?
YOU LANDED IN THE TOUGHEST PLACE IN THE COUNTY. WE NEEDED GUIDES.
DON'T WORRY, THEY'LL BE NO TROUBLE.
SHE SOUNDED AWFULLY CONFIDENT ABOUT THAT. WHAT MADE HER SO SURE? THE GUN?

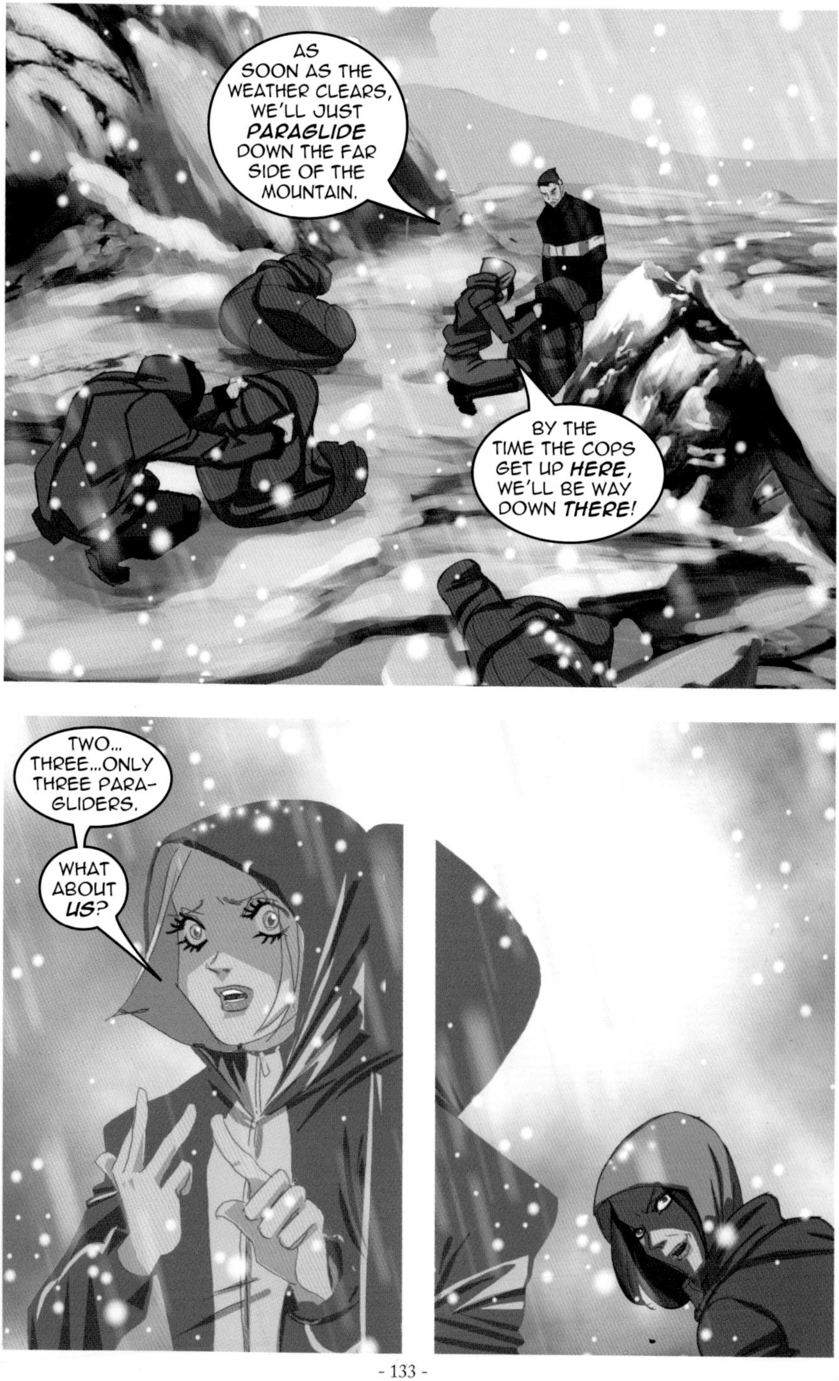
AS SOON AS THE WEATHER CLEARS, WE'LL JUST PARAGLIDE DOWN THE FAR SIDE OF THE MOUNTAIN.
BY THE TIME THE COPS GET UP HERE, WE'LL BE WAY DOWN THERE!
TWO... THREE...ONLY THREE PARA-GLIDERS.
WHAT ABOUT US?

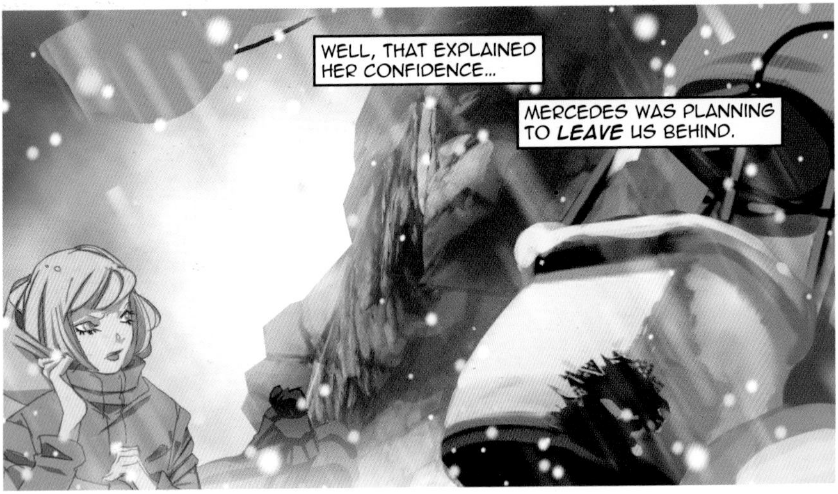
WELL, THAT EXPLAINED HER CONFIDENCE...
MERCEDES WAS PLANNING TO *LEAVE* US BEHIND.

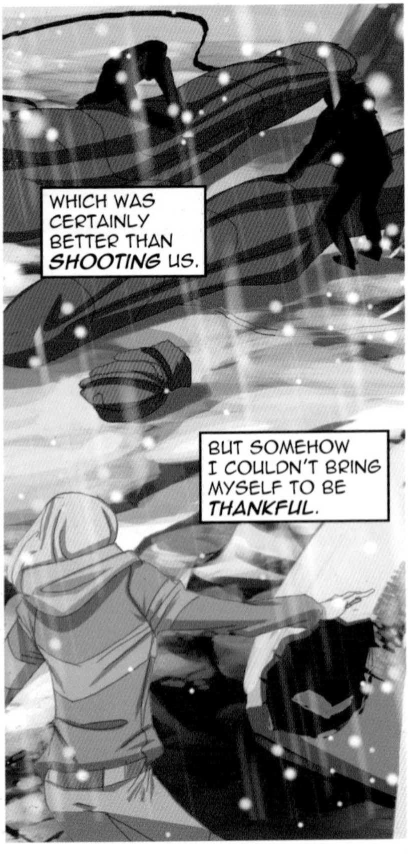
WHICH WAS CERTAINLY BETTER THAN *SHOOTING* US.
BUT SOMEHOW I COULDN'T BRING MYSELF TO BE *THANKFUL*.

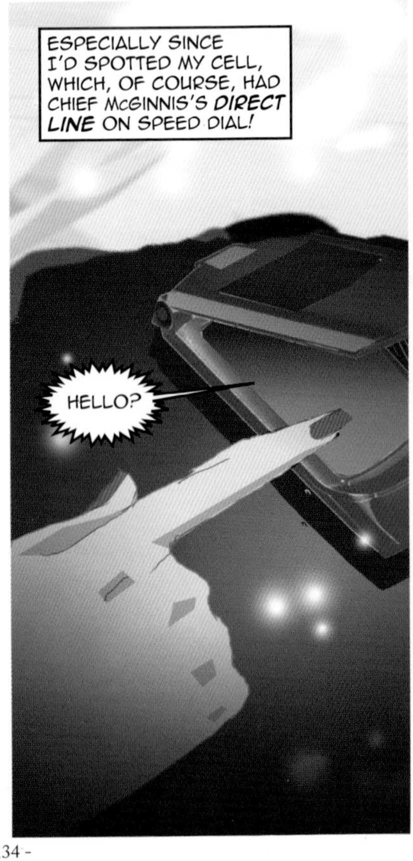
ESPECIALLY SINCE I'D SPOTTED MY CELL, WHICH, OF COURSE, HAD CHIEF McGINNIS'S *DIRECT LINE* ON SPEED DIAL!
HELLO?

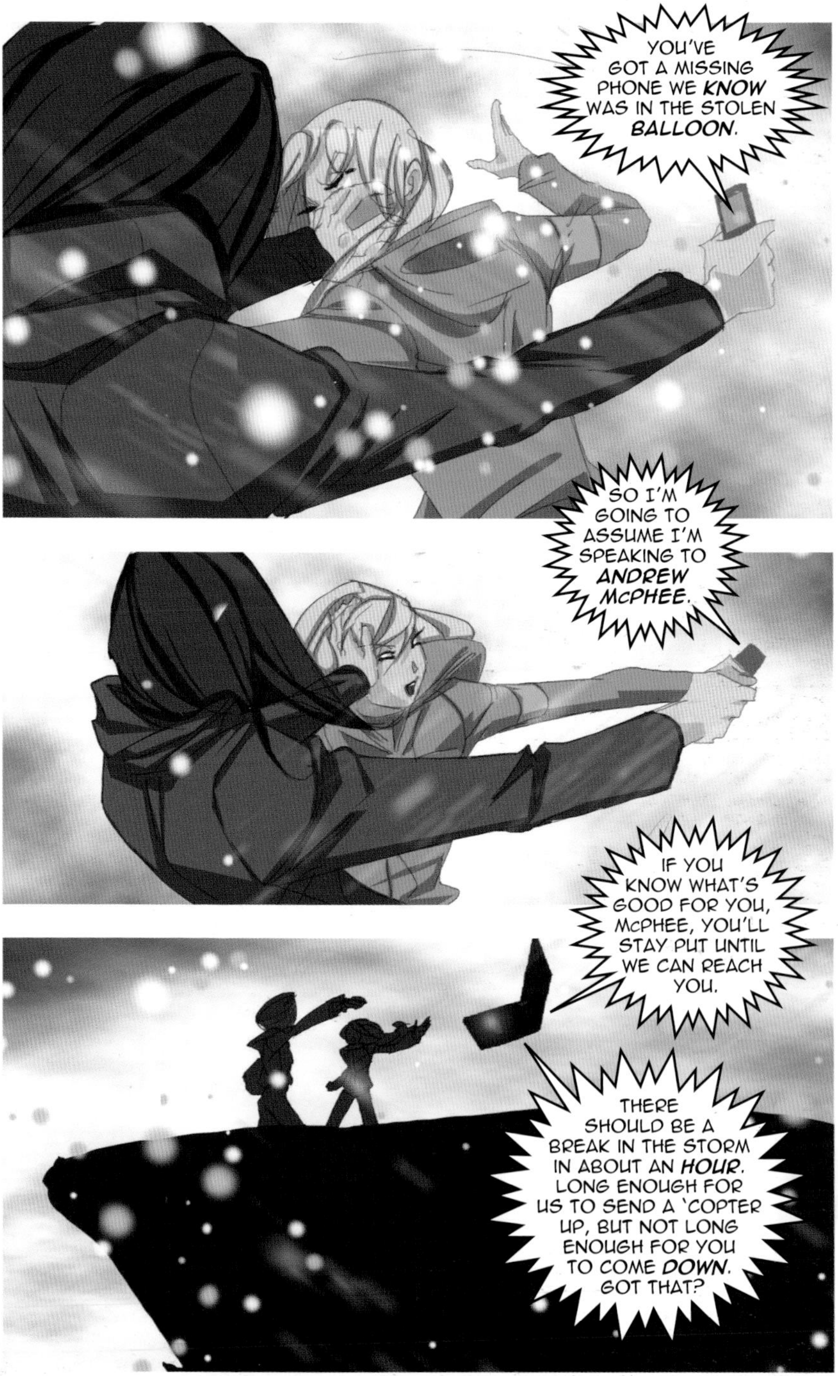
YOU'VE GOT A MISSING PHONE WE KNOW WAS IN THE STOLEN BALLOON.
SO I'M GOING TO ASSUME I'M SPEAKING TO ANDREW McPHEE.
IF YOU KNOW WHAT'S GOOD FOR YOU, McPHEE, YOU'LL STAY PUT UNTIL WE CAN REACH YOU.
THERE SHOULD BE A BREAK IN THE STORM IN ABOUT AN HOUR. LONG ENOUGH FOR US TO SEND A 'COPTER UP, BUT NOT LONG ENOUGH FOR YOU TO COME DOWN. GOT THAT?

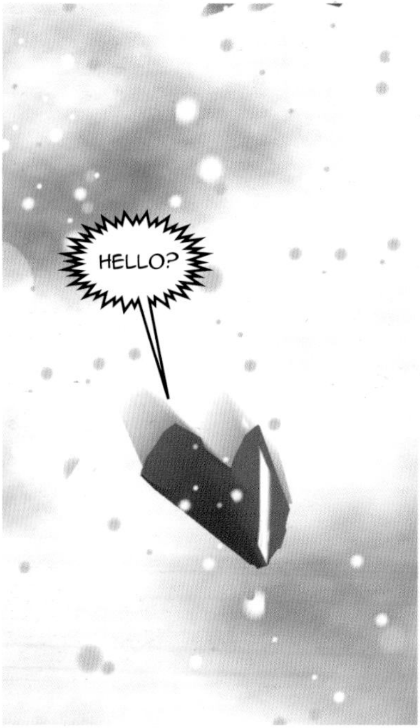
HELLO?

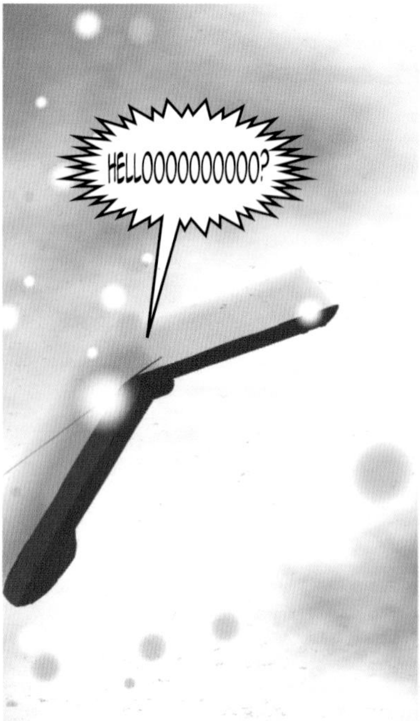
HELLOOOOOOOOOO?

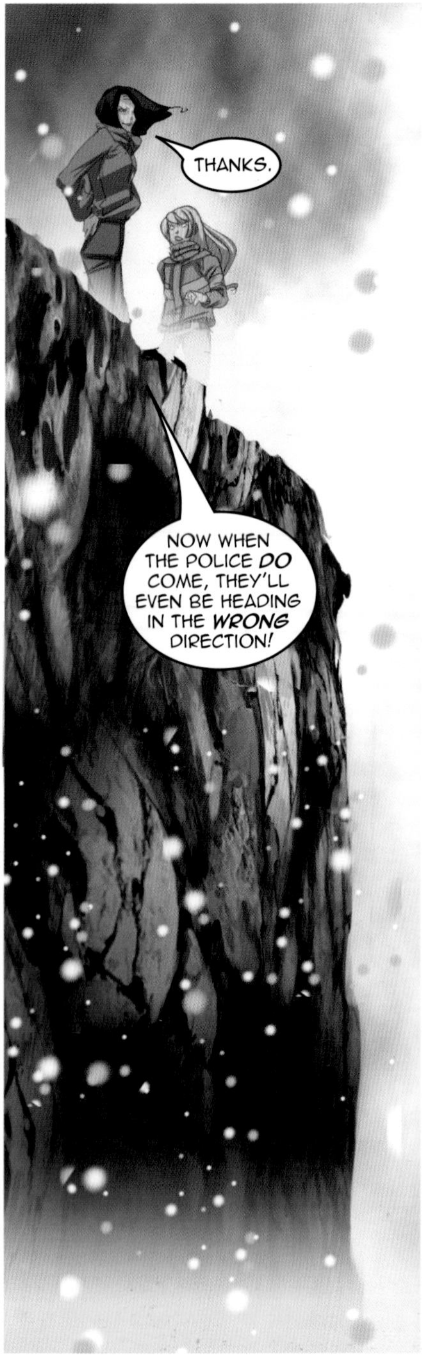
THANKS.
NOW WHEN THE POLICE *DO* COME, THEY'LL EVEN BE HEADING IN THE *WRONG* DIRECTION!

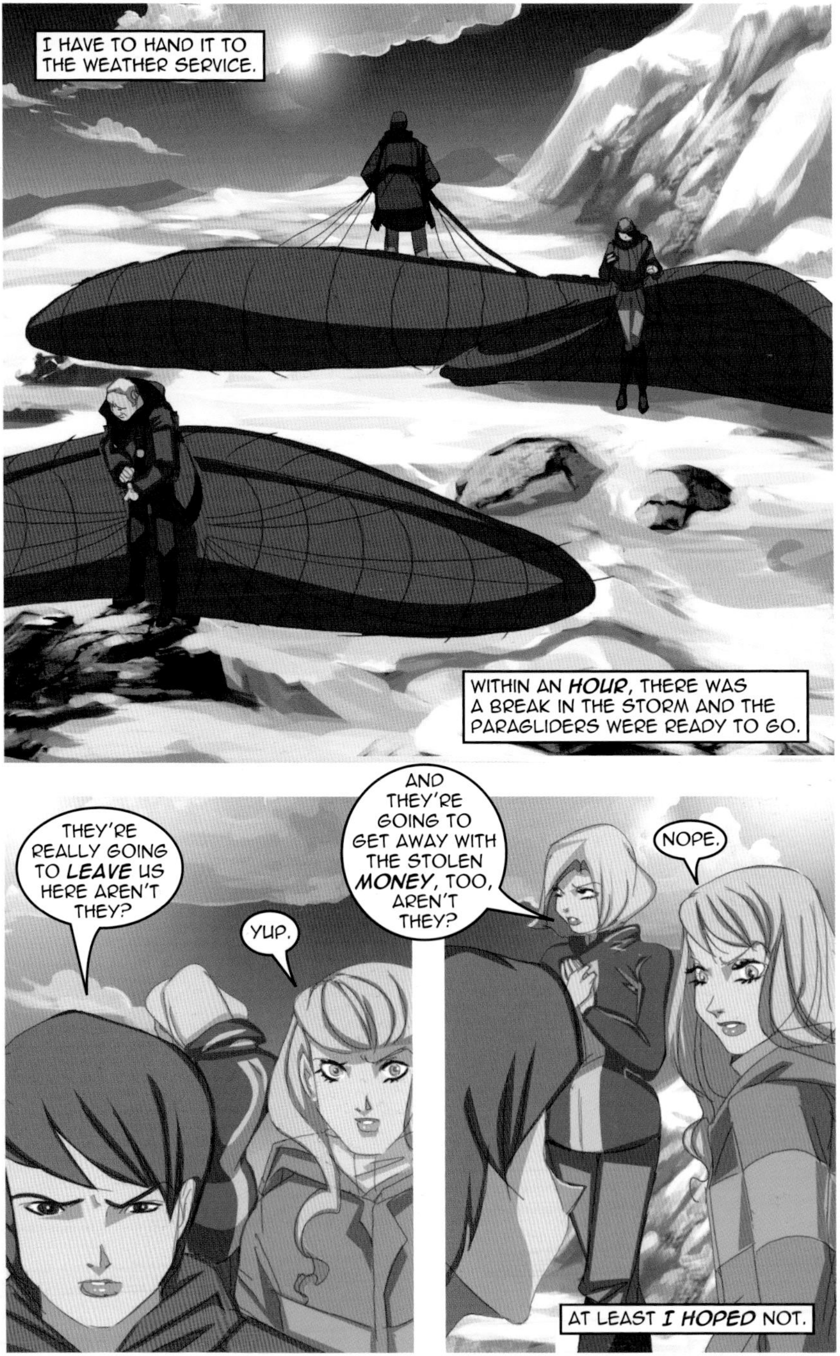
I HAVE TO HAND IT TO THE WEATHER SERVICE.
WITHIN AN HOUR, THERE WAS A BREAK IN THE STORM AND THE PARAGLIDERS WERE READY TO GO.
THEY'RE REALLY GOING TO LEAVE US HERE AREN'T THEY?
YUP.
AND THEY'RE GOING TO GET AWAY WITH THE STOLEN MONEY, TOO, AREN'T THEY?
NOPE.
AT LEAST I HOPED NOT.

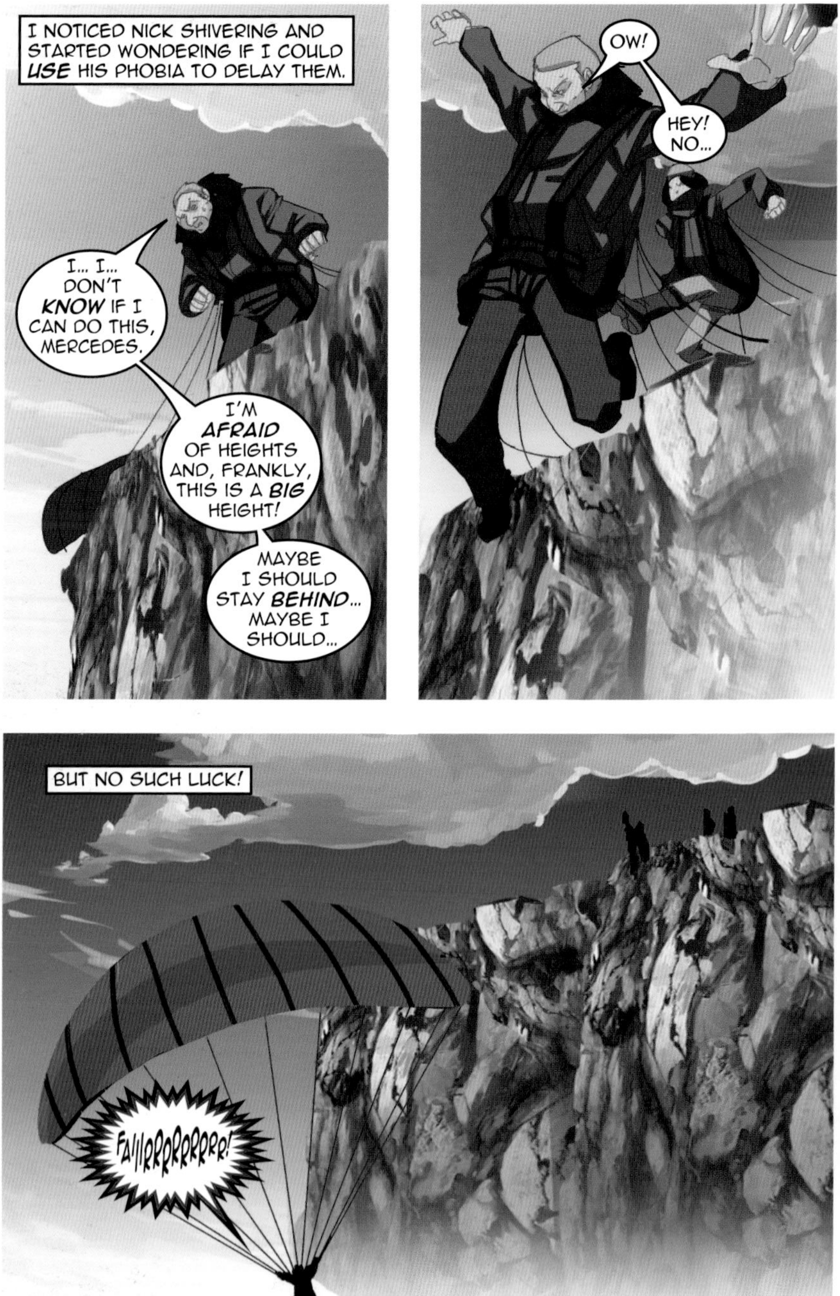
I NOTICED NICK SHIVERING AND STARTED WONDERING IF I COULD USE HIS PHOBIA TO DELAY THEM.
I... I... DON'T KNOW IF I CAN DO THIS, MERCEDES.
I'M AFRAID OF HEIGHTS AND, FRANKLY, THIS IS A BIG HEIGHT!
MAYBE I SHOULD STAY BEHIND... MAYBE I SHOULD...
OW!
HEY! NO...
BUT NO SUCH LUCK!
FWIIRRRRRRRR!

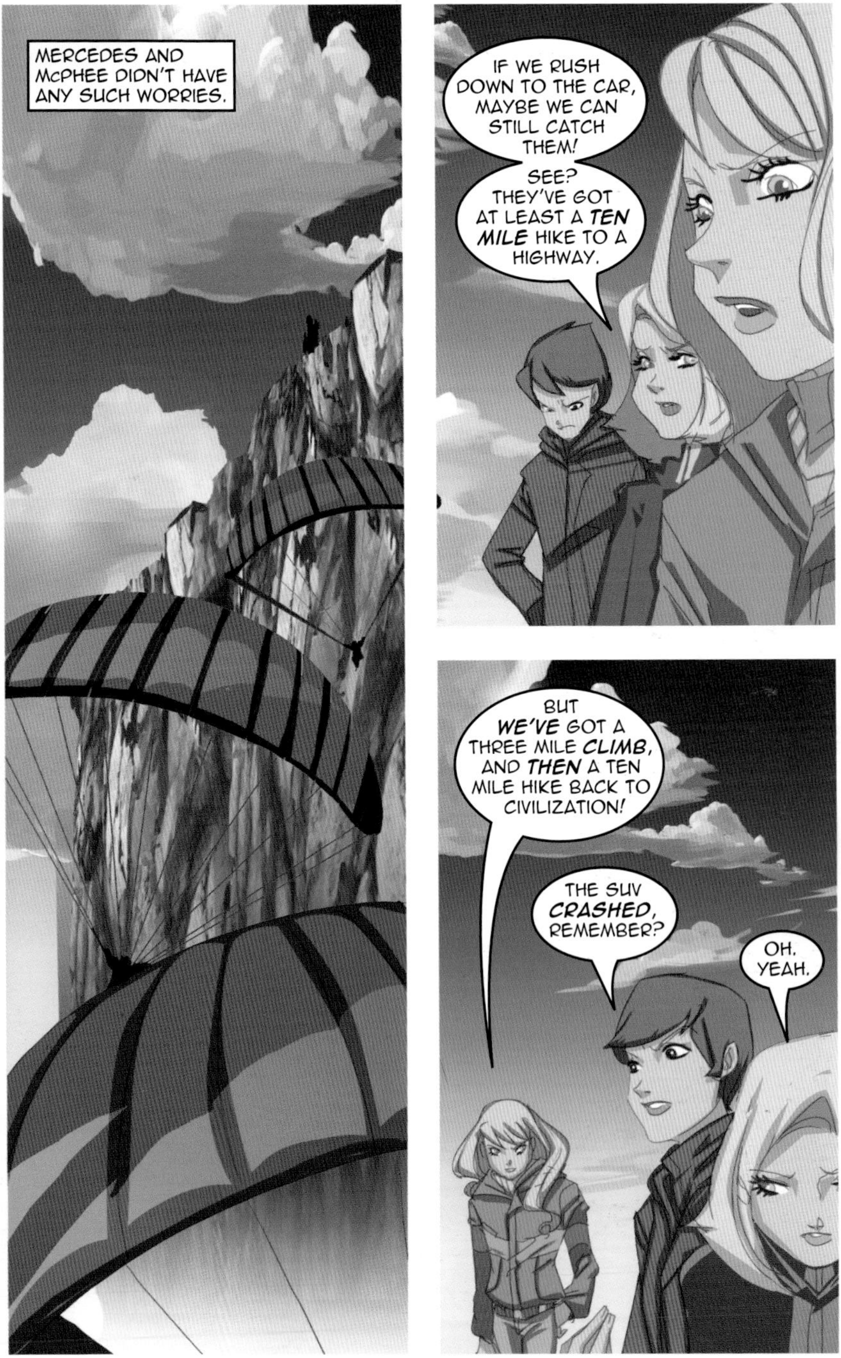

MERCEDES AND McPHEE DIDN'T HAVE ANY SUCH WORRIES.
IF WE RUSH DOWN TO THE CAR, MAYBE WE CAN STILL CATCH THEM!
SEE? THEY'VE GOT AT LEAST A *TEN MILE* HIKE TO A HIGHWAY.
BUT *WE'VE* GOT A THREE MILE *CLIMB*, AND *THEN* A TEN MILE HIKE BACK TO CIVILIZATION!
THE SUV *CRASHED*, REMEMBER?
OH. YEAH.

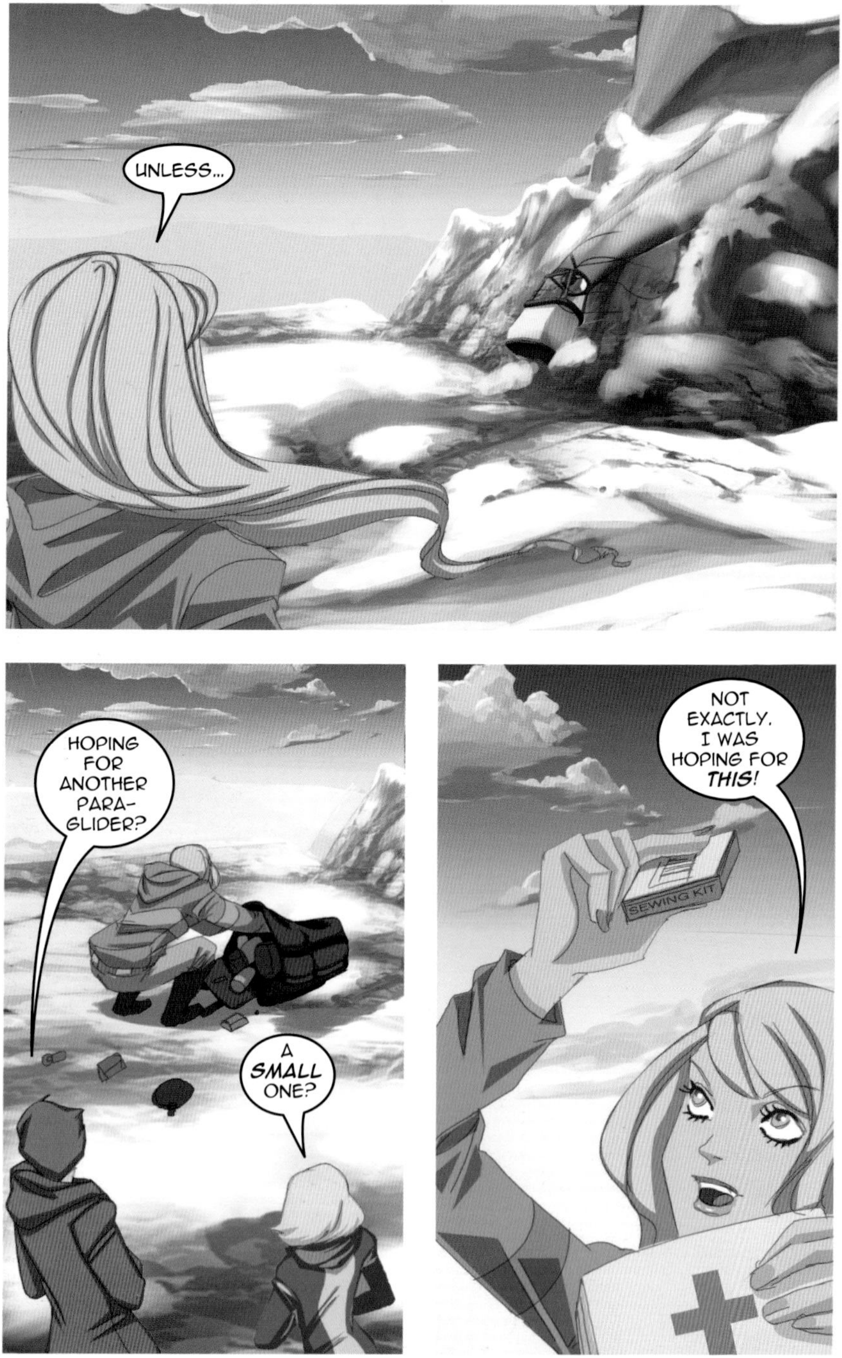
UNLESS...
HOPING FOR ANOTHER PARA-GLIDER?
A SMALL ONE?
NOT EXACTLY. I WAS HOPING FOR THIS!
SEWING KIT

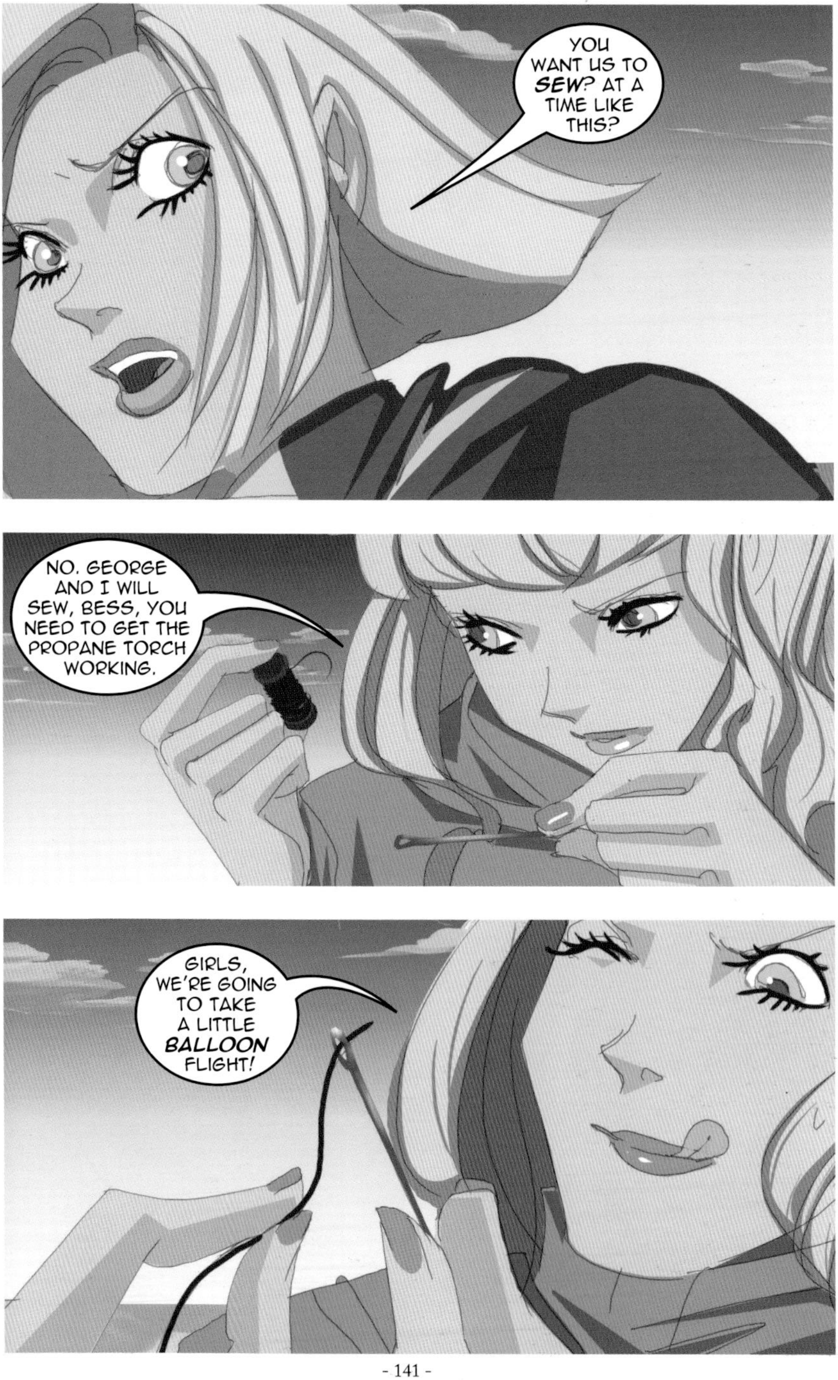
YOU WANT US TO SEW? AT A TIME LIKE THIS?
NO. GEORGE AND I WILL SEW, BESS, YOU NEED TO GET THE PROPANE TORCH WORKING.
GIRLS, WE'RE GOING TO TAKE A LITTLE BALLOON FLIGHT!

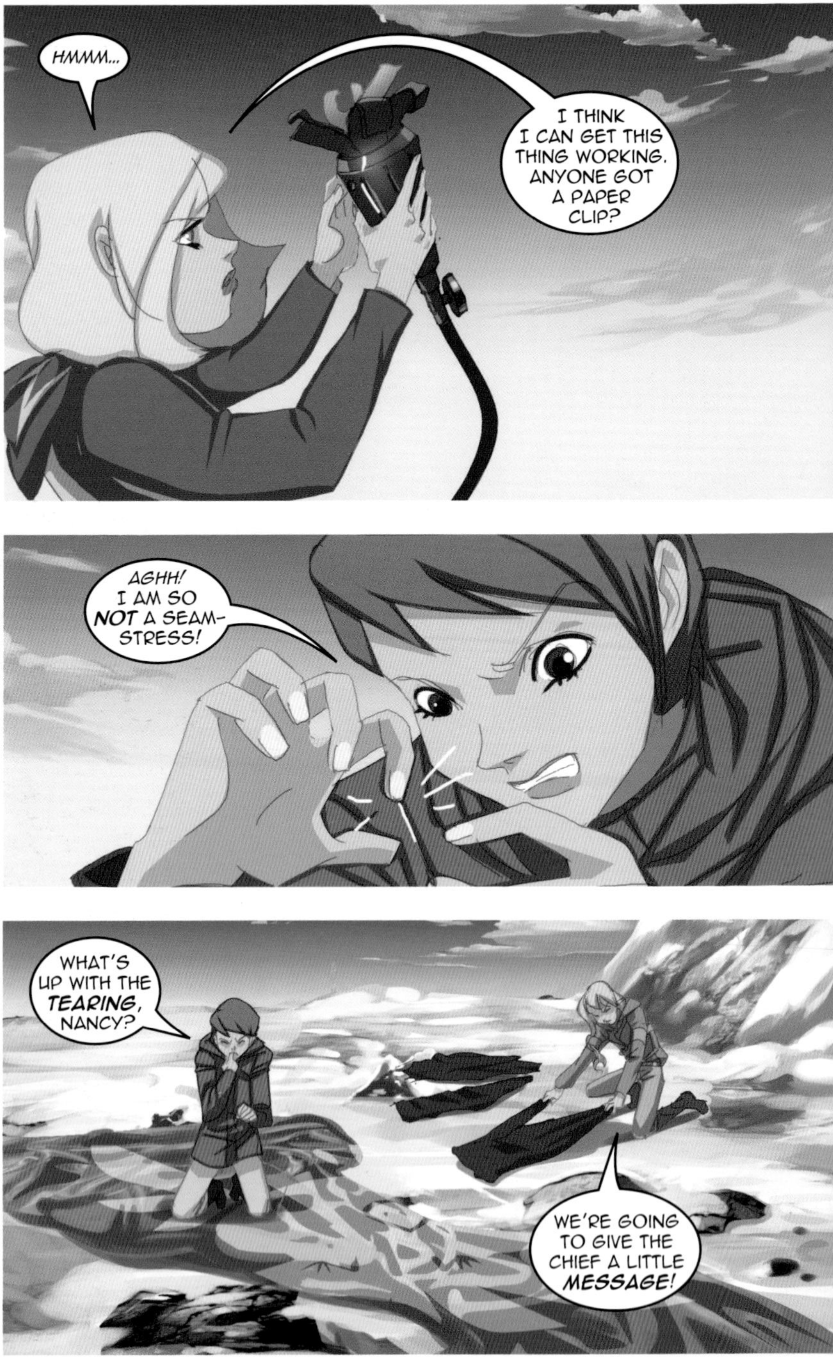
HMMM...
I THINK I CAN GET THIS THING WORKING. ANYONE GOT A PAPER CLIP?
AGHH! I AM SO NOT A SEAM-STRESS!
WHAT'S UP WITH THE TEARING, NANCY?
WE'RE GOING TO GIVE THE CHIEF A LITTLE MESSAGE!

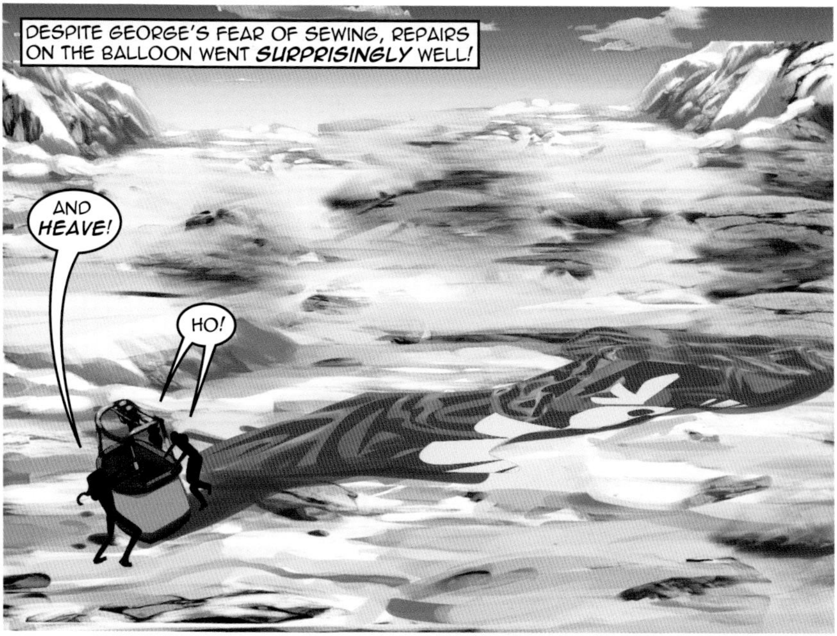
DESPITE GEORGE'S FEAR OF SEWING, REPAIRS ON THE BALLOON WENT SURPRISINGLY WELL!
AND HEAVE!
HO!

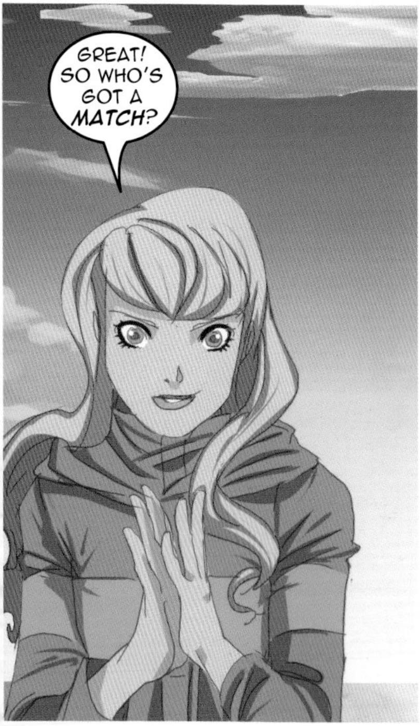
GREAT! SO WHO'S GOT A MATCH?

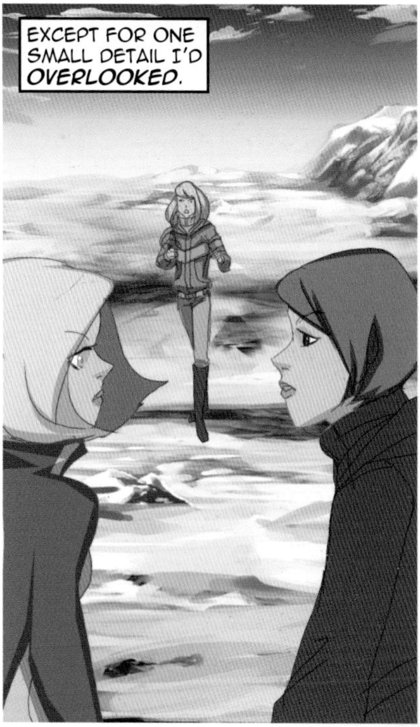
EXCEPT FOR ONE SMALL DETAIL I'D OVERLOOKED.

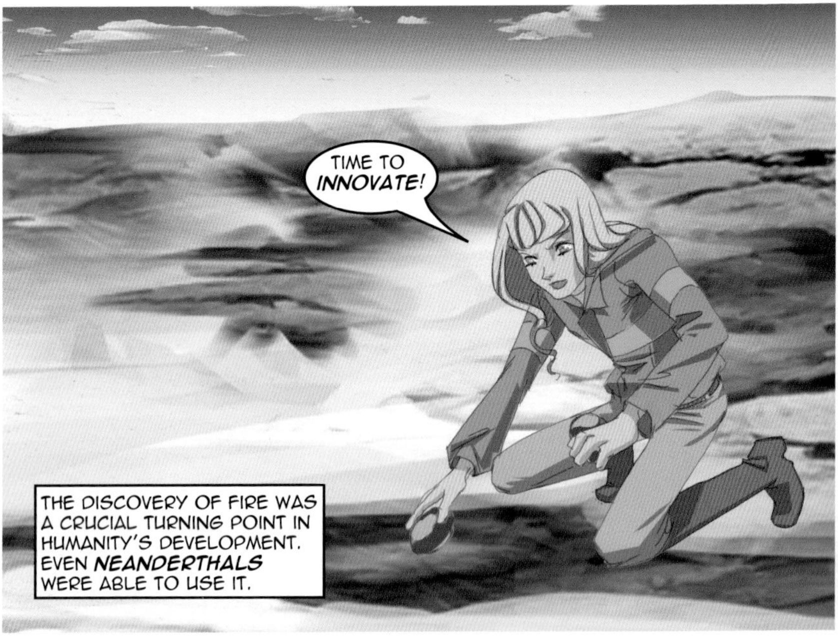
TIME TO INNOVATE!
THE DISCOVERY OF FIRE WAS A CRUCIAL TURNING POINT IN HUMANITY'S DEVELOPMENT. EVEN NEANDERTHALS WERE ABLE TO USE IT.

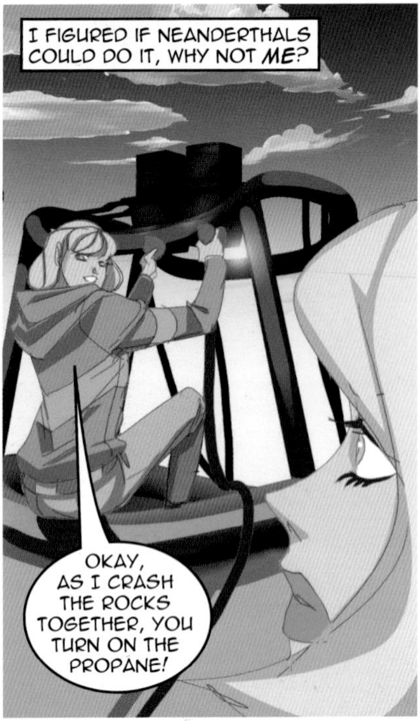
I FIGURED IF NEANDERTHALS COULD DO IT, WHY NOT ME?
OKAY, AS I CRASH THE ROCKS TOGETHER, YOU TURN ON THE PROPANE!

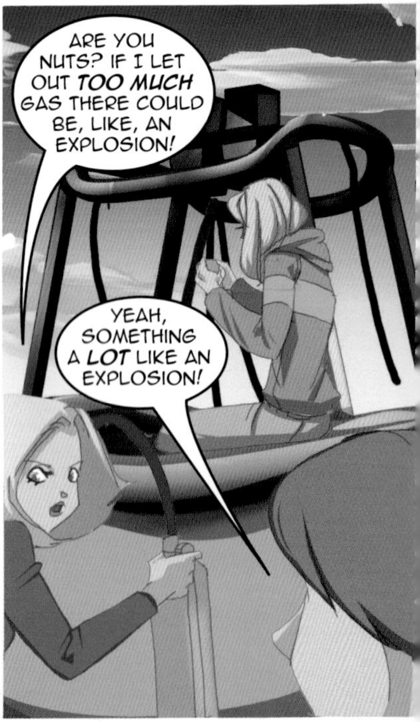
ARE YOU NUTS? IF I LET OUT TOO MUCH GAS THERE COULD BE, LIKE, AN EXPLOSION!
YEAH, SOMETHING A LOT LIKE AN EXPLOSION!

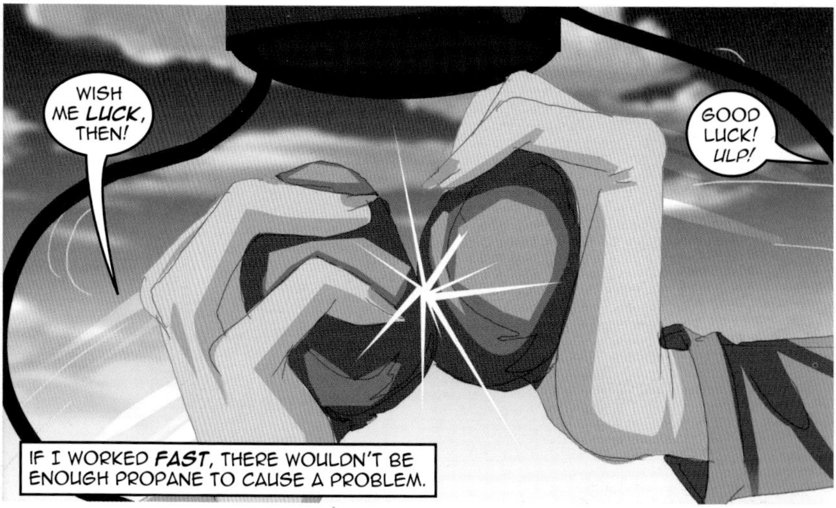
WISH ME LUCK, THEN!
GOOD LUCK! ULP!
IF I WORKED FAST, THERE WOULDN'T BE ENOUGH PROPANE TO CAUSE A PROBLEM.

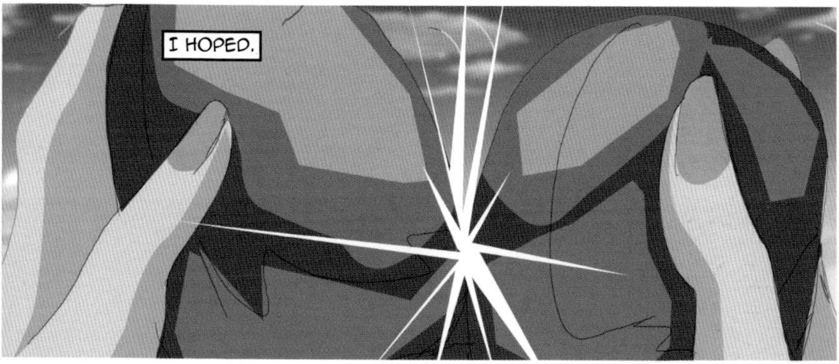
I HOPED.

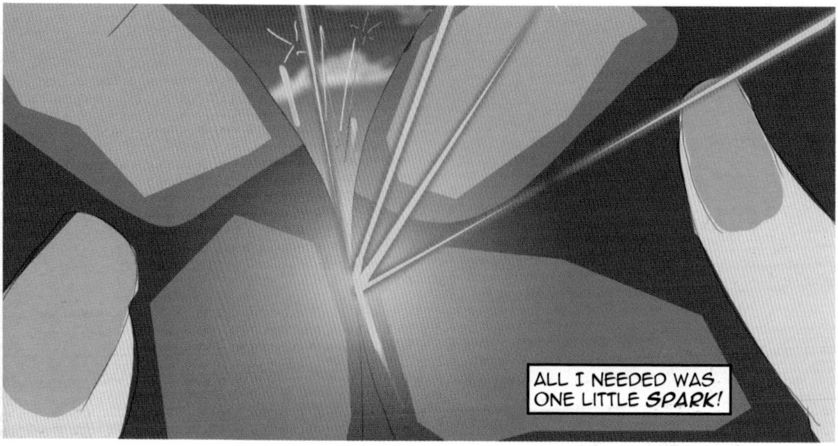
ALL I NEEDED WAS ONE LITTLE SPARK!

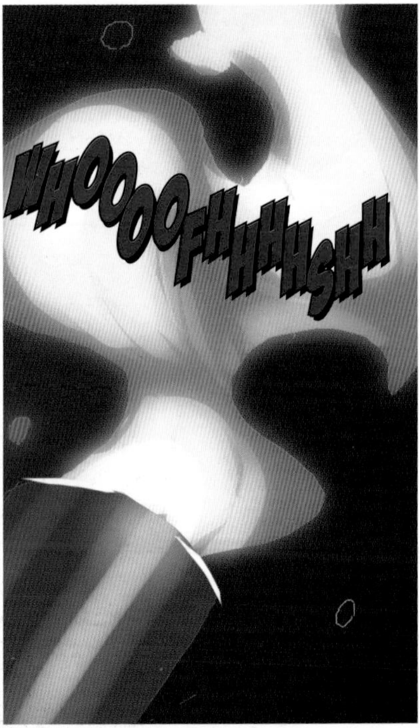
WHOOOOFHHHHSHH

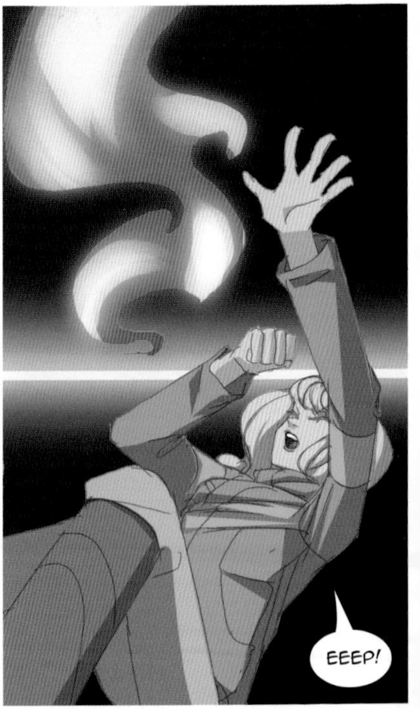
EEEP!

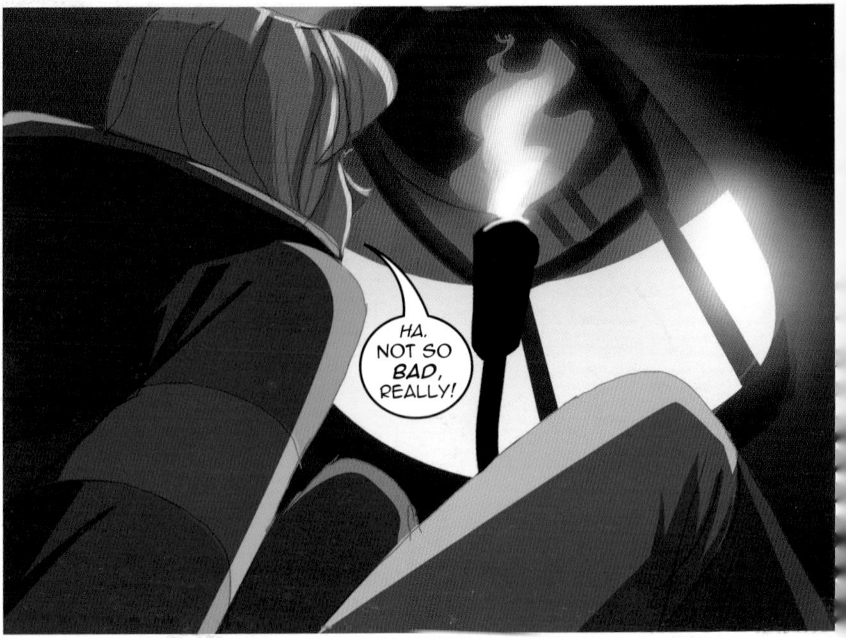
HA, NOT SO BAD, REALLY!

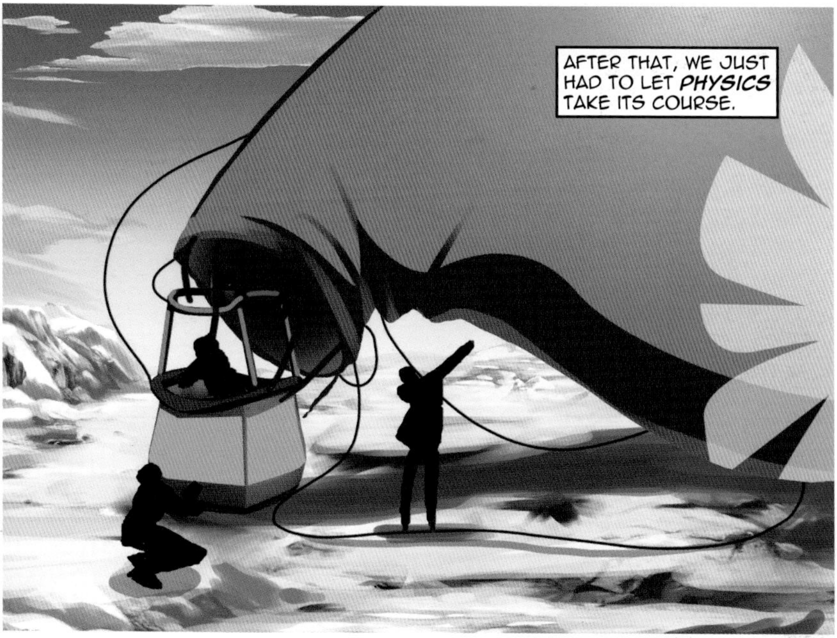
AFTER THAT, WE JUST HAD TO LET PHYSICS TAKE ITS COURSE.

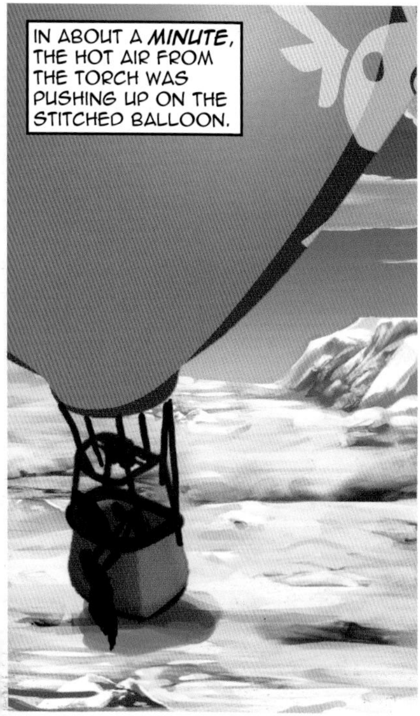
IN ABOUT A MINUTE, THE HOT AIR FROM THE TORCH WAS PUSHING UP ON THE STITCHED BALLOON.

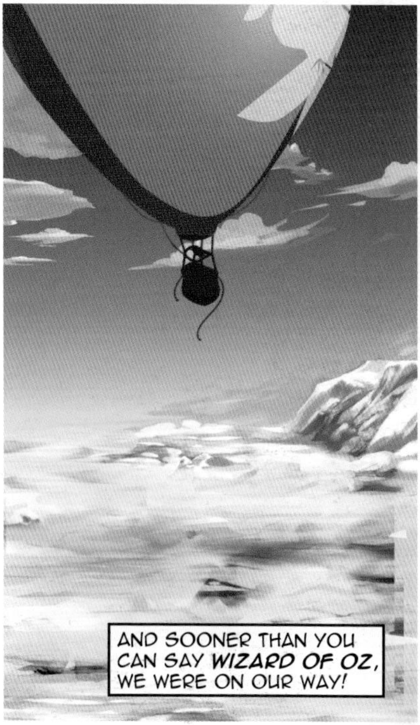
AND SOONER THAN YOU CAN SAY WIZARD OF OZ, WE WERE ON OUR WAY!

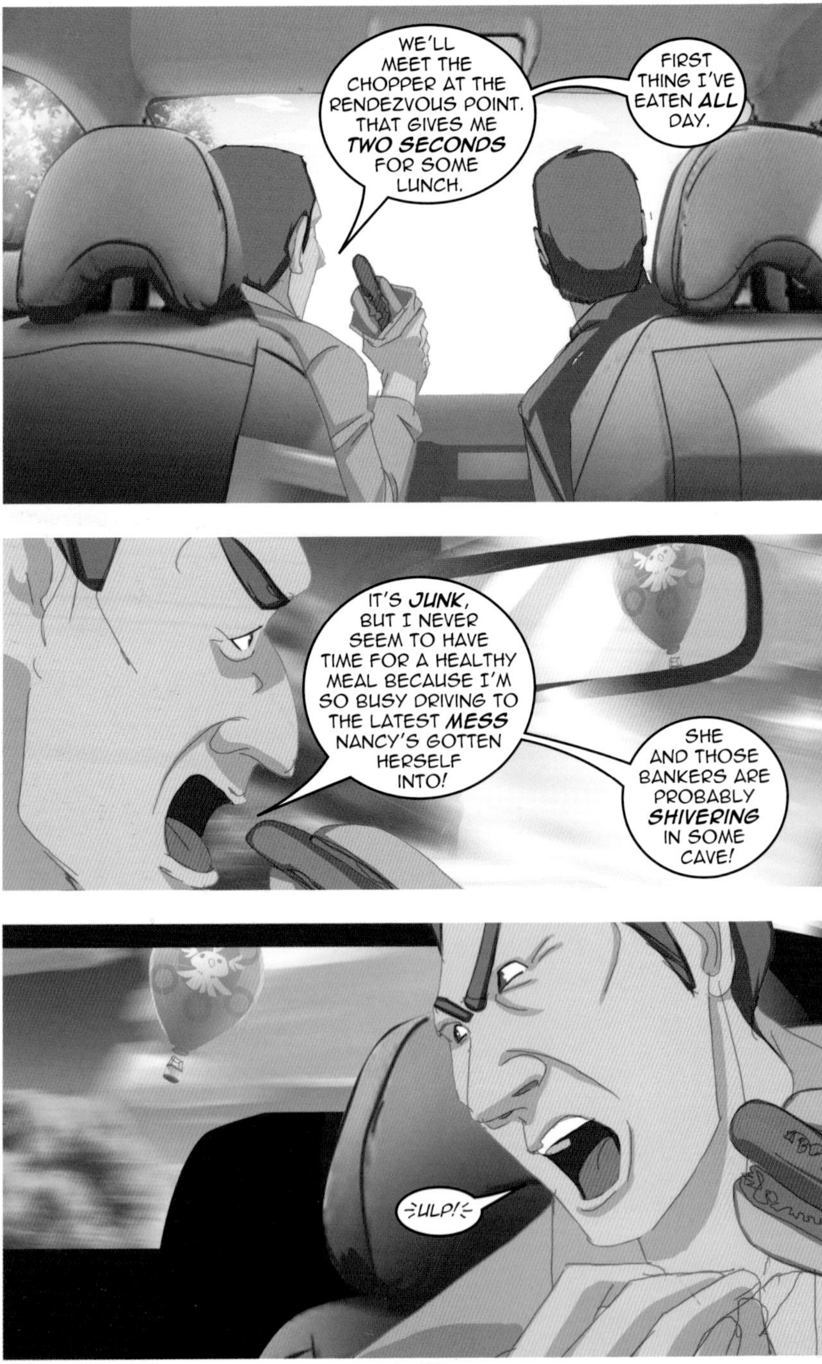
WE'LL MEET THE CHOPPER AT THE RENDEZVOUS POINT. THAT GIVES ME **TWO SECONDS** FOR SOME LUNCH.
FIRST THING I'VE EATEN **ALL** DAY.
IT'S **JUNK**, BUT I NEVER SEEM TO HAVE TIME FOR A HEALTHY MEAL BECAUSE I'M SO BUSY DRIVING TO THE LATEST **MESS** NANCY'S GOTTEN HERSELF INTO!
SHE AND THOSE BANKERS ARE PROBABLY **SHIVERING** IN SOME CAVE!
ULP!

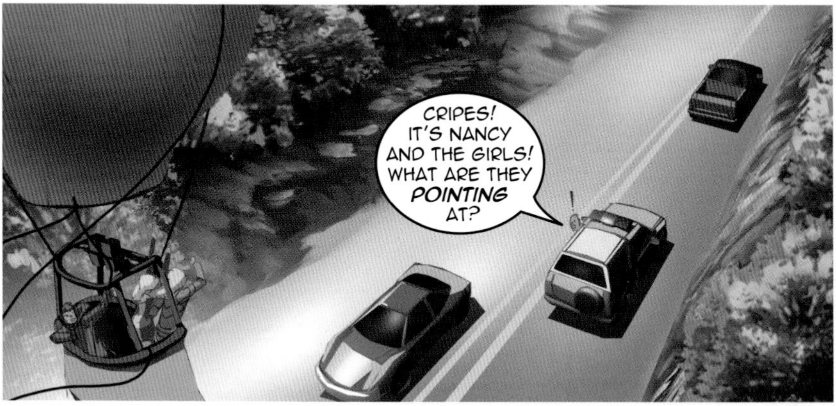
CRIPES! IT'S NANCY AND THE GIRLS! WHAT ARE THEY POINTING AT?
!

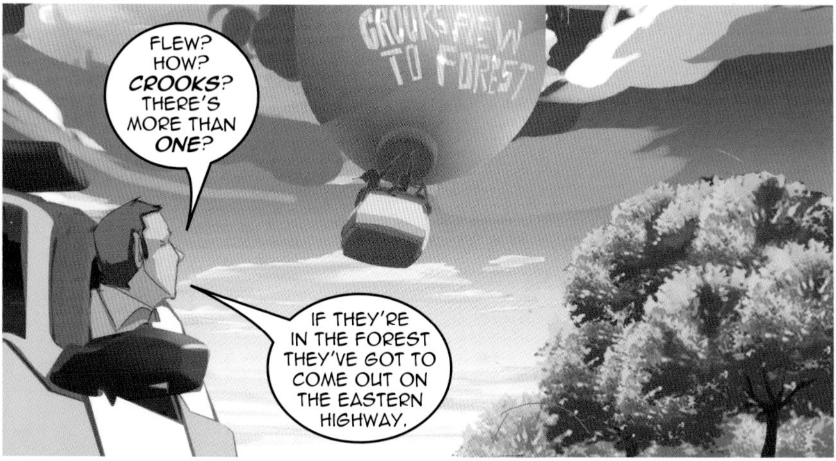
CROOKS FLEW TO FOREST
FLEW? HOW? CROOKS? THERE'S MORE THAN ONE?
IF THEY'RE IN THE FOREST THEY'VE GOT TO COME OUT ON THE EASTERN HIGHWAY.

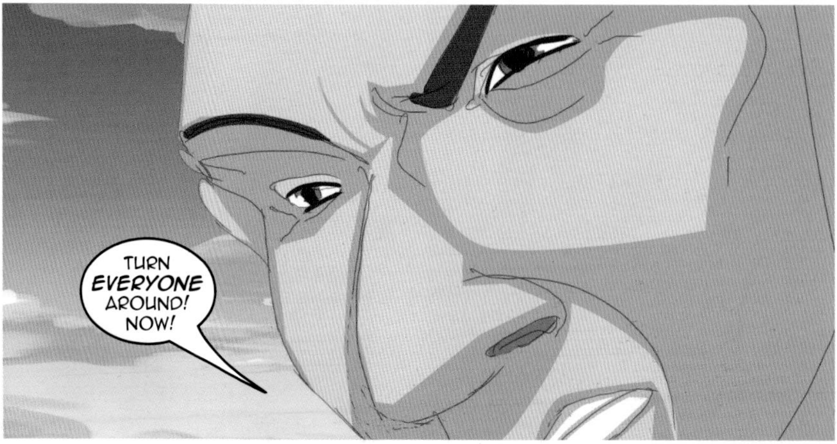
TURN EVERYONE AROUND! NOW!

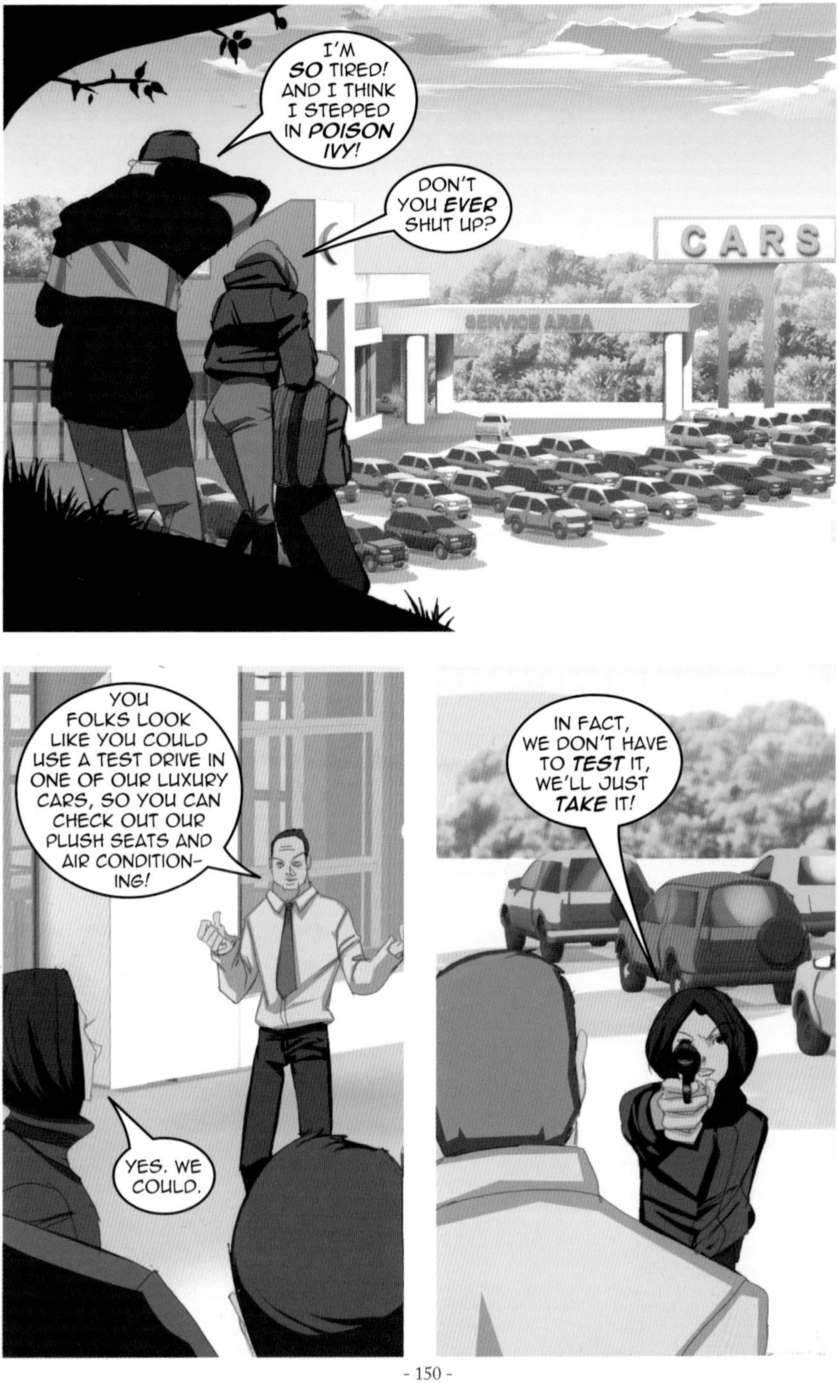
I'M SO TIRED! AND I THINK I STEPPED IN POISON IVY!
DON'T YOU EVER SHUT UP?
CARS
SERVICE AREA
YOU FOLKS LOOK LIKE YOU COULD USE A TEST DRIVE IN ONE OF OUR LUXURY CARS, SO YOU CAN CHECK OUT OUR PLUSH SEATS AND AIR CONDITION-ING!
YES. WE COULD.
IN FACT, WE DON'T HAVE TO TEST IT, WE'LL JUST TAKE IT!

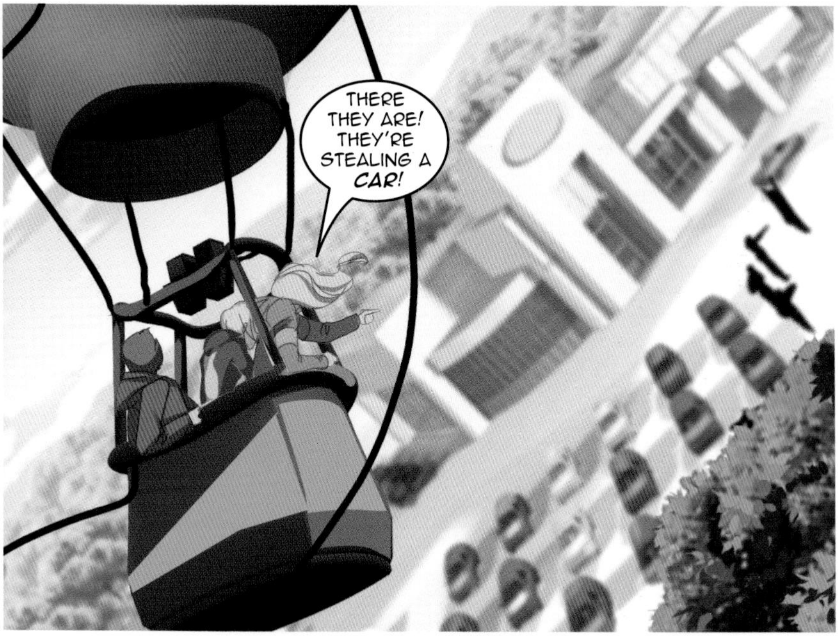
THERE THEY ARE! THEY'RE STEALING A CAR!

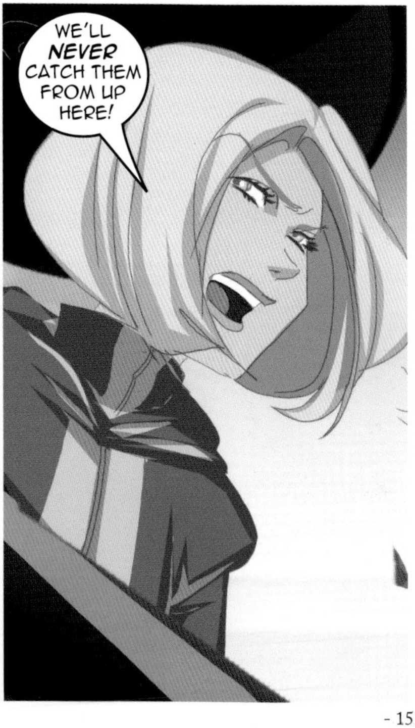
WE'LL NEVER CATCH THEM FROM UP HERE!

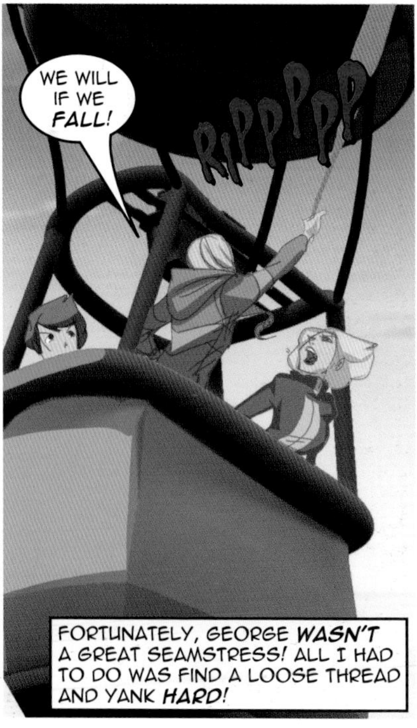
WE WILL IF WE FALL!
RIPPPPP
FORTUNATELY, GEORGE WASN'T A GREAT SEAMSTRESS! ALL I HAD TO DO WAS FIND A LOOSE THREAD AND YANK HARD!

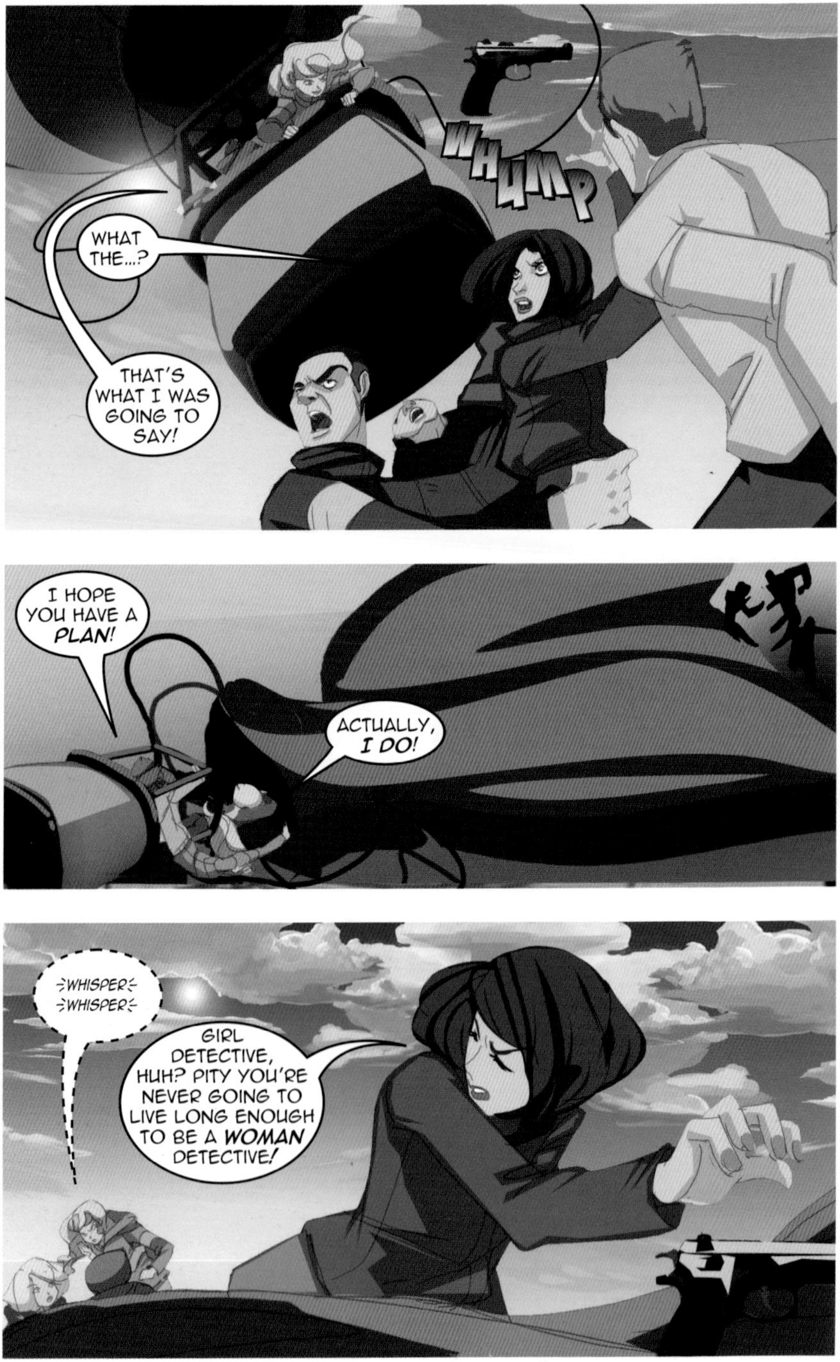
WHUMP
WHAT THE...?
THAT'S WHAT I WAS GOING TO SAY!
I HOPE YOU HAVE A PLAN!
ACTUALLY, I DO!
WHISPER WHISPER
GIRL DETECTIVE, HUH? PITY YOU'RE NEVER GOING TO LIVE LONG ENOUGH TO BE A WOMAN DETECTIVE!

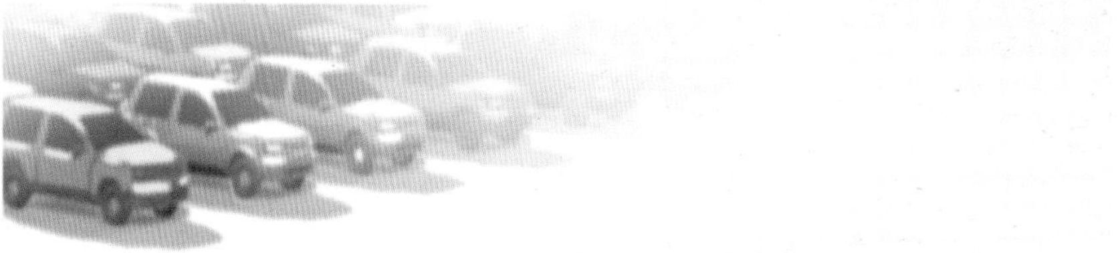

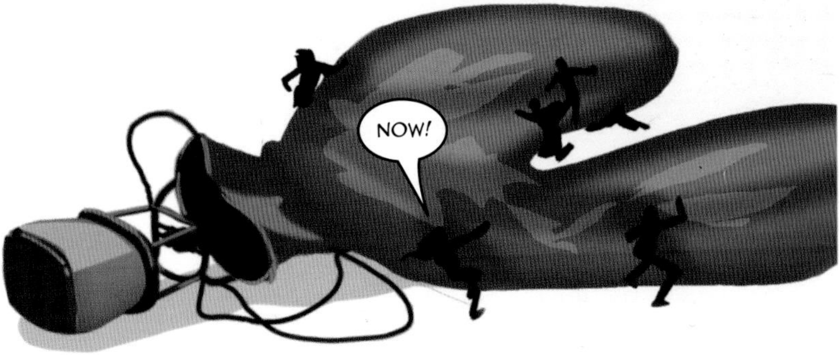
NOW!

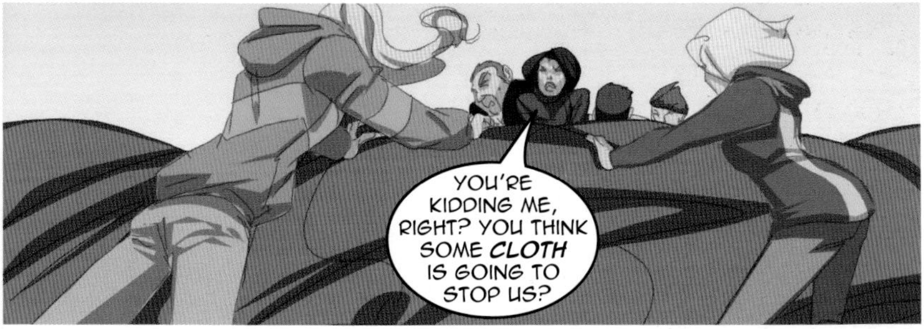
YOU'RE KIDDING ME, RIGHT? YOU THINK SOME *CLOTH* IS GOING TO STOP US?

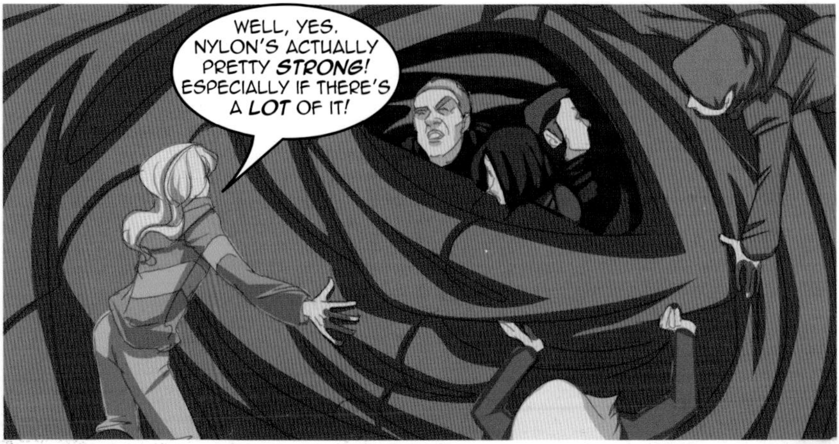
WELL, YES. NYLON'S ACTUALLY PRETTY *STRONG*! ESPECIALLY IF THERE'S A *LOT* OF IT!

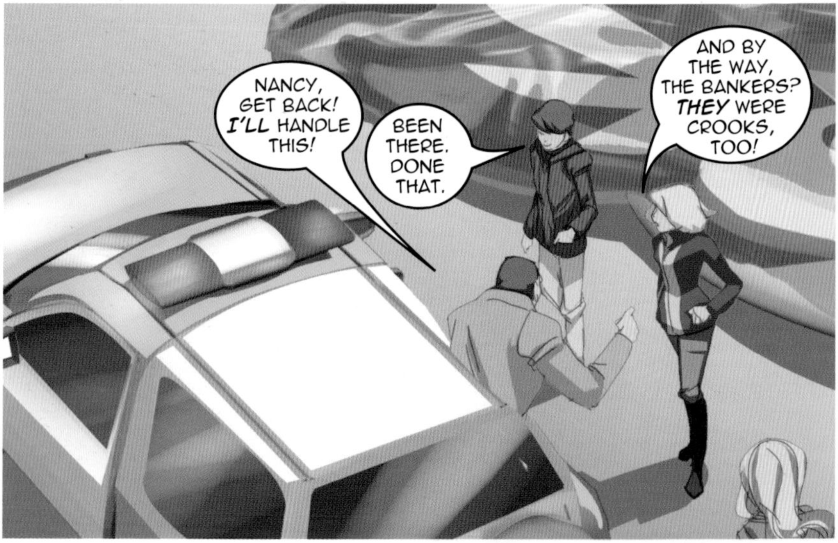
NANCY, GET BACK! I'LL HANDLE THIS!
BEEN THERE. DONE THAT.
AND BY THE WAY, THE BANKERS? THEY WERE CROOKS, TOO!

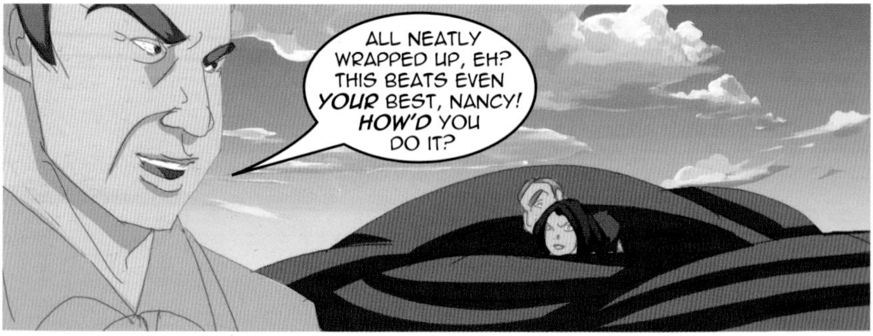
ALL NEATLY WRAPPED UP, EH? THIS BEATS EVEN YOUR BEST, NANCY! HOW'D YOU DO IT?

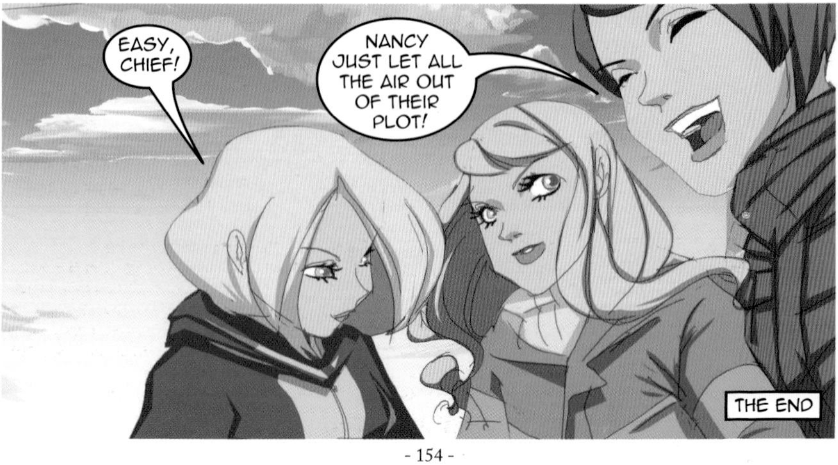
EASY, CHIEF!
NANCY JUST LET ALL THE AIR OUT OF THEIR PLOT!
THE END

NANCY DREW GRAPHIC NOVELS AVAILABLE FROM PAPERCUTZ

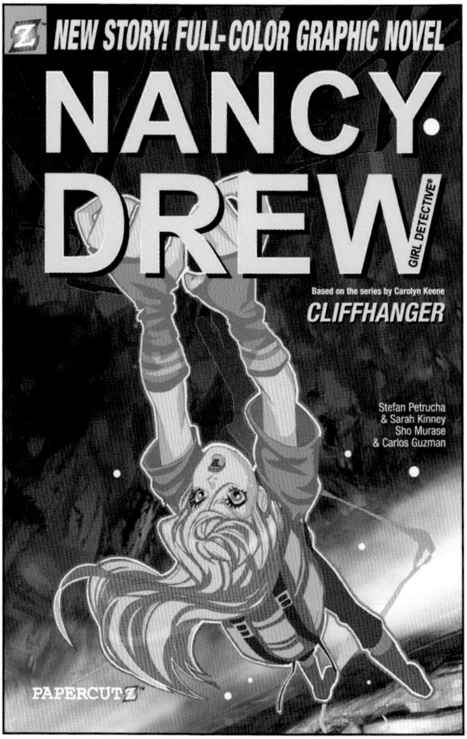
NEW STORY! FULL-COLOR GRAPHIC NOVEL
NANCY DREW
GIRL DETECTIVE
Based on the series by Carolyn Keene
CLIFFHANGER
Stefan Petrucha
& Sarah Kinney
Sho Murase
& Carlos Guzman
PAPERCUTZ

#19 "Cliffhanger"

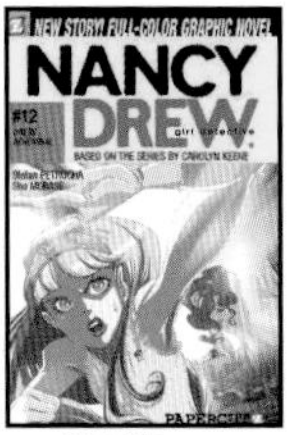
NEW STORY! FULL-COLOR GRAPHIC NOVEL
NANCY DREW
PAPERCUTZ

#12 "Dress Reversal"

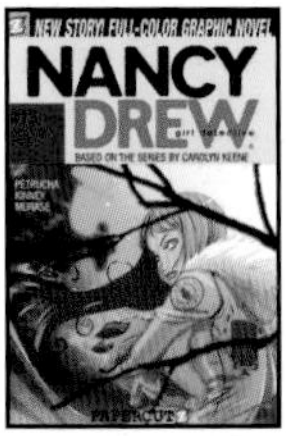
NEW STORY! FULL-COLOR GRAPHIC NOVEL
NANCY DREW
PAPERCUTZ

#13 "Doggone Town"

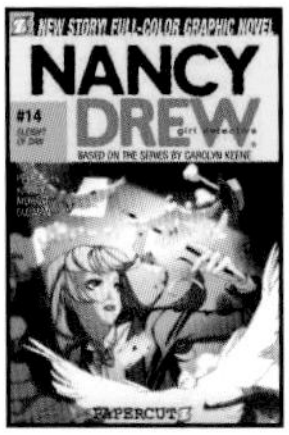
NEW STORY! FULL-COLOR GRAPHIC NOVEL
NANCY DREW
PAPERCUTZ

#14 "Sleight of Dan"

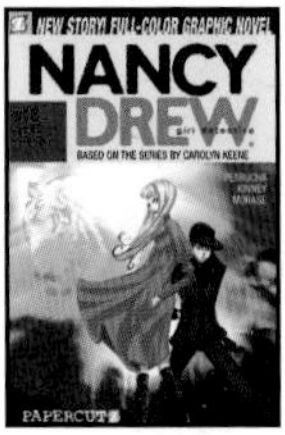
NEW STORY! FULL-COLOR GRAPHIC NOVEL
NANCY DREW
PAPERCUTZ

#15 "Tiger Counter"

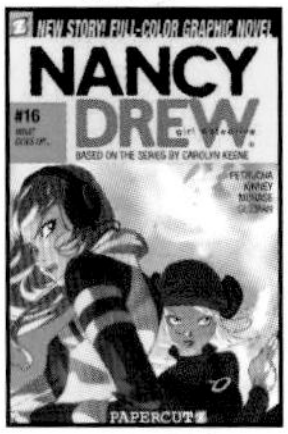
NEW STORY! FULL-COLOR GRAPHIC NOVEL
NANCY DREW
PAPERCUTZ

#16 "What Goes Up..."

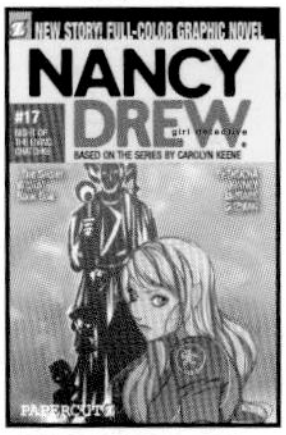
NEW STORY! FULL-COLOR GRAPHIC NOVEL
NANCY DREW
PAPERCUTZ

#17 "Night of the Living Chatchke"

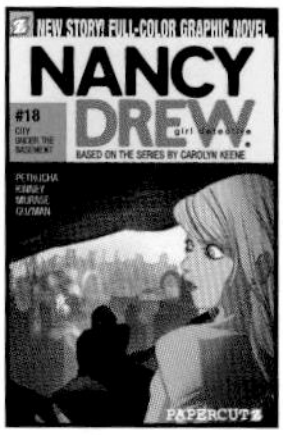
NEW STORY! FULL-COLOR GRAPHIC NOVEL
NANCY DREW
PAPERCUTZ

#18 "City Under the Basement"

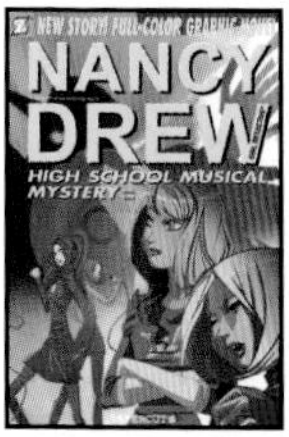
NANCY DREW
HIGH SCHOOL MUSICAL MYSTERY

#20 "High School Musical Mystery" 1

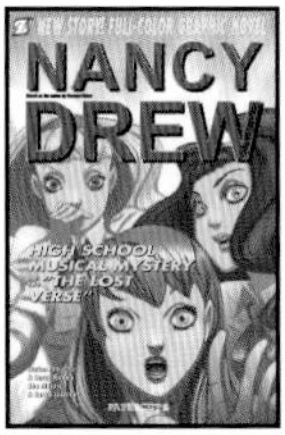
NANCY DREW
HIGH SCHOOL MUSICAL MYSTERY
THE LOST VERSE

#21 "High School Musical Mystery" 2

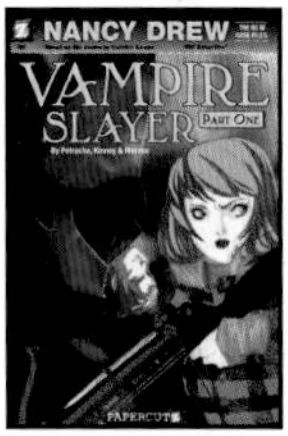
NANCY DREW
VAMPIRE SLAYER
PART ONE
PAPERCUTZ

The New Case Files #1 "Vampire Slayer" Part 1

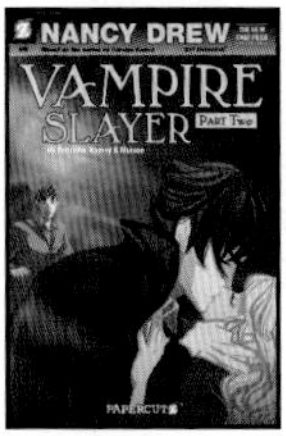
NANCY DREW
VAMPIRE SLAYER
PART TWO
PAPERCUTZ

The New Case Files #2 "Vampire Slayer" Part 2

NANCY DREW graphic novels are available at booksellers everywhere.

NANCY DREW AND THE CLUE CREW graphic novels are $7.99 each in paperback, and $11.99 in hardcover, except #1, which is $6.99 in paperback, $10.99 in hardcover. NANCY DREW GIRL DETECTIVE graphic novels are $7.95 each in paperback and $12.95 each in hardcover. except #20 and 21, $8.99PB/$13.99HC. NANCY DREW THE NEW CASE FILES are $6.99PB/$10.99HC. You may also order online at papercutz.com. Or call 1-800-886-1223, Monday through Friday, 9 – 5 EST. MC, Visa, and AmEx accepted. To order by mail, please add $4.00 for postage and handling for first book ordered, $1.00 for each additional book and make check payable to NBM Publishing. Send to: Papercutz, 160 Broadway, Suite 700, East Wing, New York, NY 10038.

NANCY DREW GIRL DETECTIVE graphic novels are also available digitally wherever e-books are sold.

papercutz.com

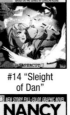

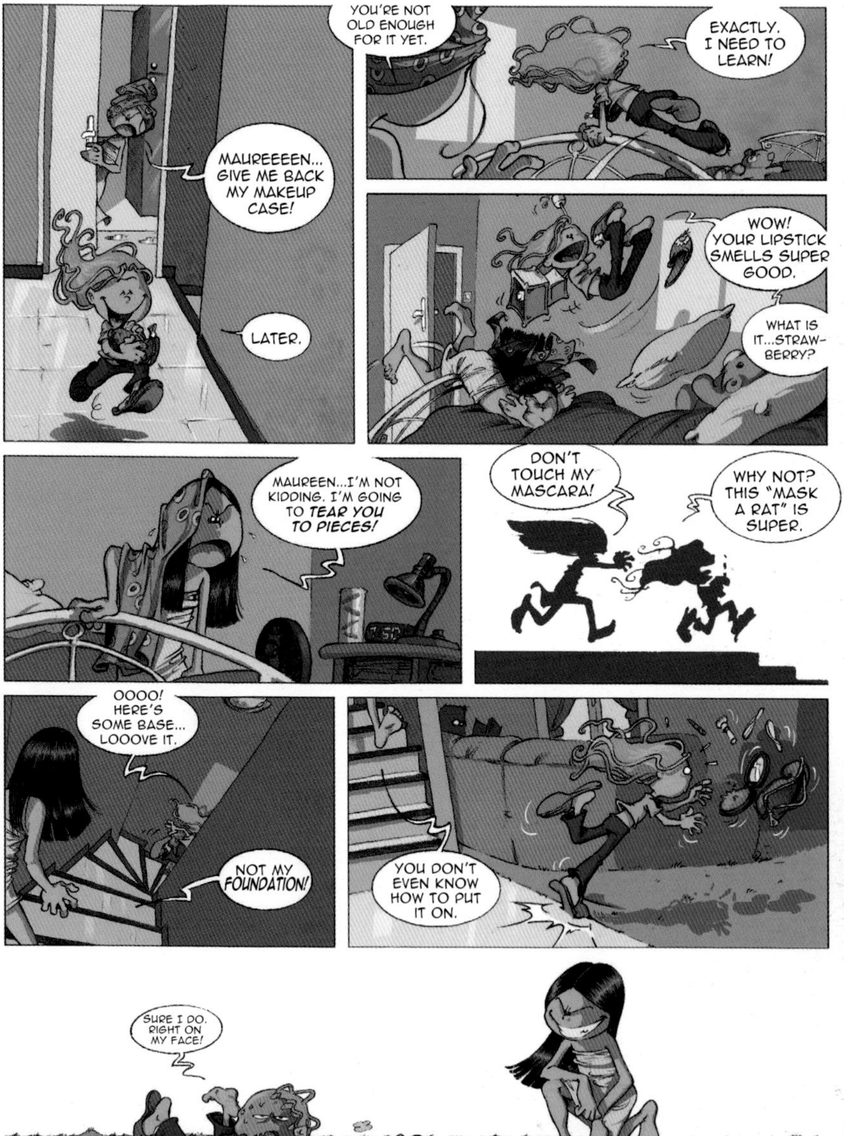
MAUREEEEN... GIVE ME BACK MY MAKEUP CASE!
LATER.
YOU'RE NOT OLD ENOUGH FOR IT YET.
EXACTLY. I NEED TO LEARN!
WOW! YOUR LIPSTICK SMELLS SUPER GOOD.
WHAT IS IT...STRAWBERRY?
MAUREEN...I'M NOT KIDDING. I'M GOING TO TEAR YOU TO PIECES!
DON'T TOUCH MY MASCARA!
WHY NOT? THIS "MASK A RAT" IS SUPER.
OOOO! HERE'S SOME BASE... LOOOVE IT.
NOT MY FOUNDATION!
YOU DON'T EVEN KNOW HOW TO PUT IT ON.
SURE I DO. RIGHT ON MY FACE!
CAZENOVE/WILLIAM

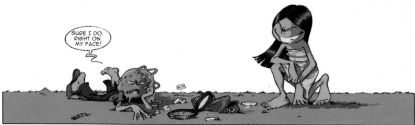

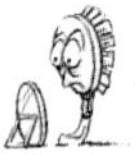

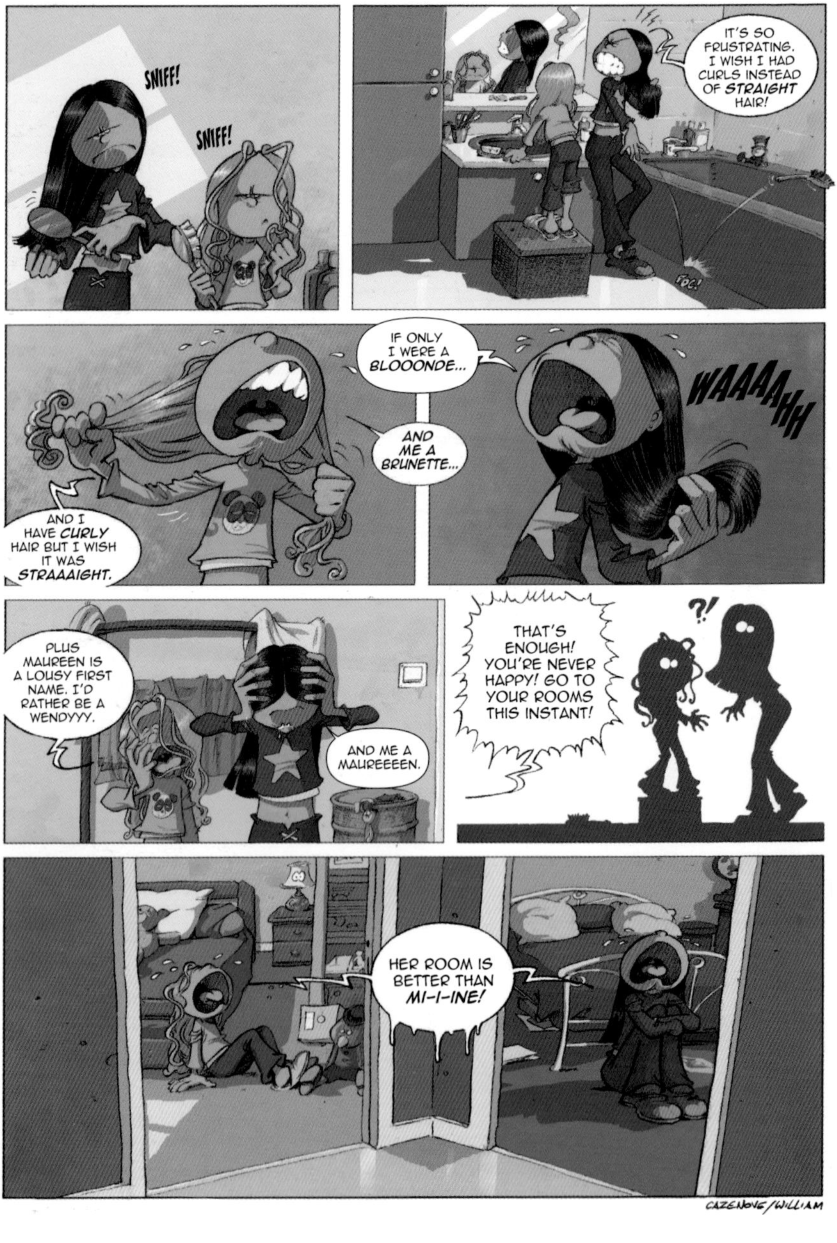
SNIFF!
SNIFF!
IT'S SO FRUSTRATING. I WISH I HAD CURLS INSTEAD OF STRAIGHT HAIR!
IF ONLY I WERE A BLOOONDE...
WAAAAHH
AND ME A BRUNETTE...
AND I HAVE CURLY HAIR BUT I WISH IT WAS STRAAAIGHT.
PLUS MAUREEN IS A LOUSY FIRST NAME. I'D RATHER BE A WENDYYY.
AND ME A MAUREEEEN.
THAT'S ENOUGH! YOU'RE NEVER HAPPY! GO TO YOUR ROOMS THIS INSTANT!
?!
HER ROOM IS BETTER THAN MI-I-INE!

CAZENOVE/WILLIAM

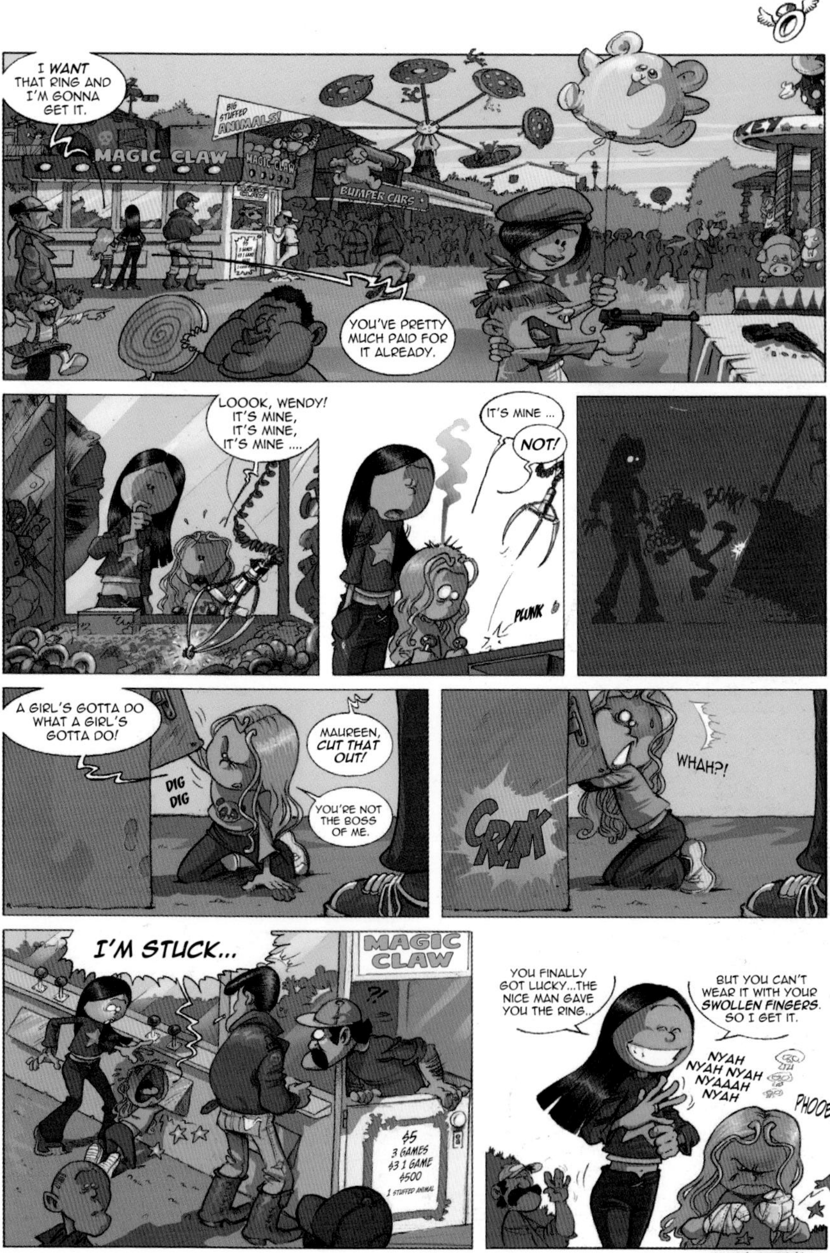
I WANT THAT RING AND I'M GONNA GET IT.
MAGIC CLAW
BIG STUFFED ANIMALS!
MAGIC CLAW
BUMPER CARS
YOU'VE PRETTY MUCH PAID FOR IT ALREADY.
LOOOK, WENDY! IT'S MINE, IT'S MINE, IT'S MINE ....
IT'S MINE ...
NOT!
PLUNK
A GIRL'S GOTTA DO WHAT A GIRL'S GOTTA DO!
DIG DIG
MAUREEN, CUT THAT OUT!
YOU'RE NOT THE BOSS OF ME.
CRAK
WHAH?!
I'M STUCK...
MAGIC CLAW
$5 3 GAMES $3 1 GAME $500 1 STUFFED ANIMAL
YOU FINALLY GOT LUCKY...THE NICE MAN GAVE YOU THE RING...
BUT YOU CAN'T WEAR IT WITH YOUR SWOLLEN FINGERS. SO I GET IT.
NYAH NYAH NYAH NYAAAH NYAH
PHOOEY!
CAZENOVE/WILLIAM

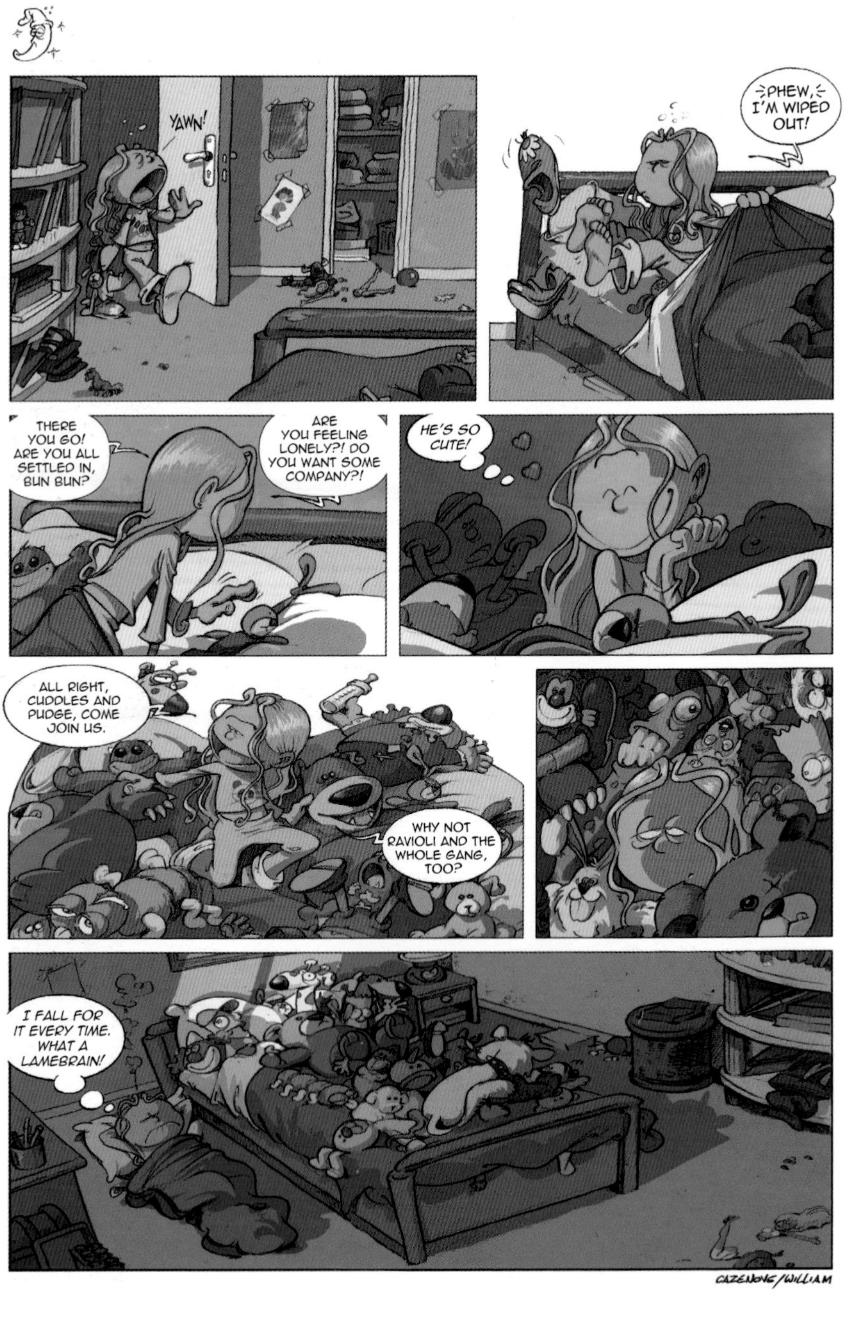
YAWN!
PHEW, I'M WIPED OUT!
THERE YOU GO! ARE YOU ALL SETTLED IN, BUN BUN?
ARE YOU FEELING LONELY?! DO YOU WANT SOME COMPANY?!
HE'S SO CUTE!
ALL RIGHT, CUDDLES AND PUDGE, COME JOIN US.
WHY NOT RAVIOLI AND THE WHOLE GANG, TOO?
I FALL FOR IT EVERY TIME. WHAT A LAMEBRAIN!
CAZENOVE/WILLIAM

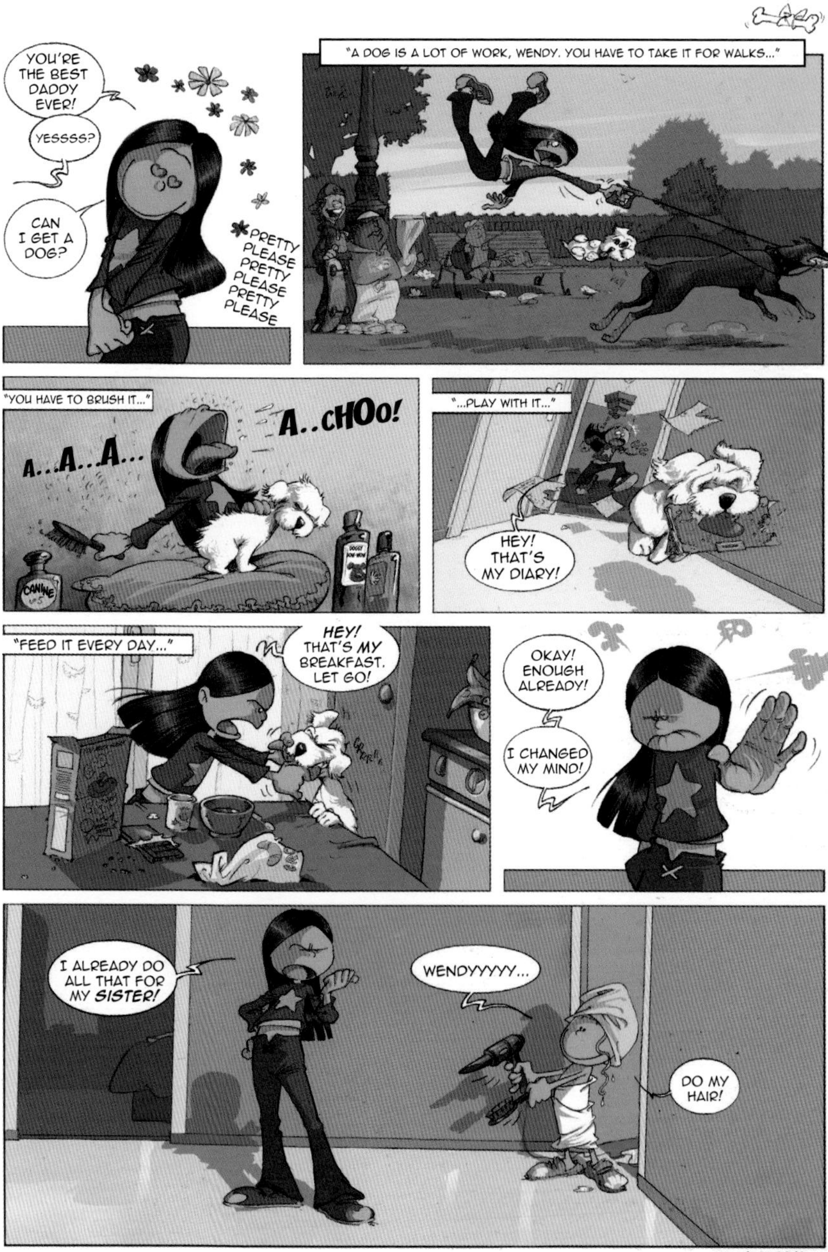
YOU'RE THE BEST DADDY EVER!
YESSSS?
CAN I GET A DOG?
PRETTY PLEASE PRETTY PLEASE PRETTY PLEASE
"A DOG IS A LOT OF WORK, WENDY. YOU HAVE TO TAKE IT FOR WALKS..."
"YOU HAVE TO BRUSH IT..."
A...A...A...
A..CHOO!
CANINE
"...PLAY WITH IT..."
HEY! THAT'S MY DIARY!
"FEED IT EVERY DAY..."
HEY! THAT'S MY BREAKFAST. LET GO!
OKAY! ENOUGH ALREADY!
I CHANGED MY MIND!
I ALREADY DO ALL THAT FOR MY SISTER!
WENDYYYYY...
DO MY HAIR!
CAZENOVE/WILLIAM

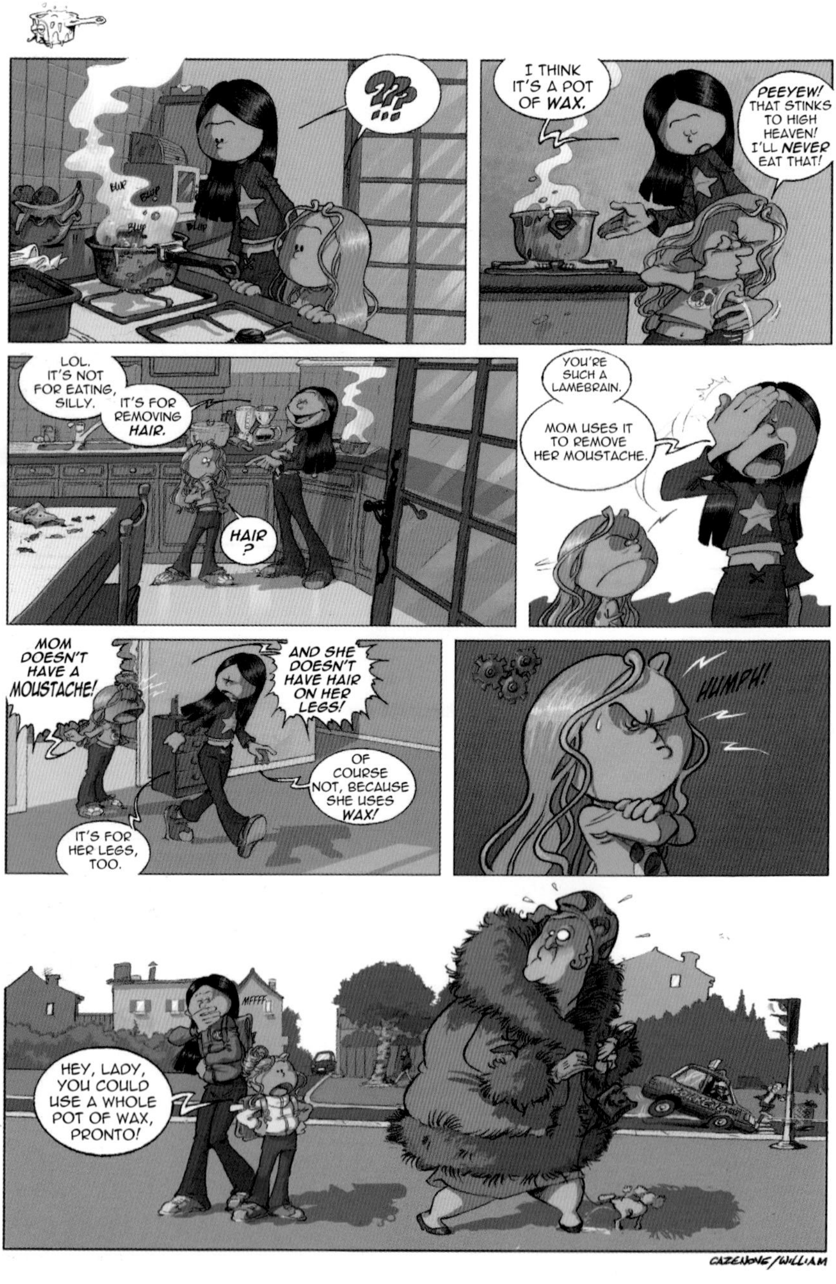
BLUP
BLUP
BLUP
BLUP
???!!!
I THINK IT'S A POT OF WAX.
PEEYEW! THAT STINKS TO HIGH HEAVEN! I'LL NEVER EAT THAT!
LOL. IT'S NOT FOR EATING, SILLY.
IT'S FOR REMOVING HAIR.
HAIR?
YOU'RE SUCH A LAMEBRAIN.
MOM USES IT TO REMOVE HER MOUSTACHE.
MOM DOESN'T HAVE A MOUSTACHE!
AND SHE DOESN'T HAVE HAIR ON HER LEGS!
IT'S FOR HER LEGS, TOO.
OF COURSE NOT, BECAUSE SHE USES WAX!
HUMPH!
MFFFF
HEY, LADY, YOU COULD USE A WHOLE POT OF WAX, PRONTO!
CAZENOVE/WILLIAM

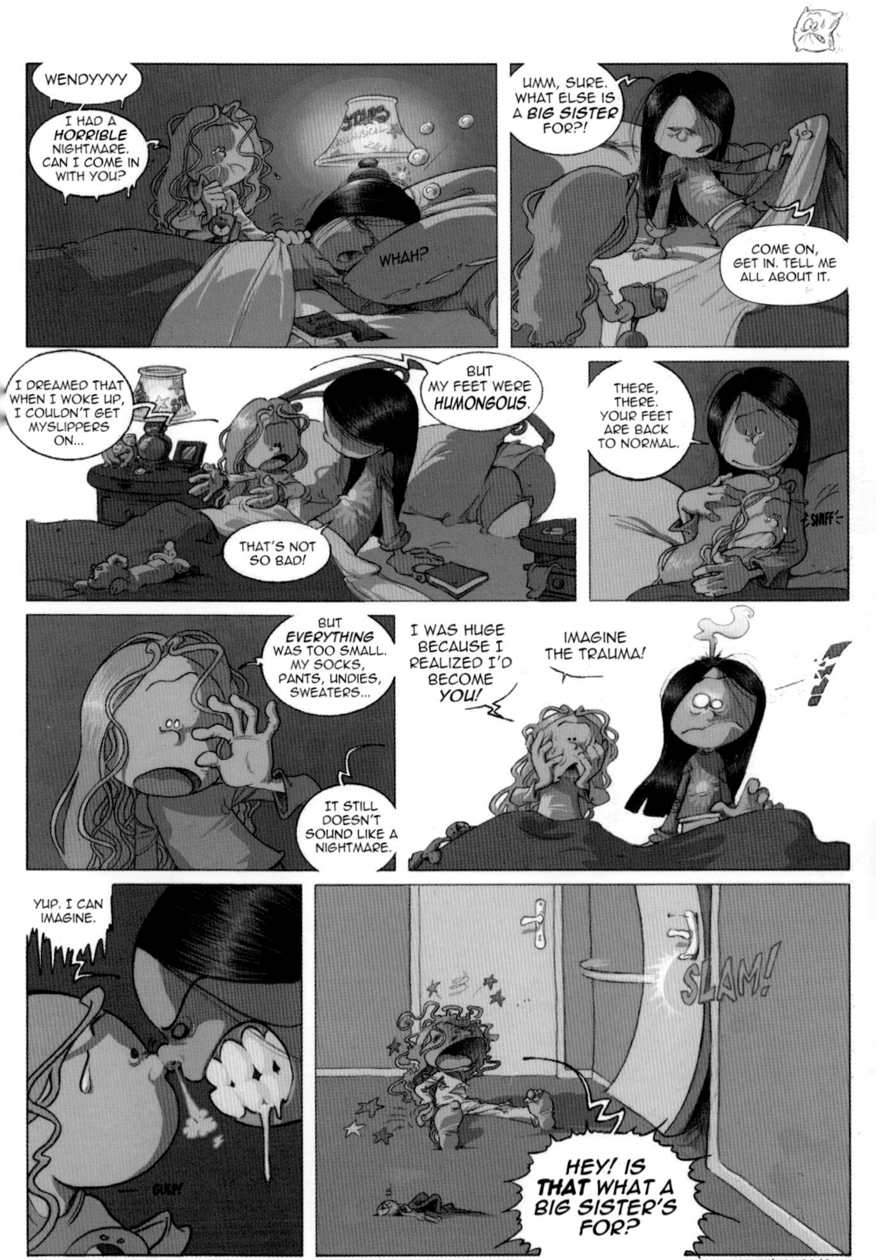
WENDYYYY
I HAD A HORRIBLE NIGHTMARE. CAN I COME IN WITH YOU?
WHAH?
UMM, SURE. WHAT ELSE IS A BIG SISTER FOR?!
COME ON, GET IN. TELL ME ALL ABOUT IT.
I DREAMED THAT WHEN I WOKE UP, I COULDN'T GET MYSLIPPERS ON...
BUT MY FEET WERE HUMONGOUS.
THAT'S NOT SO BAD!
THERE, THERE. YOUR FEET ARE BACK TO NORMAL.
SNIFF
BUT EVERYTHING WAS TOO SMALL. MY SOCKS, PANTS, UNDIES, SWEATERS...
IT STILL DOESN'T SOUND LIKE A NIGHTMARE.
I WAS HUGE BECAUSE I REALIZED I'D BECOME YOU!
IMAGINE THE TRAUMA!
YUP. I CAN IMAGINE.
GULP
SLAM!
HEY! IS THAT WHAT A BIG SISTER'S FOR?
CAZENOVE/WILLIAM

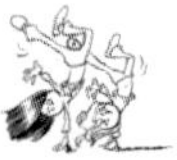

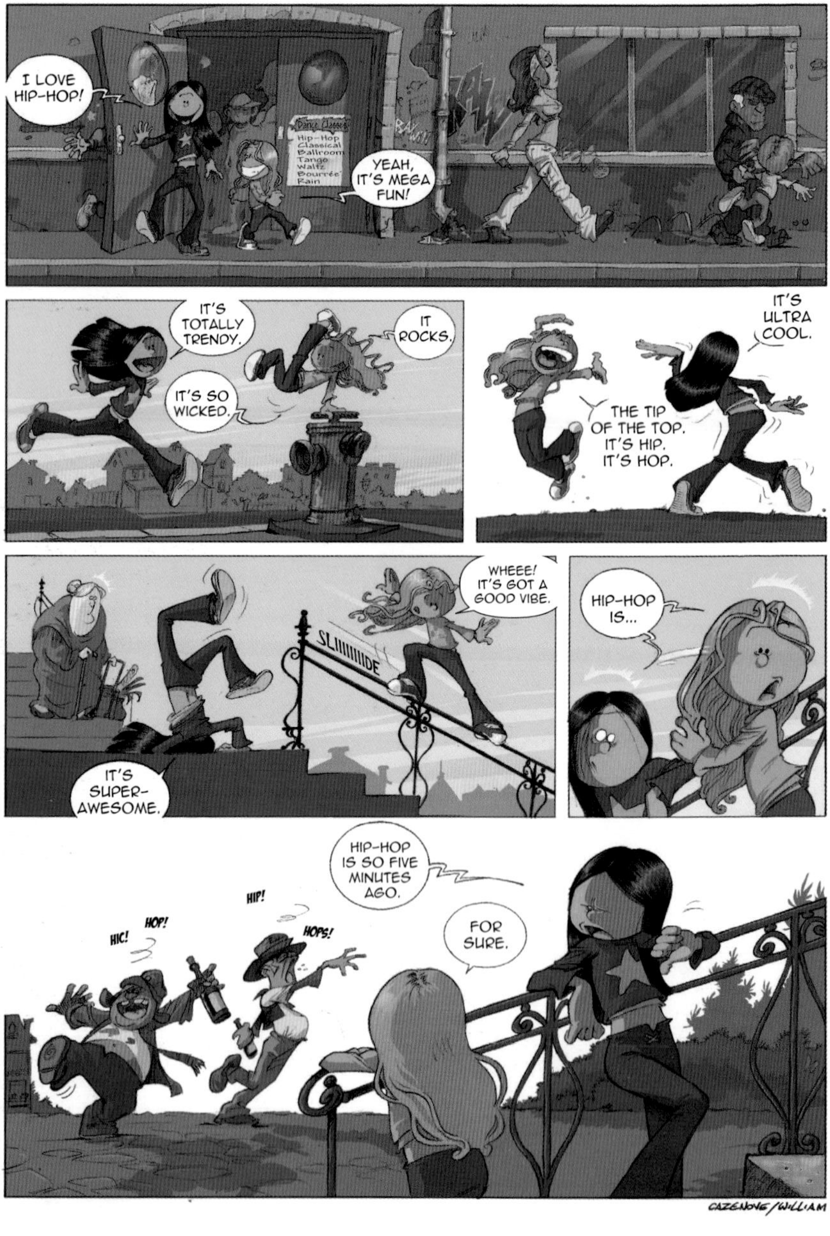
I LOVE HIP-HOP!
Dance Classes
Hip-Hop
Classical
Ballroom
Tango
Waltz
Bourrée
Rain
YEAH, IT'S MEGA FUN!
IT'S TOTALLY TRENDY.
IT ROCKS.
IT'S SO WICKED.
IT'S ULTRA COOL.
THE TIP OF THE TOP. IT'S HIP. IT'S HOP.
WHEEE! IT'S GOT A GOOD VIBE.
SLIIIIIIIDE
IT'S SUPER-AWESOME.
HIP-HOP IS...
HIP-HOP IS SO FIVE MINUTES AGO.
HIP!
HOPS!
HIC!
HOP!
FOR SURE.

CAZENOVE/WILLIAM

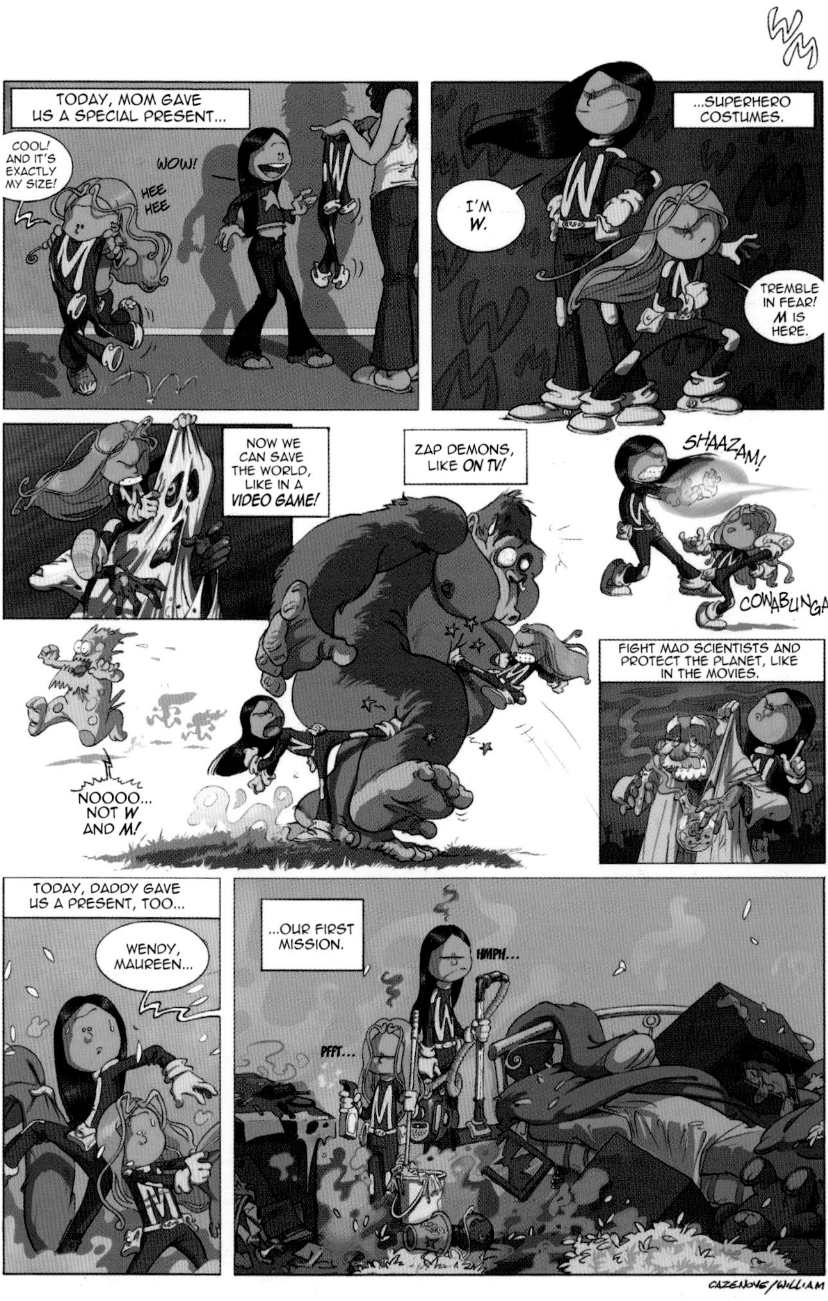
TODAY, MOM GAVE US A SPECIAL PRESENT...
COOL! AND IT'S EXACTLY MY SIZE!
WOW!
HEE HEE
...SUPERHERO COSTUMES.
I'M W.
TREMBLE IN FEAR! M IS HERE.
NOW WE CAN SAVE THE WORLD, LIKE IN A VIDEO GAME!
ZAP DEMONS, LIKE ON TV!
SHAAZAM!
COWABUNGA!
FIGHT MAD SCIENTISTS AND PROTECT THE PLANET, LIKE IN THE MOVIES.
NOOOO... NOT W AND M!
TODAY, DADDY GAVE US A PRESENT, TOO...
WENDY, MAUREEN...
...OUR FIRST MISSION.
HMPH...
PFFT...
CAZENOVE/WILLIAM

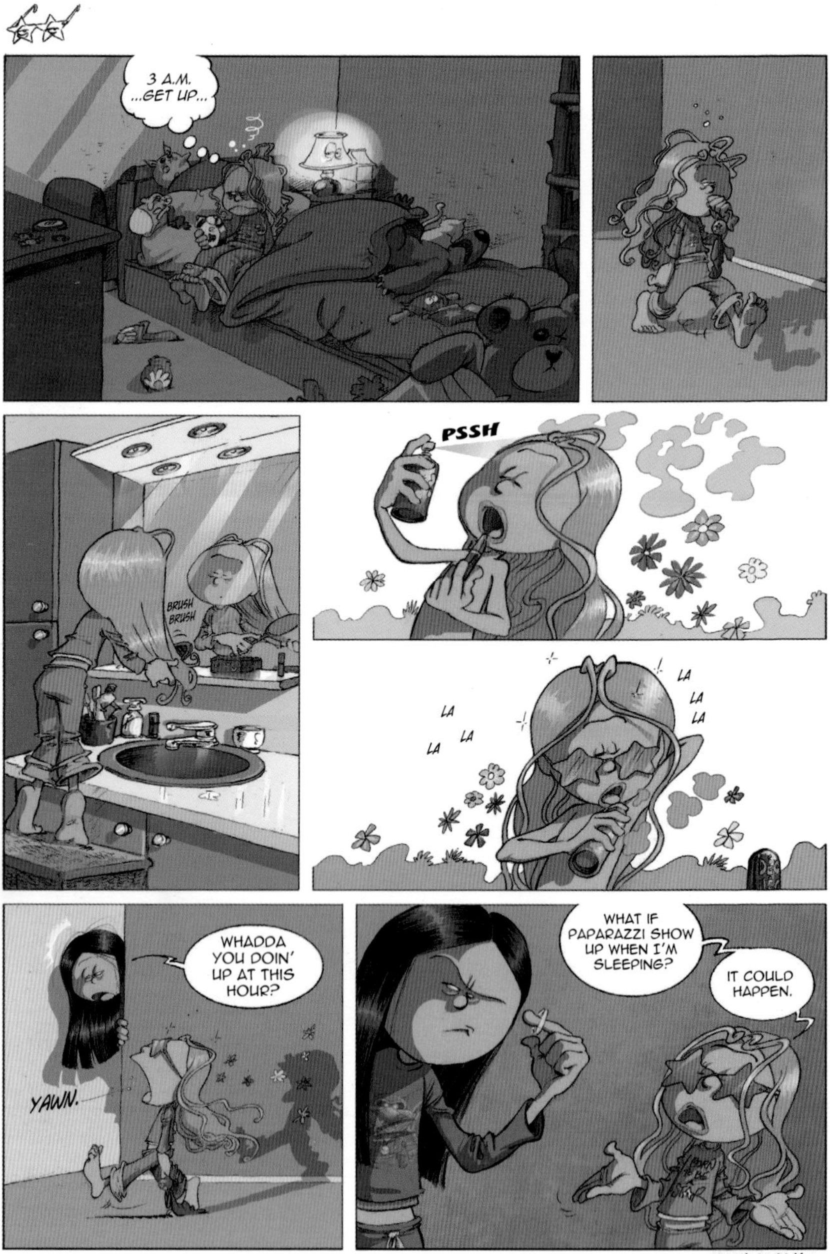
3 A.M.
...GET UP...
BRUSH
BRUSH
PSSH
LA
LA
LA
LA
LA
LA
WHADDA YOU DOIN' UP AT THIS HOUR?
YAWN.
WHAT IF PAPARAZZI SHOW UP WHEN I'M SLEEPING?
IT COULD HAPPEN.
CAZENOVE/WILLIAM

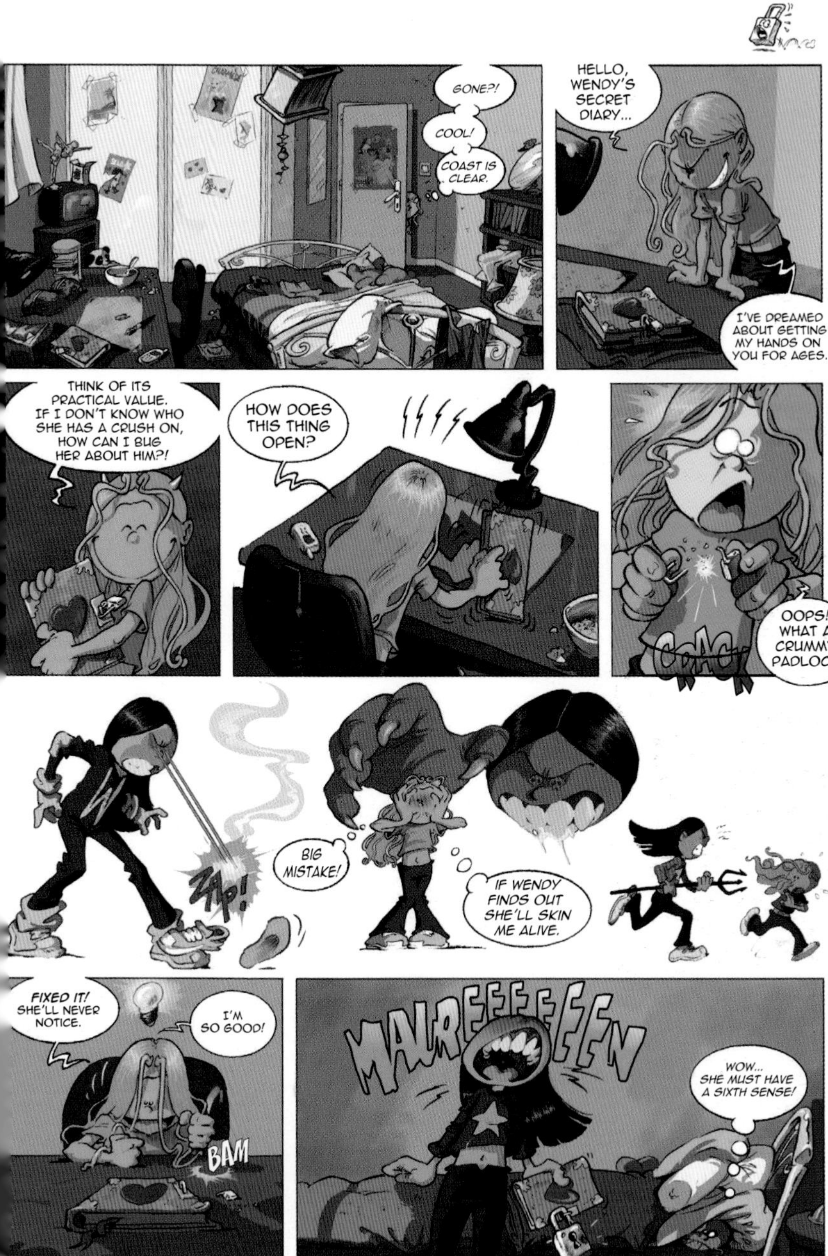
GONE?!
COOL!
COAST IS CLEAR.
HELLO, WENDY'S SECRET DIARY...
I'VE DREAMED ABOUT GETTING MY HANDS ON YOU FOR AGES.
THINK OF ITS PRACTICAL VALUE. IF I DON'T KNOW WHO SHE HAS A CRUSH ON, HOW CAN I BUG HER ABOUT HIM?!
HOW DOES THIS THING OPEN?
CRACK
OOPS! WHAT A CRUMMY PADLOCK!
ZAP!
BIG MISTAKE!
IF WENDY FINDS OUT SHE'LL SKIN ME ALIVE.
FIXED IT! SHE'LL NEVER NOTICE.
I'M SO GOOD!
BAM
MAUREEEEEEN
WOW... SHE MUST HAVE A SIXTH SENSE!
CAZENOVE/WILLIAM

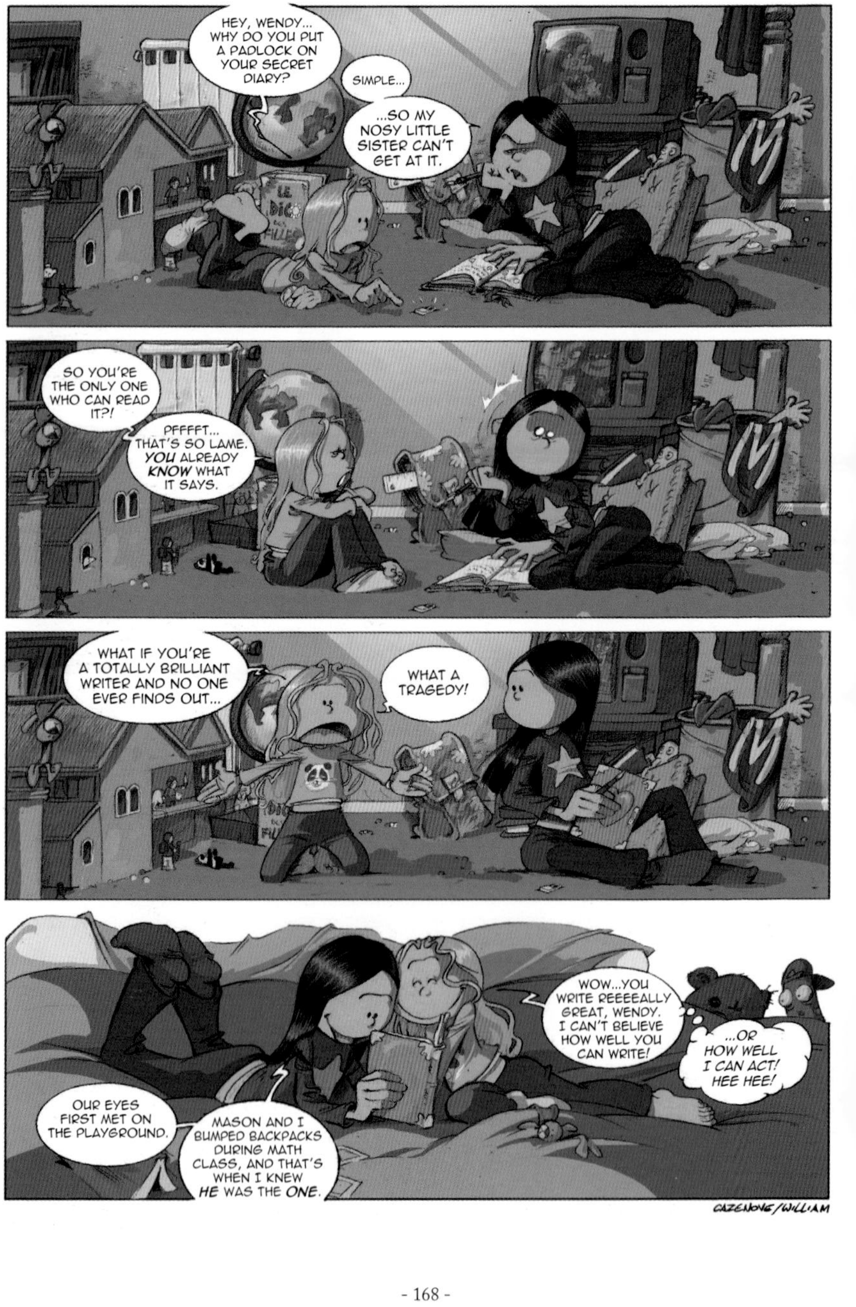
HEY, WENDY... WHY DO YOU PUT A PADLOCK ON YOUR SECRET DIARY?
SIMPLE...
...SO MY NOSY LITTLE SISTER CAN'T GET AT IT.
LE DICO DES FILLES
SO YOU'RE THE ONLY ONE WHO CAN READ IT?!
PFFFFT... THAT'S SO LAME. YOU ALREADY KNOW WHAT IT SAYS.
WHAT IF YOU'RE A TOTALLY BRILLIANT WRITER AND NO ONE EVER FINDS OUT...
WHAT A TRAGEDY!
OUR EYES FIRST MET ON THE PLAYGROUND.
MASON AND I BUMPED BACKPACKS DURING MATH CLASS, AND THAT'S WHEN I KNEW HE WAS THE ONE.
WOW...YOU WRITE REEEEALLY GREAT, WENDY. I CAN'T BELIEVE HOW WELL YOU CAN WRITE!
...OR HOW WELL I CAN ACT! HEE HEE!

CAZENOVE/WILLIAM

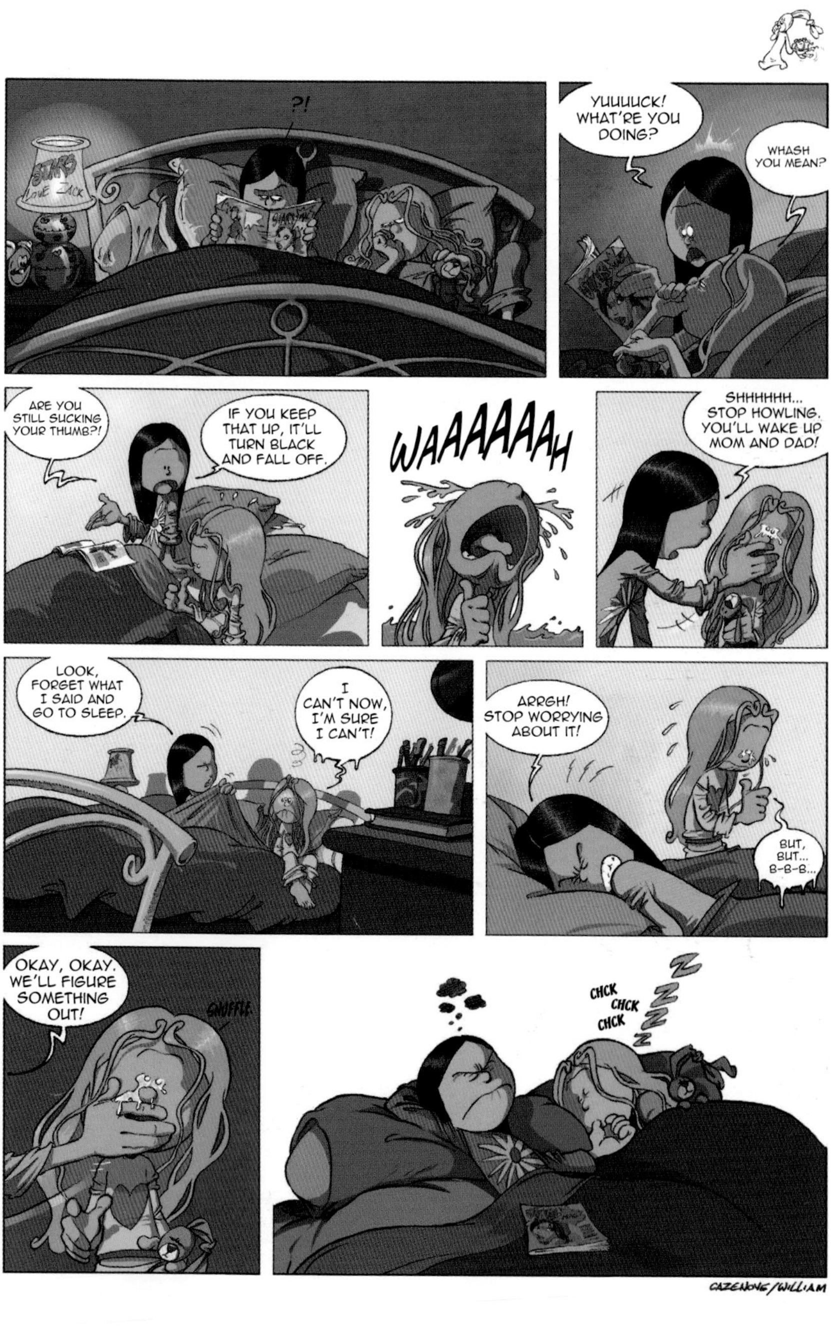
?!
YUUUUCK! WHAT'RE YOU DOING?
WHASH YOU MEAN?
ARE YOU STILL SUCKING YOUR THUMB?!
IF YOU KEEP THAT UP, IT'LL TURN BLACK AND FALL OFF.
WAAAAAAH
SHHHHHH... STOP HOWLING. YOU'LL WAKE UP MOM AND DAD!
LOOK, FORGET WHAT I SAID AND GO TO SLEEP.
I CAN'T NOW, I'M SURE I CAN'T!
ARRGH! STOP WORRYING ABOUT IT!
BUT, BUT... B-B-B...
OKAY, OKAY. WE'LL FIGURE SOMETHING OUT!
SNIFFLE
CHCK CHCK CHCK
ZZZZZ
CAZENOVE/WILLIAM

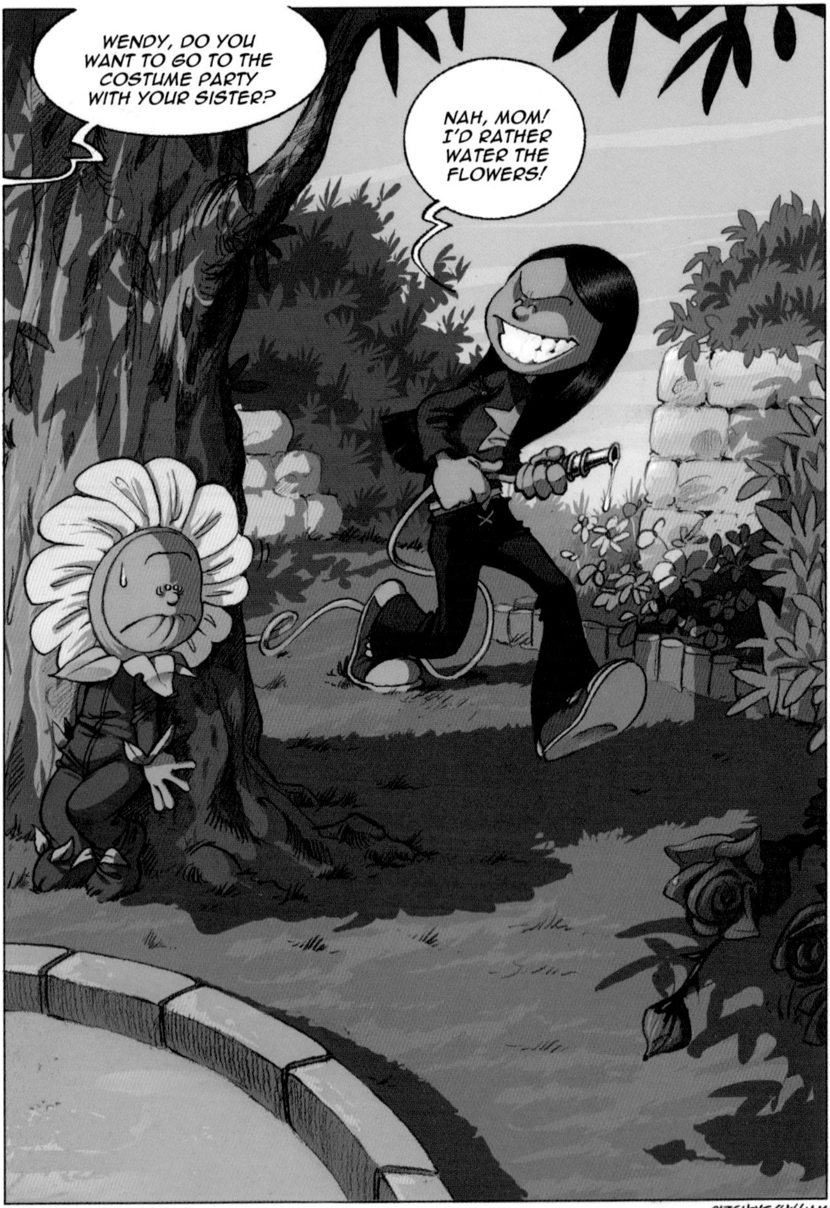
WENDY, DO YOU WANT TO GO TO THE COSTUME PARTY WITH YOUR SISTER?
NAH, MOM! I'D RATHER WATER THE FLOWERS!
CAZENOVE/WILLIAM

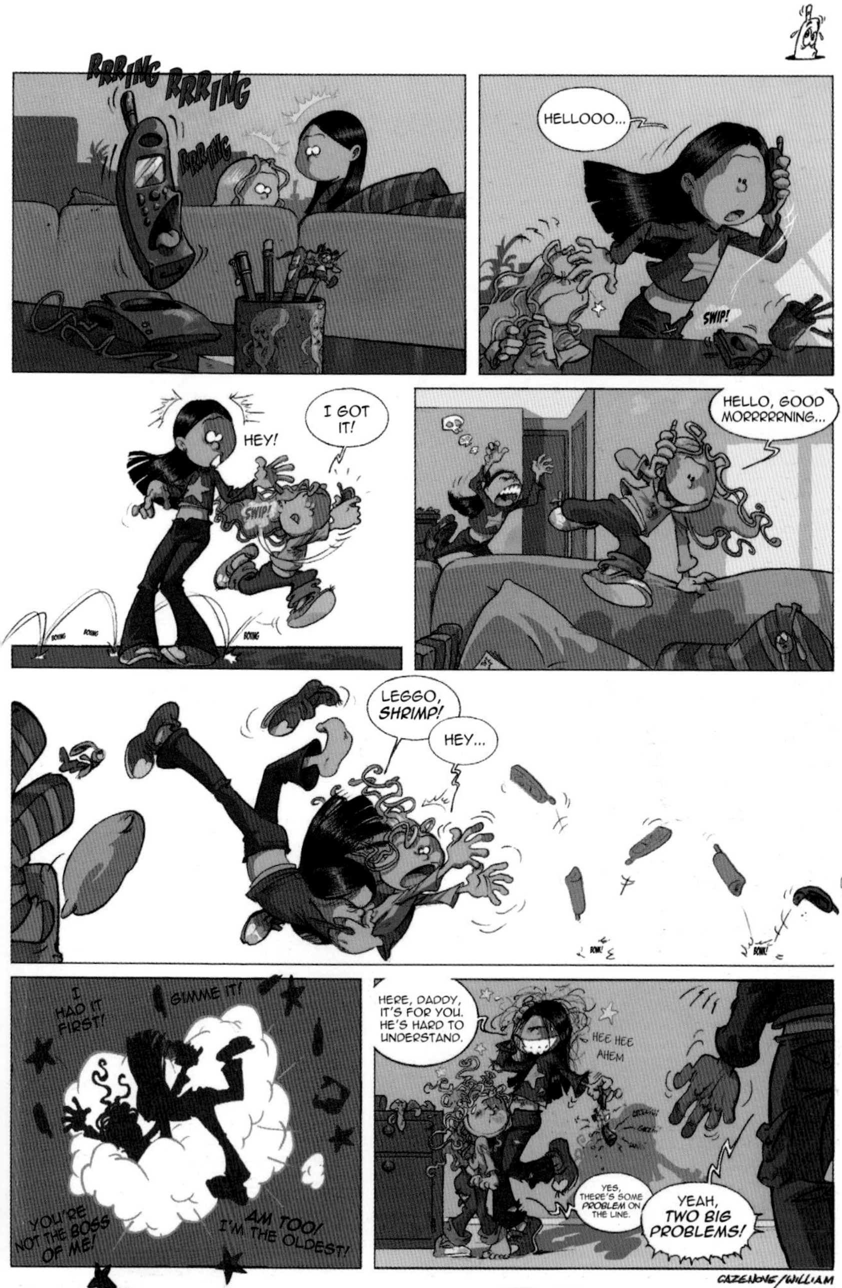
RRRING RRRING
RRRING
HELLOOO...
SWIP!
HEY!
I GOT IT!
SWIP!
HELLO, GOOD MORRRRRNING...
LEGGO, SHRIMP!
HEY...
I HAD IT FIRST!
GIMME IT!
YOU'RE NOT THE BOSS OF ME!
AM TOO! I'M THE OLDEST!
HERE, DADDY, IT'S FOR YOU. HE'S HARD TO UNDERSTAND.
HEE HEE AHEM
YES, THERE'S SOME PROBLEM ON THE LINE.
YEAH, TWO BIG PROBLEMS!

CAZENOVE/WILLIAM

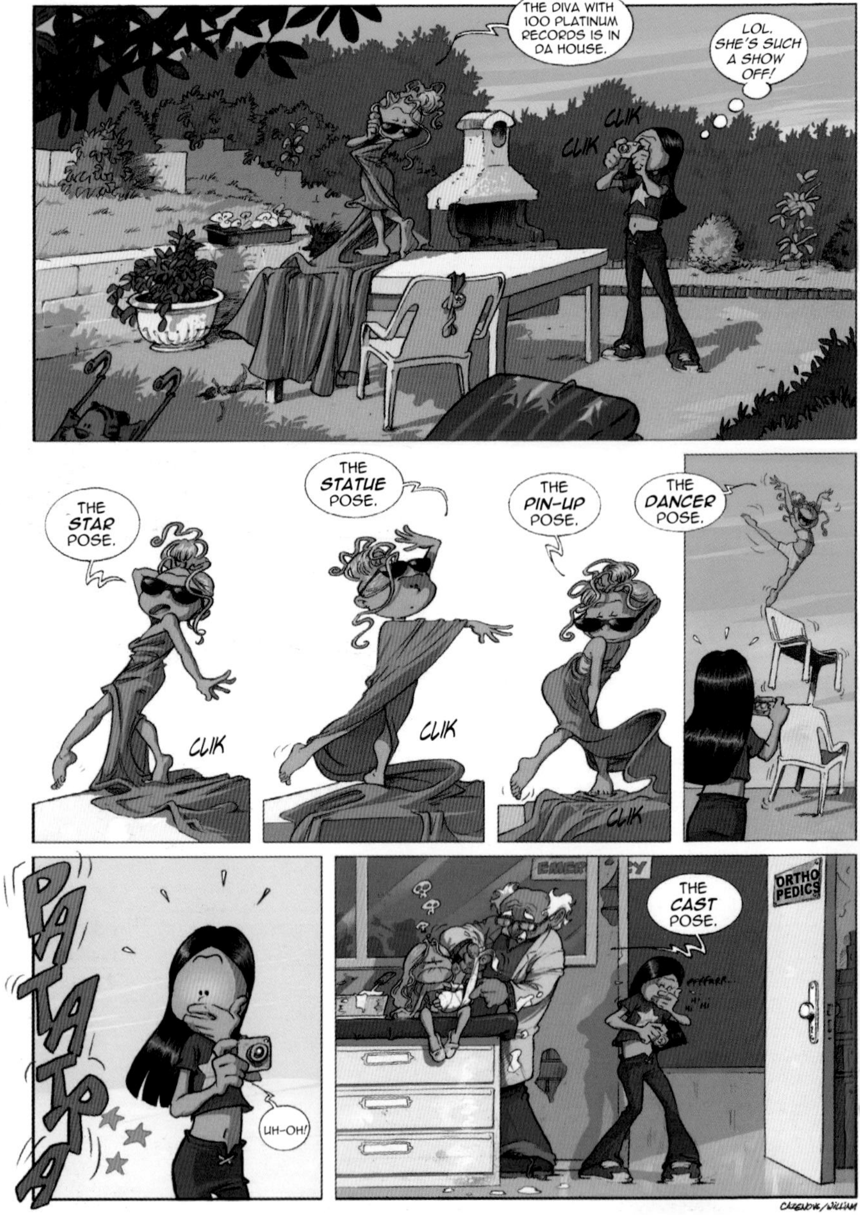
THE DIVA WITH 100 PLATINUM RECORDS IS IN DA HOUSE.
LOL. SHE'S SUCH A SHOW OFF!
CLIK
CLIK
THE STAR POSE.
CLIK
THE STATUE POSE.
CLIK
THE PIN-UP POSE.
CLIK
THE DANCER POSE.
PATATRA
UH-OH!
EMER CY
ORTHO PEDICS
THE CAST POSE.
HI HI HI
CAZENOVE/WILLIAM

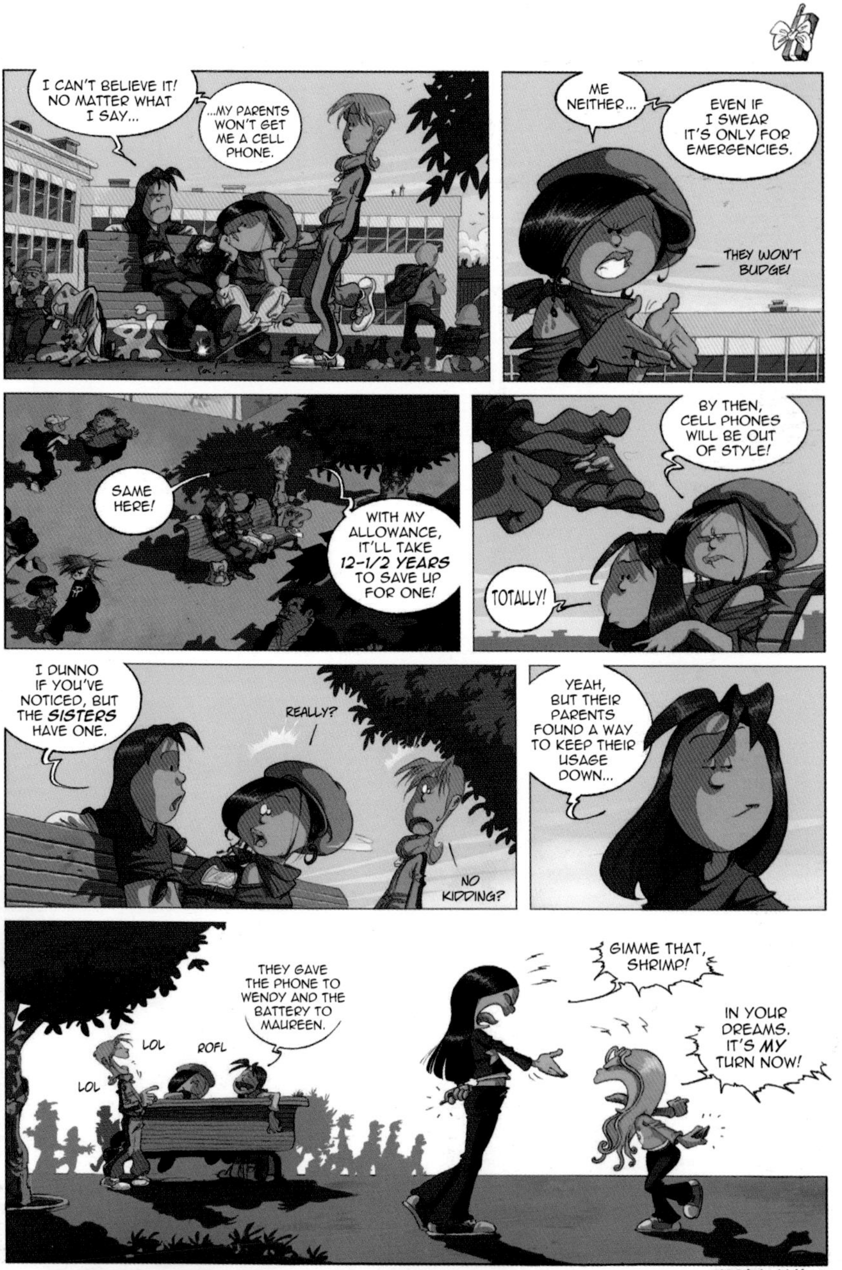
I CAN'T BELIEVE IT! NO MATTER WHAT I SAY...
...MY PARENTS WON'T GET ME A CELL PHONE.
ME NEITHER...
EVEN IF I SWEAR IT'S ONLY FOR EMERGENCIES.
THEY WON'T BUDGE!
SAME HERE!
WITH MY ALLOWANCE, IT'LL TAKE 12-1/2 YEARS TO SAVE UP FOR ONE!
BY THEN, CELL PHONES WILL BE OUT OF STYLE!
TOTALLY!
I DUNNO IF YOU'VE NOTICED, BUT THE SISTERS HAVE ONE.
REALLY?
NO KIDDING?
YEAH, BUT THEIR PARENTS FOUND A WAY TO KEEP THEIR USAGE DOWN...
THEY GAVE THE PHONE TO WENDY AND THE BATTERY TO MAUREEN.
LOL
ROFL
LOL
GIMME THAT, SHRIMP!
IN YOUR DREAMS. IT'S MY TURN NOW!
CAZENOVE/WILLIAM

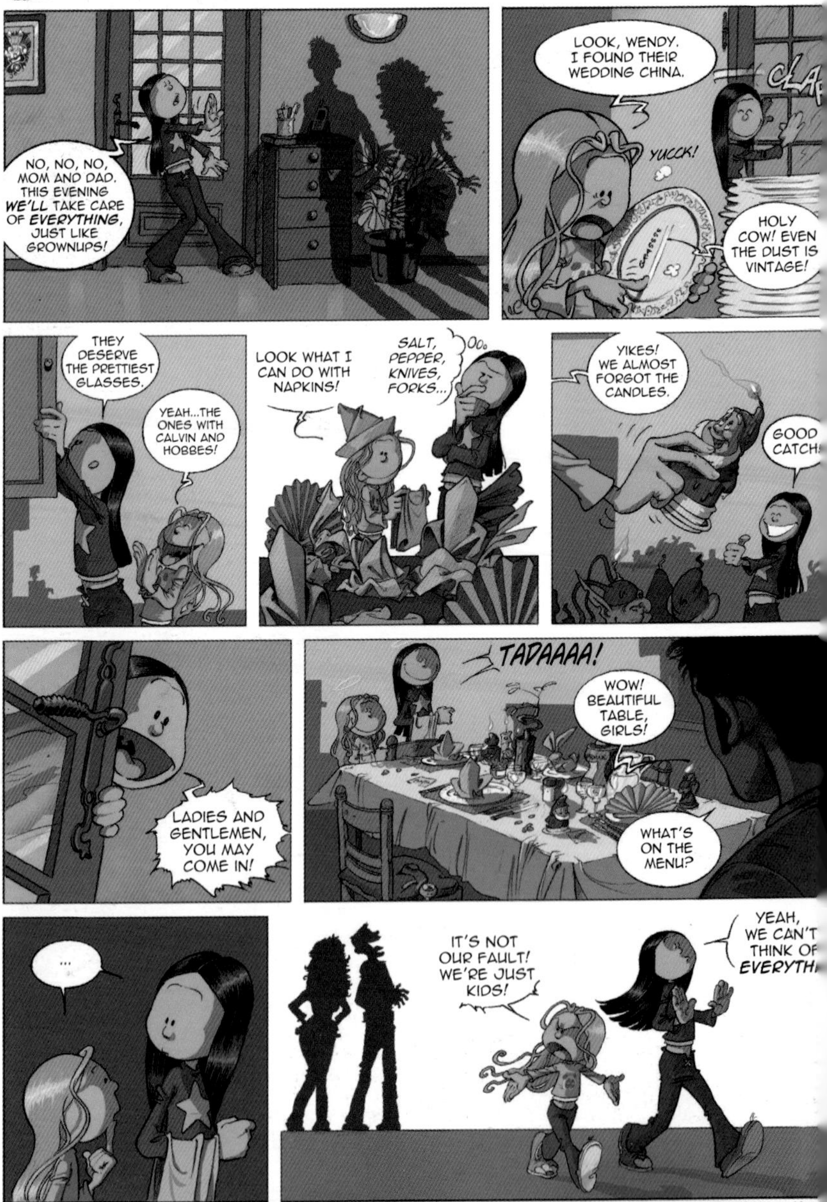
NO, NO, NO, MOM AND DAD. THIS EVENING **WE'LL** TAKE CARE OF **EVERYTHING**, JUST LIKE GROWNUPS!
LOOK, WENDY. I FOUND THEIR WEDDING CHINA.
CLA
YUCCK!
HOLY COW! EVEN THE DUST IS VINTAGE!
THEY DESERVE THE PRETTIEST GLASSES.
YEAH...THE ONES WITH CALVIN AND HOBBES!
LOOK WHAT I CAN DO WITH NAPKINS!
SALT, PEPPER, KNIVES, FORKS...
YIKES! WE ALMOST FORGOT THE CANDLES.
GOOD CATCH
LADIES AND GENTLEMEN, YOU MAY COME IN!
TADAAAA!
WOW! BEAUTIFUL TABLE, GIRLS!
WHAT'S ON THE MENU?
...
IT'S NOT OUR FAULT! WE'RE JUST KIDS!
YEAH, WE CAN'T THINK OF **EVERYTH**
CAZENOVE/WILLIA

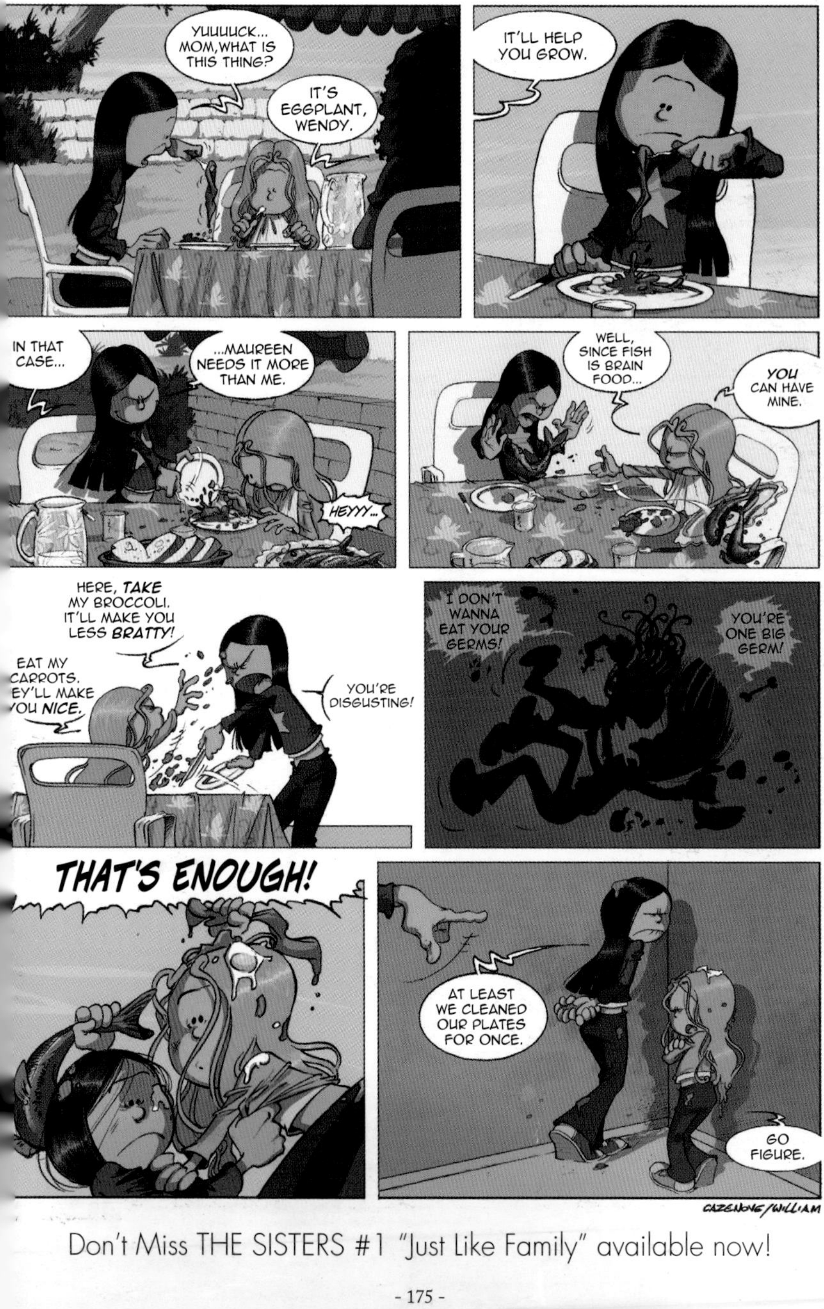
YUUUUCK... MOM, WHAT IS THIS THING?
IT'S EGGPLANT, WENDY.
IT'LL HELP YOU GROW.
IN THAT CASE...
...MAUREEN NEEDS IT MORE THAN ME.
HEYYY...
WELL, SINCE FISH IS BRAIN FOOD...
YOU CAN HAVE MINE.
HERE, TAKE MY BROCCOLI. IT'LL MAKE YOU LESS BRATTY!
EAT MY CARROTS. EY'LL MAKE YOU NICE.
YOU'RE DISGUSTING!
I DON'T WANNA EAT YOUR GERMS!
YOU'RE ONE BIG GERM!
THAT'S ENOUGH!
AT LEAST WE CLEANED OUR PLATES FOR ONCE.
GO FIGURE.
CAZENOVE/WILLIAM

Don't Miss THE SISTERS #1 "Just Like Family" available now!

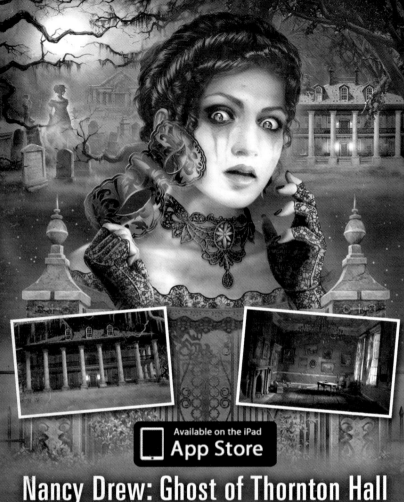